LOVE—
HER PEOPLE CALLED IT
THE TRIUMPH OVER FEAR. . . .

Now her whole being . . . and her existence, the
motion of her blood and the beating of her heart
were fused into love for this Thracian slave. . . .
He was one of those rare human beings who were
knit out of one piece. That was the first thing one
saw in Spartacus, his wholeness. He was singular.
He was content, not in where he was but in what
he was. Even in this nest of terrible, desperate
and doomed men . . . Spartacus was loved and
honored and respected. She had believed that the
desire in her loins was dead forever, but she had
only to touch him to want him. . . . She could not
conceive of having a man or loving a man who
was not . . .

SPARTACUS

Books by Howard Fast

THE ESTABLISHMENT
THE MAGIC DOOR
SECOND GENERATION
THE IMMIGRANTS
THE ART OF ZEN MEDITATION
TIME AND THE RIDDLE
A TOUCH OF INFINITY
THE HESSIAN
THE CROSSING
THE GENERAL ZAPPED AN ANGEL
THE JEWS: STORY OF A PEOPLE
THE HUNTER AND THE TRAP
TORQUEMADA
THE HILL
AGRIPPA'S DAUGHTER
POWER
THE EDGE OF TOMORROW
APRIL MORNING
THE GOLDEN RIVER
THE WINSTON AFFAIR
MOSES, PRINCE OF EGYPT
THE LAST SUPPER
SILAS TIMBERMAN
THE PASSION OF SACCO AND VANZETTI
SPARTACUS
THE PROUD AND THE FREE
DEPARTURE
MY GLORIOUS BROTHERS
CLARKTON
THE AMERICAN
FREEDOM ROAD
CITIZEN TOM PAINE
THE UNVANQUISHED
THE LAST FRONTIER
CONCEIVED IN LIBERTY
PLACE IN THE CITY
THE CHILDREN
STRANGE YESTERDAY
TWO VALLEYS

SPARTACUS

Howard Fast

A DELL BOOK

Published by
Dell Publishing Co., Inc.
1 Dag Hammarskjold Plaza
New York, New York 10017

Dell ® TM 681510, Dell Publishing Co., Inc.

ISBN: 0-440-17649-2

Reprinted by arrangement with the author

Printed in the United States of America

First Dell printing—October 1980

This book is for my daughter, Rachel, and for my son, Jonathan. It is a story of brave men and women who lived long ago, and whose names have never been forgotten. The heroes of this story cherished freedom and human dignity, and lived nobly and well. I wrote it so that those who read it, my children and others, may take strength for our own troubled future and that they may struggle against oppression and wrong—so that the dream of Spartacus may come to be in our own time.

PART ONE

How Caius Crassus journeyed along the high-road from Rome to Capua, in the month of May.

The time of the beginning of this story is 71 B.C.

It is recorded that as early as the middle of the month of March, the highroad from the Eternal City, Rome, to the somewhat smaller but hardly less lovely town of Capua, was opened to public travel once again; but this is not to say that traffic upon this road immediately reverted to normal. For that matter, during the past four years no road in the Republic had known the peaceful and prosperous flow of commerce and person which was to be expected of a Roman road. More or less of disturbance had been encountered everywhere, and it would not be incorrect to say that the road between Rome and Capua had become symbolic of this disturbance. It was well said that as the roads go, so does Rome go; if the roads know peace and prosperity, so does the city know it.

The news was posted around the city that any free citizen having business in Capua might travel there to transact it, but for the time being travel for pleasure to that lovely resort was not encouraged. However, as time passed and sweet and gentle springtime settled down over the land of Italy, restrictions were lifted, and once again the fine buildings and splendid scenery of Capua called to the Romans.

In addition to the natural attractions of the Campania countryside, those who enjoyed fine perfume yet balked at inflated prices, found profit as well as pleasure in Capua. There were situated the great perfume factories, unequaled in the whole world; and to Capua were shipped the rare essences and oils from all over the earth, exotic and ex-

7

quisite scents, Egyptian oil of roses, the essence of the lilies of Sheba, the poppies of Galilee, the oil of ambergris and of the rind of lemon and orange, the leaf of sage and mint, rosewood and sandal-wood, and so forth and so on almost without end. Perfume at Capua could be purchased at less than half the price asked in Rome, and when one considers the growing popularity of scents in that time, for men as well as for women—and the necessity for them as well—one can understand that a trip to Capua for that, if for no other reason, might well be undertaken.

II

The road was opened in March, and two months later, in the middle of May, Caius Crassus and his sister, Helena, and her friend, Claudia Marius, set off to spend a week with relatives in Capua. They left Rome on the morning of a bright, clear and cool day, a perfect day for travel, all of them young and bright-eyed and full of delight in the trip and in the adventures which would certainly befall them. Caius Crassus, a young man of twenty-five, whose dark hair fell in abundant and soft ringlets and whose regular features had given him a reputation for good looks as well as good birth, rode a beautiful white Arabian horse, a birthday present from his father the year before, and the two girls travelled in open litters. Each litter was carried by four slaves who were road broken and who could do ten miles at a smooth run without resting. They planned to spend five days on the road, putting up each evening at the country villa of a friend or relative, and this way, by easy and pleasant stages, to come to Capua. They knew before they started that the road was tokened with punishment, but they didn't think it would be enough to disturb them. As a matter of fact, the girls were quite excited by the descriptions they had heard, and as for Caius, he always had a pleasant and somewhat sensuous reaction to such things, and he was also proud of his stomach and of the fact that such sights did not inordinately disturb him.

"After all," he reasoned with the girls, "it is better to look at a crucifix than to be on one."

"We shall look straight ahead," Helena said.

She was better looking than Claudia who was blond but listless, pale skin and pale eyes and an air of fatigue which she nurtured. Her body was full and attractive, but Caius found her rather stupid and wondered what his sister saw in her—a problem he was determined to solve on this trip. He had several times before resolved to seduce his sister's friend, and always the resolution had broken down before her listless disinterest, a disinterest not specific in terms of himself, but general. She was bored, and Caius was certain that only her boredom prevented her from being utterly boring. His sister was something else. His sister excited him in a fashion that troubled him; she was as tall as he, very similar to him in appearance—better looking if anything, and considered beautiful by men who were not fended away by her purpose and strength. His sister excited him, and he was conscious that in planning this trip to Capua, he hoped for some resolution of this excitement. His sister and Claudia made an odd but satisfying combination, and Caius looked forward to rewarding incidents on the journey.

A few miles outside of Rome, the tokens of punishment began. There was a place where the road crossed a little wasteland of rock and sand, a few acres in extent, and the person in charge of the exhibit had, with an eye for effect, chosen this particular spot for the first crucifix. The cross had been cut out of fresh new wood, pitch-bleeding pine, and since the ground fell away behind it, it stood stark and bare and angular against the morning sky, so huge and impressive—over-large; since it was the first—that one hardly noticed the naked body of the man who hung upon it. It stood slightly askew, as is so often the case with the top-heavy crucifix, and this added to its bizarre, demi-human quality. Caius drew up his horse, and then walked the animal toward the crucifix; and with a little flick of her courtesy quirt, Helena ordered the litter slaves to follow.

"May we rest, oh mistress, oh mistress?" whispered the pace setter of Helena's litter, when they came to a halt before the crucifix. He was a Spaniard, and his Latin was broken and wary.

"Of course," said Helena. She was only twenty-three, but already of strong opinion, as all the women of her family were, and she despised senseless cruelty toward animals, whether slave or beast. Then the litter-bearers gently lowered the carriages, squatting gratefully beside them.

A few yards in front of the crucifix, on a straw chair shaded by a small, patched awning, sat a fat, amiable man of distinction and poverty. His distinction was manifest in each of his several chins and in the dignity of his huge paunch, and his poverty, not unmixed with sloth, was plainly evident by his poor and dirty clothes, his grimy finger nails and his stubble of beard. His amiability was the easily worn mask of the professional politician; and one could see at a glance that for years he had scavenged the Forum and the Senate and the wards as well. Here he was now, the last step before he became a beggar with only a mat in some Roman lodging house; yet his voice rolled out with the robust quackery of a barker at a fair. These were the fortunes of war, as he made plain to them. Some choose the right party with uncanny facility. He had always chosen the wrong one, and it was no use saying that essentially they were both the same. This is where it brought him, but better men fared less well.

"You will forgive me for not rising, my gentle sir and my gentle ladies, but the heart—the heart." He put his hand on the great paunch in the general area. "I see you are out early, and early you should be out, since that is the time for travel. Capua?"

"Capua," said Caius.

"Capua indeed—a lovely city, a beautiful city, a fair city, a veritable gem of a city. To visit relatives, no doubt?"

"No doubt," answered Caius. The girls were smiling. He was amiable; he was a great clown. His dignity slipped away. Better to be a clown for these young people. Caius realized that there was money involved somewhere in these proceedings, but he didn't mind. For one thing, he had never been denied money sufficient for all his needs or whims, and for another, he desired to impress the girls with his worldliness, and how better than through this worldly fat clown of a man?

"You see me a guide, a story teller, a small purveyor of bits of punishment and justice. Yet does a judge do more? The station is different, yet better to accept a *denarius* and the shame that goes with it than to beg—"

10

The girls couldn't keep their eyes from the dead man who hung from the crucifix. He was directly above them now, and they kept darting glances at his naked, sun-blackened, bird-torn body. The crows swooped around him tentatively. The flies crawled on his skin. As he hung, his body leaning out and away from the cross, he seemed always to be falling, always in motion, a grotesque motion of the dead. His head hung forward, and his long, sandy hair covered what horror might have been in his face.

Caius gave the fat man a coin; the thanks was no more than what was due. The bearers squatted silently, never glancing at the crucifix, eyes on the ground; road broken they were, and well trained.

"This one is symbolic, so as to speak," said the fat man. "Mistress mine, do not regard it as human or horrible. Rome gives and Rome takes, and more or less, the punishment fits the crime. This one stands alone and calls your attention to what will follow. Between here and Capua, do you know how many?"

They knew, but they waited for him to say it. There was a precision about this fat, jovial man who introduced them to what was unspeakable. He was proof that it was not unspeakable but ordinary and natural. He would give them an exact figure. It might not be right, but it would be precise.

"Six thousand, four hundred and seventy-two," he said.

A few of the litter-bearers stirred. They were not resting, they were rigid. If anyone had regarded them, they would have noticed that. But no one regarded them.

"Six thousand, four hundred and seventy-two," the fat man repeated. Caius made the right remark. "That much timber," Caius said. Helena knew it was a fraud, but the fat man nodded appreciatively. Now they were en rapport. The fat man extracted a cane from the folds of his gown and gestured at the crucifix.

"That one—merely a token. A token of a token, so as to speak."

Claudia giggled nervously.

"Neverthless of interest and of importance. Set apart with reason. Reason is Rome and Rome is reasonable." He was fond of maxims.

"Is that Spartacus?" Claudia asked foolishly, but the fat

man found patience for her. The way he licked his lips proved that his paternal attitude was not unmixed with emotion, and Caius thought,

"The lecherous old beast."

"Hardly Spartacus, my dear."

"His body was never found," Caius said impatiently.

"Cut to pieces," the fat man said pompously. "Cut to pieces, my dear child. Tender minds for such dreadful thoughts, but that's the truth of it—"

Claudia shuddered, but deliciously, and Caius saw a light in her eyes he had never noticed before. "Beware of superficial judgments," his father had once said to him, and while his father had weightier matters in mind than estimation of women, it held. Claudia had never looked at him as she looked at the fat man now; and he continued,

"—the simple truth of it. And now they say Spartacus never existed. Hah! Do I exist? Do you exist? Are there or are there not six thousand, four hundred and seventy-two corpses hanging from crucifixes between here and Capua along the Appian Way? Are there or are there not? There are indeed. And let me ask you another question, my young folk—why so many? A token of punishment is a token of punishment. But why six thousand, four hundred and seventy-two?"

"The dogs deserved it," Helena answered quietly.

"Did they?" The fat man raised a sophisticated brow. He was a man of the world, he made plain to them, and if they were higher in station, they were younger enough in years to be impressed. "Perhaps they did, but why butcher so much meat if one can't eat it? I'll tell you. Keeps the price up. Stabilizes things. And most of all, decides some very delicate questions of ownership. There you have the answer in a nutshell. Now this one here—" gesturing with his cane, "—have a good look at him. Fairtrax, the Gaul, most important, most important. A close man to Spartacus, yes, indeed, and I watched him die. Sitting right here, I watched him die. It took four days. Strong as an ox. My, oh my, you would never believe such strength. Never believe it at all. I have my chair here from Sextus, of the Third Ward. You know him? A gentleman—a very great gentleman, and well disposed toward me. You'd be surprised how many people came out to watch, and it was something well worth watching. Not that I could charge them a proper fee—but people give if you give them something in return. Fair measure for fair measure. I took the trouble to inform myself. You'd be surprised what profound ignorance there is here and there about, concerning the wars of Spartacus. Now see here, this young lady, she asks me, is that one Spartacus? A natural question, but wouldn't it be exceedingly unnatural if it was so. You gentle ones live a sheltered life, very sheltered, otherwise the young lady would have known that Spartacus was cut up so that not hair nor hide of him was ever found. Quite different with this one—he was taken. Cut up a little, true—see here—"

With his cane, he traced a long scar on the side of the body above him.

"Number of scars—and most interesting. Side or front. None in the back. You don't want to stress such details for the rabble, but I can tell you as a matter of fact—"

The litter-bearers were watching him now and listening, their eyes gleaming out of their long, matted hair.

"—that these were the best soldiers that ever walked on Italian soil. Bears thinking about, something like that. Come back to our friend up here. Took four days for him to die, and it would have taken a good deal longer if they hadn't opened a vein and bled him a bit. Now you may not know that, but you got to do it when you put them on the cross. Either you bleed them or they swell up like a bloater. And if you bleed them properly, then they dry properly and they can hang up there for maybe a month with no more offense than a little bit of smell. Just like curing a piece of meat, and you want plenty of sunshine to help it along. Now this was a fierce one, all right, defiant, proud—but he lost it. First day, he hung up there and cursed out every decent citizen who came along to watch. Frightful, foul language; you wouldn't want any ladies around to hear such language. Comes of no breeding, and a slave is a slave, but I bore him no ill will. Here I was and there he was, and now and then I'd say to him, Your misfortune is my fortune, and while yours may not be the most comfortable way to die, mine is by no means the most comfortable way to earn a living. And precious little I'll earn, you keep up that kind of talk. Didn't seem to move him much, one way or another, but toward evening of the second day, he closed up. Clammed up, tight as a trap. Do you know what was the last thing he said?"

"What?" whispered Claudia.

"I will return and I will be millions. Just that. Fanciful, isn't it?"

"What did he mean?" Caius wondered. In spite of himself, the fat man had woven a spell over him.

"Now what did he mean, young sir? I have no more idea than you have, and he never spoke again either. I poked him up a little the next day, but he never said a word, just looked at me out of those bloodshot eyes of his, looked at me like he could kill me, but he wasn't for killing anything else. So you see, my dear," addressing Claudia again, "he wasn't Spartacus, but was one of his lieutenants and a hard man. Close to Spartacus, but not so hard. That was a hard one, was Spartacus, hard indeed. You would not like to meet him along this highroad and never will neither, for he's dead and rotting. Now what else would you like to know?"

"I think we've heard enough," Caius said, regretting the *denarius* now. "We must be on our way."

III

In those day, Rome was like a heart which pumped its blood along the Roman roads to every corner of the world. Another nation would live a thousand years and build one third-rate road which perhaps connected its major cities. With Rome it was different. "Build us a road!" said the Senate. They had the skill. The engineers plotted it; contracts were handed out and the construction men took it under way; then the labor gangs built that road like an arrow to wherever it had to go. If a mountain stood in the way, you got rid of the mountain; if there was a deep valley, you flung a bridge across the valley; if there was a river, you bridged the river. Nothing halted Rome and nothing halted the Roman road.

This highroad, upon which these three light-hearted young people were travelling south from Rome to Capua, was called the Appian Way. It was a well-built, broad road of alternate layers of volcanic ash and gravel, and surfaced with stone. It was made to last. When the Romans put down a road, they laid it not for this year or the next, but for centuries. That was how the Appian Way was laid down. It was a symbol of the progress of mankind, the productivity of Rome, and the enduring capacity of the Roman people for organization. It stated quite clearly that the Roman system was the best system mankind had ever devised, a system of order and justice and intelligence. The evidence of intelligence and order was everywhere, and the people who travelled the road took it so much for granted that it hardly registered upon their minds.

For example, distance was specified, not estimated. Every mile of the way was marked by a milestone. Each milestone gave the pertinent information a traveller needed to know. You knew at any point precisely how far you were from Rome, from Formiae, from Capua. Every five miles, there was a public house and stables, where one could find horses, refreshments, and, if necessary, shelter for the night. Many of the public houses were quite magnificent, with broad verandas where drinks and food were served. Some had baths, where weary travellers could refresh themselves, and others had good, comfortable sleeping quarters. The newer public houses were built in the style of Greek temples, and they added to the natural beauty of the scenery along the way.

Where the ground was flat, marsh or plain, the road was terraced, with the right of way rising ten or fifteen feet above the surrounding countryside. Where the ground was broken or hilly, the road either cut its way through or crossed gorges on stone arches.

The road proclaimed stability, and over the surface of the road flowed all the elements of Roman stability. Marching on the road, soldiers could do thirty miles in a single day and repeat that same thirty miles day after day. Baggage trains flowed along the roads, loaded with the goods of the republic, wheat and barley and pig iron and cut lumber and linen and wool and oil and fruit and cheese and smoked meat. On the road were citizens engaged in the legitimate business of citizens, genteel folk going to and from their country places, commercial travellers and pleasure travellers, slave caravans going to and from the market, people of every land and every nation, all of them tasting the firmness and the orderliness of Rome's rule.

And at this time, alongside the road a crucifix was planted every few feet, and on every crucifix, a dead man hung.

IV

The morning turned out to be warmer than Caius had expected it to be, and after a while, the smell of the dead became quite unpleasant. The girls soaked their handkerchiefs with perfume and sniffed constantly, but that could not shut out the sudden waves of sweet and sickening smell which floated across the road, nor could it prevent a reaction to this smell. The girls were sick, and Caius finally had to drop behind and go to the side of the road and relieve himself. It almost spoiled the morning.

Fortunately, there were no crucifixes within half a mile of the public house where they stopped to lunch, and though they had little appetite left now, they were able to get over their sickness. This wayside inn was built in the Greek style, a rambling one story building with a pleasant veranda. The veranda, which was set out with tables, was built over a little gully through which ran a brook, and the grotto it faced upon was surrounded by banks of green and fragrant pine. There was no other smell here but the pine smell, the wet, sweet smell of the woods, and no sound except the polite hum of conversation from the diners and the music of the brook. "What an utterly delightful place," Claudia said, and Caius, who had stopped here before, found a table for them and began to order lunch with great authority. The wine of the house, a sparkling amber drink, dry and refreshing, was set before them immediately, and as they sipped it, their appetite returned. They were at the back of the house, separated from the common room in front where soldiers and draymen and foreigners ate; here it was cool and shaded, and while the issue was rarely pressed, it was recognized that only knights and patricians were served here. That made it far from exclusive, for many knights were commercial travellers, business men and manufacturers and commission merchants and slave dealers; but it was a public house and not

16

a private villa. Also, of late, the knights were aping the manners of the patricians and becoming less loud and obtrusive and unpleasant.

Caius ordered cold pressed smoked duck and glacéd oranges, and until the food came, he made conversation about the latest play to open in Rome, a rather contrived comedy in poor imitation of the Greek, as so many were.

The plot concerned an ugly and vulgar woman who made a pact with the gods to deliver them, in return for a day of grace and beauty, her husband's heart. The husband had been sleeping with the mistress of one of the gods, and the intricate and shoddy plot was based on the thin motivation of revenge. At least, that was Helena's feeling, but Caius protested that in spite of its superficiality, he thought it had many clever moments.

"I liked it," Claudia said simply.

"I think we are too concerned with what a thing says instead of the way it says it," Caius smiled. "For my part, I go to the theatre to be amused with what is clever. If one wants the drama of life and death, one can go to the arena and watch the gladiators cut each other up. I've noticed however that it isn't the particularly brilliant or profound type who frequents the games."

"You're excusing bad writing," Helena protested.

"Not at all. I just don't think the quality of writing in the theatre is of any great importance. It's cheaper to hire a Greek writer than a litter-bearer, and I'm not one of those who make a cult of the Greeks."

As he said this last, Caius became conscious of a man standing alongside the table. The other tables had filled up, and this particular man, a commercial traveller of some sort, wondered whether he might not join them.

"Just a bite and I'll be going," he said. "If you don't mind the intrusion."

He was a tall, well-fleshed, well set up man, obviously prosperous, his clothes expensive; and not deferential except to the obvious family and rank of these young people. In the old times, the knights had not had this attitude toward the landed nobility; it was only when they became very wealthy as a class that they discovered ancestry to be one of the most difficult commodities to purchase, and thereby its value increased. Caius, like so many of his friends, often remarked on the contradiction between the

17

loud democratic sentiments of these people and their intense class aspirations.

"My name is Gaius Marcus Senvius," said the knight. "Don't hesitate to refuse me."

"Please sit down," Helena answered. Caius introduced himself and the girls, and he was pleased at the other's reaction.

"I've had some dealings with some of your family," the knight remarked.

"Dealings?"

"Dealings in cattle, that is. I'm a sausage maker. I've a plant in Rome and another in Tarracina, where I'm coming from now. If you've eaten sausage, you've eaten my sausage."

"I'm sure," Caius smiled—thinking, "He hates my guts, look at him. Now he hates my guts, but he's still pleased to sit here. What swine they are!"

"Dealings in swine," said Senvius, as if he had read the other's mind.

"We are very pleased to meet you and we will carry back to our father your kindest wishes," said Helena gently. She smiled sweetly at Senvius, and he looked at her newly. As if to say, "So you are a woman, my dear, patrician or no." That was how Caius read it—"How would you like to go to bed with me, you little bitch?" They smiled at each other, and then Caius could have killed him, but hated his sister more.

"I didn't mean to interrupt your conversation," Senvius said. "Please go on with it."

"We were talking tedious talk about a tedious play."

The food came then, and they began to eat. Suddenly, Claudia halted a piece of duck halfway to her mouth and said what Caius afterwards considered a most astonishing thing.

"You must have been so disturbed by the tokens."

"Tokens?"

"The crucifixion."

"Disturbed?"

"By a waste of so much fresh meat," said Claudia calmly, not cleverly at all, but just calmly, and then went on eating her duck. Caius had to fix his face to keep from bursting out with laughter, and Senvius went red and then white. But Claudia, not knowing at all what she had done, just went on eating. Only Helena sensed something harder than ordinary in the sausage maker, and her skin prickled in anticipation. She wanted him to hit back, and was pleased when he did.

"Disturbed isn't the word," Senvius said finally. "I don't like waste."

"Waste?" asked Claudia, breaking the glacéd orange into little pieces and placing each little piece so delicately between her lips. "Waste?" Claudia drew pity from some men and anger from a few; it took an extraordinary man to see beyond that.

"They were well set up, those men of Spartacus," explained Marcus Senvius, "and well fed too. Suppose they averaged a weight of one hundred and fifty pounds each. There are more than six thousand of them mounted out there like stuffed birds. That's nine hundred thousand pounds of fresh meat—or it was fresh at any rate."

"Oh, no, he can't mean it," thought Helena. Her whole body prickled with expectation now; but Claudia, who went on eating the glacéd orange, knew that he did mean it, and Caius asked,

"Why didn't you make an offer?"

"I did."

"But they wouldn't sell?"

"I managed to buy a quarter of a million pounds."

What is he up to, Caius wondered, and thought, "He's trying to shock us. In his vulgar, filthy way, he's going to pay us back for what Claudia said." Helena, however, saw the substance of the truth, and Caius had the satisfaction of knowing that something had finally gotten under her skin.

"Of men?" whispered Claudia.

"Of tools," said the sausage maker precisely, "to quote that admirable young philosopher, Cicero. Worthless tools. I smoked them, minced them, and mixed it with pork, spice and salt. Half goes to Gaul, half to Egypt. And the price is just right."

"I think your humor is ill taken," Caius muttered. He was very young, and he found it hard to stand up to the mature bitterness of the sausage maker. The knight would never in all his life forget Claudia's insult, and he would always hold it against Caius because Caius had made the error of being present.

"I am not trying to be humorous," Senvius said matter of factly. "The young lady asked a question, and I answered it. I bought a quarter of a million pounds of slave to be turned into sausage."

"That's the most frightful and disgusting thing I ever heard," said Helena. "Your natural boorishness, sir, has taken an odd turn."

The knight rose and looked from one to another. "Pardon me," he said, and to Caius, "Ask your uncle, Sillius. He handled the transaction, and he made a nice little bit for himself in doing it."

Then he moved away. Claudia went on eating the glacéd orange calmly, only stopping to remark, "What an impossible person he turned out to be!"

"Nevertheless, he was telling the truth," Helena said.

"What?"

"Of course he was. Why should you be so shocked?"

"It was a stupid lie," said Caius, "created solely for our benefit."

"The difference between us, my dear," said Helena, "is that I know when someone is telling the truth."

Claudia became whiter than usual. She rose, excused herself, and then moved with stately dignity toward the rest room. Helena smiled a little, almost to herself, and Caius said,

"Nothing shocks you, really, does it, Helena?"

"Why should it?"

"At least, I will never eat sausage again."

"I never ate it," said Helena.

V

As they were moving along the road, early that afternoon, they fell in with a Syrian amber-trader whose name was Muzel Shabaal, whose carefully curled beard glistened with fragrant oil, and whose long embroidered gown swept down on either side of the fine white horse he rode, and whose fingers sparkled with expensive jewels. Behind him trotted a dozen slaves, Egyptians and Bedouins, each of them carrying a massive bundle on his head. Throughout the Roman domain, the road was a great leveler, and Caius found himself engaged in a rather one-sided conversation with the worldly merchant, even though the young man's contribution was little more than an occasional nod. Shabaal was more than honored to meet any Roman, for he had the most profound admiration for Romans, all Romans, but particularly the well-bred and well-situated Roman, such as Caius most obviously was. There were some Easterners who did not understand certain things about the Romans, as for example, the freedom with which their women moved about; but Shabaal was not one of those. Scratch a Roman and you found a vein of iron, as witness these tokens alongside the road—and he was very pleased at the lesson his slaves learned simply by seeing these most instructive crucifixes.

"You would hardly believe it, young sir," said Muzel Shabaal, in his fluent but curiously accented Latin, "but there were people in my land who fully expected Rome to fall to Spartacus, and there was even a small uprising among our own slaves, which we had to quell with harsh measures. How little you understand Rome, I said to them. You equate Rome with what you knew in the past or what you see around you. You forget that Rome is something new for this earth. How can I describe Rome to them? For example, I say *gravitas*. What does it mean to them? Indeed, what does it mean to anyone who has not seen Rome at first hand, and had the company of and discourse with the citizens of Rome? *Gravitas*—the earnest ones, those with a sense of responsibility, to be serious and to have serious intentions. *Levitas* we understand, it is our curse; we trifle with things, we are eager for pleasure. The Roman does not trifle; he is a student of virtue. *Industria, disciplina, frugalitas, clementia*—for me those splendid words are Rome. That is the secret of the peace of the Roman road and the Roman rule. But how does one explain that, young sir? For my part, I look with serious satisfaction at these tokens of punishment. Rome does not trifle. The punishment fits the crime, and thereby you have the justice of Rome. The effrontery of Spartacus was that he challenged all that was best. He offered rapine and murder and disorder; Rome is order—and thereby Rome rejected him . . ."

Caius listened and listened, and finally some of his boredom and distaste communicated itself. Whereupon the

Syrian, with many bows and apologies, presented Helena and Claudia each with an amber necklace. He recommended himself to them and their families and all their possible business acquaintances, and then he took himself off.

"Thank the lord," said Caius.

"My earnest one," smiled Helena.

VI

Later that afternoon, shortly before they turned off the Appian Way onto the little side road which led to the country villa where they were to spend the night, an incident occurred which broke the monotony of the journey. A maniple of the 3rd Legion, on road patrol, was resting at a way station. *Scuta, pila,* and *cassis galeae* were stacked in rows of little three-sided tents, the long shields braced on the short spears, with three helmets nodding from each pile, for all the world like a close field of sheaved grain. The soldiers crowded the common court, pushing together under the shade of the awning, calling for beer and more beer, drinking it from the pint-sized wooden bowls called foot-baths. They were a tough, hard-faced, bronzed body of men, full of the strong smell of their sweat-soaked leather pants and jerkins, loud-voiced and foul-mouthed, and still conscious of the fact that the tokens of punishment along the highroad were the result of their recent work.

As Caius and the girls stopped to watch them, their captain came out of the pavilion, a goblet of wine in one hand, the other waving greeting to Caius—the more eagerly since Caius had two very good-looking young ladies with him.

He was an old friend of Caius's, a young man, Sellus Quintius Brutas by name, making a career as a professional, and very dashing and good-looking too. Helena, he already knew, and Claudia he was only too pleased to meet, and he became very professional and offhand as he asked them what they thought of his boys.

"A loud-mouthed, filthy lot," said Caius.

"That they are—but good."

"I shouldn't be afraid of anything, with them along," said Claudia, and added, "But them."

"And they are *your* slaves now, and they shall be along with you," answered Brutas gallantly. "Where to?"

"We stay at the *Villa Salaria* tonight," said Caius, "and if you recall, the road branches about two miles from here."

"Then for two miles, you shall fear nothing on earth," cried Brutas, and asked Helena,

"Have you ever marched with a legionary guard of honor?"

"I am not and have never been that important."

"That's precisely how important you are to me," said the young officer. "Just give me a chance. Just observe. I lay them at your feet. The company is yours."

"They are the last thing in the world I would want at my feet," protested Helena.

He finished the wine, tossed the cup at the door-slave, and piped on the little silver whistle he carried around his neck. There was a weird, demanding trill of four ascending and four descending notes, and in response the legionaries gulped their beer, swore under their breath, and moved on the double to where their spears, shields and helmets were stacked. Brutas sounded his whistle again and again, the notes stringing themselves into a sharp, insistent melody, and the maniple responded as if the notes played directly upon their nervous system. They fell in, grouped into squads, wheeled, broke apart, and then ranged themselves into two columns, one on either side of the road, in a truly amazing display of controlled discipline. The girls broke out in applause, and even Caius, somewhat annoyed at the antics of his friend, was forced to admire the precision of the company.

"Do they fight as well?" he demanded.

"Ask Spartacus," said Brutas, and Claudia cried, "Bravo!"

Brutas bowed and saluted her, and she burst out laughing. It was an unusual response for Claudia, but much about her had struck Caius as unusual today. There was bright color in her cheeks, and her eyes sparkled with excitement at the drill which the maniple had executed.

Caius felt less excluded than amazed at the way she began to chat with Brutas, who had ranged himself between the two litters and taken the whole procession in hand.

"What else can they do?" asked Claudia.

"March, fight, swear—"

"Kill?"

"Kill—yes, they're killers. Don't they look it?"

"I like the way they look," said Claudia.

Brutas studied her coolly, and then replied softly, "Really I think you do, my dear."

"What else?"

"What else do you want?" asked Brutas. "Do you want to hear them? March to cadence!" he shouted, and the deep voices of the troops chanted to step,

"Sky, earth, road, stone! Steel cuts to bone!"

The doggerel was blurred and coarsened in their throats, and the words were difficult to understand. "What does it mean?" Helena wanted to know.

"Nothing actually. It's just a marching cadence. There are hundreds of them, and they don't mean anything. Sky, earth, road, stone—nothing really, but they march better. This one came out of the Servile War. Some are not for the ears of a lady."

"Some are for my ears," said Claudia.

"I'll whisper it to you," he smiled, and bent to her as he walked along. Then he straightened up, and Claudia turned her head to stare at him. Once again, the crucifixes lined the road, the hanging bodies strung like beads along the way. Brutas waved at them. "Did you want it to be genteel? That's their work. My maniple crucified eight hundred of them. They're not nice; they're tough and hard and murderous."

"And that makes them better soldiers?" asked Helena.

"It's supposed to."

Claudia said, "Have one of them come over here."

"Why?"

"Because I want you to."

"All right," he shrugged, and shouted, "Sextus! Break out and attend!"

A soldier broke out of ranks, swung on the double in front of and between the litters, saluted, and swung into step in front of the officer. Claudia sat up, folded her arms, and studied him intently. He was a middle-sized, dark-skinned, heavily muscled man. His bare forearms, neck, throat and face were tanned almost to a mahogany brown. He had sharp, jutting features, tight-stretched with skin, moist with sweat. He wore a metal helmet, and his great, four-foot shield hung on his back over his haversack. In one hand he carried the pilum, a thick, six-foot spear of hardwood, two inches in diameter and shod at one end with a wicked, heavy, eighteen-inch triangular iron point. He wore a short, heavy Spanish sword, and his leather jerkin had laced on to it three iron plates across the chest, and three more hooked on to each shoulder. Three additional iron plates were hooked from his waist and swung against his legs as he marched. He wore leather pants and high leather shoes, and under that enormous weight of metal and wood, he marched easily and apparently without effort. The metal he carried was oiled, just as his armor was oiled; the stench of oil, sweat and leather mixed and became the singular smell of a trade, a force, a machine.

From where he rode behind them, Caius could see Claudia's face in profile, the lips parted, the tongue stroking them, the eyes fixed on the soldier.

"I want him next to the litter," Claudia whispered to Brutas.

He shrugged and threw an order at the soldier, whose lips twitched in just the faintest smile as he dropped back and marched next to Claudia. Just once his eyes fixed on her, and then he looked straight ahead. She reached out and touched his thigh, just barely touched it where the muscles were bunching under the leather, and then said to Brutas,

"Tell him to go away. He stinks. He's foul."

Helena's face was rigid. Brutas shrugged again and told the soldier to fall back into ranks.

VII

The *Villa Salaria* had a rather ironic name, which recalled the time when so much of the land to the south of Rome had been a malaria-infested salt marsh. But this section of the marsh had long since been reclaimed, and the pri-

vate road, which turned off the Appian Way and led to
the estate, was almost as well built as the main road itself.
Antonius Caius, who owned the estate, was related to
Caius and Helena through their mother; and though his
country place was not as elaborate as some, being rather
near to the city, it was still a great plantation in its own
right and ranked high as a showplace among the *latifundia*.

After Caius and the two girls had turned off the Appian
Way, there was still four miles of private road before they
came to the house itself. The difference was immediately
noticeable; every inch of land was manicured and cared
for. The woods were pruned and park-like. The hillsides
were terraced, and among the terraces were many fields
of fingerlike grape vines, just beginning to put forth their
first springtime shoots. Other fields were planted in barley
—a practice becoming less and less common and profitable
as the small peasant landholds gave way to the great
latifundia—and still others showed endless rows of olive
trees. Everywhere, there was that evidence of elegant land-
scaping which can only be provided by an almost unlimited
supply of slave labor, and again and again, the three young
people noticed lovely little grottos, mossy and green and
cool, with small replicas of Greek temples within them,
marble benches, fountains of transluscent alabaster, and
white stone paths which wound in and out of the woodland
glens. Seen as it was now, in the cooling late afternoon
with the sun dropping behind the low hills, the scene had
a fairy enchantment which caused Claudia, who had not
been there before, to cry out again and again in delight.
It was in keeping with the "new Claudia," and Caius reflected upon how a delicate and rather plethoric young lady
could flower so under the stimulus of tokens of punishment, as they were called by the nicer-minded.

At this time of the day, the cattle were being driven in,
and the tinkle of cow-bells and the sad call of the cow-
herds' horns sounded constantly. Goatherds, young
Thracians and Armenians, naked except for shreds of hide
across their loins, ran through the woods, halooing at the
scampering animals, and Caius wondered which looked
the more human, the goats or the slaves. He reflected now,
as he had so often before, on the wealth of this uncle of
his. By law, any sort of commercial transaction was forbidden to the old and noble families; but Antonius Caius—

26

as with many of his contemporaries—found the law a convenient cloak rather than a chain. It was said that he had, through his agents, over ten million *sesterces* out at interest, interest which frequently amounted to one hundred per cent. It was also said that he owned a controlling interest in fourteen *quinqueremes* in the Egyptian trade and that he owned half of one of the largest silver mines in Spain. Although no one but knights sat on the boards of the great joint stock companies which had arisen since the Punic Wars, the wishes of Antonius Caius were scrupulously observed by these boards.

It was impossible to say how wealthy he was, and though the *Villa Salaria* was a place of taste and beauty, with over ten thousand acres of fields and woodland belonging to it, it was by no means the largest or the most splendid of the *latifundia*. Nor did Antonius Caius make the ostentatious display of wealth that had become habitual with so many noble families of late, the sponsoring of great gladiatorial games, the setting of a table of indescribable luxury, and entertainment in the Eastern style. The table of Antonius was good and plentiful, but it was not graced with peacock breast, hummingbird tongues, or stuffed entrails of Libyan mice. This sort of fare was still frowned upon, and the scandals of the family were not paraded. Antonius himself was a Roman of old-fashioned dignity, and Caius—who respected him but did not particularly like him—never felt wholly at ease in his presence.

Part of this unease was due to the man himself, for Antonius Caius was not the most outgoing personality in the world; but more of the unease stemmed from the fact that Caius always felt an estimation on the part of his uncle of the difference between what the nephew actually was and what Antonius Caius would like the young Roman to measure up to. Caius suspected that the legend of the virtuous and austere Roman youth, dedicated to civic duty, a brave soldier first moving through the steps of officer advancement, marrying some upright Roman maiden, rearing a family like the Gracchi, serving the state unselfishly and well, moving from post to post, becoming consul finally, revered and honored by the plain and simple folk as well as the people of title and wealth, moral and upright throughout, was never less of a reality than now; and Caius himself knew of no such young Romans. The young men who surrounded Caius in the social life of Rome were interested in a number of things; some of them were dedicated to the conquest of astronomical numbers of young ladies; others caught the disease of money at a tender age and were already, in their twenties, engaged in a number of illegal commercial enterprises; still others learned the trade of ward heeling, plodding doggedly through the dirty routine of day to day work in the wards, buying and selling votes, bribing, fixing, conniving, learning from the bottom up the trade their fathers practiced so ably; still others made careers of food, becoming discerning gourmets; and a very few went into the army which, as a career for a young gentleman, was becoming less and less popular. So Caius, who as a member of that largest group of all—which dedicated itself to the dull task of passing days as idly and as pleasantly as possible—considered himself to be a harmless if not indispensable citizen of the great republic, resented the unspoken accusation which Antonius, his uncle, so frequently expressed. To Caius, live and let live summed up a civilized and workable philosophy.

He thought of this as they entered the vast expanse of formal garden and lawn which surrounded the villa itself. The extensive barns, corrals and slave quarters which constituted the industrial base of the plantation, were separate from the living quarters, and no hint of them no hint of ugliness or struggle was allowed to intrude upon the classic serenity of the house. The villa itself, an enormous square house built around a central court and pool, stood on top of a slight elevation. Whitewashed, roofed with weathered red tile, it was not unlovely in itself, and the hardness of its plain lines was relieved by the tasteful arrangement of tall cedars and poplars all around it. The grounds were landscaped in what was known as the Ionian style, with many flowering shrubs trained to grow into unusual shapes, smooth lawns, summer houses of colored marble, alabaster basins for tropical fish, and numerous pieces of traditional lawn statuary, nymphs and pans and fawns and cherubs. Antonius Caius had a standing purchase offer at the highest price in the Roman markets where skilled Greek sculptors and landscapers were sold; he never stinted on this—although it was said that he had no taste himself and merely followed the advice of his wife, Julia. Caius believed this, for he was not without taste himself and he saw no trace of it in his uncle. While there were many other villas more splendid than the *Villa Salaria,* some like the palaces of oriental potentates, Caius could think of none in better taste or lovelier in setting. Claudia agreed with him. As they came through the gates and onto the brick road that approached the house, Claudia gasped with surprise, and said to Helena,

"It's like nothing I ever dreamed of! It's like something out of the Greek myths."

"It's a very pleasant place," Helena agreed.

The two young daughters of Antonius Caius saw them first and raced across the lawns to greet them, followed more sedately by their mother, Julia, a pleasant looking, dark-skinned and rather plump woman. Antonius himself came out of the house a moment later, followed by three other men. He was punctilious in matters of behavior for himself as well as others, and he greeted his niece and his nephew and their friend with grave courtesy—and then formally introduced his guests. Two of them were well known to Caius, Lentelus Gracchus, a shrewd, successful city politician, and Licinius Crassus, the general who had made such a name for himself in the Servile War and who was the talk of the city and had been for a year. The third man in the party was a stranger to Caius; he was younger than the others, not much older than Caius himself, diffident with the subtle diffidence of one who was not patrician born, arrogant with the less subtle arrogance of the intellectual Roman, calculating in his estimation of the newcomers, and moderately good-looking. His name was Marcus Tullius Cicero, and he acknowledged his introduction to Caius and the two pretty young women with modest self-effacement. Yet he could not effact his restless curiosity, and even Caius, who was not the most perceptive of persons, realized that Cicero was examining them, assessing them, trying to compute their background, aggregate family wealth, and influence as well.

Claudia, meanwhile, had fixed upon Antonius Caius as the most desirable male element, the master of the imposing house and the endless acres. Having only a nominal sense of politics and a rather vague notion of war, she was not particularly impressed by either Gracchus or Crassus, and Cicero was not only unknown—which meant of no consequence to Claudia—but obviously one of the money-grubbing race of knights whom she had been taught to despise. Julia already was pressing up to Caius, a favorite of hers, purring against him like a large, ungainly kitten, and Claudia made a shrewder estimate of Antonius than Caius ever had. She saw the big, hook-nosed, powerfully muscled land-owner as a mass of repressions and unsatisfied hungers. She sensed the sensual lining to his patently assumed puritanism, and Claudia preferred men who were powerful yet powerless. Antonius Caius would never be indiscreet or annoying. All this, she let him know with her apparently listless smile.

The whole party had come to the house now. Caius had dismounted before, and now an Egyptian house slave led away his horse. The litter-bearers, weary from all the miles they had come, sweating, crouched beside their burdens and shivered in the evening coolness. Now their lean bodies were animal-like in weariness, and their muscles quivered with the pain of exhaustion, even as an animals does. No one looked at them, no one noticed them, no one attended them. The five men, the three women and the two children went into the house, and still the litter-bearers crouched by the litters, waiting. Now one of them, a lad of no more than twenty, began to sob, more and more uncontrollably; but the others paid no attention to him. They remained there at least twenty minutes before a slave came to them and led them to the barracks where they would have food and shelter for the night.

VIII

Caius shared his bath with Licinius Crassus, and he was relieved to find that the great man was not of the school which took him, Caius, personally to task for all the effete qualities of well born youth today. He found Crassus pleasant and affable, and he had that winning manner which seeks for the opinions of others, even when others are persons of no particular importance.

They lolled in the bath, treading water lazily, floating back and forth, luxuriating in the warm, scented water, so heavily impregnated with fragrant salts. Crassus's body was well kept, not the paunchy affair of middle age, but hard and flat, and he was youthful and alert. He asked Caius whether they had come down the road from Rome.

"Yes, we did, and we're going on to Capua tomorrow."

"You didn't mind the tokens of punishment?"

"We were very curious to see them," answered Caius. "No, as a matter of fact, we didn't mind them particularly. Here and there, you would see a body that the birds had torn open, and that did become somewhat unpleasant, especially if the wind was coming to you, but that can't be helped, and the girls simply drew their curtains. But, you know, the litter-bearers were affected, and sometimes they were sick."

"I suppose they identified," the general smiled.

"Possibly. Do you think there is that sort of feeling among slaves? Our litter-bearers are stable-bred for the most part, and most of them were whip-broken in childhood at the school of Appius Mundellius, and while they're strong, they're not much better than animals. Would they identify? I find it hard to believe that there would be such uniform qualities among slaves. But you would know better. Do you think that all slaves felt something for Spartacus?"

"I think most of them did."

"Really? You can get quite uneasy over that."

"Otherwise, I wouldn't like this business of the crucifixion," Crassus explained. "It's wasteful, and I don't like waste for the sake of waste. Also, I think that killing can backfire—too much killing. I think it does something to us that may hurt us later."

"But slaves?" Caius protested.

"What is Cicero so fond of saying—the slave is the *instrumentum vocale,* as distinguished from the beast, the *instrumentum semi-vocale,* as distinguished from the ordinary tool, which we might call the *instrumentum mutum.* This is a very clever way of putting it, and I'm sure that Cicero is a very clever person, but Cicero did not have to fight Spartacus. Cicero did not have to estimate Spartacus's potential for logic because he did not have to lie awake nights, as I did, trying to anticipate what

31

Spartacus was thinking. When you fight against them, you suddenly discover that the slaves are something more than *instrumenta vocalia.*"

"Did you know him—I mean personally?"

"Him?"

"Spartacus, I mean."

The general smiled reflectively. "Not really," he considered. "I made my own picture of him, putting this and that together, but I don't know that anyone *knew* him. How could you know him? If your pet dog suddenly ran amuck and did so intelligently, he would still be a dog, wouldn't he? Hard to know. I made my image of Spartacus, but I wouldn't presume to write a portrait of him. I don't think anyone can. Those who might have are hanging along the Appian Way, and already the man himself is like a dream. We will now remake him back into a slave."

"Which he was," said Caius.

"Yes—yes, I suppose so."

It was difficult for Caius to pursue the matter. It was not that he had so little experience in war; the truth of the matter was that he was uninterested in war; yet war was the obligation of his caste, his class, his station in life. What did Crassus think of him? Could the politeness and the considerate attention be real? In any case, Caius's family could not be ignored or belittled, and Crassus had need of friends; for ironically enough, this general who fought the bitterest war in perhaps all Roman history had little enough glory out of it. He had fought against slaves and defeated them—when those slaves had almost defeated Rome. The whole thing was a curious contradiction, and the humility of Crassus might very well be real. About Crassus, the legends would not be made nor the songs sung. The necessity of forgetting the whole war would belittle his victory increasingly.

They climbed out of the bath, and the slave women waiting there enveloped them with the warm towels. Many a more ostentatious place than that of Antonius Caius would not have been fitted one half so well with everything to anticipate and satisfy the needs of a guest. Caius thought of this as he was rubbed dry; in the old times, as he had been taught, there was a world full of petty princelings, little kingdoms and dukedoms, but few of them would have been able to live or entertain in the style of Antonius Caius, a not too powerful or important landholder and a citizen of the Republic. Say what you would, the Roman way of life was a reflection of those most fit and most able to rule.

"I have never quite gotten used to being dressed and handled by women," said Crassus. "Do you like it?"

"I never gave it much thought," answered Caius, which was not entirely true, for there was a definite pleasure and excitement in being handled by slave women. His own father did not allow it, and in certain circles, it was frowned upon; but in the past five or six years, the attitude toward slaves had altered considerably, and Caius, like so many of his friends, had divested them of most elements of humanity. It was a subtle conditioning. At this moment, he did not actually know what these three women in attendance looked like, and if he had been asked abruptly, he could not have described them. The general's question made him observe them. They were out of some tribe or part of Spain, young, small in bone, not uncomely in their dark, silent way. Barefoot, they were dressed in short, plain tunics, and their dresses were damp from the steam of the bath and spotted with perspiration from their efforts. They excited him only a little in terms of his own nakedness, but Crassus drew one of them to him, handling her oafishly and smiling down at her, while she cringed against him but made no resistance.

It embarrassed Caius enormously; he felt a sudden contempt for this great general who was fumbling around a bath house girl; he didn't want to watch. It seemed to him small and dirty, and it divested Crassus of dignity, and Caius also felt that when Crassus remembered it later he would hold it against Caius that he had been present.

He walked to the rubbing table and lay down, and a moment later Crassus joined him. "A pretty little piece," said Crassus. Was the man a complete idiot in terms of women, Caius wondered? But Crassus was not perturbed. "Spartacus," he said, picking up the thread of his conversation before, "was as much of an enigma to me as he is to you. I never saw him—with all the devil's dance he led me."

"You never saw him?"

"Never did, but that doesn't mean that I didn't know

33

him. Piece by piece, I composed him. I like that. Other people composed music or art. I composed a picture of Spartacus."

Crassus stretched and luxuriated under the clever, kneading fingers of the masseuse. One woman held a little pitcher of scented oil, pouring a constant, careful lubrication under the fingers of the masseuse, who flexed the tension out of muscle after muscle. Crassus twisted like a great cat being stroked, sighing with pleasure.

"What was he like—your picture, I mean?" asked Caius.

"I often wonder what I was like in his mind," grinned Crassus. "He called to me in the end. Or so they say. I can't swear that I heard him, but they say he sang out, Crassus—wait for me, you bastard! Or something like that. He wasn't more than forty or fifty yards from me, and he began to cut his way to me. It was an astonishing thing. He wasn't a very big man—not a very powerful man either, but he had a fury. That's the word, precisely. When he fought with his own arms, it was like that, a fury, an anger. And he actually cut his way half the distance to me. He must have killed at least ten or eleven men in that last wild rush of his, and he wasn't stopped until we cut him to pieces."

"Then it's true that his body was never found?" asked Caius.

"That's right. He was cut to pieces, and there was just nothing left to find. Do you know how a battlefield is? There is meat and blood, and whose meat and whose blood, it is very hard to say. So he went the way he came, out of nothing into nothing, out of the arena into the butcher shop. We live by the sword and we die by the sword. That was Spartacus. I salute him."

What the general said recalled to Caius the conversation with the sausage maker, and it was on the tip of his tongue to raise the question. But then he thought better of it and asked instead,

"You don't hate him?"

"Why? He was a good soldier and a damned, dirty slave. What should I hate particularly? He's dead and I'm alive. I like this—" twisting gratefully under the masseuse's fingers, but taking it for granted that his words were something apart from her and beyond her. "—but my experience is limited. You wouldn't think so, would you, but your generation looks at things differently. I don't mean sluts, I mean niceties, like this. How far does one go, Caius?"

The young man at first did not know what the general was talking about, and glanced at him curiously. The muscles on Crassus's neck were swelling with passion, and passion was all over his body now. It troubled Caius and frightened him a little, he wanted to get out of the room quickly, but there was no way to do it decently; and less because he minded what would happen than he minded his being there to see it happen.

"You might ask her?" Caius said.

"Ask her? Do you suppose the bitch speaks Latin?"

"They all do, a little."

"You mean ask her directly?"

"Why not?" muttered Caius, and then turned onto his belly and closed his eyes.

IX

While Caius and Crassus were in the bath, and while the last fading hour before the sunset cast its golden glow over the fields and garden of *Villa Salaria*, Antonius Caius took his niece's friend on a walk across the grounds toward the horse run. Antonius Caius did not indulge in such ostentatious displays as, for example, a private race course or his own arena for games. He had a theory of his own that to survive in the possession of wealth, one had to display it discreetly, and he had none of the social insecurity that called for gaudy prominence, such as was common with the new social class of business men arising in the republic. But like his friends, Antonius Caius loved horses and paid out fantastic sums of money for good breeding stock, and took a good deal of pleasure in his stables. At this time, the price of a good horse was at least five times the price of a good slave—but the rationale was that one sometimes needed five slaves to raise a horse properly.

The horse run, fenced in, sprawled over a broad meadow. The stables and pens were at one end, and a little distance from there, a comfortable stone gallery, capable of holding up to fifty people, commanded both the course and a large pen.

As they approached the stables, they heard the shrill, demanding cry of a stallion, a note of insistence and rage new to Claudia, thrilling yet frightening.

"What is that?" she asked Antonius Caius.

"A stallion aroused. I bought him at the market only two weeks ago. Thracian blood, big boned, savage, but he's a beauty. Would you like to see him?"

"I love horses," said Claudia. "Please show him to me."

They walked to the stables, and Antonius told the foreman, a withered, shrunken little Egyptian slave, to put him in the big display pen. Then they went to the gallery to watch, seating themselves in a nest of cushions which a slave arranged for them. Claudia did not fail to notice how well-trained and how sedulous Antonius Caius's body servants were, how they anticipated every wish, every glance of his. She had grown up among slaves and she knew the difficulties one was likely to have with them. When she mentioned it to him, he remarked,

"I don't whip my slaves. When there is trouble, I kill one. That exacts obedience, but it does not break their spirit."

"I think they have wonderful spirit," Claudia nodded.

"It isn't easy to handle slaves—slaves, horses—men are the easiest."

Now they brought the stallion into the pen, an enormous yellow beast with bloodshot eyes and a lathered mouth. His head was lashed in check, yet the two slaves hanging onto his bridle could hardly keep him from rearing and plunging. He dragged them half way across the pen, and then when they released him and ran for safety, he reared and slashed at them with his hoofs. Claudia laughed and clapped her hands in delight.

"He's splendid, splendid!" she cried. "But why is he that way—so full of hate?"

"Don't you know?"

"I should think it would be love, not hate."

"The two mix. He hates us because we keep him from what he wants. Would you like to see?"

Claudia nodded. Antonius said a few words to the slave who stood a little distance from them, and the man ran down to the stables. The mare was chestnut brown, lithe and nervous. She fled across the pen, and the stallion whirled to cut her off. But Antonius Caius was not watching her; his eyes were fixed on Claudia, who was enthralled in the scene being enacted before her.

X

Through with his bath, shaved, perfumed, his hair oiled slightly and curled delicately, his clothes fresh for dinner, Caius went into the fern room to have a glass of wine before the call to dinner. The fern room at the *Vilia Salaria* combined rose-colored Phoenician tile with a delicately-tinted, pale yellow glass roof. The result at this time of the day was a gentle glow of fading sunlight which transformed the dark ferns and heavy-leafed tropical plants into a phantasy. When Caius entered, Julia was already there, sitting on an alabaster bench, with one of her little girls on either side of her, the fading light both flattering and kind. As she sat there in her long white gown, her dark hair dressed tastefully on top of her head, an arm around each of the children, she was the very picture of a Roman matron, comely and calm and dignified; and if she had not been so obviously and childishly posed, she would have quite naturally recalled to Caius every painting of the mother of the Gracchi he had ever seen. He repressed his impulse to applaud or say, "Bravo, Julia!" It was too easy to destroy Julia, for her pretense was always pathetic, never hostile.

"Good evening, Caius," she smiled in a fine combination of simulated surprise and real pleasure.

"I didn't know you would be here, Julia," he apologized.

"But please stay. Stay and let me pour you a glass of wine."

"All right," he agreed, and when she started to send the girls away, protested, "Let them stay if they want to—"

"It's really time for their supper." When the children had gone, she said, "Come and sit beside me, Caius. Do sit beside me, Caius." He sat down, and she poured wine for both of them. She touched her glass to his and drank with her eyes on him. "You are too handsome to be good, Caius."

"I have no desire to be good, Julia."

"What do you desire, Caius, if anything?"

"Pleasure," he answered frankly.

"And it becomes harder and harder, young as you are, doesn't it, Caius?"

"Really, Julia, I don't look particularly mournful, do I?"

"Or particularly happy."

"The role of vestal virgin, Julia, is not very becoming."

"You're much cleverer than I am, Caius. I can't be as cruel as you."

"I don't want to be cruel, Julia."

"Will you kiss me and prove that?"

"Here?"

"Antonius won't walk in. Right now, he is putting his new stallion to stud for the edification of that little blonde you brought here."

"What? For Claudia? Oh, no—no." Caius began to chuckle deep inside himself.

"What a little beast you are. Will you kiss me?"

He kissed her lightly on the lips.

"Just that? Will you—tonight, Caius?"

"Really, Julia—"

"Don't say no to me, Caius," she interrupted him. "Don't—please. You won't have your Claudia tonight in any case. I know my husband."

"She isn't my Claudia, and I don't want her tonight."

"Then—"

"All right," he said. "All right, Julia. We won't talk about it now."

"You don't want to—"

"It isn't that I want to or don't want to, Julia. I just don't want to talk about it any more now."

XI

The evening meal at the *Villa Salaria* demonstrated, as did other practices of the household, a certain resistance to changes already common in cosmopolitan Rome. On the part of Antonius Caius, it was less an ingrained conservatism than a desire to separate himself from the new class of rich merchants who had made their fortunes out of war, piracy, mining and trade—and who lapped eagerly at every Greek or Egyptian innovation. As far as eating went, Antonius Caius could not enjoy a meal sprawled out on a couch; it impaired his digestion and diverted him from real food to the little tidbits of sweet-and-sour delicacies which were becoming so fashionable now. His guests sat at the table and ate from the table, and while he presented them with game and fowl, with fine roasts and elegant pastries, with the best of soup and the most succulent of fruits, there were none of the weird concoctions that were showing up at the boards of so many Roman noblemen. Nor did he favor music and dancing during a meal; good food and good wine and good conversation. His father and his grandfather had both been able to read and write fluently; himself, he considered an educated man, and while his grandfather had gone out to work the fields of the farm alongside of his slaves, Antonius Caius ruled his great *latifundium* much as a minor Eastern prince might have ruled his little empire. Nevertheless, he was fond of thinking of himself as an enlightened ruler, well versed in Greek history, philosophy and drama, able to practice at least competent medicine, and a person of political affairs as well. His guests reflected his taste, and when they reclined in their chairs after the meal, sipping their dessert wine—the women having repaired to the fern room for the moment—Caius recognized in them and his host the cream of the quality which had made Rome and which ruled Rome so tenaciously and so ably.

Caius admired it less than he recognized it; he had no ambitions in that direction himself. In their opinion, he was of no value and of no particular importance, a young wastrel of good family with real talent only in the direction of food and stud; which in some respects was a new direction, a product of only the last generation or two. Yet he had some importance; he had family connections which were enviable; when his father died, he would be very wealthy, and it was even possible that some twist of fortune would turn him into a person of political consequence. Thus, he was a little more than tolerated and treated a little better than one might treat a young, perfumed fop with good features, oiled hair, and little brains.

And Caius feared them. There was a disease in them but the disease did not appear to weaken them. Here they sat, having eaten their fine food, sipping their mellow wine, and those who contested their power were crucified for miles and miles along the Appian Way. Spartacus was meat; simply meat; like the meat on the cutting table at a butcher shop; not even enough of him to crucify. But no one would ever crucify Antonius Caius, sitting so calmly and surely at the head of the table, speaking of horses, making the extremely logical point that it was better to harness two slaves to a plow than one horse, since there never was a horse which could stand the half-human treatment of slaves.

A slight smile on Cicero's face as he listened. More than the others, Cicero disturbed Caius. How could one like Cicero? Did he want to like Cicero? Once Cicero had glanced at him, as if to say, "Oh, I know you, my lad. Top and bottom, up and down, inside and out." Were the others afraid of Cicero, he wondered? Stay away from Cicero, God damn him to hell, he said to himself. Crassus was listening with polite interest. Crassus had to be polite. He was the picture of the Roman military man, erect, square face, firm, hard features, bronzed skin, fine black hair—and then Caius thought of him in the bath and winced. How could he? Across the table from Caius, sat the politician, Gracchus, a big man with a deep booming voice, his head sunk in collars of fat, his huge hands fat and puffy, with rings on almost every finger. He responded with the deeply conditioned responses of the professional politician; his laugh was a great laugh; his approval was a mighty approval, whereas his disagreement was always conditional. His statements were pompous but never stupid.

"Of course you would do better with slaves on your plow," observed Cicero, after Gracchus had expressed some disbelief. "The beast which can think is more desirable than the beast which cannot think. That stands to reason. Also, a horse is a thing of value. There are no

40

tribes of horses whom we can war against and bring back a hundred and fifty thousand to the auction block. And if you use horses, the slaves will ruin them."

"I don't see that," said Gracchus.

"Ask your host."

"It's true," nodded Antonius. "Slaves will kill a horse. They have no respect for anything which belongs to their master—except themselves." He poured another glass of wine. "Are we to talk about slaves?"

"Why not?" reflected Cicero. "They are always with us, and we are the unique product of slaves and slavery. That is what makes us Romans, if you come right down to it. Our host lives on this great plantation—for which I envy him—by the grace of a thousand slaves. Crassus is the talk of Rome, because of the slave uprising which he put down, and Gracchus has an income from the slave market—which is in a ward he owns body and soul—which I hesitate even to compute. And this young man—" Nodding at Caius and smiling. "—this young man is, I suspect, the unique product of slaves even a little more, for I am certain they nursed him and fed him and aired him and doctored him and—"

Caius turned red, but Gracchus burst out laughing and cried, "And yourself, Cicero?"

"For me, they constituted a problem. To live decently in Rome these days, one needs a minimum of ten slaves. And to buy them, feed them and house them—well, there is my problem."

Gracchus continued to laugh, but Crassus said, "I can't agree with you, Cicero, that slaves are what makes us Romans." The rumbling laughter of Gracchus continued. He took a long drink of wine, and went into a story of a slave girl he had purchased in the market the month before. He was a little tight, his face flushed, the chuckles rumbling out of his enormous paunch and interspersing his words. In great detail, he described the girl he had purchased. Caius thought the story pointless and vulgar, but Antonius nodded sagely and Crassus was carried away by the earthiness of the fat man's description. Cicero smiled thinly and reflectively through the telling.

"Yet I return to Cicero's statement," said Crassus doggedly.

"Did I offend you?" asked Cicero.

"No one is offended here," said Antonius. "We are a company of civilized people."

"No—no offense. You puzzle me," said Crassus.

"It's strange," nodded Cicero, "how when the evidence of a thing is all around us, we nevertheless resist the logic of its component parts. The Greeks are different. Logic has an irresistible lure for them, regardless of the consequences; but our virtue is doggedness. But look around us—" One of the slaves who stood in attendance at the table, replaced the emptying decanters with full ones, and another offered fruit and nuts to the men. "—What is the essence of our lives? We are not just any people; we are the Roman people, and we are that precisely because we are the first to understand fully the use of the slave."

"Yet there were slaves before there was Rome," Antonius objected.

"Indeed there were, a few here, a few there. It is true that the Greeks had plantations—so did Carthage. But we destroyed Greece and we destroyed Carthage, to make room for our own plantations. And the plantation and the slave are one and the same thing. Where other people had one slave, we have twenty—and now we live in a land of slaves, and our greatest achievement is Spartacus. How about that, Crassus? You had an intimate acquaintance with Spartacus. Could any other nation but Rome have produced him?"

"Did we produce Spartacus?" Crassus wondered. The general was troubled. Caius guessed that it bothered him to think profoundly under any circumstances—and even more so when confronted with a mind like Cicero's. There was actually no meeting ground between the two. "I thought that hell produced Spartacus," Crassus added.

"Hardly."

Undisturbed, Gracchus rumbled comfortably and drank wine and observed to Cicero, somewhat apologetically, that being a good Roman, he, Gracchus, was a poor philosopher. In any case, here was Rome and here were the slaves, and what did Cicero propose to do about it?

"Understand it," Cicero answered.

"Why?" Antonius Caius demanded.

"Because otherwise they will destroy us."

Crassus laughed and caught Caius's eye as he did so. It

was the first real rapport between them, and the young man felt a shiver of excitement race down his spine. Crassus was drinking heavily, but when Caius felt like this, he had no desire for wine.

"Did you come down the road?" Crassus asked.

Cicero shook his head; it was never easy to convince a military man that all matters were not decided by the sword. "I don't mean the simple logic of a butcher shop. Here is a process. Here on the land of our good host, there were once at least three thousand peasant families. If you consider five to a family, that is fifteen thousand people. And those peasants were damned good soldiers. What about that, Crassus?"

"They were good soldiers. I wish there were more of them around."

"And good farmers," Cicero continued. "Not for lawns and formal gardens, but take barley. Just barley—but the Roman soldier marches on barley. Is there any acre of your land, Antonius, which produces half as much barley as an industrious peasant used to squeeze out of it?"

"Not one quarter as much," Antonius Caius agreed.

It had all become exceedingly dull and boring to Caius. He was riding on his inner images, and his face felt hot and flushed. Excitement coursed through him, and he imagined that a soldier felt like this when going into battle. He hardly heard Cicero any more. He kept glancing at Crassus, asking himself why Cicero persisted in this tedious subject.

"And why—why?" Cicero was demanding. "Why can't your slaves produce? The answer is very simple."

"They don't want to," Antonius said flatly.

"Precisely—they don't want to. Why should they want to? When you work for a master, your only achievement is to spoil your work. It's no use sharpening their plows, because they'd blunt them immediately. They break sickles, crack flails, and waste becomes a principle with them. This is the monster we have created for ourselves. Here on ten thousand acres, there once lived fifteen thousand people; and now there are a thousand slaves and the family of Antonius Caius, and the peasants rot in the slums and alleys of Rome. We must understand this. It was a simple matter when the peasant came back from war and his land was overgrown with weeds and his wife had

43

gone to bed with someone else and his children didn't know him, to give him a handful of silver for his land and let him go into Rome and live on the streets. But the result is that now we live in a land of slaves, and this is the basis of our lives and the meaning of our lives—and the whole question of our freedom, of human freedom, of the Republic and the future of civilization will be determined by our attitude toward them. They are not human; this we must understand and get rid of the sentimental nonsense the Greeks talk of the equality of all that walks and talks. The slave is the *instrumentum vocale*. Six thousand of these tools line the road; this isn't wasteful, this is necessary! I am sick to death of the talk of Spartacus, of his courage—yes, of his nobility. There is no courage and there is no nobility in a cur that snaps at his master's heels!"

The coldness of Cicero had not dissipated; it had instead become transported into a livid anger, just as cold—but an anger which transfixed his listeners and made him their master, so that they stared at him, half-enchanted, half-afraid.

Only in the slaves who moved around the table, serving fruits and nuts and sweetmeats, replenishing the wine, was there no reaction. Caius noticed this, for now he was sensitized all over and the world was different for him and he was a creature of excitement and reaction. He saw how unchanged the faces of the slaves remained, how wooden their expression, how lethargic their movements. It was true then, what Cicero said—they were not made human by virtue of the fact that they walked and talked. He did not know why this should have comforted him, but it did.

XII

Caius excused himself while they were still drinking and talking. His stomach was constricting now, and he felt that he would go insane if he had to sit there and listen to any more of this. He excused himself on the grounds of weariness from his journey; but when he had left the dining room, he felt that he needed a breath of fresh air desperately, and he went through the back entrance of the house to the terrace, which extended from the rear of the house, white marble except in the center, where there was a pool of water. In the center of this pool, a nymph rose out of a cluster of sea serpents. A stream of water poured out of the conch shell she held, dancing and sparkling in the moonlight. Benches of alabaster and green volcanic stone were placed here and there on the terrace, and they were artfully given a degree of privacy by cypress trees, set in great jugs carved out of black lava. The terrace, which ran the whole width of the huge house and extended some fifty feet out from the house, was enclosed by a marble railing, except in the center, where a flight of broad white steps led down to the less formal gardens below. It was like Antonius Caius to hide this extravagant display of wealth behind his house, and so used was Caius to expenditure in stone and stonework that he hardly gave the details of the place a second glance. Perhaps Cicero would have observed the genius of a people displayed in the use of stone and the smugness that laid out incidental decoration in terms of eternity; but the thought never occurred to Caius.

Even in the normal course of things, few thoughts occurred to him which were not introduced by another; and generally they concerned food or sex. It was not that Caius lacked imagination or was stupid; it was simply that his role in life had never called for either imagination or original thought, and the only problem he faced at the moment was to understand completely the glance Crassus had given him before he left the dining room. He was thinking of that, staring out over the moonlit slopes of the plantation, when a voice interrupted him.

"Caius?"

The last person he wanted to be alone with on that terrace was Julia.

"I'm glad I came out here, Caius."

He shrugged his shoulders without answering, and she walked up to him, laid a hand on either arm, and looked up at his face.

"Be decent to me, Caius," she said.

"Why doesn't she stop slobbering and whining," he thought.

"What you give so little—it costs you so little, Caius.

45

And it costs me so much to ask for it. Don't you understand that?"

He said, "I'm very tired, Julia, and I want to go to bed."

"I suppose I deserve it," she whispered.

"Please don't take it that way, Julia."

"How shall I take it?"

"I'm just tired—that's all."

"That isn't all, Caius. I look at you, and wonder what you are, and hate myself. You're so handsome—and so rotten—"

He didn't interrupt her. Let her say it all; he would be rid of her so much more quickly.

She went on, "No—no more rotten than anyone else, I suppose. Only with you, I bring it out. But we're all rotten, we're all sick, diseased, full of death, bags of death—we're in love with death. Aren't you, Caius, and that's why you came down the road where you could look at the tokens of punishment? Punishment! We do it because we love it—the way you do the things you do, because you love them. Do you know how beautiful you are out here in the moonlight? The young Roman, the cream of the whole world in the full flush of beauty and youth— and you have no time for an old woman. I'm as rotten as you are, Caius, but I hate you as much as I love you. I wish you were dead. I wish someone would kill you and cut your miserable little heart out!"

There was a long moment of silence, and then Caius asked calmly, "Is that all, Julia?"

"No—no, not all. I wish I were dead too."

"Both of these are desires which can be satisfied," said Caius.

"You contemptible—"

"Good night, Julia," Caius said sharply, and then left the terrace. His determination not to be annoyed had been broken, and he was provoked at the senseless outburst of his aunt. If she had any sense of proportion, she would have seen how ridiculous she was making herself with her cheap sentimental whining. But Julia never had that kind of sense, and it was no wonder that Antonius found her trying.

Caius went straight to his room. A lamp was burning and there were two slaves in attendance, young Egyptians whom Antonius favored as house servants. Caius dismissed them. Then he stripped off his clothes, flushed and trembling. He rubbed himself all over with a mild perfume, powdered parts of his body, slipped on a linen robe, blew out the lamp and lay down on his bed. When his eyes got used to the dark, he was able to see fairly well, for a broad shaft of moonlight came in through the open window. The room was pleasantly cool, full of the fragrance of perfume and the spring shrubs in the garden.

It couldn't have been more than a few minutes that Caius lay there waiting, but it seemed like hours to him. Then there was a very light knock on the door.

"Come in," Caius said.

Crassus entered, closing the door behind him. The great general had never looked more manly than now, as he stood there smiling at the young man who awaited him.

XIII

The beam of moonlight had changed its position, and Caius was tired and satiated and sensual as a stretching cat—which was the image he evoked of himself for himself as he said, apropos of nothing at all,

"I hate Cicero."

Crassus was fatherly and pleased with himself and mellow, and he asked, "Why do you hate Cicero—the just Cicero? Cicero the just. Yes? Why do you hate him?"

"I don't know why I hate him. Must I know why I hate people? Some, I love and some, I hate."

"Did you know that it was Cicero's notion—not his alone, but a good deal his—to make the tokens of punishment, the six thousand crucifixes along the Appian Way? Is that why you hate him?"

"No."

"How did you feel when you saw the crucifixes?" asked the general.

"Sometimes it excited me but mostly it didn't. It excited the girls more."

"Yes?"

"But tomorrow I'll feel different," Caius smiled.

"Why?"

"Because you put them there."

"Not really—Cicero, others. I didn't care, one way or another."

"But you destroyed Spartacus."

"Does that matter?"

"I love you for it—I hate him."

"Spartacus?" asked Crassus.

"Yes, Spartacus."

"But you never knew him."

"It doesn't matter. I hate him—more than Cicero. I don't care about Cicero. But him, that slave, him I hate. If I could have killed him myself! If you could have brought him to me and said, here, Caius, cut his heart out! If you could have—"

"Now you're talking like a child," the general said indulgently.

"Am I? Why not?" Caius said, a whining note in his voice. "Why shouldn't I be a child? Is it so rewarding to be grown?"

"But why did you hate Spartacus so when you never saw him?"

"Maybe I did see him. You know, I went to Capua four years ago. I was only twenty-one then, I was very young."

"You are still very young," the general said.

"No—I don't feel so young. But then I was. A party of five or six of us went. Marius Bracus took me with him, he was very fond of me." Caius said that deliberately for the effect it would have; Marius Bracus had died in the Servile War, so there would be no question of current involvement, but let Crassus know that he was not the only one and not the first one. The general stiffened but did not speak, and Caius went on,

"Yes, there was Marius Bracus and myself and a man and a woman, friends of his, and two others, I think, whose names I have forgotten, and Marius Bracus was acting in the grand manner—yes, very much in the grand manner."

"Did you care for him greatly?"

"I was sorry he died," Caius shrugged, and the general thought,

"What a little animal you are! What a filthy little animal!"

"Anyway, we went to Capua and Bracus promised us a special circus, which was more expensive then than now. You had to be a rich man to do it in Capua."

"Lentulus Batiatus had the school there then, didn't he?" asked Crassus.

"He did, and it was supposed to be the best school anywhere in Italy. The best and the most expensive, and you could buy an elephant for what it cost to fight a pair of his boys. They say that he made a million out of this, but he was a pig in any case. Did you know him?"

Crassus shook his head. "Tell me about him, I'm very interested. It was before Spartacus broke loose, wasn't it?"

"Eight days before, I think. Yes, Batiatus made a name for himself because he kept a regular harem of slave women and people don't like that sort of thing. Not out in the open. It's all right if you do it in a room with the doors closed, but it's rather tasteless to do it on a public highway. That's practically what he did. Also, he used his boys for stud and the women for breeding, which is all right, I suppose, but he didn't know how to do anything delicately. He was a big, fat ox of a man, black hair, black beard, and I remember how dirty his clothes were, food stains all over them. An egg stain when he talked with us, a fresh egg stain right on the front of his tunic."

"The things you remember!" the general smiled.

"I remember that. I went to see him with Bracus, and Bracus wanted two turns to the death; but Batiatus was reluctant to do it. Batiatus said that there was no point trying to develop anything in the way of style or technique or precision play when every rich and bored gentleman in Rome came down for his own particular circus. But Bracus had a purse, and money talks."

"It talks with that kind," said the general. "All *lanistae* are contemptible, but this Batiatus was a pig. You know, he owns three of the biggest tenements in Rome, and a fourth that fell in last year, and half his tenants were killed in the rubbish. He'll do anything for money."

"I didn't know you knew him."

"I spoke with him. He was a mine of information on Spartacus—the only one, I suppose, who really knew about Spartacus."

"Tell me," sighed Caius.

"You were telling me—that perhaps you saw Spartacus."

"Tell me," said Caius petulantly.

"You are remarkably like a girl sometimes," the general smiled.

"Don't say that! I don't want you ever to say that!" Like a cat, Caius tensed and bristled.

"Now what have I said to anger you so?" the general soothed him. "You want me to tell you about Batiatus? It's of no great interest, but I will if you want me to. It was over a year ago, I think, and we were being clawed badly by the slaves. That was why I wanted to find out about this Spartacus. You know a man, and it's easier to beat him . . ."

Caius smiled as he listened. He didn't wholly know why he hated Spartacus so much; but sometimes he found a deeper satisfaction in hatred than in love.

PART TWO

Being the story which Crassus, the great general, told to Caius Crassus, concerning a visit to his encampment by Lentulus Batiatus, who kept a school for gladiators in Capua.

(This, then, said Crassus, as he lay beside the young man, happened shortly after I had been given the command—the kind of an honor that you take with you to a quick grave. The slaves had torn our legions to shreds, and to all effects and purposes, they ruled Italy. This, they told me to rescue. Go out and defeat the slaves, they said. My worst enemies honored me. I had encamped my troops in Cisalpine Gaul then, and I sent out a message for your fat friend, Lentulus Batiatus.)

And rain was falling lightly as Lentulus Batiatus approached the camp of Crassus. The whole landscape was miserable and desolate, and he was also desolate, being a long way from home and from the warm sunshine of Capua. Not even the comfort of a litter was his; he rode on a skinny yellow horse, thinking:

"When military men take over, honest men dance to the strings they pull. Your life is no longer your own. People envy me because I have a little money. It's fine to have money if you are a knight. It's even better to have money if you are a patrician. But if you are neither of them, only an honest man who made his money honestly, you can never lay your head down in peace. If you are not bribing an inspector, you're paying off a ward heeler; and if you're rid of both, you have a Tribune on your payroll. And every time you wake up, you're surprised you weren't knifed in your sleep. And now a damned general does me the honor of dragging me halfway across Italy—to ask me questions. If my name was Crassus or Gracchus or Silenus, or Menius, it would be a very different story indeed. That's Roman justice and Roman equality in the Republic of Rome."

And then Lentulus Batiatus entertained a series of uncomplimentary thoughts concerning Roman justice and a certain Roman general. In these thoughts, he was interrupted by a sharp interrogation from road guards stationed before the encampment. He halted his horse obediently and sat there in the cold, fine rain while two troopers advanced and examined him. Since they had to stand in the rain anyway for their time on guard, they were in no haste to relieve his discomfort. They examined him coldly and unpleasantly and asked him who he was.

"My name is Lentulus Batiatus."

Because they were ignorant peasants, they didn't recognize the name, and they wanted to know where he thought he was going.

"This road leads to the camp, doesn't it?"

"It does."

"Well, I'm going to the camp."

"For what?"

"To speak with the commander."

"Just like that. What are you selling?"

"Why, the dirty bastards!" thought Batiatus, but he said, patiently enough, "I'm selling nothing. I'm here by invitation."

"Whose invitation?"

"The commander's." And he went into his wallet and brought out the order Crassus had sent him.

They couldn't read, but even a piece of paper was sufficient to pass him on, and he was allowed to walk his yellow nag down the military road to the encampment. Like so many other rising citizens of that time, Batiatus assessed everything in terms of money; and he could not help wondering, as he proceeded, what it would cost to build this kind of a road—a temporary road just thrown down for the convenience of the encampment, but nevertheless a better road than he was able to build as an approach to his school at Capua. On a dirt and gravel base, easily-cut slabs of sandstone were laid, a whole mile of it straight as an arrow to the encampment.

"If these cursed generals would think more of fighting and less of roads, we'd all be better off," he thought; yet at the same time he glowed a little with pride. You had to admit that even in a dirty, rainy, miserable hole like this, Roman civilization made itself felt. No question about that.

Now he was approaching the encampment. As always, the temporary stopping place of the legions was like a city; where the legions went, civilization went; and where the legions camped, if only for a night, civilization arose. Here was a mighty, walled area, almost half a mile square, laid out as precisely as a draftsman might lay out a diagram on his drawing board. First there was a ditch, twelve feet wide and twelve feet deep; behind this ditch was a heavy log palisade, twelve feet high. The road crossed the ditch to the entrance, where heavy wooden gates opened at his approach. A trumpeter sounded him in, and a maniple revolved around him as he entered. It was no tribute to him, but discipline for the sake of discipline. It was no idle boast that never before in the history of the world had there been troops so disciplined as the legions. Even Batiatus, with his own enormous love of blood-letting and fighting—and thereby his inherent contempt for the drafted soldier—was impressed by the machine-like precision of everything connected with the army.

It was not simply the road or the palisade or the ditch, two miles in length, or the broad streets of the encampment-city, or the drainage ditches, or the sandstone pavement laid in the center of the streets, or the whole multiple life and motion and order of this Roman encampment of thirty thousand men; but rather the knowledge that this mighty production of man's reason and effort was the casual nightly effort of the legions in motion. It was not lightly said that barbarians were more easily defeated by seeing a legion encamp for the night than by going into battle with one.

As Batiatus dismounted, rubbing his fat behind where it had too long and too intimate contact with the saddle, a young officer came up and asked him who he was and what his business there was.

"Lentulus Batiatus of Capua."

"Oh, yes—yes," the young man drawled, a young fellow of no more than twenty, a pretty one, a scented, groomed product of one of the best families. The kind Batiatus hated most. "Yes," said the young man. "Lentulus Batiatus of Capua." He knew; he knew all about Lentulus Batiatus of Capua and who he was and what he represented and why he had been summoned here to the army of Crassus.

"Yes," thought Batiatus, "you hate me, don't you, you little son of a bitch, and you stand there despising me; but you come to me and you whine to me and you buy from me, and it's your kind that makes me what I am; but you're too good to come close to me, because you might be soiled by my breath, you little bastard!" That he thought, but he only nodded and said nothing at all.

"Yes," the young man nodded. "The commander has been expecting you. I know that. He wants you to come to him immediately. I'll take you there."

"I want to rest—eat something."

"The commander will see to that. He's a very thoughtful man," the young officer smiled, and then snapped at one of the soldiers, "Take his horse and water it and feed it and bed it down!"

"I haven't eaten anything since breakfast," said Batiatus, "and it seems to me that if your commander has waited this long, he can wait a while longer."

The eyes of the young man narrowed, but he kept his voice pleasant and observed, "That's for him to say."

"You feed the horse first?"

The young officer smiled and nodded. "Come along," he said.

"I'm not in your damned legion!"

"You're in a legion encampment."

They faced it out for a moment; then Batiatus shrugged, decided that there was no point in continuing the argument there in that needle-like rain, wrapped his wet cloak around him, and followed what he characterized as a dirty little patrician snotnose—but to himself, thinking too that, after all, he had seen more blood run in a single afternoon than this whelp, whose mother's milk was scarcely dry on his lips, had seen in all his fancy military career. But think what he might, the fat man remained as a small butcher in a slaughterhouse—his only comfort being a knowledge that he was not entirely apart from the forces which had brought the legions to this place.

He followed the young man down the broad central

avenue of the encampment, looking curiously from side to side at the dirty, mud-stained tents, good enough as roofs but open in front, and at the soldiers who sprawled on their grass beds, talking, swearing, singing and throwing dice or knuckle-bones. They were hard, clean-shaven, olive-skinned Italian peasants for the most part. Some of the tents had little stoves, but generally they took the cold as they took the heat, as they took the endless drill and the merciless discipline, the weak among them dying quickly, the tough ones becoming tougher and tougher, steel and whalebone attached to a small, efficient knife, which had become the most dreadful instrument of mass destruction ever known.

Directly in the center of the camp, at an intersection of two lines stretched between the four corners, stood the general's pavilion, the *praetorium*, which was merely a large tent divided into two sections or rooms. The flaps of this tent were closed, and on either side of the entrance stood a sentry, each of whom carried a long, slender dress spear instead of the heavy and murderous *pilum*, and a light, circular buckler and curved knife in the Thracean style, instead of the regular massive shield and Spanish shortsword. They wore white woolen cloaks which were sodden with rain, and stood as if they were carved from stone, the rain running from their helmets, their clothes and their weapons. For some reason this impressed Batiatus more than anything else he had seen. He was pleased when flesh did more than flesh was calculated to do, and this pleased him.

As they approached, the sentries saluted and then held the flaps aside. Batiatus and the young officer passed through, into the dim light of the tent, and Batiatus found himself in a room forty feet in width and some twenty in depth, the front half of the *praetorium*. Its only furnishings consisted of a long wooden table with a dozen folding stools set around it. At one end of the table, elbows upon it, staring at a map that was spread out in front of him, sat the commander in chief, Marcus Licinius Crassus.

Crassus rose as Batiatus and the officer entered, and the fat man was pleased to note how readily the general walked forward, giving him his hand in greeting.

"Lentulus Batiatus—of Capua? I imagine so."

Batiatus nodded and shook hands. This general was

really very personable, with fine, strong manly features and nothing condescending about him. "I'm happy to meet you, sir," said Batiatus.

"You've come a long way, and very decently, and very good of you too, I'm sure, and you're wet and hungry and tired."

He said this with concern and a certain misgiving, which put Batiatus at his ease; the young officer, however, continued to regard the fat man as superciliously as before. If Batiatus had been more sensitive he would have realized that both attitudes were equally meaningful. The general had a program of work before him; the young officer maintained the attitude of a gentleman toward such as Batiatus.

"I am all of that," answered Batiatus. "Wet and tired, but most of all starved to death. I asked this young man whether I could eat, but he thought it was an unreasonable request."

"We are conditioned to follow orders very precisely," said Crassus. "My orders were to bring you to me as soon as you came. Now, of course, your every wish will be mine to please. I am quite conscious of what an arduous journey you had here. Dry clothes, of course—immediately. Do you want a bath?"

"The bath can wait. I want to put something between my ribs."

Smiling, the young officer left the tent.

II

They had finished with broiled fish and baked eggs, and now Batiatus was devouring a chicken, breaking it apart and cleaning every bone thoroughly. At the same time, he dipped regularly into a wooden bowl of porridge and washed the food down with huge draughts from a beaker of wine. The chicken and porridge and wine smeared his mouth; bits of food were already dirtying the clean tunic Crassus had given him; and his hands were greasy with chicken fat.

Crassus watched him with interest. As with so many Romans of his class and generation, he had a particularized social contempt for the *lanista,* the man who schooled and trained gladiators, who bought them and sold them and hired them out for the arena. It was only in the past twenty years that the *lanistae* had become a power in Rome, a political and financial power, and frequently men of enormous wealth, such as this fat, gross man who sat at the table here with him. Only a generation ago, arena fighting was an intermittent and not too important feature of society. It had always been present; it was more popular with certain elements, less popular with others. Then, suddenly, it had become the rage of Rome. Everywhere, arenas were built. The smallest town had its wooden arena for fights. The fighting of one pair turned into the fighting of a hundred pairs, and a single set of games would go on for a month. And instead of reaching a point of satiation, the lust of the public grew seemingly without end.

Cultured Roman matrons and street hoodlums took equal interest in the games. A whole new language of the games had arisen. Army veterans looked forward to nothing else but the public dole and the games, and ten thousand workless, homeless citizens lived for no other apparent reason than to watch the games. Suddenly, the market in gladiators was a seller's market, and the gladiatorial schools came into being. The school at Capua, which Lentulus Batiatus operated, was one of the largest and most prosperous. Just as the cattle from certain *latifundia* were desired in every market place, so were the gladiators of Capua esteemed and desired in every arena. And from a street man, a third rate ward heeler, Batiatus had become a rich man and one of the most notable trainers of *bustuarii* in all Italy.

"Yet," thought Crassus as he watched him, "he is still a street man, still a crafty, vulgar, scheming animal. See how he eats!" It was always difficult for Crassus to comprehend how so very many poorly-born and ill-mannered men had more money than many of his friends could ever hope to have. Certainly, they were not less clever than this gross trainer. Take himself; he knew his own value as a military man; he had the Roman virtues of thoroughness and doggedness, and he did not look upon military tactics as something that came to one instinctively. He had studied every campaign recorded, and he had read all the best of the Greek historians. Nor did he make—as every previous general in this war had made—the mistake of underestimating Spartacus. Yet he sat here across the table from this gross man and in some curious way, he felt inferior.

He shrugged and said to Batiatus, "You must understand that I have no feelings about Spartacus in relation to yourself, or the war either, for that matter. I am not a moralist. I had to talk to you because you can tell me what no other can."

"And just what is that?" asked Batiatus.

"The nature of my enemy."

The fat man poured more wine and squinted at the general. A sentry entered the tent and placed two lighted lamps upon the table. It was evening already.

In the light of the lamps, Lentulus Batiatus was a different person. Twilight had been kind to him. Now the light roved up on his face as he massaged it with a napkin, hooking slabs of shadow over the pendulous layers of flesh. His large flat nose quivered constantly and incongruously, and bit by bit, he was getting tight. A cold glint in his eyes told Crassus not to misjudge him, not to think that this was an amiable fool. No fool indeed.

"What do I know of your enemy?"

Trumpets sounded outside. Evening drill had finished, and the roll of leather-shod feet on the double rocked the encampment.

"I have only one enemy. Spartacus is my enemy," Crassus said carefully.

The fat man blew his nose into his napkin.

"And you know Spartacus," Crassus said.

"I do, by God!"

"No one else. Just you. No one who ever fought Spartacus knew him. They went to fight slaves. They expected to blow their trumpets, beat their drums, cast their *pilum* —and then the slaves were to run away. No matter how many times the legions were torn to shreds, they still expected that. What was couldn't be, and so today Rome makes the last effort and if it fails, there will be no Rome. You know that as well as I do."

The fat man roared with laughter. He held his belly and rocked back on his stool.

"You find it funny?" Crassus asked.

"The truth is always funny."

Crassus contained himself and his temper and waited for the laughter to subside.

"There will be no Rome—there will only be Spartacus." The fat man had subsided to a giggle now, and Crassus, watching him, wondered whether he was quite in his right mind, or only drunk. What things a land produced! Here was the *lanista*, who bought slaves and trained them to fight; of course, he was laughing over that. He, Crassus, also trained men to fight.

"You should hang me, not feed me," Batiatus whispered ingratiatingly, pouring another glass of wine for himself.

"I would have a dream," said the general, pulling the conversation back to his own needs, "a sort of nightmare. One of those dreams that one has over and over again—"

Batiatus nodded understandingly.

"—and in this dream I would still fight with my eyes bandaged. That is horrible, but logical. You see, I don't believe that all dreams are omens. Certain dreams are simply reflections of the problems one faces when awake. Spartacus is the unknown. If I go to battle with him, my eyes are bandaged. That isn't the case in any other circumstances. I know why the Gauls fight; I know why the Greeks and the Spaniards and the Germans fight. They fight for the same reasons—with natural variations—that I do. But I don't know why this slave fights. I don't know how he takes a rabble, all the filth and sweepings of the whole world, and uses them to destroy the best troops the world has ever known. It takes five years to make a legionary—five years to make him understand that his life is of no consequence, that the legion and only the legion counts, that an order must be obeyed, any order. Five years of training, ten hours a day, every day—and then you can take them to a cliff and order them to march over the edge and they will obey. And yet these slaves have destroyed the best legions of Rome.

"That is why I asked you to come here from Capua—to tell me about Spartacus. So I can take the bandage away from my eyes."

Batiatus nodded somberly. He was mellowing now. He was the confidant and adviser of great generals, and that was as it should be.

"Firstly," said Crassus, "there is the man. Tell me

about him. What does he look like? Where did you get him?"

"Men never look like what they are."

"True—profoundly true, and when you realize that, you know about men." Which was the very best flattery to offer Batiatus.

"He was gentle, so gentle, almost humble, and he's a Thracian; that much about him is true." Batiatus dipped one finger in his wine and tallied his points on the table. "They say he is a giant—no, no, not at all. He's no giant. He's not even particularly tall. About your height, I would say. Black, curly hair; dark brown eyes. His nose was broken; otherwise I guess, you would call him handsome. But the broken nose gave a sheep-like expression to his face. A broad face, and gentle, and all of this deceived you. I would have killed anyone else who did what he did."

"What did he do?" asked Crassus.

"Ah—"

"I want you to speak frankly because I must have a frank picture," Crassus said slowly. "I want you to know that everything you say to me will be held in the strictest confidence." He laid aside for the moment the specific incident for which Batiatus would have killed Spartacus. "I also want to know his background—where did you buy him and what was he?"

"What is a gladiator?" smiled Batiatus, spreading his hands. "Not just a slave, you understand—or at least the gladiators of Capua are not just slaves. They are special. If you fight dogs, you do not buy house pets that are reared by little girls. If you fight men, you want men who will fight. Men who chew their gall. Men who hate. Men with spleen. So I inform the agents that I am in the market for men with spleen. That kind are no good for house slaves and they are no good on the *latifundia* either."

"Why not on the *latifundia*?" asked Crassus.

"Because if a man is broken, I don't want him. And if you can't break a man, you must kill him, but you can't work him. He spoils the work. He spoils the others who work. He is like a disease."

"Then why will he fight?"

"Ah—and there you have the question, and if you can't answer that question, you can't work with gladiators.

In the old days, they called the arena fighters *bustuarii*, and those fought for the love of fighting, and they were sick in the head, and there were only a few of them, and *they were not slaves.*" He touched his head meaningfully. "No one wants to fight to the blood unless he is sick here. No one likes it. The gladiator doesn't like to fight. He fights because you give him a weapon and take off his chains. And when he has that weapon in his hand, he dreams that he is free—and that is what he wants, to have the weapon in his hand and dream that he is free. And then it's your wit against his wit, because he is a devil, so you have to be a devil too."

"And where do you find such men?" asked Crassus, intrigued and captured by the flat, straightforward account of a man who knew his trade.

"There is only one place where you can find them—the kind I want. Only one place. The mines. It must be the mines. They must come from a place compared to which the legion is paradise, the *latifundia* is paradise, and even the gallows is a blessed mercy. That is where my agents find them. That is where they found Spartacus—and he was *koruu*. Do you know what that word means? It is an Egyptian word, I think."

Crassus shook his head.

"It means three generations of slaves. The grandson of a slave. In the Egyptian, it also means a certain kind of loathsome animal. A crawling beast. A beast who is untouchable by the company of beasts, yes, even by the company of beasts. *Koruu.* We may ask, why did this arise in Egypt? I will tell you. There are worse things than being a *lanista.* When I came into this encampment of yours, your officers looked at me. Why? Why? We are all butchers, aren't we, and we deal in carved meat. Then why?"

He was drunk. He was full of pity for himself, this fat trainer of gladiators who kept the school at Capua. His soul came forth; even a fat and dirty pig who has a *ludus* where the sand turns into stuffing for blood sausage has a soul.

"And Spartacus was *koruu*," said Crassus softly. "Did Spartacus come from Egypt?"

Batiatus nodded. "A Thracian, but he came from Egypt. The Egyptian gold operators buy from Athens and when they can, buy *koruu,* and Thracians are valued."

"Why?"

"There is a legend that they are good under ground."

"I see. But why is it said that Spartacus was purchased in Greece?"

"Do I know why all the garbage spoken is spoken? But I know where he was purchased because I purchased him. In Thebes. Do you doubt me? And I a liar? I am a fat *lanista,* a lonely man sitting in this lousy rain in Gaul. Why do I live with loneliness? What right have you to look down on me? Your life is your life. Mine is mine."

"You are my honored guest. I don't look down on you," said Crassus.

Batiatus smiled and leaned toward him. "Do you know what I want? Do you know what I need? We are two men of the world, both of us. I need a woman. Tonight." His voice became hoarsely soft and entreating. "Why do I need a woman? Not out of lust, but out of loneliness. To heal the scars. You have women—men don't cut themselves off from women."

"Tell me about Spartacus and Egypt," Crassus said. "Then we will talk about women."

III

So it was that before there was a Christian hell in books and sermons—and perhaps afterwards too—there was a hell on earth that men saw and looked at and knew well indeed. For it is the nature of man that he can only write of the hells he has first created himself.

In the month of July, when it is dry and awful, go up the Nile from Thebes. Go up to the First Cataract. Already you are in the devil's own land. See how the ribbon of green along the riverside has shrunk and withered! See how the hills and mounds of the desert have changed to a finer and finer sand. Smoke and powder; the wind touches it and it bursts up here and it throws out tentacles there. Where the river flows slowly—and it does in the dry time—a crust of white powder lies upon it. The powder is in the air too, and it is already very hot.

But at least there is a little wind in this place. Now

you have passed the First Cataract, and you must strike out into the Nubian Desert, which lies southward and eastward. Go into the desert far enough to lose the little wind that survived over the river, but not far enough to catch even a breath of breeze from the Red Sea. And now go southward.

Suddenly, the wind is still and the earth is dead. Only the air is alive, and the air is glazed with heat and shimmering with heat, and man's senses are no longer valid, for he sees nothing as it is, but everything bent and warped and curved by the heat. And the desert has changed too. It is a mistaken notion many people hold that desert is everywhere the same; but desert means only a lack of water, and this lack of water varies enormously in degree, and the desert varies too according to the nature of the soil or landscape where the desert is. There is rock desert and mountain desert and sand desert, and white salt desert and lava desert—and there is also the terrible desert of drifting white powder, where death is the absolute signature.

Here, there grows nothing at all. Not the dry, twisted, tough shrubbery of the rock desert; not the lonely tumbleweeds of the sand desert, but nothing at all.

Go into this desert then. Plod through the white powder and feel how wave after wave of the dreadful heat beats down upon your back. As hot as it can be and yet allow a man to live, so it is here. Make a track through this hot and terrible desert, and time and space become boundless and monstrous. But you go on and on and on and on. What is hell? Hell begins when the simple and necessary acts of life become monstrous, and this knowledge has been shared through all the ages by those who taste the hell men make on earth. Now it is frightful to walk, to breathe, to see, to think.

But this does not go on forever. Suddenly, it is delineated, and the further aspect of hell appears. Black ridges show ahead of you, strange, nightmarish black ridges. This is the black stone escarpment. You go on toward the black stone, and then you see that it is streaked through and through with veins of shining white marble. Oh, how bright this marble is! Oh, how it gleams and shines and with what heavenly lustre! But it must have a heavenly lustre, for the streets of heaven are paved with gold, and the white marble is rich with gold. That is why men came to this place, and that is why you are coming here, because the marble is rich and heavy with gold.

Go closer and see. It was long ago that the Egyptian Pharaohs discovered this black rock escarpment, and in those days they had only tools of copper and bronze. So they could chip and scratch at the surface, but little more. But after generations of scratching at the surface, the gold gave out and it was necessary to go into the black rock and cut away the white marble. This was made possible because the age of copper was past and the age of iron had come, and now men could work the marble with picks and iron wedges and eighteen-pound sledges.

But a new kind of man was needed. The heat and the dust and the physical contortions necessary to follow the twisting gold-bearing veins into the rock made it impossible to employ peasants either from Ethiopia or from Egypt, and the ordinary slave cost too much and died too quickly. So to this place were brought war-hardened soldiers taken captive and children who were *koruu,* bred from slaves who were bred from slaves in a process where only the toughest and the hardest could survive. And children were needed, for when the veins narrowed, deep inside the black rock escarpment, only a child could work there.

The old splendor and power of the Pharaohs passed away and the purses of the Greek kings of Egypt dwindled; the hand of Rome lay over them and the slave dealers of Rome took over the operation of the mines. In any case, no one but Romans knew how to work slaves properly.

So you come to the mines as Spartacus did, one hundred and twenty-two Thracians chained neck to neck, carrying their burning hot chains across the desert all the way from the First Cataract. The twelfth man from the front of the line is Spartacus. He is almost naked, as they all are almost naked, and soon he will be entirely naked. He wears a shred of a loin cloth, and his hair is long and he is bearded, just as every man in the line is long-haired and bearded. His sandals have worn through, but he wears the little that is left of them for what protection it may offer; for though the skin of his feet is a quarter of an inch thick and as tough as leather, it is not enough protection against the burning desert sands.

What is he like, this man Spartacus? He is twenty-three years old as he carries his chain across the desert, but it is not marked on him; for his kind, there is an agelessness of toil, no youth and no manhood and no growing old, but only the agelessness of toil. From head to foot and hair and beard and face, he is covered with the powdery white sand, but underneath the sand his skin is burned brown as his dark, intense eyes, which peer out of his cadaverous face like hateful coals. The brown skin is an adjunct of life for such as he; the white-skinned, yellow-haired slaves of the Northlands cannot work in the mines; the sun fries them and kills them, and they pass away in bitter pain.

Tall or short is hard to say, for men in chains do not walk erect, but the body is whipcord, sun-jerked meat, dry and waterless but not fleshless. For so many generations there was a process of gleaning out, winnowing out, and on the stony hills of Thrace the living was never easy, so that what survived is hard and with a tight clutch on life. The handful of wheat upon which he feeds each day, the flat, hard barley cakes are sucked dry of every shred of sustenance and the body is young enough to sustain itself. The neck is thick and muscular, but there are festering sores where the bronze collar rests. The shoulders are padded with muscle, and so equal are the proportions of the body that the man looks smaller than he is. The face is broad, and because the nose was broken once by the blow of an overseer's rod, it appears flatter than it actually is, and since the dark eyes are wide-set, it takes on a gentle, sheep-like expression. Under the beard and the dust, the mouth is large and full-lipped, sensuous and sensitive, and if the lips move back—in a grimace, not in a smile—you see that the teeth are white and even. The hands are large and square and as beautiful as some hands can be; indeed, the only thing about him that is beautiful is his hands.

This, then, is Spartacus, the Thracian slave, the son of a slave who was the son of a slave. No man knows his destiny, and the future is not a book to be read, and even the past—when the past is toil and nothing else but toil—can dissolve into a murky bed of various pain. This, then, is Spartacus, who does not know the future and has no cause to remember the past, and it has never occurred to him that those who toil shall ever do other than toil, nor has it occurred to him that there will ever be a time when men do not toil with the lash across their backs.

What does he think of as he plods across the hot sand? Well, it should be known that when men carry a chain, they think of little, of very little, and most of the time it is better not to think of more than when you will eat again, drink again, sleep again. So there are not complex thoughts in the mind of Spartacus or in the minds of any of his Thracian comrades who carry the chain with him. You make men like beasts and they do not think of angels.

But now it is the end of a day and the scene is changing, and men like these clutch at little bits of excitement and change. Spartacus looks up, and there is the black ribbon of the escarpment. There is a geography of slaves, and though they do not know the shape of the seas, the height of the mountains or the course of the rivers, they know well enough of the silver mines of Spain, the gold mines of Arabia, the iron mines of North Africa, the copper mines of the Caucasus and the tin mines of Gaul. There is their own lexicon of horror, their own refuge in knowledge of another place worse than where they are; but worse than the black escarpment of Nubia is nothing in the whole wide world.

Spartacus looks at it; the others look at it, and the whole line halts its plodding, painful motion, and the camels with their burden of water and wheat also halt, even as do the overseers with their whips and their pikes. Everyone looks at the black ribbon of hell. And then the line goes on.

The sun is sinking behind the black rock when they reach it, and it has become blacker, more savage, more ominous. It is the end of the day's work and the slaves are emerging from the shafts.

"What are they, what are they?" thinks Spartacus.

And the man behind him whispers, "God help me!"

But God will not help him here. God is not here; what would God be doing here? And then Spartacus realizes that these things he sees are not some strange species of the desert, but men like himself and children such as he was once. That is what they are. But the difference in them

66

has been composed from within and from without; and to those forces which shaped them into something other than humankind, there has been an inner response, a fading away of the desire or need to be human. Just see them— see them! The heart of Spartacus, which has become in the process of years like a stone, begins to contract with fear and horror. The wells of pity in him, which he believes to be dried up, are wet again, and his dehydrated body is still capable of tears. He looks at them. The whip lays on his back for him to move on, but still he stands and looks at them.

They have been crawling in the shafts, and now when they come out, they still crawl like animals. They have not bathed since they are here, nor will they ever bathe again. Their skins are patchworks of black dust and brown dirt; their hair is long and tangled, and when they are not children, they are bearded. Some are black men and some are white men, but the difference now is so little that one hardly remarks upon it. They all have ugly calluses on knees and elbows, and they are naked, completely naked. Why not? Will clothes keep them alive longer? The mine has only one purpose, to bring profits to the Roman stockholders, and even shreds of dirty cloth cost something.

Yet they wear an article of clothing. Each has upon his neck a bronze or an iron collar, and as they come crawling down the black rock, the overseers snap each collar onto a long chain, and when there are twenty chained together, they plod to their quarters. It must be noted that no one ever escaped from the Nubian mines; no one could escape. A year in these mines, and how can one ever belong to the world of men again? The chain is a symbol more than a need.

Spartacus stares at them and seeks for his own kind, his own race, the humankind, which is race and kind when a man is a slave. "Talk," he says to himself, "talk to each other." But they do not talk. They are silent as death. "Smile," he pleads to himself. But no one smiles.

They carry their tools with them, the iron picks, crowbars and chisels. Many of them have crude lamps strapped onto their heads. The children, skinny as spiders, twitch as they walk and constantly blink at the light. These children never grow up; they are good for two years at the most, after they come to the mines, but there is no other way to follow the gold-bearing stone when the veins narrow and twist. They carry their chains by the Thracians, but they never even turn their heads to look at the newcomers. They have no curiosity. They don't care.

And Spartacus knows. "In a little while, I will not care," he says to himself. And this is more frightening than anything else.

Now the slaves go to eat, and the Thracians are taken with them. The rock shelter, which is their barracks, is built against the base of the escarpment itself. It was built a long, long time ago. No one can remember when it was built. It is built of massive slabs of rough-hewn black stone, and there is no light inside, and ventilation only from the opening at each end. It has never been cleaned. The filth of decades has rotted on its floor and hardened on its floor. The overseers never enter the place. If there should be trouble inside, then food and water are withheld; when they have been long enough without food and water, the slaves become docile and crawl out like the animals they are. When someone dies inside, the slaves bring the body out. But sometimes a little child will die deep inside the long barracks, and it will not be noticed and he will not be missed until the corruption of his body reveals him. That is the kind of a place the barracks is.

The slaves go in without their chains. At the entrance, they are unchained and given a wooden bowl of food and a leathern jack of water. The jack contains a little less than a quart of water, and this is their ration twice a day. But two quarts of water a day is not enough to replace what the heat takes in so dry a place, and thus the slaves are subjected to a gradual process of progressive dehydration. If other things do not kill them, sooner or later this destroys their kidneys and when the pain is too bad for them to work, they are driven out to the desert to die.

All these things, Spartacus knows. The knowledge of slaves is his, and the community of slaves is his. He was born into it; he grew in it; he matured in it. He knows the essential secret of slaves. It is a desire—not for pleasure, comfort, food, music, laughter, love, warmth, women or wine, not for any of those things—it is a desire to endure, to survive, simply that and no more, to survive.

He does not know why. There is no reason to this survival, no logic to this survival; but neither is the knowledge an instinct. It is more than an instinct. No animal could survive this way; the pattern for survival is not simple; it is not an easy thing; it is far more complex and thoughtful and difficult than all of the problems faced by people who never confront this one. And there is a reason for it too. It is just that Spartacus does not know the reason.

Now he will survive. He is adapting, flexing, conditioning, acclimatizing, sensitizing; he is a mechanism of profound fluidity and flexibility. His body conserves strength from the freedom of release from the chain. How long he and his comrades carried that chain, across the sea, up the River Nile, across the desert! Weeks and weeks of the chain, and now he is free of it! He is light as a feather, but that found strength must not be wasted. He accepts his water—more water than he has seen in weeks. He will not gulp it and piss it out in waste. He will guard it and sip at it for hours, so that every possible drop of it may sink into the tissues of his body. He takes his food, wheat and barley gruel cooked with dry locusts. Well, there is strength and life in dry locusts, and wheat and barley are the fabric of his flesh. He has eaten worse, and all food must be honored; those who dishonor food, even in thought, become enemies of food, and soon they die.

He walks into the darkness of the barracks, and the fetid wave of rotten smell claws at his senses. But no man dies of a smell, and only fools or free men can afford the luxury of vomiting. He will not waste an ounce of the contents of his stomach in such a fashion. He will not fight this smell; such things cannot be fought. Instead, he will embrace this smell; he will welcome it and let it seep into him and soon it will have no terrors for him.

He walks in the dark, and his feet guide him. His feet are like eyes. He must not trip or fall, for in one hand he carries food and in the other, water. Now he guides over to the stone wall and sits down with his back against it. It is not so bad here. The stone is cool and he has support for his back. He eats and drinks. And all around him are the movements and breathing and chewing of other men and children who do exactly as he does, and within him the expert organs of his body help him and expertly extract what they need from the little food and little water. He picks the last grain of food from his bowl, drinks down what is left, and licks the inside of the wood. He is not conditioned by appetite; food is survival; every small speck and stain of food is survival.

Now the food is eaten, and some of those who have eaten are more content and others give way to despair. Not all despair has vanished from this place; hope may go, but despair clings more stubbornly, and there are groans and tears and sighs, and somewhere there is a wavering scream. And there is even a little talk, and a broken voice which calls,

"Spartacus—where are you?"

"Here, I am here, Thracian," he answers.

"Here is the Thracian," another voice says. "Thracian, Thracian." They are his people, and they gather around him. He feels their hands as they press close to him. Perhaps the other slaves listen, and in any case, they are deeply silent. It is only the due of newcomers in hell. Perhaps those who came here earlier are remembering now what mostly they fear to remember. Some understand the words of the Attic tongue and others don't. Perhaps somewhere, even, there is a memory of the snow-topped mountains of Thrace, the blessed, blessed coolness, the brooks running through the pine forests and the black goats leaping among the rocks. Who knows what memories persist among the damned people of the black escarpment?

"Thracian," they call him, and now he feels them on every side, and when he stretches out a hand he feels the face of one of them, all covered with tears. Ah, tears are a waste.

"Where are we, Spartacus, where are we?" one of them whispers.

"We are not lost. We remember how we came."

"Who will remember us?"

"We are not lost," he repeats.

"But who will remember us?"

One cannot talk in such a fashion. He is like a father to them. For men twice his years, he is a father in the old tribal way. They are all Thracians, but he is the Thracian. So he chants to them softly, like a father telling a tale to his children:

"As on the beach where churning water broke,
    In close array before the western wind,
    Churning finely up from the ocean deeps,

70

And arching as it breaks upon the land,
Its white foam spewing hard and far,
Just so in such array the Danaans moved
Unhesitating to the battle line—"

He captures them, and holds their misery, thinking to
himself, "What a wonder, what a magic in the old chant!"
He eases them out of this terrible darkness and they stand
on the pearly beaches of Troy. There are the white towers
of the city! There are the golden, bronze-girt warriors!
The soft chant rises and falls and loosens the knots of
terror and anxiety, and in the darkness there is shuffling
and motion. The slaves do not have to know Greek, and
indeed the Thracian dialect of Spartacus is little enough
like the tongue of Attica; they know of the chant, where
the old wisdom of a people is preserved and kept for the
time of trial . . .

Finally, Spartacus lays himself down to sleep. He will
sleep. Young as he is, he long ago met and conquered the
terrible enemy of sleeplessness. Now he composes himself
and explores the memories of childhood. He wants cool,
clear blue sky and sunshine and soft breezes, and all of
these are there. He lies among the pines, watching the
goats graze, and an old, old man is beside him. The old
man teaches him to read. With a stick, the old man traces
letter after letter in the dirt. "Read and learn, my child,"
the old man tells him. "So do we who are slaves carry a
weapon with us. Without it, we are like the beasts in the
fields. The same god who gave fire to men gave them the
power to write down his thoughts, so that they may recall
the thoughts of the gods in the golden time of long ago.
Then men were close to the gods and talked with them at
will, and there were no slaves then. And that time will
come again."

So Spartacus remembers, and presently his memory
turns into a dream, and presently he sleeps . . .

He is awakened in the morning by the beating of a
drum. The drum is beaten at the entrance to the barracks,
and its crash echoes and re-echoes through the stone
cavern. He rises, and all about him he hears his fellow
slaves rising. They move in the pitch darkness toward the
entrance. Spartacus takes his cup and bowl with him; if
he had forgotten it, there would have been no food or

drink for him this day; but he is wise in the ways of slavery, and there is not such great variation in the manner of slavery that he should not anticipate. As he moves, he feels the press of bodies around him, and he lets himself move with them to the opening at the end of the stone barracks. And all the while, the drum continues its crashing beat.

It is the hour before the dawn, and now the desert is as cool as it will ever be. In this single hour of the day, the desert is a friend. A gentle breeze cools the face of the black escarpment. The sky is a wonderful fading blue-black, and the twinkling stars gently disappear, the only womanly things in this cheerless, hopeless world of men. Even slaves in the gold mines of Nubia—from which none ever return—must have a little surcease; and thus they are given the hour before dawn, so that a poignant bitter-sweet may fill their hearts and revive their hopes.

The overseers stand to one side, grouped together, munching bread and sucking at water. Not for another four hours will the slaves be fed or watered, but it is one thing to be an overseer and another to be a slave. The overseers are wrapped in woolen cloaks, and each carries a whip, a weighted billy and a long knife. Who are these men, these overseers? What brings them to this terrible womanless place in the desert?

They are men of Alexandria, bitter, hard men, and they are here because the pay is high, and because they get a percentage of all the gold the mines produce. They are here with their own dreams of wealth and leisure, and with the promise of Roman citizenship when they have served five years in the interest of the corporation. They live for the future, when they will rent an apartment in one of the tenements in Rome, when they will each of them buy three or four or five slave girls to sleep with and to serve them, and when they will spend each day at the games or at the baths, and when they will be drunk each night. They believe that in coming to this hell, they heighten their future earthly heaven; but the truth of the matter is that they, like all prison guards, require the petty lordship of the damned more than perfume and wine and women.

They are strange men, a unique product of the slums of Alexandria, and the language they talk is a jargon of

Aramaic and Greek. It is two and a half centuries since the Greeks conquered Egypt, and these overseers are not Egyptians and not Greeks, but Alexandrians. Which means that they are versatile in their corruption, cynical in their outlook, and believing of no gods at all. Their lusts are warped but commonplace; they lie with men and they sleep a drugged sleep over the juice of the Khat leaves, which grow on the coast of the Red Sea.

These are the men whom Spartacus watches, there in the cool hour before the dawn, as the slaves plod from the great stone barracks, shoulder their chains and go toward the escarpment. These will be his masters; and over him they will hold the power of life and the power of death; and so he watches for small differences, habits, mannerisms and indications. In the mines, there are no good masters, but it may be that there will be some less cruel and less sadistic than others. He watches them detach themselves, one by one, to take over where the slaves are shaping up. It is still so dark that he cannot distinguish subtleties of face and feature, but his is a practiced eye in such matters, and even in the walk and heft of a man there is definition.

It is cool now, and the slaves are naked. Not even a loincloth hides their pitiful, futile, sun-blackened organs of sex, and they stand and shiver and wind their arms around their bodies. Anger comes slowly to Spartacus, for anger is not productive in the life of a slave, but he thinks, "All things but this we can bear, but when there is not even a scrap of cloth to cover our parts, we are like animals." And then revises it in his mind, "No—less than animals. For when the Romans took the land where we were owned and the plantation where we labored, the beasts were left in the field and only we were sorted out for the mines."

Now the drum stops its wracking sound and the overseers uncoil their whips and crack the stiffness out of the bull-hide, so that the air is full of a snapping and cracking music. They lay the whips in the air, for it is too early to lash the flesh, and the gangs move forward out of the shapeup. It is lighter now, and Spartacus can clearly see the skinny, shivering children who will crawl down into the belly of the earth and claw at the white stone where the gold is found. The other Thracians also see, for they

73

crowd close around Spartacus, and some of them whisper,

"Father, oh father, what kind of a hell is this!"

"It will be all right," Spartacus says; for when you are called father by those old enough to be your father, what else is there to say? So he says the words which he must say.

Now all the gangs have gone toward the escarpment, and only the huddled group of Thracians remain. A half dozen overseers are left, and led by one of their group, their whips dragging tracks through the sand, they move toward the newcomers. One of the overseers speaks and demands, in his thick jargon,

"Who is your leader, Thracians?"

No answer.

"It is too early for the whip, Thracians."

Now Spartacus says, "They call me father."

The overseer looks him up and down and takes his measure. "You are young to be called father."

"It is the custom in our land."

"We have other customs here, *father*. When the child sins, the father is whipped. Do you hear me?"

"I hear you."

"Then listen, all of you Thracians. This is a bad place, but it can be worse. When you live, we ask work and obedience. When you die, we ask little. In other places, it is better to live than to die. But here we can make it better to die than to live. Do you understand me, Thracians?"

The sun is rising now. They are chained and they carry their chain to the escarpment. Then the chain is removed. The brief coolness of the morning is already gone. They are given tools, iron picks, sledges, and iron wedges. They are shown a streak of white in the black rock at the base of the escarpment. It may be the beginning of the vein; it may be nothing at all. They are to cut away the black rock and expose the gold-bearing stone.

Now the sun is in the sky, and the terrible heat of the day begins again. Pick and sledge and wedge. Spartacus swings a hammer. Each hour, there is a pound more of weight in the feel of the hammer. Hard he is, but never before in his life of toil did he do such work as this, and soon every muscle of his body strains and whimpers with the tension. It is simple to say that a hammer weighs eighteen pounds; but there are no words to tell the tortures of a man who swings such a hammer hour after hour. And here, where water is so precious, Spartacus begins to sweat. It oozes from his skin; it runs from his forehead down into his eyes; he wills with all the strength of his will that the sweat should stop; he knows that in this climate, to sweat is to perish. But the sweat will not stop, and thirst becomes a savage, aching, terrible animal inside of him.

Four hours are forever; four hours are eternity. Who knows better than a slave how to control the desires of a body, but four hours are forever, and when the water bags are passed through the gangs, Spartacus feels that he is dying of thirst. As do all the Thracians, and they drain the leathern jacks of the crawling green and blessed fluid. And then they know what a thoughtless thing they have done.

These are the gold mines of Nubia. By midday, their strength and power to work is ebbing, and then the whips begin to urge them on. Oh, there is a great mastery of the whip in the hands of an overseer; it can touch any part of the body, delicately, lightly, threateningly, warningly. It can touch a man's groin or his mouth or his back or his brow. It is like an instrument, and it can play music on the body of a man. Now thirst is ten times worse than before, but the water is gone, and there will be no more water until the day's work is over. And such a day is eternity.

And yet it ends. Everything ends. There is a time of beginning and a time of ending. Once again, the drum beats, and the day's work is over.

Spartacus lets go of the hammer and looks at his bleeding hands. Some of the Thracians sit down. One, a lad of eighteen, rolls over and lies on his side, his legs drawn up in tight agony. Spartacus goes to him.

"Father—father, is that you?"

"Yes, yes," Spartacus says, and he kisses the lad on his brow.

"Then kiss me on my lips, for I am dying, my father, and what is left of my soul I want to give to you."

Then Spartacus kisses him, but he cannot weep, for he is dry and singed, like burnt leather.

IV

So Batiatus finished his tale of how Spartacus and other Thracians came to the gold mines of Nubia and how they labored naked on the face of the black escarpment. It had taken a long time in the telling. The rain had stopped. Darkness had fallen, profoundly and wholly under the leaden sky, and the two men, the one a trainer of gladiators and the other a patrician soldier of fortune who would some day be the wealthiest man in his world, sat in the flickering area of light which the lamps cast. Batiatus had drunk a good deal, and the loose muscles of his face had become looser. He was the kind of sensualist who combines sadism with an enormous power of self pity and subjective identification, and his tale of the gold mine had been told with power and color and pity too, and Crassus was moved in spite of himself.

Crassus was neither an ignorant nor an insensitive man, and he had read the mighty cycle which Aeschylus wrote on Prometheus, and he saw something of what it meant for a Spartacus to emerge from where he had been to a point where no power Rome could assemble might stand up against his slaves. He had an almost passionate need to understand Spartacus, to envision Spartacus—yes, and to crawl a little inside of Spartacus, as difficult as that might be, so that the eternal riddle of his class, the riddle of the man in chains who reaches for the stars, might resolve itself somewhat. He squinted at Batiatus now, telling himself that actually he owed this fat and ugly man a great deal and wondering which of the bedraggled maidens of the camp might be found to share his couch for this night. Such generalized lust was not within the comprehension of Crassus, whose desires operated differently, but the commander was meticulous in small, personal debts.

"And how did Spartacus escape from that place?" he asked the *lanista*.

"He did not escape. No one escapes from such a place. The virtue of such a place is that it so quickly destroys the desire of the slave to re-enter the world of men. I bought Spartacus out of there."

"Out of there? But why? And how did you know he was there, or who he was or what he was?"

"I didn't know. But you think my reputation for gladiators is a legend, a fiction—you think that I'm a fat and useless hulk, knowing nothing about anything. But there is an art even to my profession, I assure you—"

"I believe you," nodded Crassus. "Tell me how you bought Spartacus."

"Is wine forbidden to the Legion?" asked Batiatus, holding up the empty bottle. "Or must I add drunkenness to the contempts in which you hold me? Or is it said that a fool holds a tight rein on his tongue which only liquor loosens?"

"I'll bring you more wine," answered Crassus, and he rose and went through the curtain to his sleeping chamber, returning with another bottle. Batiatus was his comrade, and Batiatus did not bother with the stopper, but knocked the neck off the bottle against the table leg and poured until his glass dripped over.

"Blood and wine," he smiled. "I would have liked to have been born differently and to command a legion. But who knows? Your own pleasure might be to see the gladiators fight. I am bored with it."

"I see enough fighting."

"Yes, of course. But there is a style in the arena and a courage in the arena that your own mass butchery cannot quite match. They send you to retrieve the fortune of Rome after Spartacus has smashed three quarters of the armed power of Rome. Do you hold Italy? The truth of it is that Spartacus holds Italy. Yes, you will defeat him. No enemy can stand against Rome. But for the moment, he has you one better. Yes?"

"Yes," answered Crassus.

"And who trained Spartacus? I did. He never fought in Rome, but the best fighting is not at Rome. A butcher shop is what Rome appreciates, but the truly great fighting is at Capua and in Sicily. I tell you, no legionary knows how to fight, all covered up with *galea, pectoralis,* and *humeralia,* like a child in the womb, poking with that stick of yours. Go naked into the arena, with a sword in hand and nothing else. Blood on the sand, and you smell it as you walk in. The trumpets are playing and the drums are beating and the sun is shining down and the ladies are waving their lace handkerchiefs and can't keep their eyes off your parts, hanging all naked in front of you, and they will all have thrills enough before the afternoon is done, but your own orgasm comes when your belly is sliced, and you stand there crying while your guts pour out on the sand. That is fighting, my commander—and to do that well, ordinary men are no good. You need another breed, and where do you find them? I am willing to spend money to make money, and I send my agents out to buy what I need. I send them to places where weak men die quickly and where cowards kill themselves. Twice a year, I send to the Nubian mines. Once, I was there myself—yes, and that once was sufficient. To keep a mine operating, you must use up slaves. Most are good for two years, no more; many are good for only six months. But the only profitable way to work a mine is to use up slaves quickly and always buy more. And since the slaves know this, there is always the danger of desperation. That is the great enemy in the mines, desperation. A catching disease. So when you have a desperate man, a strong man who is not afraid of the whip and to whom other men listen, why the best thing to do is to kill him quickly and spike him out in the sunshine, so that the flies can feed on his flesh and everyone can see the fruit of desperation. But that kind of killing is waste and adds to no one's purse, so I have an arrangement with the overseers and they keep such men for me and sell them at a fair price. The money goes into their pockets, and no one is the loser. Such men make good gladiators."

"And that is how you bought Spartacus?"

"Precisely. I bought Spartacus and another Thracian called Gannicus. You know that at the time there was a great vogue for Thracians, because they are good with the dagger. One year it's the dagger, the next year the sword, the next year the *fuscina*. As a matter of fact, many Thracians have never touched the dagger, but legend has it, and the ladies don't want to see a dagger in the hands of anyone else."

"You bought him yourself?"

"Through my agents. They shipped the two of them in

chains from Alexandria, and I keep a port agent at Naples and ship inland by litter."

"Yours is not a small business," admitted Crassus, who was always alert for a place to invest a little money profitably.

"So you appreciate that," nodded Batiatus, the wine running from the corners of his mouth as he stretched his ponderous jowls. "So few people do. What do you think is my investment in Capua?"

Crassus shook his head. "It never occurred to me. One sees gladiators, and one doesn't stop to think of what was the investment before they walk into the arena. But that's common. One sees a legion, and one says, there have always been legions and therefore there always will be legions."

It was superb flattery. Batiatus put down his glass and stared at the commander, and then he rubbed a finger up and down his bulbous nose.

"Guess."

"A million?"

"Five million *denarii*," Batiatus said, slowly and emphatically. "Five million *denarii*. Only consider. I deal with agents in five countries. I keep a port agent in Naples. I feed only the best, whole wheat, barley, beef and goat cheese. I have my own arena for small shows and pairs, but the amphitheatre has a stone grandstand and it cost a cool million. I quarter and feed a maniple out of the local garrison. Not to mention the bribes in the same direction— begging your pardon. Not all military men are like yourself. And if you fight your lads in Rome, it's fifty thousand *denarii* a year for the tribunes and the ward bosses. Not to mention the women."

"Women?" asked Crassus.

"A gladiator is not a plough-hand on the *latifundia*. If you want him to have tone, you must provide something for him to sleep with. Then he eats better and he fights better. I have a house for my women and I buy only the best, no sluts or withered old bags, but every one is strong and healthy and virgin when she comes into my hands. I know; I try them." He drained his glass, licked his lips, and looked plaintive and lonely. "I need women," he complained, pouring the wine slowly. "Some men don't— I do."

"And this woman they call the wife of Spartacus?"

"Varinia," said Batiatus. He had turned in upon himself, and in his eyes there was a world of hatred, anger and wanting. "Varinia," he repeated.

"Tell me about her."

A measure of silence told Crassus more than the words which followed. "She was nineteen when I bought her. A German bitch, but good to look at if you like the yellow hair and the blue eyes. A dirty little animal and I should have killed her, so help me God! I gave her to Spartacus instead. It was a joke. He didn't want a woman and she didn't want a man. It was a joke."

"Tell me about her."

"I told you about her!" snarled Batiatus. He got up and stumbled through the flaps of the tent, and Crassus heard him urinating outside. It was a virtue of the commander that he pursued his goals single-mindedly. Batiatus stumbling back to the table did not disturb him. It was not his goal or need to make a gentleman out of the *lanista*.

"Tell me about her," he insisted.

Batiatus shook his head ponderously. "Do you mind if I get drunk?" he asked with aggrieved dignity.

"I have no feelings upon the matter. You may drink what you please," answered Crassus. "But you were telling me that you had Spartacus and Gannicus brought inland by litter. In chains, I suppose?"

Batiatus nodded.

"You had not seen him before, then?"

"No. What I saw, you would have thought little of, but I judge men differently. The two of them were bearded, filthy, covered all over with ulcers and sores and marked from head to foot with the whip. The stink of them was so bad it turned your stomach to go near them. Their own dry excrement was all over them. They were pared down to the limit and only their eyes demonstrated the *desperantes*. You would not have taken them to clean your latrines, but I looked at them and I saw something, because that is my own art. I put them in the baths, had them shaved and had their hair cut, had them rubbed with oil and fed well—"

"Will you tell me of Varinia now?"

"Damn you!"

The *lanista* reached for his goblet of wine, but clumsily,

overturning it. He lay forward on the table, staring at the red stain. What he saw therein, no one can say. Perhaps he saw the past, and perhaps he saw something of the future too. For the art of the augur is not wholly a fraud, and only men, not animals, have the power to judge the consequences of their acts. This was the man who trained Spartacus; he had threaded himself into a future that has no ending—even as all men do—but for ages unknown and unborn, he would be remembered. The trainer of men who had trained Spartacus sat facing the leader of men who would destroy Spartacus; but they shared in augury the vague and puzzled understanding that no one could destroy Spartacus. And because they shared even a glimmer of this, they were both of them similarly damned.

V

(Your fat friend, Lentulus Batiatus, said Crassus, the commander, but Caius Crassus, the lad who lay beside him on the bed, was dozing, eyes closed—and had heard only fragments of the story. Crassus was not a story teller; the tale was in his mind, his memory, his fears and hopes. The Servile War was done and Spartacus was done. The *Villa Salaria* signifies peace and prosperity, and that Roman peace which has blessed the earth, and he lay abed with a boy. And why not? he asked himself. Is it worse than other great men did?

(Caius Crassus brooded on the crosses that lined the road from Rome to Capua, for he was hardly entirely asleep. It did not trouble him that he shared a bed with the great general. His generation no longer felt a need to assuage guilt by rationalizing homosexuality. It was normal for him. The *passion* of six thousand slaves who hung from the crosses by the roadside was normal for him. He was much happier than Crassus, the great general. Crassus, the great general, was a man beset by devils; but Crassus, the young man of noble birth—distantly related, perhaps, for the family called Crassus was one of the largest in Rome at the time—struggled against no devils.

(It is true that the dead Spartacus affronted him. He hated a dead slave; but when he opened his eyes and looked

81

into the shadowed face of Crassus, he was at a loss to explain his hatred.

(You are not sleeping, said Crassus, no you are not sleeping after all, and there's the story, for what it is—if you heard any of it—and why do you hate Spartacus, who is now dead and gone forever?

(But Caius Crassus was lost in his own memories. It was four years before, and his friend had been Bracus. And with Bracus, he had journeyed down the Appian Way to Capua, and Bracus had wanted to please him. To please him gallantly and richly and abundantly, for what can be better than to sit next to a man you want in the cushions of the arena and to see men fight to the death? At that time, four years before now, four years before this strange evening at the *Villa Salaria,* he had shared a litter with Bracus, and Bracus had flattered him, and promised him that he would see the best of fighting, which was at Capua —and that the cost would be no barrier. There would be blood on the sand, and they would drink wine as they watched it.

(And then he had gone with Bracus to see Lentulus Batiatus, who kept the best school and trained the finest gladiators in all of Italy.

(And all of it, Caius reflected, was four years before— before there had been any Servile War, before anyone had heard the name of Spartacus. And now, Bracus was dead and Spartacus was also dead, and he, Caius, lay in bed with the greatest general of Rome.)

PART THREE

Being the tale of the first journey to Capua, made by Marius Bracus and Caius Crassus, some four years before the evening at the Villa Salaria, *and of the fighting of two pairs of gladiators.*

One fine spring day, when Lentulus Batiatus, the *lanista,* sat in his office, belching intermittently, his large breakfast making a comfortable bulk in his stomach, his Greek accountant entered the room and informed him that two young Romans were waiting outside, and that they wished to talk with him about fighting some pairs.

Both the office and accountant—a well-educated Ionian slave—were indications of wealth and prosperity on the part of Batiatus. His apprenticeship in ward politics and organized street fighting, his shrewd ladder of attachment to one important family after another, and the organizational ability which had permitted him to create one of the largest and most efficient street gangs in the city, had paid off well—and the investment of his carefully hoarded earnings in a small school for gladiators at Capua had been a wise one. As he often liked to put it, he rode on the wave of the future. A gangster could go so far and no further, and no gangster is shrewd enough always to select the winning side. More powerful gangs than his had been wiped off the Roman scene by the unexpected victory of an opponent and the savage fury of a new Consul.

On the other hand, the fighting of pairs—as it was commonly called—was a new field for investment and profit; it was legitimate; it was a recognized business; and anyone who read the signs of the times properly knew that it was only in its infancy. A casual entertainment would soon become the overwhelming craze of a whole social system. Politicians were beginning to realize that if one cannot have the glory of successful war on foreign soil, one can do almost as well by creating a minor replica at home, and the fighting of a hundred pairs, stretching through days and weeks, was already not uncommon. The demand for trained gladiators could never be filled, and prices were going higher and higher. Stone arenas were being built in city after city, and finally, when one of the most beautiful and imposing arenas in all Italy was built at Capua, Lentulus Batiatus decided to go there and start a school.

He had started in a very small way, with just a little shack and a crude fighting pen, training one pair at a time; but his business had grown rapidly, and now, five years later, he had a great establishment where he trained and stocked better than one hundred pairs. He had his own stone cellblock, his own gymnasium and bath house, his own training course, and his own arena for private shows—nothing like the public amphitheatres, of course, but capable of seating parties of fifty or sixty and large enough to fight three pairs at the same time. In addition, he had established sufficient local connections with the military—with appropriate bribes—to have a sufficient force of regular troops available at all times, and therefore spare himself the expense of creating his own private police force. His kitchen served a small army, for with the gladiators, their women, the trainers, house slaves and litter slaves, his household consisted of more than four hundred people. He had reason to be satisfied with himself.

The office in which he sat on this sunny spring morning was his latest acquisition. At the beginning of his career, he had resisted any and all window dressing. He was not patrician, and he made no pretense toward being one. But as his profits mounted, he found that it behooved him to live accordingly. He began to buy Greek slaves, and both an architect and an accountant were included in the purchases. The architect had persuaded him to build an office in the Greek style, flat-roofed and columned, with only three walls, the fourth side being open to the pleasantest prospect his situation afforded. With the drapes drawn back, a whole side of the room was open to fresh air and sunshine. The marble floor and the lovely white table upon which he conducted his affairs were in excellent taste. The open side was at his back, and he faced the doorway. Beyond that, he had a room for his clerks and a waiting room. It was a far cry, indeed, from gang warfare in the alleys of Rome.

Now the accountant said, "Two of them—*rosillae*. Perfume, rouge, and very expensive rings and clothes. A lot of money, but they are *rosillae,* and they will be a nuisance. One is just a young boy, about twenty-one, I would guess. The other is trying to please him."

"Let them come in," Batiatus said.

A moment later, the two young men entered, and Batiatus rose with excessive politeness, indicating two stools in front of his table.

As they seated themselves, Batiatus observed them quickly and expertly. They had an air of wealth, but only enough of it to show that they did not have to exhibit their wealth. They were young men of good family, but not in the great tradition—for what they were was entirely too obvious to have been tolerated by one of the sterner city *gens*. The younger one, Caius Crassus, was as pretty as a girl. Bracus was somewhat older, harder, playing the dominant role of the two. He had cold blue eyes and sandy hair, thin lips and a cynical expression. He did the talking. Caius merely listened, only glancing at his friend occasionally with respect and admiration. And Bracus talked of gladiators with the easy familiarity of the devotee of the games.

"I am Lentulus Batiatus, *lanista,*" said the fat man, giving himself a title of contempt which, he vowed, would cost them at least 5,000 *denarii* before the day was over.

Bracus introduced both of them and came to the point immediately. "We would like a private showing of two pairs."

"For just the two of you?"

"Ourselves and two friends."

The *lanista* nodded gravely and placed his fat hands together, so that his two diamonds, his emerald and his ruby showed to good advantage.

"That can be arranged," he said.

"To the death," said Bracus calmly.

"What?"

"You heard me. I want two pairs, Thracians, to the death."

"Why?" demanded Batiatus. "Why, whenever you young folk come down from Rome, must it be to the death?

You can see just as much blood and just as good fighting—
no, better!—to a decision. Why to the death?"

"Because we prefer it."

"That is no answer. Look, look," said Batiatus, spreading his hands for calm and thought and scientific consideration among men who knew the game, "you ask for Thracians. I have the best Thracian play in the world, but you will not see good play or good dagger work if you ask for the death. You know that as well as I do. It stands to reason. You pay your money—and then, zoot! it is finished. I can give you a day's play on points that will be like nothing you ever saw in Rome. As a matter of fact, you could go to the theatre and see better than anywhere in Rome. But if you come to me for private pleasure, then I stand on my reputation. My reputation is not as a butcher. I want to give you good fighting, the best fighting that money can buy."

"We want good fighting," smiled Bracus. "We want it to the death."

"That's a contradiction!"

"To your way of thinking," Bracus said softly. "You would like to keep both my money and your gladiators. When I pay for something, I buy it. I am buying two pairs to the death. If you don't wish to serve me, I can go elsewhere."

"Did I say I didn't want to serve you? I want to serve you better than you think. I can give you two pairs in rounds from morning until night, eight hours a day in the arena if you wish. And I will replace if any part of a pair is cut up too badly. I will give you all the blood and excitement you or your ladies could possibly desire, and I will charge you no more than 8,000 *denarii* for the whole thing. That includes food and wine and services of any kind you may desire."

"You know what we desire. I don't like to haggle," Bracus said coldly.

"All right. It will cost you 25,000 *denarii*."

Caius was impressed—indeed somewhat frightened at the enormous figure, but Bracus shrugged.

"Very well. They are to fight naked."

"Naked?"

"You heard me, *lanista!*"

"All right."

"And I want no fakery—no double cuts for them both to suck the sand and pretend that they are finished. If they are both down, one of your trainers will cut the throats of both. And they are to understand that."

Batiatus nodded.

"I will give you ten thousand on account and the rest when the pairs have finished."

"All right. Please pay my accountant. He will give you a receipt and draw contracts for you. Do you want to see them before you leave?"

"Can we have the arena in the morning?"

"In the morning—yes. But I must warn you that this kind of a fight may be over very quickly."

"Please don't warn me, *lanista*." He turned to Caius and asked, "Do you want to see them, child?"

Caius smiled shyly and nodded. They went out, and after Bracus had paid and signed the contract, they crawled into their litters and were carried to the exercise yard. Caius could not take his eyes off Bracus. Never, he thought, had he seen a man conduct himself so admirably. Not merely the 25,000 *denarii*—his own allowance of a thousand *denarii* a month was considered munificent by everyone he knew—but the manner of spending and the casual dealing with human life. It was a kind of cynical contempt to which Caius aspired, and which marked, for him, the highest level of cosmopolitanism; and in this case it was combined with a wonderfully cool sophistication. Never in a thousand years would he have had the courage to demand that the gladiators fight naked; yet that was one of the reasons why they were having a show for their own amusement at Capua instead of going to the arena in Rome.

At the exercise yard, the slaves set down their litters. The exercise yard was an iron-barred enclosure, one hundred and fifty feet long and forty feet wide, caged in iron on three sides, with the cellblock where the gladiators lived as its fourth side. Caius realized that here was a higher and more dangerous art than the training and keeping of wild beasts; for a gladiator was not only a dangerous beast, but one who could think as well. A delightful thrill of fear and excitement went through him as he watched the men in the exercise yard. There were about a hundred of them, clad in loin cloths and nothing else, clean-shaven, their hair cropped close to their heads, going through their paces with wooden sticks and staffs. About six trainers walked among them, and these, like all trainers, were old veterans of the army. The trainer carried a short Spanish sword in one hand and heavy brass knuckles in the other, and he walked warily and gingerly, his eyes nervous and alert. A maniple of regular army troops were spread at intervals all around the enclosure, their heavy, murderous *pila* exacting an extraordinary discipline. No wonder, Caius thought, the price of the death of a few of these men was high.

The gladiators themselves were superbly muscled and as graceful as panthers in their motions. Roughly, they fell into three classes, the three classes of fighters so popular in Italy at this time. There were the Thracians—a grouping or profession more than a race, for there were numerous Jews and Greeks among them—who were most desired at this time. They fought with the *sica*, a short, slightly curved dagger, the common weapon in Thrace and in Judea, where most of them were recruited. The *retiarii* were just beginning their epoch of popularity, and they fought with two curious weapons, a fish net and a long, three-pronged fish fork called a *tridens*. For this category, Batiatus preferred Africans, tall, long-limbed black men from Ethiopia, and they were always matched against the *murmillones*, a loose category of fighters who carried either a sword alone or sword and shield. The *murmillones* were almost always Germans or Gauls.

"Note them," said Bracus, pointing to the black men. "There is the finest play and the most skillful, but it can be a bore. To see it at its best, you must see Thracians. Don't you agree?" he asked Batiatus.

The *lanista* shrugged. "Each has its virtues."

"Match me a Thracian against a black man."

Batiatus looked at him a moment, then shook his head. "It is no match. The Thracian has only a dagger."

"I want it," said Bracus.

Batiatus shrugged, caught the eye of one of the trainers, and nodded for him to come. Fascinated, Caius watched the lines of gladiators go through their precise, dance-like exercises, the Thracians and Jews doing their dagger work with little sticks and little wooden bucklers, the black men casting nets and darting long wooden sticks that were for all the world like broom handles, and the big, blond Germans and Gauls fencing with wooden swords. Never in all his life had he seen men so conditioned, so agile, so graceful, so apparently tireless, as they went through the paces of the dance, over and over and over. There, in the sunlight behind the iron bars, they communicated even to Caius—even to his poor, warped, twisted conscience—a sense of pity that life so splendid and vital should serve only for butchery. But only a flicker of this; never before had Caius experienced such intense excitement at the prospect of a future event. Boredom had entered his life when he was only a child. He was not bored now.

The trainer was explaining, "The dagger has only one keen edge. Once the dagger is in the net, the Thracian is finished. It makes for bad blood in the school. It's no match."

"Get them," Batiatus said shortly.

"Why not with a German—"

"I'm paying for Thracians," Bracus said coldly. "Don't argue with me!"

"You heard him," said the *lanista*.

The trainer carried a little silver whistle on a string around his neck. Now he blew it sharply three times and the lines of gladiators came to rest.

"Who do you want?" he asked Batiatus.

"Draba."

"Draba!" the trainer shouted.

One of the black men turned and walked toward them, dragging net and stick. A giant of a man, his dark skin glistening with a sheen of sweat.

"David."

"David!" the trainer shouted.

This was a Jew, lean, hawk-faced, thin bitter lips, and green eyes in a clean-shaven, tanned face and head. His wooden dagger was hooked in fingers that kept flexing and unflexing, and he stared through the guests without seeing them.

"A Jew," said Bracus to Caius. "Have you ever seen a Jew?"

Caius shook his head.

"It will be exciting. Jews are very good with the *sica*. It is all they know of fighting, but they are very good."

"Polemus."

"Polemus!" the trainer shouted.

This was a Thracian, very young and graceful and handsome.

"Spartacus!"

He joined the other three. The four men stood there, separated from the two Roman youths, the *lanista* and the litter slaves by the heavy iron fence of the exercise yard. Looking at them, Caius realized that they were something new, something different and strange and terrible in his own terms. It was not only the sullen, brooding masculinity of them—a masculinity that almost never existed in his own circle of acquaintances—but the way they were closed off from him. They were men trained to fight and kill, not as soldiers fought, not as animals fought, but as gladiators fought, which was something else entirely. He was looking at four frightening masks.

"How do you like them?" Batiatus asked.

Not for the life of him could Caius have answered or spoken at all, but Bracus said coolly,

"All except that one with the broken nose. He doesn't look like a fighter."

"Looks can be deceiving," Batiatus reminded him. "That's Spartacus. He is very good, very powerful, and very quick. I chose him for a purpose. He is very quick."

"Who will you match him with?"

"With the black man," answered Batiatus.

"Very well. I hope it's worth the price," said Bracus.

That was when and how Caius saw Spartacus; although four years later he had forgotten the names of any of the gladiators and only remembered the hot sunshine, the feel and smell of the place, the smell of men's bodies running sweat.

II

This is Varinia, who lies awake in the darkness, and she has not slept this night, not at all, not even for a few moments; but Spartacus, who lies beside her, sleeps. How soundly he sleeps and how completely! The soft flow of his breath, the intaking and outgiving of air, which is the fuel for the fire of life within him, is as regular and as even as all the timely ebbing and flowing in the world of life, and Varinia thinks of that and knows that what is at peace and at grips with life has this same regularity, whether it be the motion of the tides, the passing of the seasons, or the fruition of the egg within the woman.

But how can a man sleep in such a fashion, when he knows what he faces on waking? How can he slumber at the edge of death? Where does his peace come from?

Very lightly, most lightly, Varinia touches him and traces out his skin, his flesh and his limbs as he lies there in the darkness. The skin is elastic and fresh and alive; the muscles are relaxed; the limbs are loose and resting. Sleep is precious; sleep is life for him.

(Sleep, sleep, sleep, my beloved, my darling, my gentle one, my good one, my terrible one—sleep. Sleep and husband your strength, my man, my man.)

Gently and carefully, her whole motion like a whisper, Varinia closes with him, so that more and more of her own flesh is touching his, her long limbs pressed against his, her full breasts cushioned to him, her face finally touching his, cheek to cheek, her golden hair spread like a crown above him, her terror eased by memories now and by love, for fear and love do not live easily together.

(She had said to him once, I want you to do something. I want you to do something that we do in the tribe because we believe something. He smiled at her, What do you believe in with the tribe? She said, You will laugh, and then he answered, Do I ever laugh? Have I ever laughed? Then she said to him, In the tribe we believe that the soul goes into the body, through the nose and the mouth, a little with the breath each time. You are smiling. Then he answered, I am not smiling at you. I am smiling at the wonderful things people believe; to which she cried, Because you are a Greek, and Greeks believe nothing at all. He told her then, I am not a Greek but a Thracian, and it is not true that the Greeks believe nothing at all, but the best and the richest things people can believe, these things the Greeks believe. To this, her answer was that she didn't care what the Greeks believed, but would he do what they did in the tribe? Would he put his mouth to her mouth and breathe his breath and his soul into her? And then she would do the same to him, and forever and for all time their souls would be mingled and they would be one person in two bodies. Or was he afraid? And this he answered by saying, Can't you guess the things I am afraid of?)

She lies with him now on the thin pallet on the floor of their cell. The cell is their home. The cell is their castle. All their being together has been in this stone cubicle, which measures five feet by seven feet and which contains only a chamber pot and a pallet. But even these are not theirs; nothing is theirs, not even each other, and she lies by him now, touching his face and limbs and weeping softly—she whom no one ever saw weep in the daylight.

(I do not give women, I lend women, Batiatus was fond of saying. I lend them to my gladiators. A man is no good in the arena if his parts shrivel up. A gladiator is not a litter slave. A gladiator is a man, and if he's not a man, no one will pay ten *denarii* for him. And a man needs a woman. I buy the incorrigibles because they are cheap, and if I can't tame them, my boys will.)

The night is passing, and the first faint gray of the dawn enters the cell. If Varinia were to stand up, rising to her full, tall lissome height, her head would be on a level with the single window of the cell. If she were to look out of the cell, she would see the iron-walled stretch of the exercise ground and beyond it the sleepy soldiers who stand guard day and night. She knows it well. Cell and chains are not the natural habitat for her, as they are for Spartacus.

(This particular woman filled Batiatus with eagerness and delight. His agent had purchased her in Rome for very little, as a matter of fact, for only 500 *denarii,* so he knew that the merchandise was hardly unblemished, but just to look at her filled him with eagerness and delight. For one thing, she was tall and beautifully formed, as many of the German tribe women were, and Batiatus admired tall, shapely women. For another thing, she was very young, no more than twenty or twenty-one years, and Batiatus enjoyed young women. For still another thing, she was quite beautiful and had a grand head of yellow hair, and Batiatus preferred beautiful women with fine hair. So it is not difficult to understand why she filled the *lanista* with eagerness and delight.

(But the blemish was there, and he discovered that the first time he tried to take her to bed. She became a wild cat. She became a kicking, spitting, scratching, clawing monster—and since she was large and strong, he had a bad time beating her into unconsciousness. In the struggle, all the expensive objects which decorated his bedroom were smashed, including a beautiful Greek vase which he had to use to beat her over the head until she ceased to struggle. His rage and frustration were such that he would —he felt—have been entirely justified in killing her; but when he added the fine vases, lamps and statuettes to her original cost, he considered that the investment was entirely too high to allow himself to be carried away by his anger. Nor could he in all good faith sell her in the market for a price in accordance with her appearance. Perhaps because he had started as a gang leader in the alleys of Rome, Batiatus had an extraordinary concern for business ethics. He prided himself on the fact that he sold nothing on false pretenses. Instead, he decided to let the gladiators tame her, and because he had already taken an unreasonable dislike to the strange, silent Thracian called Spartacus— whose sheep-like exterior covered a flame respected by every gladiator in the school—he chose him for her mate.

(It pleased him to watch Spartacus as he handed Varinia over to him, saying, This is a mate to lie with. Bring her to child or not, as you please. Make her obey you, but don't injure her or deform her. That is what he said to Spartacus, as Spartacus stood silent and impassive, looking calmly at the German girl. Varinia was not beautiful on that occasion. There were two long gashes on her face. One eye was swollen closed, yellow and purple, and there were green and purple bruises on her forehead, her neck and her arms.

(See what you are getting, said Batiatus, tearing off the already torn dress which he had given her, and then she stood naked in front of Spartacus. At that moment, Spartacus saw her and loved her, not for her nakedness, but because without clothes she was not naked at all and did not cringe or attempt to cover herself with her arms, but stood simply and proudly, showing no pain nor hurt, not looking at him or at Batiatus, but contained within herself, contained with her eyesight and her soul and her dreams, and containing all those things because she had decided to surrender life which was worth nothing any more. His heart went out to her.

(That night, she huddled at the farthest corner of his cell, and he left her alone, made no move toward her except to ask her, when the chill settled, You speak Latin, girl?—no answer. Then he said, I will talk to you in Latin because I don't speak German, and now the night chill is coming, and I want you to lie on my mat, girl—and still there was no answer from her. So he pushed the pallet toward her, and left it between them, and in the morning it was there, and they had both slept on the stone. But this was the first thoughtful kindness Varinia had encountered since they had taken her in the German forests, a year and half before.)

And on this damp night, turning into morning, the memory of that first night, returns to her, and with the memory there goes from her into the man sleeping beside her, such a wave of love that he would have to be made of stone not to sense it. He stirs, and suddenly, he opens his eyes, seeing her dimly in the half light of the dawning, but seeing her wholly with his inward sight, and not yet awake, he takes her to him and begins to caress her.

"Oh, my darling, my darling," she says.

"Let me."

"And where will you find the strength for today, my beloved?"

"Let me, I am full of strength."

Then she lies in his arms, the tears flowing silently.

III

The morning is for fighting, and it's in the air and all over the place, and every one of the two hundred and some odd gladiators knows and responds to the electric knowledge. Two pairs will bleed on the sand because two young men have come down from Rome with a lot of money and a taste for excitement. Two Thracians, a Jew and an African, and since the African is trained to net and fork, the odds will be off. This is the kind of thing that many *lanistae* would not permit, for even if you breed a dog you don't set him against a lion, but Batiatus will do anything for money.

The black man, Draba, awakens on this morning, and in his own tongue, he says, "I greet thee, day of death."

He lies on his pallet and thinks about his life. He muses over the strange fact that all men, even the most miserable, have memories of love and care and kisses and play and joy and song and dance, and all men are afraid to die. Even when life is worth nothing at all, men cling to it. Even when they are lonely and a long way from home and bereft of any hope whatsoever of returning to their home and subject to every indignity and pain and cruelty and fed like sleek beasts and trained to fight for the amusement of others—even when this is so, they still cling to life.

And he, who was once an honest homesteader, with home and wife and children of his own, a voice listened to in peace and honored in war—he who was all that is now given a fish net and a fish fork and sent to fight, so that people can laugh at him and clap their hands at him.

He whispers the empty philosophy of his kind and his profession, *"Dum vivimus vivamus."*

But it is empty and without solace, and his bones and muscles ache as he stands up to begin his day and force his body and mind to the task of killing Spartacus—whom he loves and values above all other white men in the place. Yet isn't it said, "Gladiator—make no friends of gladiators."

IV

They went to the baths first, the four of them walking together in silence. It was no use to talk, because there was nothing for them to talk about now, and since they would be together from now until they entered the arena, talking would only worsen the situation.

Already, the baths were steaming hot, and they plunged into the murky water quickly, as if everything had to be gotten through without thought or consideration. The bath house was quite dark, forty feet long and twenty feet deep, and lit, once the doors were closed, only by a small mica skylight. Under this pale light, the water of the bath was dull gray, overlaid by the hot mist rising from it, steaming from the red-hot stones which had been dropped into it, filling the whole bath house with the heavy texture of vapor-saturated air. It penetrated every pore of Spartacus's body, relaxed his tense muscles, and gave him a strange, divorced feeling of ease and comfort. The hot water was a never-ending wonder to him, and never did the dry death of Nubia wash entirely from him; and never could he enter the bath house without reflecting on the care given to the bodies of those who were bred for death and trained to produce only death. When he had produced the things of life, wheat and barley and gold, his body was a dirty, useless thing, a thing of shame and filth, to be beaten and kicked and whipped and starved—but now that he had become a creature of death, his body was as precious as the yellow metal he had mined in Africa.

And strangely enough, it was only now that hatred had come to flower in him. There was no room for hatred before; hatred is a luxury that needs food and strength and even time for a certain kind of reflection. He had those things now, and he had Lentulus Batiatus as the living object of his hatred. Batiatus was Rome and Rome was Batiatus. He hated Rome and he hated Batiatus; and he hated all things Roman. He had been born and bred to accept the tilling of the fields, the herding of cattle and the mining of metal; but only in Rome had he come to see the breeding and training of men so that they could cut each other to pieces and bleed on the sand to the laughter and excitement of well bred men and women.

From the baths, they went to the rubbing tables. As always, Spartacus closed his eyes as the fragrant olive oil was poured onto his skin and each separate muscle of his body was loosened under the facile and knowing fingers of the masseur. The first time this had happened to him, his feeling was that of a trapped animal, panic and terror, the small freedom of all he owned or had ever owned, his own flesh invaded by these probing, writhing fingers. By now, however, he could relax and take full advantage of what the masseur gave him. Twelve times, he had lain like this; twelve times he had fought, eight times in the great amphitheatre of Capua, with the screaming, blood-maddened crowds urging him on, four times in the private arena

96

of Batiatus for the edification of the wealthy connoisseurs of slaughter who travelled down from the mighty, legendary *urbs,* which he had never seen, to spend a day with their ladies or their male lovers watching men fight.

Now, as always when he lay upon the rubbing table, he lived over those times. It was all graven on his mind. No horror of mine or field was like the horror which gripped you when you stepped onto the hard-packed sand of the arena; no fear was like that particular fear; no indignity was like this particular indignity of being chosen to kill.

And so he learned that no form of human life was lower than the gladiator, and his very nearness to the beasts was rewarded with the same anxious care bestowed upon fine horses, even though Lentulus Batiatus or any other Roman would have been revolted at the thought of destroying a good horse in the arena. He wore his own mantle of fear and indignity, and now the fingers of the masseur traced the weave of each thread and cross thread of scar tissue.

He had been lucky. Never had he suffered a severed nerve, a scraped bone, a gouged eye, a dagger point in the eardrum or the neck or any others of those special and particular wounds his comrades feared so and dreamed of at night in a sweat of agony and terror. Never had he been hamstrung or had his intestines pierced. All his wounds were simple *mementa,* as they called them, and he could not ascribe this to skill and did not want to. Skill in this butchery! *No slave makes a soldier,* they said. But he was quick as a cat, almost as quick as the green-eyed Jew, the creature of hate and silence who lay on the table beside him, and very strong and very thoughtful. That was hardest—to think and not to become angry. *Ira est mors.* And those who became angry in the arena, they died. Fear was something else, but no anger. It was not hard for him. All his life, his thoughts had been his tools of survival. Few people knew that. "The slave—he thinks of nothing at all." And, "The gladiator is a beast." That was obvious, but within it was its very reverse. Once in a while, a free man survives by thought; but from day to day, the slave must think to live—another kind of thought, yet thought. Thought was the philosopher's companion, but the slave's adversary. When Spartacus left Varinia this morning, he blotted her out. She must not exist for him. If he lived, she would live, but now he was neither alive nor dead.

The masseurs finished. The four slaves slid off the tables and wrapped around them the long woolen cloaks, shrouds as they were called, and walked across the yard into the mess hall. Already the gladiators were at their morning meal, each man sitting cross-legged on the floor and eating from a little table in front of him. Each man had a cup of sour goatmilk and a bowl of wheat porridge cooked with bits of fat pork. The *lanista* fed well, and many a man who came to his school ate his fill for the first time, even as the condemned man does before he is nailed to the crucifix. But for the four who were to perform in the arena, there was only a little wine and a few strips of cold sliced chicken. One does not fight well on a heavy stomach.

In any case, Spartacus was not hungry. They sat apart from the others, the four of them, and they shared a distaste for food. They sipped at the wine. They took a bite or two of the meat, and sometimes they looked at each other. But no one spoke, and theirs was a little island of silence in the rumble of speech which filled the hall. Nor did the other gladiators look at them or pay them overmuch attention. This was the courtesy of the last breakfast.

It was common knowledge now how they were paired. Everyone knew that Spartacus would fight the black man, and that it would be dagger against net and fork. Everyone knew that the Thracian and the Jew were paired. Spartacus would die and the young Thracian would die. It was the fault of Spartacus. Not only did he lie with the German girl and speak of her always as his wife and in no other way than as his wife—but he made the men love him. No one of the gladiators seated there in the hall could have expressed that explicitly. They didn't know why it had happened or precisely how it had happened. A man has a manner; a man has a thousand little gestures and actions. The gentle manner of the Thracian, the sheep-like face with the full lips and the broken nose—all of that belied a quality which would make men accept his judgment, come to him with fears and quarrels, come to him for comfort and decision. Yet when he decided, they did as he said. When he spoke to them in his soft, curiously-accented

Latin, they accepted his words. He spoke to them and they were comforted. He seemed to be a happy man. He held his head upright, which was a strange thing in a slave; he never bowed his head; he never raised his voice, nor was he angry. His contentment singled him out, and he walked that way in this unholy company of trained killers and lost men.

"Gladiators are animals," Batiatus often said. "If one thinks of them as people, one loses all perspective."

The simple fact was that Spartacus refused to be an animal, and for that reason he was dangerous, and for all his skill with the dagger and for all his value for hire, Batiatus preferred him profitably dead.

The breakfast was over. The four men who were *privilegio,* as it was put in the irony of their own slang, walked by themselves. They were forbidden this morning. They were not to be spoken to or touched. But Gannicus went over to Spartacus and embraced him and kissed his lips; it was a strange thing to do, and the price was high, thirty lashes, but there were few among the gladiators who did not have a sense of why he had done it.

V

Many times in the years that followed, Lentulus Batiatus recalled that morning, and many times he subjected it to his scrutiny and attempted to understand whether the earth-shaking events which followed could be ascribed to it. Yet he was not certain that they could, and it was not possible for him to accept the fact that what happened afterwards happened because two Roman fops desired to see a private combat to the death. Never a week went by but that there was a private showing of one or two or three pairs in his own arena, and he could not see that this was too different. It made him think of the fate of certain tenement houses he owned in the city of Rome. These tenement houses, or *insulae,* as they were called, were commonly recognized as one of the best investments a business man could make. They were subject to none of the vicissitudes of merchant enterprise; they paid a steady and for the most part a rising rate of income, and this income could be increased. But a certain danger was contained within this increase of income. In the beginning, Batiatus bought two houses, one four stories and one five stories high. Each had twelve apartments to a floor, and each apartment cost its tenant about nine hundred *sesterces* a year.

It did not take Batiatus long to realize that a man interested in profit kept adding stories. Unenterprising scavengers owned low houses; rich men owned skyscrapers. Promptly the *lanista* ran the five story house up to seven stories, but the first addition to the four story house brought it crashing down in ruins, saddling him not only with a huge loss, but with the death of over twenty of his tenants —which meant the additional spending of a fortune in bribes. Something of the same addition of quantity and resulting change in quality existed here, in terms of his gladiators, yet Batiatus knew that he was no worse in his practice than most *lanistae,* and, indeed, better than many.

It was true that this was a bad morning. Firstly, there was the lashing of Gannicus. It was not good to lash gladiators, but at the same time, the discipline of a school had to be the most stringent discipline in the world. The breaking of any small feature of discipline by a gladiator had to be punished—and punished quickly and mercilessly. Secondly, there was the resentment among the gladiators that a dagger man was to be pitted against net and fork. Thirdly, there was the fighting itself.

Batiatus was waiting at the arena for the guests to arrive. Regardless of what Batiatus thought of these Romans in a personal sense, there was an honor due to money which he was keenly aware of. Whenever he encountered a millionaire—not merely a man who had millions but one who could spend millions—he was overwhelmed by his own sense of being so small a frog in so small a puddle. When he was a gang leader on the streets of the *urbs,* his own dream was to accumulate the 400,000 *sesterces* which would entitle him to admittance into the order of knighthood. When he became a knight, however, he first began to realize what wealth meant, and for all he had climbed— by his own shrewdness too—there was an endless vista of ladder ahead of him.

Honor where honor is due. That is why he waited here for Caius and Bracus and the others; and thereby did not know that Gannicus had earned thirty lashes. Instead, he escorted the honored guests to the box which had been prepared for them, a box built just high enough to view every corner of the little arena without craning or stretching. He himself adjusted the pillows of their couches, so that they might recline in the greatest ease and comfort as they watched the fighting. Cool wine was brought to them and little pots of sweetmeats and honied squab, so that thirst and appetite might always be satisfied. A striped awning protected them from the morning sun, and two household slaves stood by with feather fans, in case the coolness of the morning should give way to a sultry forenoon. As he superintended the arrangement of the scene, Batiatus's heart swelled with pride—for certainly, here was all that anyone, no matter how delicate his tastes, could ask. And to fill in the boredom between now and the moment when the game began, there were two musicians and a dancing girl on the floor of the arena.

Not that they paid much attention to either the music or the dancing; they were keyed higher than that, and the married friend of Bracus—Cornelius Lucius was his name —prattled nervously of what one needed to live decently in Rome these days. Batiatus lingered and listened; he was eager to know what one needed to live decently in Rome these days, and the conversation caught him when he learned that Lucius had paid 5,000 *denarii* for a new *libarius*, a fortune for a man to bake pastry.

"But one can't live like a pig—or can one?" asked Lucius. "Or even the way my father lived. If one wants to eat decently, one needs at least four, the pastry cook, the *cocus*, the *pistores* and certainly a *dulciarius*, or else one sends to the market for cooked sweets and one could just as well do without that."

"I don't see how one could do without that," his wife said. "Every month a new *tonsores*; no one but a god could shave you properly, but if I claim an extra hairdresser or masseur—"

"It is not requiring a hundred slaves," Bracus told her gently, "but training them—and even when you have trained them, I sometimes think that it's hardly worth the effort. I have a *privata* for my clothes, a Greek from Cyprus who can quote you Homer by the hour. Mind you, he neither cleans nor washes. All I ask of him is that he keep some order among my clothes. I have a closet for cloaks. All I desire is that when I am through with a particular cloak, it should be placed in that closet. A tunic in the closet where my tunics are kept. One could train a dog to do that, no? So if I say, Raxides, give me my yellow tunic, he can do it. But he can't do it. And it would take more time to teach him to do it properly than to do it myself."

"You can't do that yourself," Caius protested.

"No—of course not. Child, see what kind of wine the *lanista* serves."

Batiatus was quicker. "Cisalpine," he boasted, holding the jug before them.

Bracus spat delicately, a finger alongside his nose. "How did you think of cushions, if I didn't say to you, we want cushions? Do you have Judean wine, *lanista?*"

"Of course—the very best. A light rose—the lightest rose." He screamed at one of the slaves to bring Judean wine immediately.

"Tell him," said Lucius to his wife, who was whispering to him.

"No—"

Bracus stretched himself toward her, took her hand and pressed it to his lips. "Darling, is there anything you can't tell me?"

"I'll whisper it."

She whispered it, and Bracus answered, "Of course, of course." And then told Batiatus, "Bring the Jew here before he fights."

The thread which ran through the actions of well bred people always eluded Batiatus. He knew there was such a thread, but for the life of him, he could not define it with any consistency, and he could not locate a rhyme or reason of pattern which would enable him to conceal his origin in a scheme of behavior. Each party which hired his arena for a private showing behaved differently; how do you know?

Batiatus sent for the Jew.

He came between two trainers and he walked to the box and stood there waiting. He was still wrapped in his long, rough woolen cloak, and his pale green eyes were like cold stones. He saw nothing out of those eyes. He just stood there.

The woman simpered. Caius was frightened. This was the first time a gladiator had ever stood within arm's reach

102

of him, with neither wall nor bars between them, and the two trainers were not sufficient to reassure him. This was nothing human, this Jew with the green eyes and the thin mouth, the fierce hooked nose and the close-cropped skull.

"Tell him to shed his cloak, *lanista*," said Bracus.

"Unclothe," Batiatus whispered.

The Jew stood there for a little while; then, suddenly, he dropped his cloak and stood naked before them, his lean, muscular body as motionless as if it were carved from bronze. Caius stared fascinated. Lucius pretended to be bored, but his wife stared with her mouth slightly open, her breath coming hard and fast.

"*Animal bipes implume,*" Bracus said tiredly.

The Jew bent, retrieved his cloak, and turned away. The two trainers followed him.

"Let him fight first," Bracus said.

VI

At this time, it was not yet required by law that when Thracian or Jew fought in the arena with the traditional dagger, or perhaps better, the slightly-curved knife which was known as the *sica*, he should be given a wooden buckler for his defense, and even when that law was passed, it was frequently violated. The buckler, like the traditional brass greaves and helmet, defeated the essential drama of the knife—which was the incredible play of motion and agility called forth from the gladiators. Until about forty years before this time—and until then the combat of pairs was fairly infrequent—the usual bout in the arena was called *Samnites,* and the pairs fought in heavy armor, carrying the great oblong shield of the legion, the *scutum,* and the Spanish sword, the *spatha.* This was neither very exciting nor very bloody, and the crash of shield against shield and sword against sword could go on for hours, without either of the pair being damaged particularly. At that time, too, the *lanista* was as despised as a procurer— usually a petty gang leader who bought a few used-up slaves and let them hack at each other until they fell dead of loss of blood or sheer exhaustion. Very often, the *lanista* was a procurer, dealing in gladiators with one hand and in prostitutes with the other.

Two innovations revolutionized the fighting of pairs—and turned a dull spectacle into the craze of Rome and brought many a *lanista* to a seat in the Senate, a country villa and a fortune of millions. The first was a result of Roman military and commercial penetration of Africa. The black man, fairly rare in the past, made his appearance in the slave market, the Negro in all his great height and strength. A *lanista* conceived the notion of giving him a fish net and fish fork, a triple-pointed fish spear, and putting him into the arena against sword and shield. Immediately, this caught the fancy of the Romans; the games were no longer casual. The process was completed by the second innovation—which was the result of the penetration of Thrace and Judea and the discovery of two hardy, independent races of mountain peasants whose main weapon in war was a short, razor-sharp curved knife. Even more than the *retiarii*, the net-men, this transformed gladiatorial combat. Very rarely was buckler or body armor used. The lumbering crash of the *Samnites* was transformed into the lightning-like play of the dagger duels, long, ghastly wounds, blood and disembowelment, skill and pain and flashing motion.

As Bracus put it to his young companion, "Once you have seen Thracians, you don't want anything else, you know. Anything else is very dull, tedious and meaningless. Good Thracian play is the most exciting thing in the world."

It was time for the pairs. The dancing girl and the musicians had gone. The little arena was bare and empty in the hot morning sunshine. An aching, quivering silence hung over the whole place, and the four Romans, the lady and the three gentlemen, lay upon their couches under the striped awning, sipped at their rose-colored Judean wine, and waited for the game to begin.

VII

In the house of expectation, which was a little shed opening onto the arena, the three gladiators, the two Thracians

104

and the black man, sat and waited for the Jew to return. They sat on a bench without happiness; they were *consigned,* as it was put. Only shame was their companion, neither glory nor love nor honor. And the black man said finally, breaking the silence which they had imposed upon themselves.

"Quem di diligunt adolescens moritur." If the gods love you, you die in childhood.

"No," said Spartacus.

And then the black man asked him, "Do you believe in the gods?"

"No."

"Do you believe there is another place after we die here?"

"No."

"Then what do you believe in, Spartacus?" the black man asked.

"I believe in you and I believe in me."

"You and me," said Polemus, the young, handsome Thracian, "we are meat on the butcher table of the *lanista.*"

"What else do you believe in, Spartacus?" the black man asked.

"What else—? What does a man dream? When a man is going to die, what does he dream?"

"I tell you what I said before," the black man said softly, his deep voice resonant and sorrowful in his chest, "and I tell you this. I am too lonely and too far from home and too bitter for home. I don't want to live any more. I will not kill you, my comrade."

"Is this a place for mercy?"

"It's a place for weariness, and I'm tired."

"My father was a slave," said Spartacus, "and he taught me the only virtue. The only virtue of a slave is to live."

"We cannot both live."

"And the only kindness of life to a slave is that, like other people, he doesn't know the time of his death."

Now the guards had heard them, and they hammered with their spears on the wall of the shed for silence. The Jew returned; in any case, he would not have spoken; he never spoke. He stood inside the door, cloaked, his head bent with sorrow and shame. A trumpet sounded. The young Thracian rose, his underlip quivering with tension, and he and the Jew dropped their cloaks. The door opened, and naked, side by side, they walked into the arena.

The black man was not interested. He was wedded to death. Fifty-two times, he had fought with net and spear and emerged alive, and now the cord that bound him to life had snapped. He sat on the bench with his memories, bowed over, his head in his hands; but Spartacus leaped to the door and pressed his eye to a crack, so that he might see, so that he might know. He took no side; the Thracian was of his people, but the Jew was something that tore his heart in a peculiar and strange way. When a pair fought to the death, one had to die, but the essence of the matter was life while life persisted. The essence of Spartacus was life. People recognized that in him. It was survival pitched onto the plane of the stars, and now he pressed his eye to the crack which gave him a channel of vision down the center of the arena.

His vision at first was blocked by the pair, but they dwindled in size as they walked to the center of the arena and faced those who had purchased their flesh and blood. Their shadows flowed behind them; their bodies were dark and glistened with oil. Then they moved ten paces apart, and each stood framed at the edge of his vision, with the sand and sunlight between them. Spartacus could see the box where the Romans sat; it defined the end of his vision, a broad, gay pavilion of pink and yellow and purple color, with its striped awning, the slow motion of the feather fans of the body slaves. There they sat, who had purchased life and death, the few and the mighty—and all the thoughts that must come to one man at least in every age of time, all of the thoughts came to Spartacus . . .

Now the trainer, the master of the arena, entered. He bore the two knives on a tray of polished wood, and he offered them symbolically to those who had paid the price of the game. As he slanted the tray toward them, the sun flashed from the polished metal of the blades, twelve inches of shining steel, razor-sharp, beautifully tooled and hafted in dark walnut. The knife was slightly curved, and the merest feather touch of the blade would split the skin.

Bracus nodded, and hatred was like the touch of one of those knives on Spartacus, from head to foot—and then controlled and passionless as he watched the two gladiators select their weapons and then move apart outside of his field of vision. Yet he knew what their movements were;

every movement he knew. Eyeing each other with the wary horror and alertness of the condemned, they were each of them measuring the twenty paces of space allotted. Now they bent and rubbed sand onto the hilts, and onto the surface of their hands. Now they were crouched and every muscle was trembling like a taut spring and their hearts were pounding like machines.

The trainer blew his silver whistle and the two gladiators reemerged in Spartacus's field of vision. Naked, crouched, each with the gleaming knife cradled in the palm of his right hand, they had shed their manhood. They were two animals. They circled like animals, shuffling their feet in short, flat steps on the hot sand. Then they closed and were apart in one convulsive motion, and the Romans were applauding and the Jew's breast was marked with a thread of blood he wore like a sash.

But neither of them seemed to be aware of the damage done. Their concentration upon each other was so intense, so absolute, so demanding that the whole world appeared to pivot upon them. Time ceased; all of life and experience was concentrated upon each other, and the intensity with which they studied each other became something painful. And then again they came together in what seemed to be a single, integrated convulsion of force and decision, and then they were locked, left hand gripping right, and they stood together, bound to each other, body to body, face to face, the locked wrists straining and screaming in silence the desire to close and cut and kill. Their transition was complete now; they hated each other; they knew only one purpose, the purpose of death, since only by killing could one of them live. Gripped together as they were, muscles rigid and straining, the two became one, one entity torn within itself.

As long as flesh and blood could stand it, they strained in that grip, and then it broke and they tore apart, and now there was a ribbon of red the whole length of the Thracian's arm. A dozen paces from each other, they stood panting and hating and trembling, each of them painted all over with blood and oil and sweat, the blood trickling down and staining the sand at their feet.

Then the Thracian struck. Knife outstretched, he flung himself at the Jew, and the Jew went down on one knee, parried the knife upward and flung the Thracian who hurtled through the air. And almost before the Thracian struck the ground, the Jew was upon him. It was the moment of supreme horror and extreme excitement in the game. Death was cutting at the Thracian. He twisted, rolled, convulsed, used his bare feet to ward off the terrible knife, but the Jew was all over him, cutting and stabbing—yet, such was the convulsive desperation of the young Thracian, unable to deliver a death blow.

The Thracian found his feet; his bleeding, torn body literally sprang into the air and on its feet and he stood there, but life and strength were running out of him. The explosion which brought him to his feet had tapped his deepest well of strength. He balanced with one hand, clutched the knife with the other, and swayed back and forth, probing at the air with his blade to ward off the Jew. But the Jew stood back and away from him, making no move to close again—and indeed there was no need to close, for the Thracian was hamstrung, cut across face, hands, body and legs, and bleeding his life into the soggy spreading blot of the sand beneath his feet.

Yet the supreme drama of life and death was not played out. The Romans awoke from their trance and they began to cry at the Jew, shrilly, hoarsely, demandingly,

"Verbera! Strike! Strike!"

But the Jew did not move. He had only the single slash across his breast, but his motion had flung the blood all over his body. Now, he suddenly hurled his knife into the sand, where it stuck quivering. He stood there with his head bowed over.

In just an instant, the opportunity would pass. The naked Thracian, who now wore a suit of red blood over every inch of his skin, sank to one knee. He had let go of his knife now, and he was dying quickly. The Romans screamed, and a trainer bounded across the arena, swinging a long, heavy bullhide whip. Two soldiers followed him.

"Fight, you scum!" the trainer roared, and then the bullhide curled across the Jew's back and around his belly. "Fight!" The lash struck him again and again, but he didn't move, and then the Thracian rolled over on his face, quivered a little and began to moan with pain, low cries of pain at first, and then a rising crescendo, whipped out of his twisting body. Then the cries of pain stopped and he lay still; then the trainer stopped whipping the Jew.

The black man had joined Spartacus at the crack in the door. They watched without speaking.

The soldiers approached the Thracian and prodded him with their spears. He moved a little. One of the soldiers unhooked a small but heavy hammer that hung from his belt. The other soldier wedged his spear under the Thracian and turned him over. Then the first soldier struck him a terrible blow upon the temple with his hammer, a blow which crushed in the soft surface of the skull. After this, the soldier saluted the spectators with his brain-clotted hammer. At the same time, a second trainer led a donkey into the arena. The donkey wore a bright feather headdress and a leather harness from which a chain dragged. The chain was made fast to the Thracian's feet, and the soldiers whipped the donkey with their spears, so that he cantered around the arena at a sharp trot, dragging the bloody, brain-dripping corpse after him. The Romans applauded this and the lady waved her lace handkerchief with delight.

Then the bloody sand was turned over and smoothed, for the music and dancing before the next pair.

VIII

Batiatus had hurried into the box of his customers to make apology, to explain why, when he had been paid so well, the Jew had failed at the very end to kill the flesh in life, to sever an artery in throat or arm, so that the rich red blood could paint the proper finish to combat; but Marius Bracus, holding a wine goblet in one hand, waved him to silence with the other,

"Not a word, *lanista*. It was delightful. It was sufficient."

"Yet I have a reputation."

"Devil take your reputation. But wait—I'll tell you what. Bring the Jew here. No other punishment. When a man has fought well, that's enough, isn't it? Bring him here."

"Here? Well, really," Lucius began—

"Of course! Don't try to clean him up. Let him come as he is."

While Batiatus went on the errand, Bracus held forth, attempting, as the connoisseur so often attempts, and with the same concession of futility, to explain the precise beauty and skill of what they had just seen.

"If one sees that once in a hundred pairs, then one is fortunate. A moment of glory, better than an hour's tedious fencing. That is the famous *avis jacienda ad mortem*. A flight to death—and how better could a gladiator die? Consider the circumstances. The Thracian measures the Jew and knows he is outpointed—"

"But he drew first blood," Lucius objected.

"Which means nothing. Most likely they never fought before. That was taking the measure. They must each make a series of passes to find each other. If they were evenly mated, they would fence, which would mean skill and endurance; but when they locked, the Jew broke the lock and strung the Thracian's arm. If it had been the right arm instead of the left, it would have ended there; but as it was, the Thracian knew he was outpointed, and he staked all on a lunge—a body lunge. Nine out of ten gladiators would have blocked it and tried for a lock, yes and even taken a nasty cut to block it. Do you know what it means to parry one of those knives with all the weight of a man's body behind it? Why did I send for the Jew? I'll show you—"

While he was talking, the Jew had appeared, still naked, smelling of blood and sweat, a wild, awful picture of a man standing before them, his head bent, his muscles still quivering.

"Bend over!" Bracus ordered him.

The Jew did not move.

"Bend!" cried Batiatus.

The two trainers who were with him took hold of the Jew and forced him over onto his knees before the Romans, and Bracus exclaimed triumphantly as he pointed to his back.

"See there—there! Not the whip marks. See where the skin is broken, as if a lady's nail had scratched him. That's where the Thracian's knife touched him as he went under the lunge and flung him. *Avis jacienda ad mortem!* Let him be, *lanista*," Bracus told Batiatus. "No more whip. Let him be and you will have a fortune out of him. I'll

110

make him his reputation myself. A toast to you, gladiator!" Bracus cried.

But the Jew stood dumbly, his head hanging.

IX

"The stones would weep," said the black man, "and the sands we walk on whimper and whine in pain, but we don't weep."

"We are gladiators," answered Spartacus.

"Do you have a heart of stone?"

"I am a slave. I suppose a slave should have a heart of stone or no heart at all. You have good things to remember, but I am *koruu,* and I have nothing at all to remember that is any good."

"Is that why you can watch this and not be moved?"

"It will not help me to be moved," answered Spartacus dully.

"I don't know you, Spartacus. You are white and I am black. We are different. In my land, when a man's heart fills with sorrow, he weeps. But in you Thracians, the tears have dried up. Look at me. What do you see?"

"I see a man weeping," said Spartacus.

"And am I less a man because of that? I tell you, Spartacus, I will not fight you. May they be damned and cursed and everlastingly cursed! I will not fight you, I tell you."

"If we don't fight, we both die," Spartacus answered quietly.

"Then kill me, my friend. I am tired of living. I am sick of living."

"Quiet in there!" The soldiers hammered at the wall of the shed, but the black man turned and smashed his great fists against the wall until the whole shed shook. Then he stopped very suddenly and sat down on the bench and pillowed his face in his hands. Spartacus walked over to him and lifted his head and tenderly wiped the beads of sweat from his brow.

"Gladiator, befriend no gladiator."

"Spartacus, why is man born?" he whispered in agony.

"To live."

"Is that the whole answer?"

"The only answer."

"I don't understand your answer, Thracian."

"Why—why, my friend?" Spartacus asked, almost pleadingly. "The child knows the answer, the moment it comes out of the womb. It is such a simple answer."

"No answer for me," the black man said, "and my heart is breaking for those who used to love me."

"And others will love you."

"No more," said the black man, "no more."

X

In after years, Caius would not remember the morning of the two pairs in Capua with any great clarity. There were many sensations in his life; sensations were bought and paid for, and Spartacus was only a Thracian name. Romans held that all Thracian names sounded alike, Gannicus, Spartacus, Menicus, Floracus, Leacus. Caius might have said, telling the story, that the Jew was also a Thracian, for the growing lore of the arena and the drug-like addiction of a whole people to the arena had given the term Thracian two meanings. On the one hand, Thracian was the term for any of the folk of the hundred tribes who lived in the southern section of the Balkan area, and by the Romans, used even more loosely to define any barbarian people east of the Balkans across the steppes to the Black Sea. Those close to Macedonia spoke Greek, but Greek was by no means a language of all who were called Thracians— even as the curved knife was by no means the common weapon of all those tribes.

On the other hand, in the sporting language of the city of Rome and in the common slang of the arena, a Thracian was anyone who fought with the *sica*. Thereby, the Jew was a Thracian, for Caius neither knew nor cared that he came of the party of the *Zealots,* wild, stiff-necked peasants of the Judean hills, who had carried a banner of incessant rebellion and hatred for the oppressor ever since the old days of the Maccabees and the first agrarian war. Caius knew little of Judea and cared less; the Jew was a circumcised Thracian. He had seen a pair fight, and the second pair would follow. The second pair was more unusual, but in his memories of what had happened to the black man he forgot the black man's opponent. He remembered well, however, their entrance into the arena, the two of them walking from their cage and from the shadow into the bright, bleeding sunlight and onto the spotted yellow sand. The birds flew off—the bloodbirds, *avis sanguinaria,* the dainty little birds of spotted yellow who pecked so voraciously at the stained sand, filling their gullets. Like the sand, they were spotted yellow, and when they took flight, it was like gobs of sand flung into the air. The two men then halted at the appointed place. Here, do homage to those who have purchased your flesh and blood; here is the moment when life is worthless, when dignity and shame alter the meaning of life. This is what is arrived at; the mistress of the world amuses herself with blood.

Caius would remember how small the Thracian looked against the giant black man of Africa, for that was an engraved picture on the sunlit background of yellow sand, on the unpainted wooden boards of the amphitheatre; but he would not remember what Bracus had said. Those words were small and inconsequential, and they washed away in the river of time. The petty whims of such men are never causes; they only seem to be causes; even Spartacus was not a cause, but the result of what was normal to Caius. And the whim which had led Bracus to plan this microcosmic orgy of death and suffering for the amusement of his empty-headed, worthless companion did not seem a whim to Caius, but rather a thing of great originality and excitement.

So the pair did their homage and the Romans sipped wine and nibbled sweets. Then came the weapon-bearer. For Spartacus, the knife. For the black man, the long, heavy, three-pronged fish fork and the fish net. They were both clowns in their shame and bloody degradation. The whole world had been enslaved so that these Romans could sit here and nibble sweets and sip wine in the shady comfort of their box.

The pair took the weapons. And then as Caius saw it, the black man went mad. Madness was the only construction Caius could place upon it. Neither he nor Bracus nor Lucius could have made the journey to the black man's beginnings, and only if they had made that journey would they have known that the black man did not go mad at all. Not even in mind could they have seen the house he had by a riverside and the children his wife bore him and the land he tilled and the fruit of the land, before the soldiers came and with them the slave dealers to harvest that crop of human life so magically transmuted into gold.

So they only saw the black man go mad. They saw him cast his net aside and shout a wild warcry. And then they saw him hurtle toward the grandstand. A trainer with bared sword tried to stop him, and then the trainer was squirming on the three-pronged fork like a pricked fish, and then hurled into the air like a fish, turning over and over and screaming in the air before he struck the ground. Now a six-foot fence barred the path of the black giant, but he tore the boards from it as if they were paper. He was transformed in his strength; his strength made him like a weapon driving toward the box where the party sat.

But now soldiers were running from the sides of the arena. The foremost soldier braced himself, legs spread on the sand, and hurled his spear, the great wooden spear with the iron point which nothing in the world could resist, which had leveled the armies of a hundred nations. But it did not level the black man. The spear caught him in the back, the iron point driving through his chest and out of the front of him, yet it didn't halt him, and even with that monstrous wooden pole attached to his back, he clawed on toward the Romans. A second spear tore through his side, and yet he struggled onward. A third spear entered his back and a fourth spear pierced his neck. Now at last, he was finished—yet the fork in his outstretched hand touched the rail of the box where the Romans cowered in terror. And there he lay with the blood gushing out of him and there he died.

But it must be noted that through all of this, Spartacus had not moved. If he had moved, he would have died. He cast his knife into the sand, and remained without moving. Life is the answer to life.

PART FOUR

Which concerns Marcus Tullius Cicero and his interest in the origin of the Great Servile War.

If at the *Villa Salaria,* where a group of well-bred Roman ladies and gentlemen had come together for a night to partake of the thoughtful hospitality of a Roman plantation owner and gentleman, there was overmuch thought of Spartacus and the great revolt he had led, this was only to be expected. They had all of them reached the villa over the Appian Way, most of them coming south from Rome, and Cicero coming north toward Rome on his way from Sicily, where, as *quaestor,* he held an important government post. Thus, their hour to hour travel was filled with the presence of the tokens of punishment, the stern and uncompromising *signa poenae* which told all the world that the Roman law was both merciless and just.

Yet the least sensitive of human beings could not have travelled the great highway without pondering upon the series of terrible battles between slaves and free men which had shaken the Republic to its very roots—and indeed shaken the whole world which the Republic ruled. There was no slave on the plantation who did not toss uneasily in his sleep at the thought of so many like him hanging from the numberless crosses. It was a mighty passion, this particular crucifixion, and the pain of six thousand men who died so slowly and so cruelly pervaded the whole countryside. That was only to be expected, and it was only to be expected that a young man as thoughtful as Marcus Tullius Cicero would not be unaffected

Concerning Cicero, it is worth remarking that men like

115

Antonius Caius went out of their way to offer him a deference beyond what was due to his thirty-two years.

It was not a question of lineage, of current family importance, or even of personal charm or ingratiating quality; for even his friends did not consider Cicero to be particularly charming. Clever, he was, but others were just as clever. Specifically, Cicero was one of those young men —present in every age—who are capable of shedding every scruple, every ethic, every confusion of current morality, every impulse to ease conscience or guilt, every impulse of mercy or justice which might stand in the way of success. This should not imply that he was not concerned with justice, morality or mercy; he was, but only in terms of self-advancement. Cicero was not merely ambitious, for ambition pure and simple could contain certain elements of emotion; Cicero was coldly and shrewdly concerned with success—and if his calculations sometimes backfired, that too was not unusual in men of his type.

They had not yet backfired at this time. He was the boy wonder who had practiced law at eighteen, fought a major campaign—purely for prestige and with no bodily danger— in his twenties, and turning thirty, had stepped into an important administrative post of the government. His essays —on philosophy and government—and his orations were read and admired, and if he borrowed the thin substance they contained, most people were too ignorant to know from where he had stolen. He knew the right people and he estimated them carefully. At that time, most people in Rome searched for influential connections; the prime virtue of Cicero was that he allowed nothing to interfere with his connections with the right people.

Long ago, Cicero had discovered the profound difference between justice and morality. Justice was the tool of the strong, to be used as the strong desired; morality, like the gods, was the illusion of the weak. Slavery was just; only fools—according to Cicero—argued that it was moral. Travelling north along the highroad, he could appreciate the awful suffering of the endless crucifixions, but he did not allow himself to be moved by them. He was working, at that time—and he was always writing something—upon a short monograph on the series of servile wars which had shaken the whole world, and he was intensely interested in the various examples of slaves hanging along the Appian

Way. He had perfected himself in interest without involvement, and he was able to study the various types, the Gauls, the Africans, the Thracians and the Jews and the Germans and the Greeks who composed the host of the crucified, without experiencing either sickness or pity. It occurred to him that in this vast passion there was a reflection of some new and mighty current which had come into the world— a current with ramifications which would stretch out into ages still unborn; but it also occurred to him that in his own particular time, a person who could coldly observe and analyze and interpret this new manifestation of servile revolt would be in a position of unique power. Cicero had only contempt for those who hated without understanding the subjective needs of the objects of their hatred.

These were qualities in Cicero that some saw and others did not see. When Claudia arrived at the *Villa Salaria* that evening, she did not observe these qualities. The least complex type of strength was most understandable to Claudia. Helena, on the other hand, recognized and paid tribute. "I am like you," her eyes said to Cicero. "Shall we pursue this?" And when her brother lay in bed, awaiting the coming of a great general, she betook herself to Cicero's chamber. She was full of the contrived dignity of a person who despises herself and takes comfort from the act, but why she should have felt inferior to this man who came from a money-grubbing upper middle class family, she could not have said. She could not have admitted, even to herself, that before the evening was done, she would do a number of things for which she would subsequently hate herself.

To Cicero, however, she was a very desirable type of woman. Her tall, strong carriage, her fine, straight features and her intense dark eyes exemplified for him all the storied qualities of patrician blood. It was the particular goal toward which his own people had climbed for generations, yet found always unobtainable. And to find within such an exterior the qualities which brought a woman to a man's chamber so late at night for only one obvious reason was singularly satisfying.

At that time, it was a rare Roman who pursued his work into the night. The strangely unequal development of that society found one of its weakest spots in artificial lighting, and Roman lamps were poor, spluttering things which strained the eyes and gave at best a pale yellow glow. To work at night, therefore, especially at night after too much wine and food, was a specific sign of admirable or suspicious eccentricity—depending upon the person who did the work. With Cicero, it was rather admirable, for this was the amazing young man; and when Helena entered his chamber, the amazing young man sat cross-legged on his bed, a scroll loosely open in his lap, noting and correcting. Perhaps the situation would have been too admittedly posed in terms of an older woman; Helena was only twenty-three, and she was properly impressed. A leader in peace and a leader in war was still a constant of the old legends, and there were those Romans who were said to sleep only two or three hours a night, giving all the rest of their time to the nation. They were consecrated. She liked the idea that a *consecrated* man should have looked at her as Cicero had.

Even before she had closed the door behind her, Cicero had nodded at the foot of his bed, for her to seat herself there—a matter of necessity, since there was no other comfortable place to sit in the room—and then he went on with his work. She closed the door and sat down on the bed.

What now? It was one of the wonders of Helena's young life that no two men approached a woman in precisely the same way. But Cicero did not approach her at all, and after she had sat there for a quarter of an hour or so, she asked,

"What are you writing?"

He looked at her inquiringly. The request was perfunctory; it was a conversational opening, but Cicero wanted to talk. Like so many young men of his type, he perpetually awaited the woman who would understand him—which meant the woman who would feed his ego properly, and he asked Helena,

"Why do you ask?"

"Because I want to know."

"I'm writing a monograph on the servile wars," he stated modestly.

"You mean a history of them?" It was at a time when historical writing by upper class gentlemen of leisure was just beginning to be fashionable, and many a newly arrived aristocrat was busily manipulating the early history of the Republic so that his ancestry and great events might mesh properly.

"Not a history," Cicero answered seriously, looking at the girl gravely and steadily, a manner he had whereby he could convey an impression of honesty and integrity; notwithstanding his own process of simulation. "A history would involve a chronology. I am more interested in the phenomenon, the process. If one looked at those crosses, those tokens of punishment which line the Appian Way, one could see only the dead bodies of six thousand men. One might conclude that we Romans are a vindictive people, and it is not enough to say that we are a just people, invoking the necessity of justice. We must explain, even to ourselves, the logic of this justice. We must understand. It was not enough for the old man to say *delenda est Carthago*. That is demagoguery. For my part, I would have wanted to understand why Carthage must be destroyed and why six thousand slaves must be put to death in such a fashion."

"Some say," Helena smiled, "that if they were all thrown on the market at once, some very respectable fortunes would have been wiped out."

"A little truth and a lot of untruth," Cicero replied. "I want to see beyond the superficial. I want to see the meaning of slave revolt. Delusion has become a great Roman pastime; I don't like to delude myself. We talk of this war and that war, of great campaigns and great generals, but none of us want even to whisper about the constant warfare of our time which overshadows all other warfare, the servile war, the revolt of the slaves. Even the generals concerned hush-hush it. There is no glory in servile war. There is no glory in the conquest of slaves."

"But surely it isn't an affair of such consequence."

"No? And were the crucifixions of no consequence to you as you came down the Appian Way?"

"It was quite sickening. I don't enjoy looking at such things. My friend Claudia does."

"In other words, of some consequence."

"But everyone knows of Spartacus and his war."

"Do they? I'm not so sure. I'm not so sure that even Crassus knows a great deal. Spartacus is a mystery as far as we are concerned. According to the official records, he was a Thracian mercenary and highwayman. According to Crassus, he was a born slave out of the gold mines of Nubia. Whom do we believe? Batiatus, the swine who kept the school at Capua, is dead—his throat cut by a Greek slave who was his bookkeeper—and so is every other contact with Spartacus dead or gone. And who will write about him? People like myself."

"Why not people like yourself?" asked Helena.

"Thank you, my dear. But I know nothing of Spartacus. I only hate him."

"Why? My brother hates him too."

"And don't you hate him?"

"I don't feel anything in particular," said Helena. "He was just a slave."

"But was he? And how does a slave become what Spartacus became? That is the mystery I must solve. To find out where this began and why it began. But I'm afraid I bore you?"

There was an air of sincerity about Cicero which people caught and believed, and which made them defend him against all the charges hurled at him in later years. "Please go on talking," said Helena. The young men she knew in Rome who were Cicero's age talked about the latest perfumes, the gladiator they were betting on, the particular horse they were backing, or their latest mistress or concubine. "Please go on," she said.

"I don't wholly trust rhetoric," Cicero said. "I like to write things down and let them fall into place. I'm afraid most people feel as you do, that the rising of slaves is of no great consequence. But, you see, our whole lives are concerned with slaves, and the rising of slaves accounts for more warfare than all of our conquests. Can you believe that?"

She shook her head.

"I can prove it, you know. About a hundred and twenty years ago it began—with the rising of the Carthaginian slaves we had made captive. Then, two generations later, the great revolt of the slaves in the mines of Laurium in Greece. Then the mighty revolt of the miners in Spain. Then, a few years later, the revolt of Sicilian slaves, which shook the republic to its roots. Then, twenty years later, the servile war led by the slave Salvius. These are only the great wars, but in between are a thousand smaller uprisings —and the whole thing together is a single war, a continuing, unending war between ourselves and our slaves, a silent war, a shameful war that no one speaks of and the

120

historians are unwilling to record. We're afraid to record it, afraid to look at it; because it's something new on earth. There were wars between nations, cities, parties, even wars between brothers—but this is a new monster inside of us, inside our guts and against all parties, all nations, all cities."

"You frighten me," said Helena. "Do you know what kind of a picture you make?"

Cicero nodded and looked searchingly at her. She was moved to cover his hand with hers, and she felt a rich, outgoing sense of warmth toward him. Here was a young man, not too much older than herself, who was deeply concerned with matters concerning the fate and future of the nation. It reminded her of the stories she had heard of the old times, vaguely-remembered stories of her childhood. Cicero laid his manuscript aside and began to stroke her hand gently, and then he leaned over and kissed her. Vividly, now, she recalled the tokens of punishment, the rotting, bird-eaten, sun-baked flesh of the men who were crucified along the Appian Way; only now it was no longer horrible; Cicero had made a rationale out of it, but for the life of her, she could not recall the content of his rationale.

"We are a most singular people, filled with a great capacity for love and justice," thought Cicero. He felt, as he began to make love to Helena, that here was a woman at last who understood him. Yet that did not lessen the sense of power a conquest of her afforded him. Quite to the contrary, he felt himself full of power, the extension of power—and it was that very extension, if the truth must be told, which comprised the logic of what he wrote. In a moment of mystical revelation, he saw the power of his loins joined with that power which had crushed Spartacus, and would crush him again and again. Looking at him, Helena realized suddenly, and with horror, that his face was full of hate and cruelty. As always, she submitted with fear and self-loathing.

II

Out of sheer weariness and emotional upheaval, Helena slept finally, and the waking nightmare which always marked her relations with a man, turned into a strange and disturbing dream. The dream combined reality and unreality in a manner which made them difficult to separate. In her dream, she recalled the time in the streets of Rome when her brother, Caius, had pointed out to her Lentulus Batiatus, the *lanista*. That was only about seven months ago, and only a few days before Batiatus had his throat cut by his Greek bookkeeper—as gossip had it, in a quarrel over a woman the Greek had purchased with money stolen from the *lanista*. Batiatus had made something of a reputation for himself through his connection with Spartacus. This time, he was in Rome to defend himself in a lawsuit over one of his tenements; the house had collapsed, and the surviving families of six tenants who were killed were suing him.

In her dream, she recalled him very well and normally, a huge, waddling product of overeating and dissipation, who would not hire a litter, but walked all wrapped in a great toga, hawking and spitting constantly and driving off street urchins who begged for alms, with a cane he carried. Later, that same day, she and Caius stopped at the Forum and just by chance happened in at the court where Batiatus was defending himself. This, in the dream, was much the same as it had been in life. The court was being held out of doors. It swarmed with spectators, idlers, women with endless time on their hands, young men about town, children, people from other lands who could not leave the great *urbs* without witnessing the famous Roman justice, slaves on their way to or from some errand—indeed it seemed a miracle that any reason, much less justice, could be extracted from such a throng; but this was how the courts proceeded, week in and week out. Batiatus was being questioned, and he answered the questions in a bull-like roar, and all of this was as it had been in her actual experience.

But then, as happens in dreams, she found herself without explanation standing in the *lanista*'s bedchamber and watching the Greek bookkeeper approach with bared knife. The knife was the curved *sica* which Thracians fight with in the arena, and the floor of the bedchamber was also *arena*, or sand, since both are the same word in Latin. The Greek minced across the sand with all the wary poise of a Thracian, and the *lanista*, awake and sitting up in his bed, watched him with horror. But no word or sound from anyone. Then, alongside the Greek, a giant figure appeared, a mighty, bronzed man in full armor, and Helena knew immediately that this was Spartacus. His hand closed over the bookkeeper's wrist and squeezed just a trifle, and the knife fell to the sand. Then the bronzed, handsome giant who was Spartacus, nodded at Helena, and she picked up the knife and cut the *lanista*'s throat. The Greek and the *lanista* then disappeared, and she was left with the gladiator; but when she opened her arms to him, he spat full in her face, turned on his heel, and walked off. Then she ran after him, whimpering and pleading for him to wait for her, but he had disappeared, and she was alone in a boundless space of sand.

III

It was an ugly and cheap death which actually had overtaken Batiatus, the *lanista*, to be murdered by his own slave; and perhaps he would have avoided that and many other things if, after the abortive performance of the two pairs for Bracus, he had put to death both gladiators who survived. If he had done that, he would have been entirely within his rights; for it was an accepted practice to kill gladiators who sowed dissension. But it is questionable whether it would have changed history too much if Spartacus had perished. The forces which prodded him would simply have turned elsewhere. Just as the dream of Helena, the Roman maiden sleeping her guilt-ridden sleep at the *Villa Salaria* so long afterwards, concerned not him specifically, but the slave who takes up the sword, so were his own dreams less a singular possession than the blood-ridden memories and hopes shared by so many of his profession, the gladiators, the men of the sword. That would answer those who could not understand how the plot of Spartacus had been hatched. It was not hatched by one, but by many.

Varinia, the German girl, his wife, sat by him as he slept, kept awake by his moans and by his frantic talking in his sleep. He talked of a great many things. Now he was a child and now he was in the gold mines, and now he was in the arena. Now the *sica* had split his flesh and he screamed with pain.

When that happened, she woke him, for the nightmare he had been living in his sleep was impossible for her to endure any longer. She awakened him and made love to him tenderly, stroking his brow and kissing his wet skin. When Varinia had been a little girl, she saw what happened to men and women in her tribe when they knew love for each other. It was called the triumph over fear; even the devils and spirits of the great forests where her people lived knew that those who loved were invulnerable to fear, and you could see that in the eyes of people who loved and in the way they walked and in the way their fingers intertwined. But after she had been taken captive, she had forgotten such memories, the prime instinct of her existence had become hatred.

Now her whole being, the life within her, her being and her existence, her living and functioning, the motion of her blood and the beating of her heart were fused into love for this Thracian slave. Now she knew that the experience of the men and women in her tribe was very true and very ancient and very expressive. She no longer was afraid of anything on earth. She believed in magic, and the magic of her love was real and provable. At the same time, she realized that her man was an easy man to love. He was one of those rare human beings who were knit out of one piece. That was the first thing one saw in Spartacus, his wholeness. He was singular. He was content, not in where he was but in what he was as a human being. Even in this nest of terrible, desperate and doomed men—in this murder school of condemned murderers, army deserters, lost souls and miners whom the mines could not destroy, Spartacus was loved and honored and respected. But her love was something else. All of him was the essence of men and the being of men for women. She had believed that the desire in her loins was dead forever, but she had only to touch him to want him. Everything about him was the special way in which men should be formed, if she were the sculptor and had to do the forming. His broken nose, his large brown eyes and his full, mobile mouth were as different from the faces of the men she had known in her childhood as a face could be, but she could not conceive of having a man or loving a man who was not like Spartacus.

Why he should be as he was, she did not know. She had

been long enough a part of the cultured, genteel life of the Roman aristocracy to know what their men were, but why a slave should be what Spartacus was, she did not know.

Now her hands quieted him, and she asked him, "What were you dreaming?"

He shook his head.

"Hold me close to you and you won't dream anymore."

He held her close to him and whispered to her, "Do you ever think that we might not be together?"

"Yes."

"And then what will you do, my darling?" he asked her.

"Then I will die," she answered simply and directly.

"I want to talk to you about that," he said, awake out of his dream now and calm again.

"Why should we think of it or talk about it?"

"Because if you loved me enough, you would not want to die if I died or was taken away from you."

"Do you think that way?"

"Yes."

"And if I died, you would not want to die?" she asked.

"I would want to live."

"Why?"

"Because there is nothing without life."

"There is no life without you," she said.

"I want you to make me a promise and to keep it."

"If I make a promise, I will keep it. Otherwise, I won't make it."

"I want you to promise that you will never take your own life," said Spartacus.

She didn't answer him for a time.

"Will you promise?"

Finally, she said, "All right, I will."

Then in a little while, he was asleep, calmly and gently, with her arms around him.

IV

The morning drumbeat summoned them to exercise. There was forty minutes of simple on-the-double in the enclosure before the morning meal. Each man on awakening was

125

given a glass of cold water. His cell door was opened. If he had a woman, she was permitted to clean the cell before she went to work as a part of the slave population of the school. There was no waste in the institution of Lentulus Batiatus. The women of the gladiators scrubbed and cleaned and cooked and tilled the kitchen gardens and worked in the baths and tended the goats, and on these women Batiatus was as hard a master as any plantation owner, using the whip freely and abundantly and feeding them cheap mash. But of Spartacus and Varinia, he had a curious fear; although he would hardly have been able to say what there was in them that he feared and why he feared it.

On this particular and remembered morning, however, there was a note of impatience and hatred through the school, in the reveille drums, in the way the trainers drove the men from their cells into the enclosure, lining them up to face the iron fence where the black African was crucified in death; and the women were whipped to their tasks with the same nervous hatred. There was no fear of Varinia this morning, nor was the whip any lighter on her than on others. If anything, she was singled out by the overseer with special comments about the whore of the great warrior. And the whip touched her more often than others. She worked in the kitchen, to where she was driven.

It was the anger of Batiatus which pervaded the place, a deep and trembling anger which arose out of the one thing which could most successfully anger the *lanista*, a financial loss. Bracus had withheld half of the agreed price, and although there would be a lawsuit and all the trimmings, Batiatus knew what the chances were of his winning a lawsuit against a prominent Roman family in a Roman court. The results of his anger were everywhere in the place. In the kitchen, the cook cursed the women and beat them to their work with his long wooden rod of authority. The trainers, lashed by their employer, lashed the gladiators, and the black man in death was stretched onto the enclosure fence, to confront the gladiators as they shaped up for their morning drill.

Spartacus took his place, Gannicus on one side of him, a Gaul called Crixus on the other side. They made two lines across the face of the cellblock, and the trainers who faced them this morning were heavily armed, specially armed with knife and sword. The gates of the enclosure were opened, and four squads of regular troops, forty men, stood there at attention, their big wooden darts swinging in their fists at their sides. The morning sun flooded the yellow sand and touched the men with its warmth, but there was no warmth in Spartacus, and when Gannicus whispered to him whether he knew what this meant, he shook his head silently.

"Did you fight?" the Gaul asked.

"No."

"But he didn't kill any of them, and if a man is going to die, he could die better than that."

"Will you die any better than that?" asked Spartacus.

"He'll die like a dog and so will you," said Crixus the Gaul. "He'll die in the sand with his belly open, and so will you."

It was then that Spartacus began to realize what he must do; or it could be better said that the realization, with him so long, solidified into a reality. The reality was only beginning; the reality would never be any more than a beginning with him, the end or endlessness of it stretching into the unborn future; but the reality was connected with all that had happened to him and the men around him and with all that was going to happen now. He stared at the great body of the Negro, lashed out in the sun, the skin and flesh torn where the *pila* had driven through it, the blood clotted and dry, the head hanging between the broad shoulders.

What a contempt for life these Romans have! thought Spartacus. How easily they kill, and what a lusty delight they take in death! Yet why not, he asked himself, when the whole process of their living was built on the blood and bones of his own kind? Crucifixion had a particular fascination for them. It had come from Carthage, where the Carthagenians had adopted it as the only death fitting for a slave; but where Rome's fingers reached, crucifixion became a passion.

Batiatus came into the enclosure now, and Spartacus, barely moving his lips, asked the Gaul who stood beside him, "And how will you die?"

"The way you will, Thracian."

"He was my friend," said Spartacus of the dead Negro, "and he loved me."

"That's your curse."

Batiatus took his place before the long line of gladiators and the soldiers gathered behind him. "I feed you," said the *lanista*. "I feed you the best, roasts and chickens and fresh fish. I feed you until your bellies swell out. I bathe you and I massage you. I took the lot of you from the mines and the gallows, and here you live like kings in idleness on the fat of the land. There was nothing lower than what you were before you came here, but now you live in comfort and you eat the best."

"Are you my friend?" whispered Spartacus, and the Gaul answered, barely moving his lips, "Gladiator, make no friends of gladiators."

"I call you friend," said Spartacus.

Batiatus now said, "In the black heart of that black dog, there was neither gratitude nor understanding. How many of you are like him?"

The gladiators stood in silence.

"Pick me a black man!" said Batiatus to the trainers, and they went to where the Africans stood and dragged one out to the center of the enclosure. It had been arranged in advance. The drums began to roll, and two soldiers separated themselves from the others and lifted their heavy wooden spears. Still the drums rolled. The Negro struggled convulsively and the soldiers drove their spears one after another through his breast. He lay on his back in the sand, the two spears angled curiously. Batiatus turned to the officer who stood beside him, and said,

"Now there will be no more trouble. The dogs will not even growl."

"I call you friend," said Gannicus to Spartacus, and the Gaul who stood on the other side of him said nothing, only breathing heavily and hoarsely.

Then the morning drill began.

V

Afterward, at a Senatorial Board of Inquiry, Batiatus claimed, quite truthfully, that not only did he not know that a plot had been hatched, but that he did not believe it

128

possible for one to be hatched. In support of this, he pointed out that there were always at least two among the gladiators who were in his pay with his promise of manumission. At intervals, these two would be paired out to fight for hire. One would be freed, the other would be returned with some slight signs of combat, and then a new informer would be recruited for the pair. Batiatus insisted that a plot could not have been hatched without his knowledge.

Thus it was always, and no matter how often revolt broke out among the slaves, there was no locating it, no pinning it down, no finding the continuous root of it, which unquestionably, like the roots of strawberries, was continuous and invisible, whereas only the flowering plant could be seen. Whether it was revolt in Sicily on a grand scale or an abortive attempt on a plantation, which ended in the crucifixion of a few hundred miserable wretches, the attempt of the Senate to dig up the roots failed. Yet the roots had to be dug up. Here men had created a splendor of life and luxury and abundance never known in the world before; the warring of nations had ended in the Roman Peace; the separation of nations had ended with the Roman roads; and in the mighty urban center of the world, no man wanted for food or pleasure. This was as it should be, as all and each and every one of the gods had planned it to be, yet with the flowering of the body had come this disease which could not be rooted out.

Whereby the Senate asked Batiatus, "Were there no signs of conspiracy, discontent, plotting?"

"There were none," he insisted.

"And when you executed the African—mind you, we consider your action quite proper—was there no protest?"

"None."

"We are particularly interested in whether any sort of outside help, foreign provocation of any sort could have entered into this matter?"

"It is impossible," said Batiatus.

"And there was no outside help or funds provided for the triumvirate of Spartacus, Gannicus and Crixus?"

"I can swear by all the gods there were not," said Batiatus.

VI

Yet this was not wholly true, and no man is alone. It was the incredible strength of Spartacus that he never saw himself alone and he never retreated into himself. Not too long before the abortive fighting of the two pairs, which the wealthy young Roman, Marius Bracus, had contracted for, there was a rising of slaves on three great plantations in Sicily. Nine hundred slaves were involved and all except a handful were put to death, and it was only at the tail end of blood-letting that the owners realized how much cold cash was going down the drain. Thereby, almost a hundred survivors were sold into the galleys for a mere pittance, and it was in a galley that one of Batiatus's agents saw the huge, broad-shouldered, red headed Gaul whose name was Crixus. Since galley slaves were considered incorrigibles, the price was cheap and even the bribes which promoted the transaction were small, and since the slave dealers who controlled the naval docks at Ostia did not look for trouble, they said nothing of the origin of Crixus.

Whereby Spartacus was neither alone nor disconnected with many threads which wove a particular fabric. Crixus was in the cell next to his. On many an evening, stretched full length on the floor of his cell, his head near the door, Spartacus heard the story from Crixus of the endless warfare of the Sicilian slaves, which had begun more than half a century before. He, Spartacus, was a slave and born out of slaves, but here among his own kind were legendary heroes as splendid as Achilles and Hector and Odysseus the wise, as splendid and even prouder, though no songs were sung of them and they were not turned into gods which men worshipped. Which was well enough, for the gods were like the rich Romans and as little concerned with the lives of slaves. These were men and less than men, slaves, naked slaves who were cheaper on the market than donkeys, and who put their shoulders into harness and dragged ploughs across the fields of the *latifundia*. But what giants they were! Eunus, who freed every slave on the island and smashed three Roman armies before they dragged him down, Athenion the Greek, Salvius the Thracian, the German Undart, and the strange Jew, Ben Joash, who had escaped in a boat from Carthage and joined Athenion with his entire crew.

Listening, Spartacus would feel his heart swell in pride and joy, and a great and cleansing sense of brotherhood and communion toward these dead heroes would come over him. His heart went out to these comrades of his; he knew them well; he knew what they felt and what they dreamed and what they longed for. Race, city or state had no meaning. Their bondage was universal. Yet for all the pitiful splendor of their revolts, they always failed; always it was the Romans who nailed them to the cross, the new tree and the new fruit, so that all might see the rewards for a slave who would not be a slave.

"In the end it was always the same," Crixus said . . .

So the longer he was a gladiator, the less Crixus spoke of what had been. Neither the past nor the future can help the gladiator. For him, there is only now. Crixus built a wall of cynicism around himself, and only Spartacus dared to probe at the bitter shell of the giant Gaul. And once Crixus had said to him,

"You make too many friends, Spartacus. It's hard to kill a friend. Leave me alone."

On this morning, after the drill, they were grouped together for a while in the enclosure before going to the morning meal. Hot and sweating, the gladiators stood or squatted in little groups, their talk muffled by the presence of the two Africans who now hung crucified on the fence. There was a fresh pool of blood under the one who had been selected as a token of punishment for the other, and the blood birds pecked and gobbled the sweet stain. The gladiators were sullen and subdued. It was only the beginning, they felt. Batiatus would now contract and fight them as quickly as he could. It was a bad time.

The soldiers had gone off to eat in a little grove of trees, across the brook that ran by the school, and Spartacus, from within the enclosure, could see them there, sprawled on the ground, their helmets off, their heavy weapons stacked. He never took his eyes off them.

"What do you see?" asked Gannicus. They had been slaves a long time together, together in the mines, together as children.

"I don't know."

131

Crixus was sullen; violence had been too long capped inside of him. "What do you see, Spartacus?" he also asked.

"I don't know."

"But you know all, don't you, and for that the Thracians call you father."

"Who do you hate, Crixus?"

"Did the black man also call you father, Spartacus? Why didn't you fight him? Will you fight me when our turn comes, Spartacus?"

"I will fight no more gladiators," said Spartacus quietly. "That I know. I didn't know it a little while ago, but I know it now."

A half dozen of them had heard his words. They gathered close to him now. He no longer looked at the soldiers; he looked at the gladiators instead. He looked from face to face. The half dozen became eight and ten and twelve, and still he said nothing; but their sullenness went away, and there was a demanding excitement in their eyes. He looked into their eyes.

"What will we do, father?" asked Gannicus.

"We will know what to do when the time comes to do it. Now break this up."

Then time telescoped, and a thousand years were upon the Thracian slave. All that had not happened in a thousand years would happen in the next few hours. Now again, for the moment, they were slaves—the dregs of slavery, the butchers of slavery. They moved toward the gates of the enclosure and then they marched to the mess hall for the morning meal.

At this point, they passed Batiatus in his litter. He sat in his great eight-slave litter with his slim, cultured bookkeeper, both of them on their way to the market in Capua to purchase provisions. As they passed the ranks of gladiators, Batiatus noticed how evenly and with what discipline they marched, and he considered that even if the sacrifice of an African had been an unwonted expense, it was entirely justified.

Thereby, Batiatus lived, and his bookkeeper lived to slit his master's throat in time to come.

VII

What happened in the dining room—or mess hall, it would be better called—where the gladiators gathered to eat, would never properly be known or told; for there were no historians to record the adventures of slaves, nor were their lives considered worthy of record; and when what a slave did had to become a part of history, the history was set down by one who owned slaves and feared slaves and hated slaves.

But Varinia, working in the kitchen, saw it with her own eyes, and long afterwards she told the tale to another—as you will see—and even if the mighty sound of such a thing dies away to a whisper, it is never wholly lost. The kitchen was at one end of the mess hall. The doors which led to it were at the other.

The mess hall itself was an improvisation of Batiatus. Many Roman buildings were built in a traditional form, but the training and hiring of gladiators on a mass scale was a product of this generation, as was the craze for the fighting of pairs, and the question of schooling and controlling so many gladiators was a new question. Batiatus took an old stone wall and added three sides to it. The quadrangle thus formed was roofed in the old-fashioned manner, a wooden shed projecting inward on all sides for a width of about eight feet. The central part was left open to the sky, and the inside was paved to a central drain, where rain water could run off. This method of construction was more common a century before, but in the mild climate of Capua it was sufficient, although in the winter the place was cold and often damp. The gladiators ate cross-legged on the floor under the shed. The trainers paced the open court in the center, where they could watch all most easily. The kitchen, which consisted of a long brick and tile oven and a long work table, was at one end of the quadrangle, open to the rest of it; a pair of heavy wooden doors were at the other end, and once the gladiators were inside, these doors were bolted.

So it happened this day, in the routine fashion, and the gladiators took their places and were served by the kitchen slaves, almost all of them women. Four trainers paced in the center court. The trainers carried knives and short whips of plaited leather. The doors were duly bolted from the outside by two soldiers who were detached from the platoon for this duty. The rest of the soldiers were eating their morning meal in a pleasant grove of trees about a hundred yards away.

All this Spartacus saw and noted. He ate little. His mouth was dry and his heart hammered at his breast. No great thing was being made, as he saw it, and there was no more of the future open to him than to any other man. But some men come to a point where they say to themselves, "If I do not do such and such a thing, then there is no need or reason for me to live any more." And when many men come to such a point, then the earth shakes.

It was to shake a little before the day was over, before this morning gave way to noon and nightfall; but Spartacus did not know this. He only knew the next step, and that was to talk to the gladiators. As he told that to Crixus, the Gaul, he saw his wife, Varinia, watching him as she stood before the stove. Other gladiators watched him too. The Jew, David, read the motion of his lips. Gannicus leaned his ear near to him. An African called Phraxus leaned closer to hear.

"I want to stand up and speak," said Spartacus. "I want to open my heart. But when I speak, there is no going back, and the trainers will try to stop me."

"They won't stop you," said Crixus, the giant red headed Gaul.

Even across the quadrangle, the currents were felt. Two trainers turned toward Spartacus and the crouching men around him. They snapped their whips and drew their knives.

"Speak now!" cried Gannicus.

"Are we dogs that you snap whips at us?" said the African.

Spartacus rose to his feet, and dozens of gladiators rose with him. The trainers lashed out with their whips and knives, but the gladiators swarmed over them and killed them quickly. The women killed the cook. In all this, there was little noise, only a low growl from the milling gladiators. Then Spartacus gave his first command, gently, softly,

134

unhurriedly, telling Crixus and Gannicus and David and Phraxus,

"Go to the door and keep it secure, so that I may speak."

It was in the balance for just an instant, but then they obeyed him, and when he led them afterwards, for the most part they heeded what he said. They loved him. Crixus knew that they would die, but it didn't matter, and the Jew, David, who had felt nothing for so long, felt a rush of warmth and love for this strange, gentle, ugly Thracian with the broken nose and the sheep-like face.

VIII

"Gather around me," he said.

It had been done so quickly, and there was still no sound from the soldiers stationed outside. The gladiators and the slaves from the kitchen—thirty women and two men—pressed around him, and Varinia stared at him with fear and hope and awe and pressed toward him. They made a passage for her; she went over to him, and he put an arm around her and held her tight against his side, thinking to himself,

"And I am free. Never a moment of freedom for my father or grandfather, but right now I stand here a free man." It was something to make him drunk, and he felt it rush through him like wine. But along with it, there was the fear. It is no light thing to be free; it is no small thing to be free when you have been a slave for a very long time, for all the time that you have known and all the time your father has known. There was also, in Spartacus, the subdued and willful terror of a man who has made an unalterable decision and who knows that every step along the path he takes, death waits. And lastly, a great questioning of himself, for these men whose trade was killing had killed their masters, and they were full of the awful doubt which comes over a slave who has struck at his master. Their eyes were upon him. He was the gentle Thracian miner who knew what was in their hearts and came close to them, and because they were full of superstition and

135

ignorance, as most folk of that time were, they felt that some god—a strange god with a little pity in his heart—had touched him. Therefore, he must contrive with the future and read it as a man reads a book, and lead them into it; and if there were no roads for them to travel, he must make roads. All this, their eyes told him; all this, he read in their eyes.

"Are you my people?" he asked them, when they were pressed close around him. "I will never be a gladiator again. I will die first. Are you my people?"

The eyes of some of them filled with tears, and they pressed even closer to him. Some were more afraid, and some were less afraid, but he touched them with a little bit of glory—which was a wonderful thing he was able to do.

"Now we must be comrades," he said, "and all together like one person; and in the old times, among my people—as I heard it told—when they went out to fight, they went with their own good will, not like the Romans go, but with their own good will, and if someone did not want to fight, he went away, and no one looked after him."

"What will we do?" someone cried.

"We will go out and fight, and we will make a good fight, for we are the best fighting men in the whole world." Suddenly, his voice rang out, and the contrast to his gentle manner of before transfixed and held them; his voice was wild and loud, and surely the soldiers outside heard him cry,

"We will make a fighting of pairs so that in all the time of Rome, they will never forget the gladiators of Capua!"

There comes a time when men must do what they must, and Varinia knew this, and she was proud with a kind of happiness she had never known before; proud and full of singular joy, for she had a man who was like no other in all the world. She knew about Spartacus; in time, all the world would know about him, but not precisely as she knew about him. She knew, somehow, that this was the beginning of something mighty and endless, and her man was gentle and pure and there was no other like him.

"First the soldiers," said Spartacus.

"We are five to one, and maybe they will run away."

"They will not run away," he answered angrily. "You must know that about the soldiers, that they will not run away. Either they will kill us or we will kill them, and if we kill them, there will be others. There is no end to the Roman soldiers!"

When they looked at him as they did, he told them, "But there is also no end to the slaves."

Then they made their preparations very quickly. They took the knives from the dead trainers, and from the kitchen they took everything that could be used as weapons, the knives and cleavers and spits and roasting forks and pestles, particularly the pestles, which were used for grinding grain for porridge and of which there were at least twenty, wooden rods with a heavy lump of wood at the end; and they could be used either as clubs or as things to throw. They took the firewood too, and a man took a meat bone if there was nothing else, and they took pot covers to use as shields. In one way or another, they had weapons, and then, with the women behind them, they threw back the big doors of the mess hall and went out to fight.

They had moved very quickly, but not quickly enough to surprise the soldiers. The two who had been on guard had warned them, and they had sufficient time to put on their armor and to form in four maniples of ten, and now they stood in their formation on the other bank of the brook, forty soldiers, two officers, and a dozen trainers, armed as the soldiers were, heavily, with sword, shield and spear. Thus, fifty-four heavily armed men faced the two hundred naked and almost unarmed gladiators. It was unequal odds, but the odds were on the side of the soldiers, and they were Roman soldiers, against whom nothing on earth could stand. They hefted their spears and they moved forward on the double, one maniple after another. Their officers' orders came high and clear on the morning breeze, and they swept forward like a broom to clear this dirt from their path. Their high-stepping booted feet splashed in the water of the brook. The wild flowers bent aside as they mounted the bank, and from all over the place, the remaining slaves came running out and clustered in knots, to see this incredible thing that was happening. The terrible *pila* rocked back on bent arms, the iron points sparkling in the sunshine, and by all that Roman power meant, even the modest extension of Roman power which these four maniples represented, the slaves should have broken and run, ashes to ashes and dirt to dirt.

But at that moment the Roman power was at bay; and Spartacus became a commander. There is no clear definition for a man who leads other men; leadership is rare and intangible, the more so when it is not backed with power and glory. Any man can give orders, but to give them so that others will listen is a quality, and that was a quality of Spartacus. He ordered the gladiators to spread out, and they spread out. He ordered them to make a wide loose circle around the maniples, and they made such a circle. Now the four charging maniples slowed their pace. Indecision seized them. They halted. No soldiers on earth could match the pace of gladiators, where life was speed and speed was life, and except for their loin cloths, these gladiators were naked—whereas the Roman footsoldiers were burdened with the great weight of sword, spear, shield, helmet and armor. The gladiators raced into a broad circle, a hundred and fifty yards across, in the center of which were the maniples, turning here and there, hefting the *pila* —which was worthless at a range of more than thirty or forty yards. The Roman spear could be thrown only once; one throw and then close in. But what to throw at here?

In that moment, with startling clarity, Spartacus saw his tactics, the whole pattern of his tactics in the years to come. He saw in his mind's eye, briefly and vividly, the logic of all the tales told of armies which had hurled themselves against those iron points of Rome, to be smashed under the mighty weight of the Roman spear and then to be cut to pieces with the short, razor-sharp edge of the Roman sword. But here was the discipline of Rome and the power of Rome helpless within a circle of shouting, cursing, defiant and naked gladiators.

"Rocks!" cried Spartacus. "Rocks—the stones will fight for us!" He raced around the circle, light on his toes, light in his motions, graceful. "Throw rocks!"

And under the shame of rocks, the soldiers went down. The air became full of flying stones. The women joined the circle—the household slaves joined and the field slaves ran from the gardens to join. The soldiers shielded themselves under their huge targets, but that gave the gladiators a chance to run in, cut and run. One maniple charged the circle and hurled their spears. A single gladiator was caught by one of the terrible weapons, but the rest flung themselves on the maniple and dragged it down and slew the soldiers almost with bare hands. The soldiers fought back. Two maniples made a circle, and even when only a handful remained on their feet under the rain of stones, even when the gladiators poured onto them like a pack of wolves, they fought until they were dead. The fourth maniple tried to cut their way out of the circle and escape, but ten were too few for such a tactic, and they were dragged down and slain, even as the trainers were slain—and two of the trainers, pleading for mercy, were killed by the women who beat them to death with rocks.

The strange, violent little battle, which had started close to the mess hall, raged across the grounds of the school and onto the Capuan road, where the last soldier was dragged down and killed, and all over that space and distance lay dead men and wounded men, fifty-four dead who were Romans and trainers, and more who were gladiators.

Yet it was only the beginning. Full of victory, blooded with it and exulting with it, it was only a beginning—and now as he stood on the highroad, Spartacus could see the walls of Capua in the distance, a misty golden city in the golden haze of the forenoon, and he could hear the beat of the garrison's drums. Now there would be no rest, for things were happening and word was on the wind, and there were many soldiers garrisoned in Capua. The whole world had exploded. He rode on currents mighty and tumultuous as he stood panting on the paved highroad with blood and death around him, and he saw Crixus, the red headed Gaul, laughing, Gannicus exultant, David the Jew with blood on his knife and life in his eyes, and the huge Africans deliberately calm, murmuring their battle chant. He took Varinia in his arms then. And other gladiators were kissing their women, whirling them up in their arms and laughing with them, while house slaves came running with skins of Batiatus's wine. Even the wounded made less of their wounds, and stifled their cries of pain. And the German girl looked at Spartacus, laughing and crying at once, and touched his face, his arms and the hand in which he held his knife. The wine sacks were being tilted when Spartacus brought them back to themselves. They could have stepped out of history then, drunken and exultant, for already the soldiers were beginning to march out of the gates of Capua, but Spartacus caught them and held them. He ordered Gannicus to strip the dead soldiers of their arms, and he sent Nordo, an African, to see whether the armory could be broken into. His gentleness had gone now, and his single-minded intentness upon their escape burned like a bright flame and transformed him. All his life had been for this, and all his patience had been in preparation for this. He had waited for centuries; he had waited since the first slave was shackled and whipped to hew wood and draw water, and he would not be turned from it now.

Before, he had asked them; now he commanded them. Who could use Roman arms? Who had fought with the *pilum?* He made a rank in four maniples.

"I want the women inside," he said. "They are not to be exposed. They are not to fight."

The fury of the women had surprised him. It was beyond and more than the fury of the men. The women wanted to fight; they wept with him out of their need to fight. They pleaded for some of the precious knives, and when he denied that, they belted their tunics and filled them with rocks to throw.

Near the school were sloping, hilly fields of plantations. The field slaves, seeing that something was different and terrible and wild, ran to watch, gathered on the stone walls and in little clumps here and there and, seeing them, the manner of his future, in all its simplicity, became plain to him. He called the Jew, David, and told him what to do, and the Jew ran toward the field slaves. Spartacus had not guessed wrong; three quarters of the field slaves returned with David. They came running up and saluted the gladiators and kissed their hands. They carried with them their hoes, and all of a sudden their hoes were not tools but weapons. Now the Africans returned. They had not been able to break into the main armory; it would take at least a half hour to do so; but they had broken open a newly arrived chest of *tridents,* the long, three-pointed fish forks. There were thirty of these three-pointed spears, and Spartacus distributed them among the *retiari,* and the Africans kissed the weapons, stroked them, and made their strange pledges upon them in their own strange tongues.

All this had taken only a very short time, yet the need for haste weighed even more heavily upon Spartacus. He wanted to be away from the place, away from the school, away from Capua. "Follow me!" he cried. "Follow me!" Varinia stayed next to him. They went off the road and across the fields, mounting up onto the sloping hills. "Never leave me behind, never leave me behind," said Varinia. "I can fight like a man can fight."

Now they saw the soldiers coming on the road from Capua. There were two hundred of the soldiers. They came on the double until they saw that the gladiators were taking to the hills. Then their officers swung them on a tangent, so that they might cut off the gladiators, and the soldiers charged onto the fields. And beyond them, the citizens of Capua were pouring through the gates to watch this rising of slaves put down, to see a fighting of pairs without cost and without quarter.

It could have ended here or an hour before or a month afterwards. At any one of an endless number of points, it could have ended. Slaves had run away before. If these slaves had run away, they would have gone into the fields and the woods; they would have lived like animals on what they could steal and on the acorns from the ground. They would have been hunted down one by one, and they would have been crucified one by one. There was no sanctuary for a slave; the world was made that way. And as Spartacus looked at the garrison soldiers, racing toward them, he knew this simple fact. There was no place to hide, no hole to crawl into. The world had to be changed.

He stopped running away, and he said, "We will fight the soldiers."

X

Long afterwards, Spartacus asked himself, "Who will write of our battles and what we won and what we lost? And who will tell the truth?" The truth of the slaves was contrary to all the truth of the times they lived in. The truth was impossible—in every case the truth was impossible, not because it did not happen, but because there was no explanation for it within the context of those times. There were more soldiers than slaves, and the soldiers were heavily armed; but the soldiers did not expect the slaves to fight and the slaves knew that the soldiers would fight. The slaves poured down on them from the slopes, and the soldiers, who were running in open order, the way men run after a flushed hare, could not meet the shock, flung their spears wildly, and cowered under the rain of stones the women showered upon them.

So the truth was that the soldiers were beaten by the slaves and ran away from them, and halfway back to Capua the slaves pursued them and dragged them down. In the first battle, the slaves suffered sorely, but in the second battle only a handful of them died, and the Roman soldiers fled before them. This was the fact of the matter, but the tale was told in a hundred different ways, and the first report was that written out by the commander of the forces at Capua.

"There was a rising of the slaves at the training school of Lentulus Batiatus," he wrote, "and a number of them escaped and fled southward along the Appian Way. Half a cohort of garrison troops were sent out against them, but some of them managed to break through and escape. It is not known who their leaders are or what their intentions are, but already they have caused dissension among the slaves of the countryside, and it is felt by the citizens here that the noble Senate should spare no effort to reinforce the garrison at Capua, so that the revolt may be put down promptly." Possibly as an afterthought, the commander added, "A series of outrages have already taken place. It is feared that the countryside will suffer from looting and rapine."

And, of course, Batiatus told his story to crowds of Capuan citizens who were eager to hear it. No one was really disturbed—except Batiatus, who saw years of work go down the drain—but everyone realized that the countryside would be an uneasy place until the last of these terrible men (the gladiators) were run down and either slain or nailed upon a cross, so that others might profit by the example. The telling was a process; the story was told and retold by hundreds of people whose whole lives were built on the uneasy structure of slaves, and they told the tale out of their fears and needs. Thus it has always been. Years later, it would be,

"Yes, I happened to be taking the waters at Capua when Spartacus broke loose. I saw him, yes indeed. A giant of a man. I saw him skewer a little child on his spear. It was a terrible thing to see."

Or any one of a thousand other versions. But the truth was something Spartacus himself only caught glimpses of at that time. His vision had broken loose from the fetters of his time. In two small engagements, the slaves he led had beaten Roman soldiers. It was quite true that these were only a handful of second-rate garrison troops, soft from easy living in a resort city, and they were opposed by the best professional swordsmen in all of Italy. But even with that factor considered, for the slave to strike down his master twice in a single day is an earth-shaking fact. Nor did they throw it away when the soldiers fled. They came back when Spartacus called them—they were disciplined people, and already in a few hours, he was like a god to them. They were full of pride, and their fears had gone away. They kept touching each other; in a fashion, it was a caressing of each other—as if the remorseless maxim, *Gladiator, make no friends of gladiators,* had suddenly reversed itself. And thereby, they were filled with an awareness of each other. They did not think this through or reason it out; they were in great part simple and ignorant folk, but they had been suddenly exalted and purified. They looked at each other as if they had never seen each other before, and perhaps there was some truth in that. They had never really dared to look at each other before. Can the executioner look at his victim? But now they were no longer victim and executioner in inevitable partnership; now they were a brotherhood in triumph, and now Spartacus knew how it had happened in Sicily and in so many other places. He felt their strength because a part of it swelled up within himself, and this very current that coursed through him cleansed him of all the suffering that made up his past, all the fears and shames and indignities. He had clung to life for so long, made an exact science of maintaining the life within him for so long, that one might readily have supposed that life would become a careful and cautious matter with him. But here was the sum of his savings, and he suddenly no longer feared death or thought of death because death was of no consequence . . .

About five miles south of Capua, a little distance from the Appian Way, the gladiators and their women and the slaves who had joined them, gathered on a hillside within sight of one of the great manor houses which marked the plantation of some Roman gentleman. It was well onto midday now, and in the process of the two fights and the subsequent march southward, the gladiators had become a little army. From a distance, were it not for the black men among them, they might have been taken for a detachment of Roman soldiery. The weapons had been shared out among them, as had been the helmets and body armor and spears and shields of the soldiers. No one was unarmed now, and armed and tested as they were, it was doubtful whether any force closer than Rome could seriously challenge them. Aside from their women, but with the hand slaves and the field slaves who had joined them, they numbered two hundred and fifty men. Each of the three major groupings, the Gauls, the Africans and the Thracians, marched as a detachment—each with its own leading men as its nominal officers. Because for so long they had seen the Roman maniple of ten as a unit, they fell into it quite naturally. Spartacus led them. There was no discussion of that. They would have died for him. They were full of the legends of men who had been touched by the gods. When they looked at Spartacus, that belief was in their faces.

While they marched, he was at their front, and the German girl, Varinia, walked beside him, her arm around his waist. Sometimes, she looked at him. This was not news to her. Long ago, she had married this man who was the best and bravest of all men, and hadn't she known that then —as well as she knew it now? When their eyes met, she smiled at him. She had fought the soldiers. She didn't know whether he was pleased or not that she had fought the soldiers, but he made no objection to the knife she carried in her hand. They were equals. The world was full of old legends of the Amazons, the women who had gone onto the battlefield like men in the old, old days—and there were many other legends still current at the time of Spartacus of a past where all men and women too had been equals

144

and there was neither master nor slave and all things had been held in common. That long ago was obscured by a haze of time; it was the golden age. It would be the golden age again.

It was a golden age now with the sun tipped over the lovely countryside and the fierce men of the arena, the men of the *sand,* pressing around him and the German slave girl, full of questions. The grass was soft and green in the meadow where they gathered. Yellow flowers topped it like butter, and everywhere butterflies and bees swarmed and the air was full of their song. They called him *father* in the Thracian way.

"What will we do now and where will we go?"

He stood in the circle of them. Varinia sat in the grass, her cheek against his leg. They sat or crouched in the grass around him, the long-limbed black men, the Gauls with their ruddy faces and blue eyes, the Thracians with their dark hair and close-knit bodies. "We are a tribe," he said. "Is that your will?" They nodded at him. The tribe held no slaves and all men spoke equally, and it was not so long ago but that they remembered at least the memory.

"Who will speak?" he asked. "Who will come as your leader? Stand up if you want to lead us. We are free men now."

No one stood up. The Thracians beat their bucklers with the hilts of their knives, and the drumming roused a flight of thrushes from the meadow. Some people appeared in the distance around the manor house, but so far away that it was impossible to say who or what they were. The black men saluted Spartacus by clapping their hands in front of their faces. They were all strangely content, and for the moment they were living in a dream. Varinia's cheek kept pressing against her man's leg. Gannicus cried,

"Hail, gladiator!"

A man who was dying stood up weakly. He had been stretched on the grass, his arm cut to the bone for all the length of it and the blood draining out of him. He was a Gaul and he didn't want to be left behind, and this way he had tasted freedom a little. His arm was bound around with blood-soaked cloth, and he walked over to Spartacus who helped him to stand erect.

"I am not afraid to die," he said to the gladiators. "It is

better than to die in the pairs. But I would rather follow this man than to die. I would rather follow this man and see where he leads us. But if I die, remember me and do him no wrong. Listen to him. The Thracians call him father, and we are like little children, but he will suck the evil out of us. There is no evil left in me. I did a great thing, and I am purified and I am not afraid to die. I will sleep quietly. I will dream no dreams after I am dead."

Some of the gladiators wept openly now. The Gaul kissed Spartacus, and Spartacus returned his kiss. "Stay by my side," Spartacus said, and the man sank down on the grass next to him, and the field hands who had joined them stared openmouthed at these gladiators who had such easy intimacy with death.

"You die but we will live," Spartacus said to him. "We will remember your name and shout it aloud. We will make a noise of it all over the land."

"You will never give up?" the Gaul pleaded.

"Did we give up when the soldiers came against us? We fought the soldiers twice and we won. Do you know what we must do now?" he asked the gladiators.

They watched him.

"Can we run away?"

"Where will we run?" asked Crixus. "Everywhere, it is the same as here. Everywhere, it is master and slave."

"We will not run away," said Spartacus, who knew now and surely and as certainly as if he had never had a doubt. "We will go from plantation to plantation, from house to house, and wherever we go, we will set the slaves free and add them to our numbers. When they send the soldiers against us again, we will fight them, and the gods will decide whether they want it the Roman way or our way."

"And weapons? Where will we find weapons?" someone asked.

"We will take them from the soldiers. And we will make them too. What is Rome but the blood and sweat and hurt of slaves? Is there anything we cannot make?"

"Then Rome will go to war against us."

"Then we will go to war against Rome," said Spartacus quietly. "We will make an end of Rome, and we will make a world where there are no slaves and no masters."

It was a dream, but they were in a mood for dreaming. They had plunged into the skies, and if this strange

Thracian with the black eyes and the broken nose had told them that he intended to lead them against the gods themselves, they would have believed at that moment and followed at that moment.

"We will not dishonor ourselves," Spartacus told them, speaking softly and directly and intently, speaking in a way to each of them singly and directly. "We will not do as the Romans do. We will not obey the Roman law. We will make our own law."

"What is our law?"

"Our law is simple. Whatever we take, we hold in common, and no man shall own anything but his weapons and his clothes. It will be the way it was in the old times."

A Thracian said, "There is enough for all to be rich."

"You make the law. I will not make it," said Spartacus.

So they talked, and there were greedy men among them who dreamed of being great lords, like the Romans, and there were others who dreamed of holding Romans as slaves; so they talked and talked, but in the end it was as Spartacus had stated it.

"And we will take no woman, except as wife," said Spartacus. "Nor shall any man hold more than one wife. Justice will be equal between them, and if they cannot live in peace, they must part. But no man may lie with any woman, Roman or otherwise, who is not his lawful wife."

Their laws were few, and they agreed upon their laws. Then they took up their arms and went against the manor house. Only the slaves remained, for the Romans had fled to Capua . . . And the slaves joined the gladiators.

XI

In Capua, they saw the smoke of the first manor house which burned, and thereby the slaves were vindictive and cruel. They would have wanted for the slaves to be gentle and understanding; in more practical terms, they would have wanted the slaves to flee to the still-wild mountain heights, hiding singly or in handfuls in caves, living like animals until each was hunted down as an animal is hunted down. Even when the citizens of Capua saw the smoke of the first burning house, they were not unduly alarmed. It was to be expected that the gladiators would take out their bitterness on whatever they encountered. An express was already hammering along the Appian Way to inform the Senate of the outbreak at Capua—and this meant that in a very few days, the situation would be under control. A lesson would be taught to slaves then that they would not easily forget.

A large landowner, Marius Acanus by name, was forewarned, and gathered all his seven hundred slaves together to shepherd them to the safety of the walls of Capua; but the gladiators met him on the road and stood in grim silence and watched as his own slaves slew him and his wife, and his wife's sister, and his daughter and his daughter's husband. It was a grim and awful business, but Spartacus knew that he could not stop it, nor was he particularly anxious to stop it. They had harvested only what they had sown, and the litter slaves themselves did the work, the moment they saw that these were not Roman soldiers but the very escaped gladiators whose fame was already running all over the place, a song and a scream on the wind itself. It was late afternoon now, but the news had flown quicker than time. The original few hundred were more than a thousand, and as they marched south, slaves poured over the hills and across the valleys to join them. The field hands came with their tools of work; the goatherds drove their herds of goats and sheep with them. When they approached a house, flowing toward it, a great, shapeless mass of folk—for only the gladiators still preserved a military formation of sorts—the news ran before them, and the kitchen slaves came out to greet them with their knives and cleavers, and the house slaves came running to give them gifts of silk and fine linen. In most cases, the Romans fled; where the overseers and the Romans put up a fight, there was grisly evidence of work done.

They could not move quickly. They had become too great a host of laughing, singing men and women and children, all of them drunk with the same wine of freedom. Darkness fell before they were twenty miles from Capua, and they camped in a valley beside a bubbling stream, lighting fires, and eating their fill of fresh meat.

Whole goats and sheep, and here and there even a bullock, went onto their spits, and the crisp, savory smell of roasting meat perfumed the air. It was a great feasting for folk who went from year's end to year's end on leeks and turnips and barley porridge. They washed down the meat with wine, and their songs and laughter spiced the food. What a company they were, Gauls and Jews and Greeks and Egyptians, Thracians and Nubians and Sudanese and Lybians, Persians and Assyrians and Samarians, Germans and Slavs, Bulgars and Macedonians and Spaniards and many an Italian too out of generations which had been sold into bondage for one reason or another, Sabines and Umbrians and Tuscans and Sicilians and folk of many other tribes whose very names are lost forever, a singular company of blood and nations but united first in their bondage and now in their freedom.

In the old times, there had been the family of the *gens* and the community of the tribe—and ultimately the pride and privilege of the nation; but for the world here was something new in this peculiar comradeship of the oppressed, and in all the great throng of so many nations and peoples that night, there was no voice raised in anger or discontent. They were touched with a little love and a little glory. Many of them had hardly seen Spartacus, or had him pointed out to them from a distance only, but they were full of Spartacus. He was their leader and their god— for it was not clear in their minds that gods did not walk the earth occasionally, and hadn't Prometheus himself stolen the holy fire from heaven and given it as the most precious of all gifts to mankind? And what had happened once could happen again. Already, tales were being told around their fires, and a whole Saga of Spartacus was coming into being. There was no one among them—no, not even among the little children—who had not dreamed dreams of a world where none were slaves . . .

And meanwhile Spartacus sat among the gladiators, and they talked and weighed the things that had happened. The little brook had become a river already and a torrent was in the making. Gannicus said it. His eyes shone whenever he looked at Spartacus. "We can march across the world and turn it over, stone by stone!" This he said, but Spartacus knew better. He lay with his head in Varinia's lap, and she passed her fingers through his tight brown curls and felt the stubble on his cheeks, and inside she was full of riches and contentment. Now she was satisfied, but a fire burned in him; he had been more satisfied in slavery. He looked at the clear bright stars in the Italian night and he was filled with wild thoughts and yearning and fears and doubts and the weight of what he had to do lay upon him. He had to destroy Rome. The very thought, the insolent enormity of thinking this, made him smile and Varinia was pleased and traced his lips with her fingers, singing to him in her own tongue,

"When the hunter, from the forest,
Brings the red deer from the hunting,
Casts his eyes upon the fire,
Speaks the children, speaks the woman—"

The rhythm of a forest folk in a cold and wild land. How many of her strange forest songs he had heard. She sang, and he repeated to himself, his thoughts laying themselves against the background of the music, his dreams spaced out among the shining stars in the sky,

"You must destroy Rome—you, Spartacus. You must take these people away and be stern and strong with them. You must teach them to fight and kill. There is no going back—not one single step back. The whole world belongs to Rome, so Rome must be destroyed and made only a bad memory, and then, where Rome was, we will build a new life where all men will live in peace and brotherhood and love, no slaves and no slavemasters, no gladiators and no arenas, but a time like the old times, like the golden age. We will build new cities of brotherhood, and there will be no walls around them."

Then Varinia stopped singing and asked him. "What are you dreaming, my man, my Thracian? Are the gods in the stars talking to you? Then what are they telling you, my beloved? Are they telling you secret things that are never to be shared?" She half believed this. Who knew what was true and what was untrue concerning the gods? Spartacus hated the gods and gave them no worship. "Are there gods for slaves?" he had once asked her.

"In all my life," he said to her, "there will be nothing I won't share with you, my beloved."

"Then what are you dreaming?"

"I am dreaming that we will make a new world."

Then she was afraid of him, but he said to her, gently,

"This world was made by men. Did it just happen, my darling? Think. Is there anything in it that we did not build, the cities, the towers, the walls, the roads and the ships? Then why can't we make a new world?"

"Rome—" she said, and in the single word there was the power implicit, the power that ruled the world.

"Then we will destroy Rome," answered Spartacus. "The world has had its belly full of Rome. We will destroy Rome and we will destroy what Rome believes in."

"Who? Who?" she pleaded.

"The slaves. There have been risings of slaves before, but it will be different now. We will send out a call that slaves will hear across the world . . ."

So peace went and hope went, and long afterwards, Varinia recalled that night when her man's head was in her lap and his eyes were fixed on the far off stars. Yet it was a night of love. A few people are given a few such nights, and then they are fortunate. They lay there, among the gladiators, alongside the fire, and time went slowly. They touched each other and proved their awareness of each other. They became like one person.

PART FIVE

Being an account of Lentelus Gracchus, some of his memories, and some particulars of his stay at the Villa Salaria.

Lentelus Gracchus was fond of saying that as his weight increased, so did his ability to walk a tight rope, and the fact that thirty-seven of his fifty-six years were spent in the successful pursuit of Roman politics gave support to his claim. Politics, as he occasionally said, required three unchanging talents and no virtues. More politicians, he claimed, had been destroyed by virtue than by any other cause; and the talents he enumerated in this fashion. The first talent was the ability to choose the winning side. Failing that, the second talent was the ability to extricate oneself from the losing side. And the third talent was never to make an enemy.

All three of these talents were ideals, and ideals being what they are and people being what they are, there was no such thing as one hundred per cent fulfillment. On his own part, he had done well. Starting as the son of a simple but industrious cobbler, he was buying and selling votes at the age of nineteen, buying and selling offices and an occasional assassination at the age of twenty-five, leading a powerful political gang at the age of twenty-eight, and unopposed leader of the famous Caelian Ward at the age of thirty. Five years later he was a magistrate, and at the age of forty he entered the Senate. He knew ten thousand people in the city by name and twenty thousand more by sight. He included in his list of favors even his worst enemies, and while he never made the mistake of believing that any of his associates were honest, he never fell into the more

profound error of taking for granted the dishonesty of any
one of them.

His weight and substance befitted his position; he had
never trusted women nor had he noticed that they were
particularly profitable to his colleagues. His own vice was
food, and the huge layers of fat which he had accumulated
over the span of successful years not only turned him into
an impressive figure of a man, but made him one of those
few Romans who were never seen in public but that they
were wrapped in the folds of a toga. In a tunic, Lentelus
Gracchus was not an ingratiating figure of a man. In a
toga, he was a symbol of Roman substance and virtue. His
three hundred pounds of weight supported a bald, jowled
head, firmly set in rings of fat. He had a deep, hoarse
voice, a winning smile, and small, cheerful blue eyes which
peered out of folds of flesh. And his skin was pink as a
baby's.

Gracchus was less cynical than informed. The formula
of Roman power had never been a mystery to him, and he
was rather amused by Cicero's ponderous advance toward
what Cicero liked to think was the last and most important
truth. When Antonius Caius asked him his opinion of
Cicero, Gracchus replied shortly,

"A young fogey."

With Antonius Caius, Gracchus was on the best of terms,
as he was with so many patricians. Aristocracy was the one
mystery and shrine he permitted himself. He liked aristocrats. He envied them. He also, within a certain area, despised them, for he considered all of them rather stupid,
and he never got over the fact that they seemed to derive so
little advantage from birth and station. Nevertheless, he
cultivated them, and it gave him a feeling of pride and
pleasure to be invited to one of their splendid plantations,
such as the *Villa Salaria*. He did not put on airs and he
made no attempt to pass as an aristocrat. He did not speak
their clipped, genteel Latin, but rather the easy language
of the plebs. Though he could well afford it, he made no
attempt to set up a plantation of his own. For their part,
they appreciated his practicality and fund of useful information; and his immense size communicated assurance.
Antonius Caius liked him because Gracchus was a man
utterly unmoved by moral judgment, and he often referred

to Gracchus as the only wholly honest man he had ever known.

On this evening, Gracchus missed little of what went on. He weighed and assessed, but he did not judge. For Caius, he had nothing but contempt. The great and wealthy general, Crassus, amused him, and concerning Cicero, he said to his host,

"He has everything but greatness. I think he would cut his mother's throat if it advanced the cause of Cicero."

"But the cause of Cicero is not that important."

"Precisely. And therefore he will fail at practically everything. He is nobody to fear since he is nobody to admire."

That was a most penetrating comment to make to Antonius Caius, who was someone to admire, even though his sexual tendencies and practices were pitched at the level of a twelve year old. Gracchus was willing to admit to himself that the ground he stood upon was turning to slime. His world was disintegrating, but since the process of disintegration was exceedingly slow and since he himself was far from immortal, he had no interest in deceiving himself. He was able to see what went on without taking sides; there was no necessity in his makeup for him to take sides.

On this particular evening, he remained awake after the rest of the household had gone to sleep. He slept little and poorly, and now he took a turn around the grounds in the bright moonlight. If anyone had asked him, he would have been able to report fairly accurately on how partners had been chosen for bed that evening; but he had observed this without prying, and he felt no resentment. This was Rome. Only a fool considered otherwise.

As he walked, he saw Julia sitting on a stone bench, a mournful figure in the night, dispossessed and stricken with terror at her own inadequacy and by the manner of her rejection. He turned toward her.

"Two of us for the night," he said to her. "It is a most beautiful night, isn't it, Julia?"

"If you feel beautiful."

"And you don't, Julia?" He arranged his toga. "Would you like me to sit for a while?"

"Please do."

He sat in silence for a little, mildly responsive to the moonlit beauty of the grounds, the great white house rising so finely out of its bed of shrubs and evergreens, the terrace, the fountains, the pale gleam of sculpture here and there, the arbors with their lovely benches of pale pink or deep black marble. How much beauty Rome had managed! Finally, he said,

"It would seem, Julia, that this should content us."

"Yes, it would seem so."

He was her husband's friend and guest. "A privilege to be a Roman," he remarked.

"You never make these stupid platitudes except when you are with me," Julia answered quietly.

"Yes?"

"Yes, I think so. Tell me, did you ever hear of Varinia?"

"Varinia?"

"Do you ever commit yourself on anything without turning it over in your mind at least five times? I'm not trying to be clever, my dear." She rested her hand on his great paw. "I can't be. Varinia was the wife of Spartacus."

"Yes, I have heard of her. As a matter of fact, you people out here are obsessed with Spartacus. I've heard of little else tonight."

"Well, he spared the *Villa Salaria*. I don't know whether to be grateful or not. I suppose it's the tokens of punishment. I haven't been out to the road yet. Are they very terrible?"

"Terrible? I don't know that I gave it much thought. There they are, and that's about all. Life is cheap, and slaves are worth just about nothing these days. Why did you ask me about Varinia?"

"I've been trying to think of whom I envy. I think I envy her."

"Really, Julia? A little barbarian slave girl. Shall I have a dozen like her picked up at the market tomorrow and sent here?"

"You're never serious about anything, are you, Gracchus?"

"Very little worth being serious about. Why do you envy her?"

"Because I hate myself."

"That's too complex for me," Gracchus rumbled. "Can you see her, dirty, picking her nose, hawking, spitting, her nails broken and unclean, her face covered with pimples? That's your slave princess. Do you still envy her?"

"Was she like that?"

Gracchus laughed. "Who knows! Julia, politics is a lie. History is the recording of a lie. If you go down to the road tomorrow and look at the crosses, you will see the only truth about Spartacus. Death. Nothing else. Everything else is sheer fabrication. I know."

"I look at my slaves—"

"And you don't see Spartacus? Of course. Stop eating your heart out, Julia. I'm older than you. I take the privilege of advice. Yes, at the risk of intruding where I've no business to go. Take a young buck out of your slave quarters—"

"Stop it, Gracchus!"

"—and he might be Spartacus for all that."

She was crying now. Gracchus did not see many women of his class in tears, and he felt suddenly awkward and stupid. He began to ask her whether it was his fault. Nothing he had said was particularly insulting; but was it his fault?

"No, no, please, Gracchus. You're one of the only friends I have. Don't stop being my friend because I'm such a fool." She dried her eyes, excused herself, and left him there. "I'm very tired," she said. "Please don't come with me."

II

Like Cicero, Gracchus had a sense of history; the important difference was that Gracchus never confused himself concerning his own place and role; and therefore he saw many things far more clearly than Cicero did. He sat now all alone in the warm and gentle Italian night and turned over in his mind the strange case of a Roman matron and patrician who envied a barbarian slave woman. First, he considered whether Julia was telling the truth. He decided that she was. For some reason, the essence of Julia's own pitiful tragedy was spotlighted by Varinia—and he wondered whether in the same way the meaning of their own lives was not contained in the endless tokens of punishment which lined the Appian Way. Gracchus was not troubled by morality; he knew his own people, and he was not taken in by the legendry of the Roman matron and the Roman family. But for some strange reason, he was most deeply troubled by what Julia had said, and the question would not leave him.

The answer was in a flash of understanding which left him cold and shaken in a way he had rarely been shaken before; and it left him full of fear of death and of the awful and utter darkness and non-existence which death brings; for the answer took away a great deal of the cynical certainty which supported him and left him sitting there on the stone bench bereft, a fat and paunchy old man whose personal doom had suddenly become linked with an enormous movement of the currents of history.

He saw it clearly. The thing which had come into the world so newly was a whole society built upon the backs of slaves, and the symphonic utterance of that society was the song of the whip-lash. What did it do to the people who wielded the whip? What did Julia mean? He had never married; a germ of this present understanding had kept him from ever taking a wife, so he bought women and the concubines in his house were there when he needed them. But Antonius Caius also kept a stable of concubines, even as every gentleman he knew kept a quantity of women as one keeps a quantity of horses or dogs, and the wives knew and accepted and equalized matters with the male slaves. It was not a simple matter of corruption, but a monster which had turned the world over; and these people, gathered together for a night at the *Villa Salaria,* were obsessed with Spartacus because Spartacus was all that they were not. Cicero might never understand whence came the virtue of this mysterious slave, but he, Gracchus, he understood. Home and family and honor and virtue and all that was good and noble was defended by the slaves and owned by the slaves—not because they were good and noble, but because their masters had turned over to them all that was sacred.

As Spartacus had a vision of what might be—the vision arising out of himself—so did Gracchus have his own vision of what might be, and what he saw in the future made him cold and sick and afraid. He rose and gathered his toga about him, and plodded with heavy steps toward his room and bed.

But he could not sleep easily. He took up Julia's wish, and like a little boy he wept noiseless and dry tears for a companion in his loneliness, and like a little boy, he pretended that the slave girl Varinia shared his bed with him. Terror gave force to his plaintive desire for virtue. His fat, ringed hands stroked a ghost on his bedsheet. The hours passed, and he lay there with his memories.

They all hated Spartacus. This house was filled with Spartacus; no one knew his form or shape or thoughts or manner, but this house was filled with his presence and Rome was filled with his presence. It was a complete fiction that he, Gracchus, was free from that hatred. Quite to the contrary, his hatred, which he had always so carefully concealed, was more violent, more bitter, more poignant than their hatred.

As he struggled with his memories, his memories took shape and form and color and reality. He remembered how he was sitting in the Senate—and he never sat in the Senate chamber but that he felt and resented his own pride at being there among the great, the aristocrats—when news came by fast post from Capua that there had been an uprising among the gladiators at the school of Lentulus Batiatus and that it was spreading over the countryside. He remembered the wave of fear that spread through the Senate, and how they began to cackle like a great flock of geese, all of them talking at once, all of them saying wild, frightened things simply because a handful of gladiators had killed their trainers. He remembered his disgust with them. He remembered how he rose, gathering his toga together and throwing it over his shoulder with the sweeping gesture which had become a hallmark of his, and thundering at his august colleagues,

"Gentlemen—gentlemen, you forget yourselves!"

They stopped their cackling and turned to him.

"Gentlemen, we are faced with the crime of a handful of miserable, dirty butcher slaves. We are not faced with a barbarian invasion. But even if we were, gentlemen, it would seem to me that the Senate might comport itself somewhat differently! It would seem to me that we owe ourselves a certain dignity!"

They were enraged with him, but he was enraged with them. He made it a point of pride never to lose his temper, but this was one time he had, and he, a person of low birth and breeding, a commoner, had insulted and humbled the most august body in the whole world. "The devil with that!" he said to himself, and he stalked out of the chamber with their pious defense of their dignity ringing in his ears, and he went home.

That day lived with him. Every minute of that day lived with him. He had been frightened at first. He had violated his own sacred rules of conduct. He had lost his temper. He had made enemies. He walked through the streets of his beloved Rome, and he was full of fears at what he had done. But the fear was mingled with contempt for his colleagues and contempt for himself, in that he could not even now overcome his awe of the Senate and his ingrained veneration for the fools who occupied its seats.

For once, he was blind to the smell and the sound and the sight of his beloved Rome. Gracchus was city born and bred, and the *urbs* was his habitat. It was part of him and he was part of it, and he nursed a consummate contempt for far horizons and green valleys and babbling brooks. He had learned to walk and run and fight in the twisting alleys and dirty gutters of Rome. He had scrambled like a goat in his childhood over the tall roofs of the endless tenement houses. The smell of charcoal fires, which pervaded the city, was the sweetest perfume he knew. This was one area in his life where cynicism never conquered. To go through the narrow market streets, with their rows of pushcarts and stalls, where the merchandise of the whole world was displayed and sold, was always a new adventure for him. Half the city knew him by sight. It was "Ho, Gracchus!" here, and "Ho, Gracchus!" there, with no ceremony or bother about it, and the venders and cobblers and beggars and loafers and draymen and masons and carpenters liked him because he was one of them and had fought and clawed his way up to the top. They liked him because when he bought votes, he paid the highest price. They liked him because he put on no airs and because he preferred to walk rather than ride in a litter and because he always had time to greet an old friend. That he offered no cure for their increasing misery and hopelessness in a world where slaves were driving them to become loafers and beggars who lived on the dole of the state, made little difference. They knew of no cure. And he, in turn, loved their world, the world of gloom where the towering tenements almost met over the dirty alleys and had to be propped apart with timbers, the world of the streets, the noisy, dirty, wretched streets of the world's greatest city.

But on this day which he remembered so vividly, he was blind and shut off from all that. He walked through the streets without heeding the greetings. He bought nothing at the stalls. Even the tasty morsels of fried bacon, stuffed derma and smoked sausage which cooked on so many pushcarts did not attract him. Usually he could not resist the street cooking, the honey cakes and smoked fish and dried salted sardines and pickled apples and cured roe; but on this day he was unaware of it and sunk in his own gloom, he returned to his home.

Gracchus, who was almost as wealthy as Crassus, never permitted himself to build or purchase one of the private villas which were going up in the new part of the city, among the gardens and parks along the river. He preferred to occupy the ground floor of a tenement in his old ward, and his doors were always open to those who desired to see him. It must be remarked that many well-to-do families lived in these ground floors. They were the choice tenement dwellings, and in a Roman tenement, the price decreased and the misery increased as one mounted the rickety stairs that led to the upper stories. Usually it was only the two lowest floors which had water piped in and any toilet or bathing facilities to speak of; but the old tribal commune was not so far in the past that an absolute separation of rich and poor had been achieved everywhere, and many a wealthy merchant or banker had a veritable nest of poverty towering for seven stories over his head.

So Gracchus remembered how he had come back to his home that day with never a word of cheer or greeting for anyone, and how he had gone into his office, giving his slaves the rather unusual request that he be left alone. His slaves were all women; that he insisted upon and would have no man share his quarters with him; nor did he overdo it, as so many of his friends did. Fourteen women did for all of his needs. He kept no special harem, as bachelors frequently did; he used those of his slave women who attracted him at the times when he wanted a bedmate, and since he desired no complications in his home, whenever one of his women became pregnant, he sold her to a plantation owner. He reasoned that it was better for children to grow up in the country, and he saw nothing either immoral or cruel in his procedure.

He had no favorites among his women—since he never was capable of anything more than the most casual relationship with any woman—and he was fond of saying that his was a better ordered and more peaceful household than most. But now, as he lay in bed at the *Villa Salaria* and recalled that day, his memories of his household had no joy or warmth. A moral measure had taken hold of him, and it sickened him to think of how he lived. Yet he pursued the incidents of that day. He saw himself from a vantage point, a fat, gross man in a toga sitting all alone in the bare room he called his office, and he must have sat there for better than an hour before there was any interruption. Then a knock at the door.

"What is it?" he asked.

"There are some gentlemen to see you," the slave said.

"I don't want to see anyone." How childish he was being!

"These are *fathers* and honorable persons from the Senate."

So they had come to him, and he was not lost and cast out of their circle. What had made him think that he would be? Of course, they would come to him! He lived again. His ego returned. He sprang up and threw open the door, and he was the old Gracchus, smiling, assured, competent.

"Gentlemen," he said. "Gentlemen, I bid you welcome."

There were five in the committee. Two of them were *consulares;* the other three were patricians of distinction and shrewdness. The committee had come less in terms of the present emergency than to re-cement whatever political breaks Gracchus might be in the process of making. So they were bluff and intimate and they scolded him.

"Why, Gracchus? Have you been sitting there this whole year waiting for an opportunity to insult us?"

"I have neither the wit nor the grace to beg your pardon properly," Gracchus apologized.

"You have both. But that is beside the point."

He called for chairs, and they seated themselves in a circle around him, five men of age and dignity, wrapped in the fine white togas which had become the symbol of Roman rule the world over. He had wine brought and a tray of sweets. The *consularis* Caspius became the spokesman. He flattered Gracchus and puzzled him, for Gracchus did not see the occasion as being one of such monumental crisis. He had often dreamed of playing the part of consul, but that was not his dish and he had none of the talents or particular family connections required. He tried to guess what they were after, and could only presume that it was connected with Spain, where the revolt against the Senate—and Rome, of course—led by Sertorius, had turned into a contest for power between Sertorius and Pompey. Gracchus had his own estimation of this. He despised both the rivals, and was determined to sit by and allow them to destroy each other. As were, he knew, the five gentlemen who faced him.

"You see then," said Caspius, "that this revolt in Capua has enormous implications of danger."

"I don't see that at all," answered Gracchus flatly.

"Taking into consideration what we have suffered from slave revolts—"

"What do you know about this revolt?" asked Gracchus, more gently now than before. "How many slaves are there involved? Who are they? Where have they gone? How real is your worry?"

Caspius answered the questions one by one. "We have maintained constant communication. Initially, only the gladiators were involved. There is one report that only seventy escaped. A later report has it that over two hundred escaped, Thracians and Gauls and a number of black Africans. The later reports increase their numbers. This may be the result of panic. On the other hand, there may have been disturbances on the *latifundia*. They seem to have been responsible for considerable damage, but no details are available. As to where they have gone, it would seem that they are moving in the direction of Mount Vesuvius."

"Nothing more than *it would seem*," snapped Gracchus impatiently. "Are they idiots at Capua that they can't assess what has happened in their own courtyard? They have a garrison there. Why didn't the garrison put an end to this thing quickly and expeditiously?"

Caspius looked coolly at Gracchus. "They had only one *cohort* at Capua."

"One cohort! How many troops do you need to pull down a few wretched gladiators?"

"You know as well as I do what must have happened at Capua."

"I don't know, but I can guess. And my guess would be

that the garrison commander is in the pay of every filthy *lanista* operating in the place. Twenty soldiers here, a dozen there. How many were left in the city?"

"Two hundred and fifty. There it is. No need for righteousness, Gracchus. The troops were defeated by the gladiators. That is what is so worrisome, Gracchus. Our feeling is that the City Cohorts should be dispatched immediately."

"How many?"

"At least six cohorts—at least three thousand men."

"When?"

"Immediately."

Gracchus shook his head. This was precisely what he might have expected. He thought of what he intended to say. He thought it over very carefully. He gathered in his mind all that he knew and had known of slave psychology.

"Don't do it."

He had a habit of opposing them. They all demanded to know why.

"Because I don't trust city cohorts. Leave the slaves alone for the time being. Let a little rot start in them. Don't send city cohorts."

"Who will we send?"

"Recall one of the legions."

"From Spain. And Pompey?"

"Let Pompey rot and be damned! All right—leave Spain alone. Bring the Third down from Cisalpine Gaul. Don't rush. These are slaves, a handful of slaves. It will not be anything unless you make it something . . ."

So they argued, and in his memory, Gracchus lived the argument again and lost again and saw them, in their incredible fear of slave revolt, determine to send six of the City Cohorts. Gracchus slept just a little. He woke at the break of dawn, as he always did, regardless of time and place. He took his morning water and fruit to the terrace to eat.

III

Daylight eases the fears and the perplexities of man, and most often it is like a balm and a benediction. Most often, but not always; for there are certain categories of human beings who do not welcome the light of day. A prisoner hugs the night, which is a robe to warm and protect him and comfort him, and daylight brings no cheer to a condemned man. But most often, daylight washes out the confusions of the night. Great men assume the mantle of their greatness anew each morning, for even great men become like all other men in the night time, and some of them do despicable things and others of them weep and still others huddle in fear of death and of a darkness deeper than that which surrounds them. But in the morning they are great men again, and Gracchus, sitting on the terrace, mantled in a fresh snow-white toga, his big fleshy face cheerful and confident, was a picture of what a Roman senator should be. It has been said many times, then and later, that no finer and nobler and wiser body of men ever came together for legislative debate than the Senate of Republican Rome, and looking at Gracchus, one was inclined to accept this. It was true that he was not nobly born and that the blood in his veins was of exceedingly dubious ancestry, but he was very rich, and it was a virtue of the Republic that a man was measured in terms of himself as much as in terms of his ancestors. The very fact that the gods gave a man wealth was an indication of his inborn qualities, and if one wanted proof of this, one had only to see how many were poor and how few were rich.

As Gracchus sat there, he was joined by the others of the company which graced the *Villa Salaria*. It was an extraordinary group of men and women who had gathered there for the night, and they enjoyed the knowledge that they were remarkable and very important persons. It put them at ease with each other, and it underlined their trust in Antonius Caius, who never made the mistake of mixing people improperly at his plantation. But in general terms of Roman country life, they were not too unusual. It is true that among them were two of the richest people in the world, a young woman who would become a remarkable whore of the ages, and a young man who through a life of calculated and cold intrigue and plotting would remain famous for many centuries to come, and another young man whose degeneracy would become a matter of fame in itself; but at almost any time, similar folk would be found at the *Villa Salaria*.

This morning, they grouped themselves around Gracchus. He was the only one among them who wore a toga. He was the immovable senior magistrate, sitting there with his scented water, peeling an apple, and granting a word here or there. "They recover well," he said to himself, looking at the well groomed men and the carefully painted women, their hair done expertly and beautifully, their lipstick and rouge so artfully placed. They made conversation about this thing and that thing, and their conversation was clever and well-rehearsed. If they spoke about sculpture, Cicero took an official position, as might be expected:

"I am tired of all this talk of the Greeks. What have they done that the Egyptians did not achieve a thousand years before? In both cases, you have a particular degeneracy, a people unfit for growth or command. Which their sculpture reflects. At least a Roman artist portrays what is."

"But what is can be very boring," Helena protested, the prerogative of youth and an intellectual and a woman. It was expected of Gracchus that he should deny knowing anything at all about art. However, "I know what I like." Gracchus knew a good deal about art. He bought Egyptian art, because it struck some chord in him. Crassus had no strong opinions about art; it was remarkable how few strong opinions he had, yet he was a good general as such things went. At the same time, he resented Cicero's cocksure statement. It was all very well to talk about degeneracy when you didn't have to fight the so-called degenerates.

"I must say I favor Greek sculpture," Antonius Caius remarked. "It's cheap, and it's very pleasing once the color washes off. Of course, it's those old pieces without any color that one finds around, but they look well in a garden and I prefer them that way."

"Then you might have bought the monuments of Spartacus—before our friend Crassus had them smashed to pieces," Cicero smiled.

"Monuments?" asked Helena.

"They had to be smashed," Crassus said cooly.

"What monuments?"

"If I'm not mistaken," Cicero said, "it was Gracchus who signed the order for their destruction."

"You're never mistaken, are you, young man?" Gracchus rumbled. "You're quite right." He explained to Helena, "There were two great monuments carved out of volcanic stone that Spartacus raised up on the eastern slope of Vesuvius. I never saw them, but I signed the order for their destruction."

"How could you?" Helena demanded.

"How could I not? If filth raises an emblem of filth, you wash it out!"

"What were they like?" Claudia asked.

Gracchus shook his head, smiling ruefully at the manner in which the ghosts of the slaves and the ghost of their leader intruded, no matter where the conversation began. "I never saw them, my dear. Crassus did. Ask him."

"I can't give you an artist's opinion," Crassus said. "But these things looked like what they were supposed to be. There were two of them. One was the figure of a slave, about fifty feet tall, I'd say. He stood with his feet apart and he had burst his chains, so that they hung loose about him. With one arm, he clasped a child to his breast, and in the other hand, hanging loose, there was a Spanish sword. That was one, and you might call it a colossus, I suppose. It was very well done as far as I could see, but as I said, I'm no judge of art. But it was plainly done, and the man and the child were well formed even to such details as the calluses and sores the chains would naturally raise. I remember young Caius Taneria pointing out to me the heavy shoulder development of the slave and the raised veins in the hands, just as you would see in any ploughman. You know, Spartacus had a good many Greeks with him, and the Greeks are very clever at this kind of thing. They never had an opportunity to paint it, or perhaps they couldn't get any pigment, and all in all it reminded me of some of the old carvings you see in Athens, the ones where the paint has washed off, and I agree with Caius that they're pleasing that way—and very cheap too.

"The other monument was not as tall; the figures were no more than twenty feet high, but they were also well done. There were three gladiators, a Thracian, a Gaul and an African. The African, interestingly enough, was carved out of black stone; the other figures were white. The African stood in the center, somewhat taller than the others, grasping his trident in both hands. On one side of him stood the Thracian, knife in hand, and on the other side, the Gaul, sword in hand. It was well done, and you could see that they had been fighting, for they were badly cut about the arms and legs. Behind them, a woman stood —and very proudly, and they say Varinia was the original of that. The woman held a trowel in one hand and a mattock in the other. I must confess, I never quite understood the significance of that."

"Varinia?" Gracchus asked softly.

"Why did you have to destroy them?" Helena asked.

"Could you leave their monuments standing?" countered Gracchus. "Could you leave it there, for all to point to and say, Here is what slaves did?"

"Rome is strong enough to afford to leave them—yes, and point to them," Helena declared.

"Nicely said!" Cicero remarked, but Crassus thought of how it had been then, with ten thousand of his best troops lying in a bloody field, and the slaves moving away like an angry lion that is only annoyed but hardly hurt.

"What did the sculpture of Varinia look like?" Gracchus asked, trying to make the question seem as casual as possible.

"I don't know that I can recall it very well. You would take her for a German or Gaulish woman, long hair, loose gown and all that. The hair in braids and bound the way the Germans and Gauls do it. A good bust—a fine, strong figure of a woman, like some of those German wenches you see in the market today, and everyone so eager to buy them. Of course, one doesn't know whether it actually was Varinia or not. Like everything else in the Spartacus business, we know almost nothing about it. Unless you want to swallow the propaganda whole and let it go at that. All I know about Varinia is what that dirty old *lanista*, Batiatus, told me, and that was precious little, except that his tongue was out and he slobbered over the memory of her. So she must have been attractive—"

"And you destroyed that too!" Helena declared.

Crassus nodded. He was not a man easily disturbed. "My dear," he said to Helena, "I was a soldier and I carried out the instructions of the Senate. You will hear it said that the Servile War was a small thing. It's quite natural that such a view should be taken, since it profits Rome little to tell the world what a job we had with some slaves. But here, on this pleasant terrace at the home of my dear and good friend, Antonius Caius, with the company we have, we can dispense with legends. No one ever came as close to destroying Rome as Spartacus did. No one ever wounded her so terribly. I don't want to build up my own case. Let Pompey be the hero, and there's a little virtue in putting down slaves. But the truth remains, and if the tokens of punishment are unpleasant, think of how I felt when I saw the ground carpeted with the bodies of the finest troops in Rome. So I didn't shrink from destroying some rock carving that the slaves had made. Quite to the contrary, I took a certain satisfaction in it. We destroyed the images most thoroughly and ground them into rubble—so that no trace of it remains. So did we destroy Spartacus and his army. So will we in time—and necessarily—destroy the very memory of what he did and how he did it. I am a fairly simple man and not particularly clever, but I know this. The order of things is that some must rule and some must serve. So the gods ordained it. So it will be."

It was a quality of Crassus that he could evoke passion without being in the slightest degree passionate himself. His fine, strong military features gave emphasis to what he said. He was so much and so completely the bronze hawk of the Republic!

Gracchus watched him from under dropped lids. Gracchus sat there and watched each of them, the thin-faced, predatory Cicero, the young fop, Caius, Helena, the silent, suffering and somewhat ridiculous Julia, Claudia, sleek and satisfied, Antonius Caius—and Crassus—all of them, he watched, and he listened too, and he thought again of how the Senatorial Committee had come after him when he stalked away. That was the beginning, of course—when the six cohorts were sent. And the beginning would be forgotten, and the end too, as Crassus said. Unless—as it might be—the end was still to come.

IV

In the beginning, the decision of the Senate was to send six of the City Cohorts to Capua immediately to put down the revolt of the slaves. This was the decision which Gracchus had opposed, and which was, in some measure, carried through to teach him elements of humility. In the light of what followed, the question of humility was recalled by Gracchus with certain bitter satisfaction.

Each of the City Cohorts consisted of five hundred and sixty soldiers—who were armed as the average legionary was, only better and more expensively. The city was a good place to be. The legions went to the ends of the earth, and often enough they never returned but found their graves in foreign soil, and often enough they returned five or ten or fifteen years later. The legions marched all day on a handful of meal, and sweated and worked, built roads and cities in the wilderness, and sometimes the great *urbs* became only a memory to them. The City Cohorts lived on the fat of the land, and for them there was no end of girls, wine, and games. Even a common soldier in a City Cohort was a political factor, and a trickle of money always tickled his palm. Many of these men had good off-duty flats in the city, and some of them supported as many as six female slaves. The tale was told of one city soldier who kept fourteen concubines in a large apartment in Rome and made a profitable business out of raising children to the age of six and then selling them in the public market. Many similar stories were told.

They wore handsome uniforms. All of the cohorts were commanded by young men of good families who were making careers out of the army, but desired their careers within walking distance of the theatre, the arena and the better restaurants. Half of them were friends of Caius, and once or twice he had even toyed with the notion of taking such an appointment himself, but had abandoned the idea as being apart from his peculiar talents. But this kind of command and also the fact that the cohorts were called upon to perform ceremonial parade duty at almost every public function, led to a natural rivalry among the young gentlemen to lead the best uniformed contingent. In the city, the dirty, sweat-soaked leather trousers of the legionary was replaced by softly-tanned and beautifully-dyed doeskin. Each regiment sported a different color, and the privilege of wearing plumes in the helmets was generally given. The *humeralia,* the iron shoulder strips which came down in front and lapped over the breast-plate, were frequently plated with gold or silver. One cohort was armored entirely in brass, and each regiment had a distinctive boot, often knee-high and ornamented with tiny silver bells. Bronze greaves, long since discarded by the frontier legions who found marching miles a day impossible to men whose legs were encased in metal, were still sported by half of the city regiments, and each cohort had a different design for the face of its shields. The quality of their arms and armor was unmatched in all Italy.

It was not that they were poorly trained. The cohorts went through their paces every day in this period. They trained, usually in the early morning, in the *Circus Maximus,* which was then an open race course in the depression of the *Vallis Murcia,* and it was a pleasure to see them go through their movements to the cadenced music of one hundred fifes. On any morning, the hillsides around the circus would be covered with the children of Rome, who watched the military spectacle with delight and envy.

But the fact of the matter was that the cohorts were not legions, and it's one thing to put down a mob of desperate and hungry unemployed or to fight through a political squabble in the narrow city streets, and quite another to go up against Spaniards or Gauls or Germans or Thracians or Jews or Africans. Yet this was no more than an uprising of a handful of slaves, and for all their failings, six of the City Cohorts included better than three and a half thousand Roman soldiers. Even Gracchus granted that in part. He did not, as a matter of principle, like to see the cohorts go more than a day's march from the city walls. But there were twenty-seven cohorts in all, and even Gracchus granted that they could do what they had to do. His opposition stemmed more from a deep-seated fear of these political regiments which consisted not of peasant soldiers but of the city born and bred, the workless, conscienceless, corrupted parasites of Rome, the cast-off and the hopeless who lived their lives in the limbo between the mass of the slaves upon which the society rested and the handful of rulers above. They outnumbered the working people of Rome, the dwindling core of artisans and shopkeepers. They spent their days in the streets or in the arena; they lived on their dole and gambled and bet on the races and sold their votes at each election and strangled their newborn children to escape the responsibility of raising them

171

and spent hours at the baths and lived in the dirty little flats in the towering tenements—and from them were recruited the City Cohorts.

The six cohorts left at the break of dawn, on the day following the decision of the Senate. Their command was given to a young senator, Varinius Glabrus, who was given the token of legate and dispatched as a direct deputy of the Senate. There was no shortage of older men with years of military experience in Rome; but Rome had been wracked for years by an internal struggle for power, and the Senate was exceedingly wary about giving military power into the hands of anyone outside their body. Varinius Glabrus was vain, rather stupid, and politically dependable.

He was thirty-nine years old at the time, and through his mother, he had excellent family connections. He was not unduly ambitious, and both he and his family welcomed the assignment as an opportunity for considerable glory with no uncertainty attached. In selecting him, the Senate majority was strengthening its position with a whole section of the patrician population. The officers under him would do what had to be done in a military way; as to the few decisions he had to make, careful and explicit instructions were given him. He was to lead his men to Capua at field pace, which meant twenty miles a day. All of this distance was along the Appian Way, which meant that wagons would take care of food and water which the ordinary legionary had to carry on his back. He was to bivouac his men outside the walls of Capua, and spend no more than a day in that city receiving intelligence on the progress of the slave revolt and making his plans to suppress it. After that, he was to report his plans to the Senate, but proceed with his plans without waiting for confirmation. He was to deal with the slaves as he found necessary, but was to make every effort to capture the leaders of the revolt, and to return them and as many more as could be taken, to Rome for public trial and punishment. If the council at Capua should request tokens of punishment, he was given the right to crucify ten slaves outside Capua—but only if that represented less than half of those taken prisoner. By explicit order of the Senate, all property rights in the slaves were forfeit to the Senate, and Varinius was instructed that no claims upon them should be honored, although writs for subsequent suits could be accepted and delivered to the Committee for Claims.

This was before there was any indication at Rome of who led the revolt. The name of Spartacus was not yet known, nor was it clearly understood how the revolt at the school of Batiatus had come about. The City Cohorts assembled for parade at the break of dawn, but there was some delay in terms of a dispute among the officers for position of the cohorts. The sun was well up in the sky when they began to march. The stirring military music of their drums and fifes sounded through the city, and when they reached the gates there was quite a crowd assembled to see them go.

Gracchus remembered that very well—well indeed. He and two other senators joined the crowd at the gates, and he recalled what a fine sight it was as the cohorts marched out, the band playing, the banners flying, the standards swaying so proudly, the plumed helmets of the soldiers nodding as they marched, and Varinius at the head of the column, wearing a burnished brass breast-plate, riding a fine white horse, and waving to the crowds who cheered him. There's nothing in the world as stirring as a parade of well-drilled soldiers. Gracchus remembered it well indeed.

V

So the Senate learned the name of Spartacus, and Gracchus could recall the first time he heard the name spoken. Possibly, that was the first time it was spoken aloud at Rome. Unobtrusively, without particular importance or note, it was commented upon by Varinius in the report which he sent by fast post from Capua to the Senate in Rome. The report of Varinius was not a specially inspiring document. It began with the customary, "May it please the noble Senate," and then it went on to detail the few incidents of the march along the Appian Way and the intelligence which had been gathered at Capua. The main feature of the march was that the three cohorts who wore bronze greaves developed painful sores on the instep. Varinius had decided that they should abandon their greaves and have one of the wagons take the armor back to Rome. The officers of the cohorts concerned felt that this was a reflection upon their regimental honor, that their men were being insulted, and that the whole thing would be solved with a little foot-grease. Varinius gave in to them, and as a result, over a hundred men would have to be left at Capua as unfit for duty. Several hundred others were limping, but it was felt that they would be fit enough to participate in the campaign against the slaves.

(Gracchus winced when he heard the word *campaign* used.)

As to the revolt, Varinius was obviously torn between a desire to report the facts—which made little of it—and the opportunity for self-advancement, which would mean making a good deal of it. He inserted a statement by Batiatus concerning the background of the revolt, and he remarked that "it would seem to be led by one, Spartacus, a Thracian, and another, Crixus, a Gaul." Both of these were gladiators, but it was impossible to tell from the report how many gladiators were involved. Varinius told in detail of three separate plantations which had been put to the torch. The slaves on these plantations were unquestionably loyal to their masters, but upon the pain of death they were forced to join the slave-rebels. Those who refused were instantly put to death.

(Gracchus nodded. That was the only way it could be put.)

Two plantation owners had attempted to take refuge in Capua, but they were intercepted by the gladiators and slain by them, and their slaves had been forced to join the revolt. In addition to that, numbers of malcontents among the slaves of the area had run off to join the rebels. Varinius added a long list of atrocities alleged to have been committed by the slaves, which had been taken and attested to. These depositions enumerated additional atrocities on the part of the slaves.

He finished by stating that as far as he knew, the slaves had made their headquarters on the wild and rocky slope of Mount Vesuvius, and that he intended to march there immediately and enforce the will of the Senate upon them.

The Senate received and accepted his report. Also, a resolution was offered and passed in the Senate that some eighty escaped slaves now held for the mines be offered

174

as tokens of punishment, "so that all slaves within the *urbs* might read a warning and a lesson in their fate." The same day, these poor wretches were crucified at the *Circus Maximus,* in an interval during the races. They hung from their crosses while the current favorite, *Aristones,* a magnificent Parthion stallion, lost unexpectedly to *Charos,* a mare from Nubia—bankrupting a considerable section of the sporting blood of Rome.

But no more was heard from Varinius or the City Cohorts for six days. And at the end of the time, a brief report came through. The City Cohorts had been defeated by the slaves. It was a brief report, with no supporting facts, and for twenty-four hours the Senate and the city waited in tense expectation. Everyone talked about the new slave uprising, but no one knew. Nevertheless, fear was all over the city.

VI

The Senate sat in whole session with locked doors, and outside the crowd gathered and grew until the plaza was full and the streets leading into it were blocked, and there was rumor everywhere, because now the Senate knew the story of the City Cohorts.

Only one or two of the chairs were empty. Gracchus, remembering that session, decided that at such moments—moments of crisis and bitter knowledge—the Senate was at its best. The eyes of the old men, who sat so silent in their togas, were full of consequence and without troubled fear, and the faces of the younger men were hard and angry. But all of them were acutely conscious of the dignity of the Roman Senate, and within that context Gracchus could relinquish his cynicism. He knew these men; he knew by what cheap and perverted means they purchased their seats and what a dirty game of politics they played. He knew each and every particular well of filth each and every one of these men kept in his own backyard; and still he felt the thrill and pride of a place among their ranks.

He was not able now to gloat over his own personal victory. His own personal victory was not separable from what they faced, and thereby they chose him as *senator inquaesitor,* and he took their grief and put away his own petty triumph. He stood before them, facing the Roman soldier who had returned, the Roman soldier raised and bred out of the streets and alleys of the city, but now for the first time in his life standing before the august Senate, a thin-faced, dark-eyed man, furtive and frightened, one eye twitching, a tongue that anxiously licked his lips again and again, still in his armor, weaponless, as one comes before the Senate, shaven and at least partially washed, but with a blood-soaked bandage on one arm, and very tired too. Gracchus did what others would not have done. Before he began the formal questioning, he had an attendant bring wine and set it down on a little table next to the soldier. The man was weak and Gracchus did not want him keeling over in a faint. That would not help. The man held in his hands the little ivory rod of the *legate,* the rod that was— they were wont to say—more potent in its power than an invading army, the arm and authority and power of the Senate.

"You may give it to me," Gracchus began.

The soldier did not understand him at first, and then Gracchus took the rod from his hands and laid it upon the altar, feeling his throat tighten and a pain around his heart. He could have contempt for men, men being what they are, but he had no contempt for that little rod which represented all the dignity and power and glory of his life, and which had been handed to Varinius only days before.

Now he asked the soldier, "Your name first?"

"Aralus Porthus."

"Porthus?"

"Aralus Porthus," the soldier repeated.

One of the senators cupped his ear and said, "Louder. Won't you have it louder? Can't hear."

"Speak up," said Gracchus. "No harm will come to you here. Here you are in the sacred chamber of the Senate, to speak the whole truth in the name of the undying gods. Speak up!"

The soldier nodded.

"Take some wine," Gracchus said.

The soldier looked from face to face, the rows of stolid, white-robed men, the stone seats in which they sat like graven images, and then he poured a glass of wine with a shaking hand, poured until it overflowed, gulped it, and licked his lips again.

"How old are you?" Gracchus asked.

"Twenty-five years."

"And where were you born?"

"Here—in the *urbs*."

"Have you a trade?"

The man shook his head.

"I want you to answer each question. I want you to say yes or no at least. If you can answer in more detail, do so."

"No—I have no trade except war," the soldier said.

"What was your regiment?"

"The Third Cohort."

"And for how long were you a soldier in the Third Cohort?"

"Two years—and two months."

"Before then?"

"I lived on the dole."

"Who was your commander in the Third?"

"Silvius Caius Salvarius."

"And your hundred?"

"Marius Gracchus Alvio."

"Very well, Aralus Porthus. Now I desire you to tell me and the honored senators assembled here exactly what happened after your cohort and the other five cohorts marched south from Capua. You are to tell it to me directly and clearly. Nothing you say will be held against you, and here in this sacred chamber, you can come to no harm."

Still, it was not easy for the soldier to talk coherently, and to Gracchus, years later, sitting in the gentle springtime morning on the terrace of the *Villa Salaria*, the memories of the sharp and ominous pictures evoked by the soldier's words were clearer than the words themselves. It was not a very satisfied or cheerful army that had marched south from Capua under the leadership of Varinius Glabrus. The weather had turned unseasonably hot, and the City Cohorts, unused to constant marching, suffered a good deal. Though they were carrying twenty pounds less per man than the legionary carried on the march, still they bore the weight of helmet and armor, shield, spear and sword. They developed sores where the edges of the hot metal rubbed against their flesh, and they discovered that the soft and

177

beautiful parade boots which showed so proudly as they strutted back and forth across the *Circus Maximus* were less useful on road and field. Afternoon showers drenched them, and as evening came they were bitter and morose.

Gracchus could picture them very well indeed, the long column of soldiers, off the Appian Way now, plodding along a dirt-surfaced cart track, the wet plumes dragging from their brazen helmets, even the voice of complaint gone in their tiredness. It was about then that they caught the four field slaves and killed them—three men and one woman.

"Why did you kill them?" Gracchus interrupted.

"We felt that every slave in that part of the country was against us."

"If they were against you, why would they come down from the hills to the road to watch the columns march by?"

"I don't know. It was in the Second Cohort that they did it. They broke ranks and grabbed the woman. The men tried to protect her, so they speared the men. It just took a minute, and the men were dead. When I got there—"

"You mean that your regiment broke ranks as well?" Gracchus demanded.

"Yes, sir. The whole army. We crowded around—those of us who could get close to what was happening. They pulled the clothes off her and had her spread-eagled naked on the ground. Then, one after another, they—"

"You need not go into the details of that," Gracchus interrupted. "Did your officers interfere?"

"No, sir."

"You mean they permitted this to go on without interference?"

The soldier stood for a moment without answering.

"I want you to answer the truth. I don't want you to be afraid to answer the truth."

"The officers didn't interfere."

"How was the woman killed?"

"She died from what they were doing to her," the soldier responded softly. Then they had to ask him to speak up again. His voice almost faded away entirely.

He told of how they made camp that night. Two cohorts did not even raise their tents. The night was warm and the soldiers bedded down on an open field. He was interrupted here.

"Did your commander make an attempt to establish a fortified camp? Do you know whether he did or not?"

It was the pride of the Roman army that no legion camped anywhere even for one night without building a fortified camp, palisaded or earth-walled, ditched, staked, laid out like a small castle or city.

"I know what the men said."

"Tell us that."

"They said that Varinius Glabrus wanted it, but the regimental commanders resisted it. The men said that even if they all agreed, there were no engineers with us, and that the whole thing hadn't been planned with any sense or meaning. They said—please, the noble—"

"Tell us what they said without fear."

"Yes, they said there was no sense or meaning in the way the thing was planned. But the officers argued that a handful of slaves didn't represent any danger. It was already on to nightfall, and as I heard it, the officers' argument was that if Varinius Glabrus wanted a fortified camp, then why had he marched us until dusk? The men were saying that too. This was the worst march of the whole journey. First on the dusty roads, so choked with dust that we couldn't breathe, and then in the pouring rain. It was all right for the officers, they said, riding on their horses, but we had to walk. But the argument was that now we had the carts with us carrying our baggage, and while the carts were with us, we should make all the distance we could."

"Where were you then?"

"Close to the mountain—"

Yes, it was better recalled in the pictures evoked than from the flat words of the frightened, unimaginative soldier who was giving the testimony. And some of these pictures were so clear in the mind of Gracchus that he could almost believe that he had seen it with his own eyes. The dirt road narrowing to the merest cart track. The lovely fields and pastures of the *latifundia* giving way to the tangled woods and lonely outcroppings of volcanic rock that bordered the crater. And over all, the brooding majesty of Vesuvius. The six cohorts strung out over a mile of roadway. The baggage carts lurching in the ruts. The men disgruntled and weary. And then, ahead of them, a great ridge of rock, and underneath it a little open field with a brook running through it, buttercups and daisies and soft grass, and night-fall coming.

They made their camp there, and Varinius gave in to the officers on the question of fortifications. That, too, Gracchus could visualize. The regimental commanders would point out that they led better than three thousand heavily armed Roman soldiers. What possibility was there of attack? What danger was there of attack? Even at the outset of the revolt, the gladiators had numbered only two hundred or so; and many of those had been killed. And the men were very tired. Some of them lay down on the grass and fell asleep immediately. A few cohorts raised tents and made an attempt at a disciplined laying out of regimental streets. Most of the cohorts prepared cook fires, but since there was a large supply of bread in the baggage carts, some dispensed with even that. Such was the picture of the camp made in the shadow of the mountain. Varinius raised his tent at the very center of the camp, and there he planted his standard and his Senatorial Ensign. The people of Capua had prepared great hampers of beautifully cooked delicacies. He would sit down with his senior officers and make a meal of it—perhaps relieved that the arduous task of building fortifications would not have to be faced. After all, it was not the worst campaign in the world, honor and perhaps a little glory, and all of it only a few days march from the great city.

So, in his memory, on his inward eye that raised him from the beasts and separated him from the beasts, Gracchus reflected and recalled the pictures that made up the beginning. Memory is the joy and sorrow of mankind. Gracchus sat sprawled in the sunshine, looking into the glass of morning water he held in his hand, and listening to the far echo of the one miserable soldier who had come back with the ivory rod of the legate in his hand. Pictures came. What is it like for those who face death in a few hours, but know it not at all? Had Varinius Glabrus ever heard the name of Spartacus? Probably not.

"I remember how night fell, and all the stars were in the sky," the soldier said to the stony-faced senators.

The simple beauty of a fool's speech. Night fell, and Varinius Glabrus and his officers must have sat in his great

180

pavilion drinking wine and nibbling the flesh from honied squabs. There must have been good talk that night, clever talk. Here were a number of young gentlemen of the most sophisticated society the world had ever seen. What had they probably talked about? Now, four years later, Gracchus tried to recall what had been popular then—in the theatre, at the track, in the arena? Wasn't it shortly after a new production of Pacuvius's *Armorum Iudicium?* And hadn't Flavius Gallis sung the leading role as it had never been sung before? (Or was that always a fancy, that a role was sung or played as it had never been sung or played before?) Yet it might have been, and perhaps the young men of the City Cohorts lifted their voices over their wine:

"Men' servasse ut essent qui me perderent?"

Rolling forth and heard through the camp—well, possibly. Memory was a fanciful thing. Tiredness must have gone away everywhere in that camp. The men of the City Cohorts lay upon their backs, munching bread and looking at the stars, those of them who hadn't raised tents. And so sleep came, gentle sleep came to the three thousand and several hundred soldiers of Rome who had marched south to Mount Vesuvius to teach slaves that slaves must not lift their hands against their masters . . .

Gracchus was *senator inquaesitor.* His to ask the questions, and between the answers of the soldier there was such a silence in the Senate chamber that one might have heard the wings of a fly brushing the air.

"You slept?" asked Gracchus.

"I slept," answered the single frightened soldier who had returned to bear witness.

"And what awakened you?"

Here the soldier groped for speech. His face became very white, and Gracchus thought he was going to faint. But he did not faint, and here his report became precise and clear, but emotionless. This is what he said happened, as he saw it:

"I went to sleep, and then I woke up because someone was screaming. At least, I thought that one man was screaming, but when I woke up I realized that there was a great scream of many men in the air, and the air was full of it. I woke up and rolled over immediately. I sleep on my belly, that is why I rolled over. Lying next to me was Callius, who has only one name, an orphan from the streets, but he was my first and favorite friend. He was my right hand support, and that is why we slept side by side, and when I rolled over my right wrist went into something wet and hot and soft, and when I looked I saw that it was the neck of Callius, but the neck cut all through, and all the time that scream kept on screaming. Then I sat up in a pool of blood, and I didn't know whether it was my blood or not, but all around me in the moonlight were the dead; lying where they had slept, and the whole camp was filled with slaves who were armed with razor-sharp knives, and up and down went these knives, flashing in the moonlight, and that was the way we were killed, half of us while we slept. And when a man sprang to his feet, they killed him too. And here and there a few soldiers made a little group, but they didn't fight long. It was the most terrible thing I ever saw in my life, and the slaves never stopped killing. Then I lost my head, and I began to scream too. I am not ashamed to say that. I drew my sword and dashed through the camp, and I cut at a slave and killed him, I think, but when I came to the edge of the meadow, there was a solid line of spears all around the camp, and most of those who held the spears were women, but they were not women such as I had ever seen or dreamed of, but terrible, wild things and their hair was blowing in the night wind and their mouths were open in a terrible scream of hate. That was part of the scream, and there was a soldier who dashed past me and drove onto the spears, because he didn't think the women would spear him, but they did, and no one escaped from that place, and when the wounded came crawling, they drove their spears into them too. I ran up to the line and they put a spear in my arm, so I tore away and ran back into the camp, and then I fell in the blood and lay there. I lay there with my ears full of that screaming. I don't know how long I lay there. It didn't seem very long. I said to myself, you will get up and fight and die, but I waited. Then the screaming became less, and then hands grasped me and pulled me to my feet, and I would have struck at them with my sword, but they knocked it out of my hand, and there was no strength in my hand because of the pain of the spear cut. Slaves held me and a knife went up to cut my throat, and then I knew it was all finished and I would die too. But someone called out, *wait!* And the knife waited. It waited an inch from my throat.

Then a slave strode up, he too with a Thracian knife in his hand, and he said to them, Wait. *I think he's the only one.* They stood there and waited. My life waited. Then a slave with red hair came up, and they talked back and forth. I was the only one. That's why they didn't kill me. I was the only one, and all the rest were dead. They took me through the camp, and the cohorts were dead. Most of them were dead where they slept. They never woke up. They took me to the pavilion of Varinius Glabrus, the legate, but the legate was dead. He lay on his couch, dead. Some officers of the cohorts were in the pavilion, where they had been killed. All dead. Then they bound up the wound in my arm and left me there with some slaves to guard me. Now the sky was becoming gray and dawn was in the air. But all the cohorts were dead."

This he said without emotion, in a straightforward, matter of fact narrative, but his eye kept twitching all the time, and he ever looked at the rows of senators who sat with such stony faces.

"How do you know they were all dead?" demanded Gracchus.

"They kept me there in the pavilion until dawn came. The sides of the pavilion were rolled up, and I could see all over the bivouac. The screaming had stopped now, but I still heard it inside of my head. I could look around, and everywhere I looked the dead lay on the ground. The smell of blood and death was in the air. Most of the women who made the circle of spears were not there now. They went away somewhere. I don't know where they went. But through the smell of blood, I could smell meat roasting. Maybe the women were cooking meat for breakfast. It made me sick to think that people could eat now. I vomited. The slaves dragged me out of the pavilion until I had finished vomiting. It was getting lighter now. I saw groups of slaves going through the camp. They were stripping the dead. Here and there they spread out our tents. I could see these white spots on the ground all over the place. They took everything that the dead were wearing, armor and clothes and boots, and made piles of it on the outspread tents. The swords and spears and armor they washed in the brook. The brook ran near the pavilion and it turned the color of rust, just from the bloody arms and armor they washed in it. Then they took our grease pots, and after they dried the metal, they greased it. One of the tents was spread out a few paces from the pavilion. They stacked the swords on that one, thousands of swords—"

"How many slaves were there?" asked Gracchus.

"Seven, eight hundred a—thousand maybe. I don't know. They were working in groups of ten. They worked very hard. Some of them harnessed our baggage wagons and loaded them with what they had stripped from the dead, and drove them away. While they worked, some of the women came back with baskets of roasted meat. One group at a time would stop to eat. They ate our bread rations, too."

"What did they do with the dead?"

"Nothing. They left them there where they were. They moved around as if the dead were not there at all, once they had stripped everything off them. The dead were everywhere. The ground was carpeted with them, and the ground was soaked with blood. Now the sun had come up. It was the worst thing I ever saw. Now I saw a group of slaves standing at one side of the field, watching what was going on. There were six in the group. One of them was a black man, an African. They were gladiators."

"How did you know?"

"When they came over to where I was, in the pavilion, I could see that they were gladiators. Their hair was cropped to their skulls and they had scar-marks all over their bodies. It's not hard to tell a gladiator. One of them was missing an ear. One had red hair. But the leader of the group was a Thracian. He had a broken nose and black eyes that looked at you without moving and without blinking—"

Now there was a change among the senators, almost imperceptible but there nevertheless. They were listening in a new way; they were listening with hatred and tension and added intensity. Very well indeed did Gracchus remember that moment, for that was when Spartacus came to life, emerged out of nowhere to rock the whole world. Other men have roots, a past, a beginning, a place, a land, a country—but Spartacus had none of these. He was born on the lips of a soldier who survived and whose survival was engineered by Spartacus for that very purpose—for the purpose of having him return to the Senate to say, it was such and such a man. It was not a giant of a man, not a wild man, not a terrible man, simply a slave; but there was something that the soldier saw which had to be told in detail.

"—and the face reminded me of a sheep. He wore a tunic and a heavy brass belt and high boots, but no armor or helmet. He had a knife in the belt, and that was all the arms he had. His tunic was splattered with blood. He had the kind of a face you don't forget. He made me afraid of him. I wasn't afraid of the others, but I was afraid of him." The soldier might have told them of seeing that face in his dreams, of waking up in a cold sweat and seeing that flat, tanned face with the broken nose and the black eyes, but those were not the details of information that one gave to the Senate. The Senate was not interested in his dreams.

"How do you know he is a Thracian?"

"I could tell from his accent. He spoke bad Latin, and I've heard Thracians speak. One of the others was a Thracian and maybe the rest were Gauls. They just looked at me, just glanced at me. It made me feel that I was dead with the others. They glanced at me and walked past to the other section of the pavilion. The bodies had been taken out of the pavilion now and thrown on the ground outside with the bodies of the soldiers. But first they had stripped Varinius Glabrus naked, and all his armor and all the things he had were stacked on his couch. His legate's staff was on the couch too. The slaves came back and gathered around the couch, looking at the armor and the possessions of the commander. They picked up the sword and examined it and passed it around. It had an ivory scabbard, covered with carving. They looked at it, and then they threw it back on the couch. Then they examined the staff. The man with the broken nose—his name is Spartacus—turned to me and held up the staff and asked me, *Roman, do you know what this is? It's the arm of the noble Senate,* I answered. But they didn't know. I had to explain it to them. Spartacus and the red headed Gaul sat down on the couch. The others remained standing. Spartacus put his chin in his hands, his elbows on his knees, and kept his eyes fixed on me. It was like having a snake look at you. Then when I had finished talking, they said nothing, and Spartacus kept on staring at me. I could feel the sweat pouring from all over my skin. I thought they were going to kill me. Then he told me his name. *My name is Spartacus,* he said. *Re-*

member my name, Roman. And then they stared at me
again. And then Spartacus said, *Why did you kill the three
slaves yesterday, Roman? The slaves did you no harm.
They came down to look at the soldiers marching past.
Are the women of Rome so virtuous that a whole legion
must rape one poor slave woman? Why did you do it,
Roman?* I tried to tell him what had happened. I told him
that the Second Cohort had raped her and killed the slaves.
I told him that I was in the Third Cohort, and that I had
nothing to do with it and that I had not raped the woman.
I don't know how they found out about that, because there
seemed to be no one else around when the three slaves
were killed. But they knew everything that we did. They
knew when we came to Capua. They knew when we left
Capua. It was all in his black snake eyes that never blinked.
It was all in his voice. He never raised his voice. He talked
to me the way someone talks to a child, but he didn't fool
me talking to me like that. He was a killer. It was in his
eyes. It was in the eyes of all of them. All killers. I know
gladiators like that. Gladiators become killers. No one else
but gladiators could have killed the way they killed that
night. I know gladiators who—"

Gracchus interrupted him. He was in and under the spell
of his own speech, like a man in a trance, and rather
sharply Gracchus said to him,

"We are not interested in what you know, soldier. We
are interested in what happened between you and the
slaves."

"This happened," the soldier began, and then he stopped.
He came awake and looked from face to face of the noble
Senate of mighty Rome. He shivered and said,

"Then I waited for them to tell me what they were going
to do with me. Spartacus sat there, and he had the staff in
his hand. He ran his fingers up and down its length and then
he suddenly thrust it at me. I didn't know at first what he
meant or what he wanted. *Take it, soldier,* he said. *Take it,
Roman. Take it.* I took it. *Now you are the arm of the
noble Senate,* he said. He didn't seem angry. He never
raised his voice. He was just stating a fact—I mean it was
a fact to him. That was what he wanted. There was nothing
I could do. Otherwise, I would have died before I touched
the sacred rod. I would not have touched it. I'm a Roman.
I'm a citizen—"

"You will not be punished for that," Gracchus said. "Go on."

"Now you are the arm of the noble Senate, Spartacus said again. *The noble Senate has a long arm, and all there is on the end of it now is yourself.* So I took the rod—I held it, and still he sat there with his eyes fixed on me, and then he asked me, *Are you a citizen, Roman?* I told him I was a citizen. He nodded and smiled a little. *Now you are a legate,* he said. *I will give you a message. Take it to the noble Senate. Word for word—take it to them as I give it to you."* Then he stopped. He stopped speaking, and the Senate waited. Gracchus waited too. He didn't want to ask him for the message of a slave. Yet it would have to be spoken. Spartacus had come out of nowhere—but now he stood in the midst of the Senate Chamber, and Gracchus saw him then as he saw him so many times afterwards, even though he never saw the flesh and blood that was Spartacus.

And finally, Gracchus told the soldier to speak.

"I can't."

"The Senate commands you to speak."

"These were the words of a slave. May my own tongue dry up—"

"That's enough of that," Gracchus said. "Tell us what this slave told you to tell us."

So the soldier spoke the words of Spartacus. This was what Spartacus said to him—as nearly as Gracchus could recall it all the years later; and recalling it, Gracchus had a picture of how the *praetorium* must have been, the great pavilion of a Roman commander with its gay blue and yellow stripes, standing in the center of that field of naked dead, the slave Spartacus sitting on the commander's couch, his general staff of gladiators grouped around him, and in front of him the frightened, wounded Roman soldier, the single survivor, held by two slaves and holding in turn the delicate rod of power, the legate's staff, the arm of the Senate!

"Go back to the Senate (said Spartacus) and give them the ivory rod. I make you legate. Go back and tell them what you saw here. Tell them that they sent their cohorts against us, and that we destroyed their cohorts. Tell them that we are slaves—what they call the *instrumentum vocale.* The tool with a voice. Tell them what our voice says. We say that the world is tired of them, tired of your rotten

187

Senate and your rotten Rome. The world is tired of the wealth and splendor that you have squeezed out of our blood and bone. The world is tired of the song of the whip. It is the only song the noble Romans know. But we don't want to hear that song any more. In the beginning, all men were alike and they lived in peace and they shared among them what they had. But now there are two kinds of men, the master and the slave. But there are more of us than there are of you, many more. And we are stronger than you, better than you. All that is good in mankind belongs to us. We cherish our women and stand next to them and fight beside them. But you turn your women into whores and our women into cattle. We weep when our children are torn from us and we hide our children among the sheep, so that we may have them a little longer; but you raise your children like you raise cattle. You breed children from our women, and you sell them in the slave market to the highest bidder. You turn men into dogs, and send them into the arena to tear themselves to pieces for your pleasure, and as your noble Roman ladies watch us kill each other, they fondle dogs in their laps and feed them precious tidbits. What a foul crew you are and what a filthy mess you have made of life! You have made a mockery of all men dream of, of the work of a man's hands and the sweat of a man's brow. Your own citizens live on the dole and spend their days in the circus and the arena. You have made a travesty of human life and robbed it of all its worth. You kill for the sake of killing, and your gentle amusement is to watch blood flow. You put little children into your mines and work them to death in a few months. And you have built your grandeur by being a thief to the whole world. Well, it is finished. Tell your Senate that it is all finished. That is the voice of the tool. Tell your Senate to send their armies against us, and we will destroy those armies as we destroyed this one, and we will arm ourselves with the weapons of the armies you send against us. The whole world will hear the voice of the tool—and to the slaves of the world, we will cry out, Rise up and cast off your chains! We will move through Italy, and wherever we go, the slaves will join us—and then, one day, we will come against your eternal city. It will not be eternal then. Tell your Senate that. Tell them that we will let them know when we are coming. Then we will tear down the walls of

Rome. Then we will come to the house where your Senate sits, and we will drag them out of their high and mighty seats, and we will tear off their robes so that they may stand naked and be judged as we have always been judged. But we will judge them fairly and we will hand them a full measure of justice. Every crime they have committed will be held against them, and they will make a full accounting. Tell them that, so that they may have time to prepare themselves and to examine themselves. They will be called to bear witness, and we have long memories. Then, when justice has been done, we will build better cities, clean, beautiful cities without walls—where mankind can live together in peace and in happiness. There is the whole message for the Senate. Bear it to them. Tell them it comes from a slave called Spartacus . . ."

So the soldier told it, or in some such fashion—it was so long ago, thought Gracchus—and so the Senate heard it, their faces like stone. But it was long ago. It was so long ago, and most of it forgotten already, and the words of Spartacus not written down, and existing nowhere except in the memories of a few men. Even from the records of the Senate those words were expunged. It was right. Of course it was—just as right as it was to destroy those monuments the slaves had set up and to pound them into a rubble of stone. Crassus understood that, even though Crassus was something of a fool. A man had to be a little bit of a fool to be a great general. Unless he was Spartacus, for Spartacus had been a great general. Had he been a fool too? Were those words the words of a fool? Then how does a fool, for four long years, resist the power of Rome, smashing one Roman army after another and making Italy a graveyard for the legions? How then? They say he is dead, but others say that the dead live. Is this the living image of him walking toward Gracchus—a giant in size, a giant of a man, and yet so much the same, the broken nose, the black eyes, the tight curls against his skull? Do the dead walk?

VII

"Look at old Gracchus," said Antonius Caius, smiling at the way the politician's big head had fallen forward—yet he kept his goblet of scented water balanced so that not a drop spilled.

"Don't make fun of him!" said Julia.

"Who laughs at Gracchus? No one, I say, my dear Julia," said Cicero. "I will strive all my life for such dignity."

"And always fall a good deal short of it," thought Helena.

Gracchus woke up, blinking. "Was I sleeping?" It was typical of him that he turned to Julia. "My dear, I beg your pardon. I was daydreaming."

"Of good things?"

"Of old things. I don't think man is blessed with memory. More often he is cursed with it. I have too many memories."

"No more than the next man," offered Crassus. "We all have our memories, equally unpleasant."

"And never pleasant?" asked Claudia.

"My memory of you, my dear," Gracchus rumbled, "will be like sunshine until the day I die. Permit an old man to say that."

"She would permit a young man too," laughed Antonius Caius. "Crassus was telling us, while you slept—"

"Must we talk of nothing but Spartacus?" cried Julia. "Is there nothing but politics and war? I detest that talk—"

"Julia," Antonius Caius interrupted.

She stopped, swallowed hastily, and then looked at him. He spoke to her as one does to a difficult child.

"Julia, Crassus is our guest. It is pleasing to the company to hear him tell us things we could not learn in any other way. I think it might be pleasing to you, too, Julia, if you would listen."

Her mouth tightened and her eyes became red and watery. She inclined her head, but Crassus was gracious in his apology.

"It bores me as much as it does you, Julia, my dear. Forgive me."

"I think Julia would like to listen, wouldn't you, Julia?" Antonius Caius said. "Wouldn't you, Julia?"

"Yes," she whispered. "Please continue, Crassus."

"No—no, not at all—"

"I was foolish and behaved badly," Julia said, as if repeating a lesson. "Please continue."

Gracchus stepped into what was degenerating into an exceedingly unpleasant situation. He turned it away from

Julia onto Crassus, saying, "I'm sure I can guess the general's thesis. He was telling you that the slaves won their battles because they had no regard for human life. Their hordes poured onto us and overwhelmed us. Am I correct, Crassus?"

"You could hardly be more incorrect," Helena laughed.

Gracchus allowed himself to be the butt, and was even tolerant of Cicero when the young man said, "I always suspected, Gracchus, that anyone whose propaganda was as good as yours had of necessity to believe it."

"Some of it," Gracchus admitted tolerantly. "Rome is great because Rome exists. Spartacus is contemptible because Spartacus is no more than those tokens of punishment. That is the factor one must consider. Wouldn't you agree, Crassus?"

The general nodded. "Yet," said Cicero, "there were five great battles Spartacus won. Not those battles where he drove back the legions—not even those where he put them to flight. I refer to the five times he destroyed Consular Armies, destroyed them and wiped them from the face of the earth and took their arms. Crassus was making the point that Spartacus was less a brilliant master of tactics than a fortunate—or unfortunate, as you look at it—leader of a particular group of men. They were undefeatable because they could not afford the luxury of defeat. Isn't that the point you were making, Crassus?"

"To an extent," the general admitted. He smiled at Julia. "Let me illustrate with a story that will please you more, Julia. Some war, some politics, and something of Varinia. That was the woman of Spartacus, you know."

"I know," Julia answered softly. She looked at Gracchus with relief and with gratitude. "I know," Gracchus said to himself. "I know, my dear Julia. We are both somewhat pathetic and somewhat ridiculous, the main difference being that I am a man and you are a woman. You could not become pompous. But essentially we are the same, with the same empty tragedy in our lives. We are both in love with ghosts, because we never learned how to love or be loved by human beings."

"I always thought," said Claudia, rather unexpectedly, "that someone had invented her."

"Why, my dear?"

"There are no such women," Claudia said flatly.

"No? Well, perhaps. It is hard to say what is true and what isn't true. I read of an action I myself fought in, and what I read had very little to do with the reality. That's how it is. I don't vouch for the truth of this, but I have every reason to believe it. Yes, I think I believe it."

There was a strange note in his voice, and looking at him sharply, Helena realized suddenly how handsome he was. Sitting there on the terrace in the morning sunshine, his fine, strong face was reminiscent of the legendary past of the young republic. But for some reason, the thought was not pleasant, and she glanced sidewise at her brother. Caius had his eyes fixed upon the general in a sort of rapt worship. The others did not notice this. Crassus commanded attention; his low, sincere voice gripped them and held them, even Cicero who looked at him with a new awareness. And Gracchus remarked again what he had noticed earlier, the quality whereby Crassus could evoke passion without being the least bit passionate.

"Just a word in general to preface this," Crassus began. "When I took command, the war had been going on for a good many years, as you know. It's always delicate to step into a lost cause, and when the war is servile, there's precious little glory in victory and unspeakable shame in defeat. Cicero is quite correct. Five armies had been destroyed by Spartacus, wholly destroyed." He nodded at Gracchus. "Your propaganda is tempting, but you will admit that I had to look at the situation as it was?"

"Of course."

"I found there were no hordes of slaves. There was never an occasion when we did not outnumber them, if the whole truth is to be told. That was true at the beginning. It was true at the end. If Spartacus ever had under his command anything like the three hundred thousand men he was supposed to have led, then we would not be sitting here today on this pleasant morning at the loveliest country home in Italy. Spartacus would have taken Rome and the world too. Others may doubt that. But I fought against Spartacus enough times not to doubt it. I know. The whole truth is that the mass of the slaves of Italy never joined Spartacus. Do you think, if they were made of such metal, that we would be sitting here like this on a plantation were the slaves outnumber us a hundred to one? Of course, many joined him, but he never led more than forty-five thousand fighting men—and that was only at the height of his power. He never had cavalry, such as Hannibal did, yet he brought Rome closer to her knees than Hannibal ever did—a Rome so powerful that it could have crushed Hannibal in a single campaign. No, only the best, the wildest, the most desperate, joined Spartacus.

"That was something I had to find out by myself. I was ashamed of Rome when I found what a state of panic and illusion these slaves had created. I wanted the truth. I wanted to know precisely what I was fighting, what kind of a man, what kind of an army. I wanted to know why the best troops in the world, who had fought and smashed everything from Germans to Spaniards to Jews, should throw down their shields and run away at the sight of these slaves. I had made my camp in Cisalpine Gaul then, a camp Spartacus would think twice of before attacking, and I went into the matter. I have few virtues, but one of them is thoroughness, and I must have interviewed a hundred people and read a thousand documents. Among them was Batiatus, the *lanista*. Among them was a stream of soldiers and officers who had fought against Spartacus. And this tale was told to me by one of them. And I believe it."

"If the story is as long as the introduction," Antonius Caius remarked, "we'll have our lunch here." The slaves were already bringing Egyptian melon and grapes and a light morning wine. It was cool and delightful on the terrace, and even those who planned to continue their journey this day were in no hurry to move.

"Longer. But a rich man is listened to—"

"Go on," said Gracchus gruffly.

"I intend to. This tale is for Julia. With your permission, Julia."

She nodded, and Gracchus thought, "You would not suspect him of insight. What the devil is he driving at?"

"This was on the occasion of the second destruction of a Roman army by Spartacus. The first occasion, the case of the City Cohorts, I imagine my friend Gracchus recalls only too well—as we all do, of course," Crassus said, a malicious note in his voice. "After that, the Senate sent Publius against him. A full legion and a very good one, I think. It was the Third, wasn't it, Gracchus?"

"Thoroughness is your virtue, not mine."

"I think I'm right. And if I'm not mistaken, some city

193

cavalry went with the legion—about seven thousand men in all. Julia," he said, "please believe that there is nothing particularly mysterious about warfare. It requires more brains to make money or to weave a piece of linen than it does to be a good general. Most people whose business is war are not very clever—for obvious reasons. Spartacus was quite clever. He understood a few simple rules of warfare, and he understood the strength and weaknesses of Roman arms. Few others ever had. Hannibal did, but few others. Our esteemed contemporary, Pompey, does not, I'm afraid."

"And are we to hear these sublime secrets?" Cicero asked.

"They are neither sublime nor particularly secret. I repeat them for Julia. They seem to be something impossible for a man to learn. The first rule is never to split your forces unless it is necessary for survival. The second rule is to attack if you are going to fight, and if you are not going to attack, avoid battle. The third rule is to choose the time and place of battle and never leave that choice to the enemy. The fourth rule is to avoid encirclement at all cost. And the final rule is to attack and destroy the enemy where he is weakest."

"That sort of ABC," commented Cicero, "can be found in any manual of arms, Crassus. It lacks profundity, if I may say so. It is all too simple."

"Perhaps. But nothing so simple lacks profundity—I assure you."

"And just to complete it," said Gracchus, "what are these strengths and weaknesses of Roman arms?"

"Something equally simple, and Cicero, I'm sure, will disagree with me again."

"I'm a willing student at the feet of a great general," Cicero said lightly.

Crassus shook his head. "No, indeed. Two things all men are convinced they have talent for, with neither preparation nor study involved. Writing a book and leading an army. And with good reason, since such an amazing number of idiots get to do both. I refer to myself, of course," he added disarmingly.

"That's very clever," said Helena.

Crassus nodded at her. He was concerned with women, but not really interested in them; in any case, that was

Helena's opinion. "As to our own army," Crassus went on, "its weaknesses and its strength can be summed up in one word, discipline. We have the most disciplined army in the world—perhaps the only disciplined army. A good legion drills its troops five hours a day, seven days a week. The drill provides for a series of contingencies of battle, but it cannot provide for all. The discipline is to an extent mechanical, and when the new contingency arrives, the discipline meets its test. Also, we have an excellent attack army; its whole advantage is attack and its weapons are weapons of attack. That is why the legion builds a fortified camp whenever it halts for the night. The Achilles heel of the legion is night attack. The first tactic of Roman arms is our own choice of ground for battle. But that is a luxury Spartacus rarely permitted us. And Publius, when he took the Third Legion down south, violated all of these exceedingly simple propositions. Understandably so. He had nothing but contempt for Spartacus."

The two daughters of Antonius Caius joined the party on the terrace now. They came running, flushed with laughter and play and excitement, and found refuge in Julia's arms only in time to hear the last words of Crassus.

"Did you know Spartacus?" the older one asked. "Did you see him?"

"I never saw him," smiled Crassus. "But I respected him, my dear."

Gracchus peeled an apple gravely and observed Crassus through narrowed eyes. He did not like Crassus, and he reflected that he had never met a military man whom he felt any warmth or affection for. He held up the skin of the apple in one long piece, and the little girls clapped their hands in delight. They reached for it, but he insisted that they make a wish first. "Then fold the skin around your wish. The apple contains all knowledge."

"And an occasional worm," Julia remarked. "This was a story about Varinia, Crassus."

"We meet her presently. I simply propose the background. Spartacus was still in the region of Vesuvius at this time. And Publius, like the fool he was, divided his troops into three parts, each containing somewhat more than two thousand men, and began to beat up that difficult country—looking for Spartacus. In three separate engagements, Spartacus wiped his army off the face of the earth. He did the same thing each time, caught them in a narrow defile where the maniples could not deploy, and destroyed them. However, in one of the instances, a full cohort of cavalry and the best part of a cohort of infantry managed to break loose and beat their way out, the infantry hanging on to the horses' tails, and the horses going hell for leather. If you understand how the slaves fought, you know that they don't allow something like that to divert them. They concentrate on what is at hand. Which is what they did, and the eight or nine hundred infantry and cavalry retreated through the woods, got lost, and turned up at the camp of the slaves where the women and children were. I say camp—but it was more of a small village. It had a ditch around it, a dirt wall, and a palisade on top of that. There must have been a good many legion deserters with Spartacus, for this was built the way we lay out a camp, and the huts inside were laid out on regular streets. Well, the gates were open and there were a number of children playing outside and some women watching them. You must understand that when soldiers have been beaten and have run away, most of their controls are gone. Nor do I sit in judgment on those who kill slaves, whether child or woman or man. We have reason enough to hate the filth, and those soldiers were full of hate. They swarmed down on the place, and the cavalrymen speared the children the way you spear rabbits. They killed some of the women too in the first rush, but others of the women fought back, and then the women in the village poured out of the gate, armed with knives and swords and spears. I don't know what the soldiers had in mind—if anything more than hate and revenge. They would have killed some of the women, I suppose, and raped the others. You recall that a very bad feeling was all over the country about slaves then. Before Spartacus, if a man killed one of his own women slaves, he could not go out in the street and hold up his head. It was regarded as more or less of a degrading act, and if it could be proved that he acted without reason, he could be heavily fined. That law was changed three years ago, wasn't it, Gracchus?"

"It was," said Gracchus without pleasure. "But go on with your story. It was about Varinia."

"Yes?" Crassus seemed to have forgotten for a moment.

Julia was looking past him onto the lawns. "Run off now," she said to her children. "Run off and play."

"You mean the women fought the soldiers?" Claudia wanted to know.

"That was the point," Crassus nodded. "There was a terrible battle there at the gate. Yes, the women fought the soldiers. And the soldiers went mad and forgot that they were fighting women. The battle went on for almost an hour, I guess. As it was told, the women were led by this wild berserk with blond hair, who was supposed to have been Varinia. She was everywhere. Her clothes were torn off, and she fought naked with a spear. She was like a fury—"

"I don't believe any of it," Gracchus interrupted.

"No need to believe it if you don't want to," Crassus nodded, realizing that his story had failed miserably. "I only told it for Julia."

"Why for me?" Julia demanded.

Staring at him intently, Helena said, "Please finish the story. Whether it's true or not. It has an end, hasn't it?"

"A common end. All battles have essentially the same end. You win them or you lose them. We lost this. Some slaves returned, and between them and the women, only a handful of cavalry escaped. They made the report."

"But Varinia was not killed?"

"If that was Varinia, she was certainly not killed. She turns up again and again."

"And is she alive now?" Claudia asked.

"Is she alive now?" Crassus repeated. "It doesn't matter, does it?"

Now Gracchus rose, threw his toga back in characteristic gesture, and stalked off. There was a little bit of silence, and then Cicero asked,

"What's eating the old man?"

"God only knows."

"Why do you say it doesn't matter whether Varinia is alive now?" Helena wanted to know.

"The business is over, isn't it?" Crassus said flatly. "Spartacus is dead. Varinia is a slave woman. The market in Rome is glutted with them. Varinia and ten thousand others." His voice was suddenly full of anger . . .

Antonius Caius excused himself and went after Gracchus. It disturbed him that two such men as Gracchus and Crassus, bound together as they were politically, should have a falling out about nothing at all. He had never known Gracchus to behave like this before. Could it be over Julia, he wondered? No—not with old Gracchus, not with fat, womanless old Gracchus. Gracchus was many things, but Antonius Caius could never regard him as other than a capon in matters of sex. And why should Crassus, who could have any woman in Rome, free or slave, concern himself with poor, pathetic Julia? God knows, if either of them wanted Julia, they were welcome to her, and his bed and board along with her! Nothing would make him happier.

He found Gracchus sitting moodily in the conservatory. He walked up to his old friend and nudged him gently. "All right, old man—all right?"

"Some day," said Gracchus, "the world will prove too small for Crassus and myself."

PART SIX

Which tells of the journey to Capua by part of of the company at the Villa Salaria, *of some details of that beautiful city, and of how the travellers witnessed the crucifixion of the last of the gladiators.*

On the same day, Cicero and Gracchus made their farewells and went on to Rome. Crassus and the party of young Caius, under the persuasion of Antonius, stayed another day at the *Villa Salaria,* agreeing that they would leave early in the morning and thereby get a good day's travel on the road. Crassus had already suggested to Caius that they travel together, and Helena and Claudia were pleased at the thought of being in the company of the famous general.

They left the plantation soon after sunrise. The four litters, the various attendants and baggage bearers made quite a procession on the road, and when they reached the Appian Way, Crassus picked up an honor guard of ten legionaries. Crassus had been invited to Capua for ceremonies celebrating the final crushing of the servile revolt—in the place where the revolt itself had arisen. One hundred gladiators had been selected from among the prisoners taken after the defeat and death of Spartacus, and for weeks now the games had been celebrated. These games were *munera sine missione,* the process of elimination from which there could be only a single survivor. As each pair fought, the survivor was paired with another. The dance of death was almost endless.

"I should think you would have wanted to see it," Caius said.

The four litters travelled side by side, so that they could talk as they went along the road. Traffic coming from the other direction was shunted to the edge of the road by the legionaries, and people who saw the size and wealth of the procession accepted its privilege of the right of way.

Caius and Crassus were side by side, Claudia next to Crassus, and Helena next to her brother. Because of his age and because of certain feelings he had toward them, Crassus had taken on the role of host. He had well-trained slaves, and even as the litters moved down the magnificent road, he anticipated the needs and desires of his companions, whether it was a fragrant and iced new wine from Judea, or succulent Egyptian grapes, or a spray of scent to clear the air for them. Like many very rich men, he was most thoughtful in a material way toward those of his own social class; he acted now as host, companion and guide. In answer to Caius's question, he said,

"No. It might surprise you, Caius, but I have almost no taste for games now. Yes, once in a while, if the pair is very good and very special. But I'm afraid this would only bore me. But if I had known that you would like to see it—"

"It's of no consequence."

"But one does survive the *munera*," Claudia said.

"Not necessarily, for the last pair could both be badly cut. But most likely, if one does, he will be crucified symbolically before the gates. There are seven gates, you know, and when the tokens of punishment were erected, it began with seven crosses, one in front of each gate. Whoever survives will simply replace the corpse at the Appian Gate. Have you ever been to Capua?" he asked Claudia.

"No, I haven't."

"Then you have a treat in store for you. It's such a beautiful city, the most beautiful in the whole world, I sometimes think, and on a clear day there is the glorious bay to be seen from the walls, and in the distance the white summit of Vesuvius. I don't know of anything else like it. I have a small villa there, and if you would all be my guests, I would be very pleased."

Caius explained that his great-uncle, a Flavian, was expecting them, and that they could hardly change their plans now.

"In any case, we can see something of each other. The first few days will be a bore, but when the official welcome and speeches and all the rest are done with, we can have some hours on the bay, sailing—that's the king of all sports, you know—and a picnic perhaps, and certainly an after-noon among the *unguentarii*. There is no separating Capua from its perfume, and I have an interest in a plant there and know something of the lore of the essence. Whatever perfume your heart desires," he told them generously, "it will be my pleasure to present to you."

"You are very kind," said Helena.

"Let us say that kindness costs me so little and rewards me well. In any case, I love Capua and have always felt proud of it. It is a very old city. You know, legend has it that a thousand years ago, the Etruscans built twelve cities in this part of Italy—the twelve jewels in the golden neck-lace, they were called. One of them was named *Volturnum*, and that is supposed to be the Capua of today. Of course, that is only a legend, and the Samnites, who took it from the Etruscans about three hundred and fifty years ago, re-built most of it—and when we took it from them, we built new walls and laid new streets everywhere. It is a much lovelier city than Rome."

So they travelled on down the Appian Way. By now, they paid little or no attention to the tokens of punishment. When the wind blew and brought them the odor of decay-ing flesh, a spray of perfume sweetened the air. But for the most part, they hardly looked at the crosses. There were no incidents of consequence apart from the normal traffic on the road. They spent two nights at country homes, and one night in a very luxurious mile station. By easy stages, they came finally to Capua.

II

Capua was in a gala mood, a city at the height of its fame and glory and prosperity—with the stain of servile war wiped away. Twelve hundred banners floated from the white walls of the city. The seven famous gates were wide open, for the land was at peace, and nothing troubled it. News of their coming had gone before them, and there was a mass of city dignitaries to welcome them. The civic band of one hundred and ten pieces, brasses and fifes and drums, brayed out its greeting, and the City Cohort, decked out in silver-plated armor, escorted them through the Appian

Gate. It was very thrilling for the girls, and even Caius, though he pretended indifference, was excited by the unusual and colorful welcome that they shared with their famous companion. Once within the city, they parted from Crassus and went to the house of their relatives; but a few hours later an invitation came from the general asking Caius and his sister and his friend and his family as well to be the guests of Crassus at the formal banquet to be held that very evening. It made Caius quite proud to be the object of the general's attention, and all through the long and rather tedious banquet, Crassus went out of his way to show small kindnesses to them. Caius and Claudia and Helena only tasted a few of the fifty-five courses served as a mark of the general's distinction and honor. Capua carried on the ancient Etruscan tradition of skillful and exotic preparation of insects, but Caius could not bring himself to enjoy insects, even when dissolved in honey or made into delicate cakes with minced lobster. One of the features of the evening was a new dance which had been created specifically in honor of Crassus. It portrayed the rape of Roman virgin maids by the blood-thirsty slaves, and scenes were enacted with great fidelity in the hour-long extravaganza. When the slaves were finally slain, a burst of white blossoms fluttered like snow from the ceiling of the great chamber.

Helena noticed that as the evening wore on and as the several hundred guests at the banquet became increasingly drunk, Crassus drank less and less. He only tasted the wine, and did not even taste the heavy plum brandy which Capua was so famous for, and which they distilled even as they distilled their world-famous perfume. He was a strange combination of austerity and sensuousness. They exchanged looks frequently now, and both qualities were in his eyes. Caius and Claudia, on the other hand, were quite drunk.

It was very late when the banquet finished, but Helena had a strange and willful notion that she would like to see the school of Lentulus Batiatus, the place where the servile revolt had its very beginnings, and she asked Crassus whether he wouldn't take them there and be their guide and mentor. It was a glorious night, cool and balmy and full of the scent of the spring blossoms that were in bloom everywhere in the city. A great yellow moon was just rising up into the sky, and there would be no trouble about seeing their way through the darkness.

They were standing in the plaza of the forum, a crowd around the general, and there was also a question of diplomatically separating the two girls from Helena's family; but she pressed Caius to act as their chaperone. He was so drunk that he readily agreed; he stood swaying a little, and looked at Crassus with worshipping eyes. The general managed the formalities, and a little while later they were in their litters, bound for the Appian Gate. The guards at the gate saluted the general and he joked with them a bit and distributed a handful of silver among them. He also asked them for directions.

"Then you've never been there?" Helena asked.

"No—I've never seen the place."

"How strange," remarked Helena. "I think that if I were you, I would have wanted to see it. The way your life and the life of Spartacus intertwine at this point."

"My life and the death of Spartacus," Crassus observed calmly.

"The place isn't much now," the captain of the gate told them. "It was a tremendous investment on the part of the old *lanista,* and he seemed well on his way to becoming a millionaire. But after the revolt, bad luck seemed to dog his steps, and then when he was murdered by his slave, the place was tied up in litigation. It has been ever since. The other big schools have moved into the city. Two of them took over apartment houses."

Claudia yawned. Caius was asleep in his litter.

"In the history of the rising, the one written by Flacius Monaaia," the captain of the guard continued cheerfully, "the school of Batiatus is described as being in the heart of the city. Now we take the tourists there. Believe me, my word is of no consequence as against the word of a historian. But Batiatus's place is easy enough to find. Follow that little path alongside the brook. It's almost as light as day under this moon. You can't miss the arena. The wooden grandstand just towers up."

A group of slaves carrying spades and picks came through the gate while they were talking. They also carried a ladder and a wicker basket. They went to where the great crucifix stood, the first and most symbolic of all the tokens of punishment, the first of the six thousand crosses which marked the road to Rome. As they set the ladder against the cross, a flock of crows fluttered angrily away.

"What are they doing?" Claudia asked suddenly.

"Cutting down a dog so that we may raise another dog in his place," the captain of the gate answered casually. "In the morning, the survivor of the *munera sine missione* will be honored according to his rights. There will die the last slave who was with Spartacus."

Claudia shivered. "I don't think I want to go with you," she said to Crassus.

"If you wish to go home you may—will you send two of your men with her?" he asked the captain.

But Caius, snoring comfortably, went with them. Helena wanted to walk, and Crassus nodded and left his litter to stroll with her. The litters moved on ahead, and the great financier and general and the young woman followed in the moonlight. As they passed the crucifix, the slaves were handing down the sun-blackened, bird-torn, stinking remains of the man who had died there. Others were digging at the base of the cross and driving wedges in to straighten and strengthen it.

"Nothing really disturbs you, does it?" Crassus asked Helena.

"Why should something like this disturb me?"

Crassus shrugged. "I didn't mean it as criticism, you know. I think it's quite admirable."

"That a woman should not be a woman?"

"I accept the world we live in," Crassus answered noncommittally. "I know of no other world. Do you?"

Helena shook her head without speaking, and they walked on. It was not a great distance to the school, and the landscape, lovely in the daytime, was changed by the moonlight into a veritable fairyland. Presently, they saw ahead of them the wall of the arena. Crassus told the litter-bearers that they could set down the litters together and remain beside them until he returned. Then he walked on with Helena.

The place was small and tawdry in its emptiness. Much of the iron which framed the exercise ground had been stolen. The wooden shacks were already rotting and half the wall of the arena was down. Crassus led Helena onto the sand, and they stood there looking up at the grandstand. The arena seemed very small and shabby, but the sand was silvery in the moonlight.

"I heard my brother speak of this," Helena said. "But he made so much of it, and it seems so little."

Crassus attempted to connect the fields of dead, the bloody battles, and the endless gruelling campaigns with this shabby little school, but he could not. It had no meaning to him, and he had no feeling for it.

"I want to go up in the stand," Helena said.

"If you wish. But carefully. The wood may be rotten."

They made their way up to the box which had been Batiatus's pride and joy. The striped awning hung in tatters, and mice scurried from the remains of ancient pillows. Helena sat down on one of the couches and Crassus sat beside her. Then Helena said,

"Don't you feel anything toward me?"

"I feel that you are a very lovely and intelligent young lady," Crassus replied.

"And I, great general," she said quietly, "feel that you are a swine." He leaned toward her, and she spat full in his face. Even in the dim light, she saw how his eyes lit with rage. This was the general; this was the passion that never came into his words. He struck her, and the blow flung her off the couch and against the rotten fence, which splintered under her weight. She lay there, half over the edge, with the floor of the arena twenty feet below her, but caught herself and pulled herself back—and the general never moved. Then she was on him like a wildcat, scratching and clawing, but he grasped her two wrists and held her away from him, smiling coolly at her now, and telling her,

"The real thing is different, my dear. I know."

Her spasm of anger and energy passed, and she began to cry. She cried like a little spoiled girl, and while she wept, he made love to her. She neither resisted this nor welcomed it, and when he had finished an act without either passion or urgency, he said to her,

"Was that what you wanted, my dear?"

She didn't reply, but fixed her clothes and her hair, wiped away what lipstick had smeared over her face, and wiped off the eye shadow that had run down her cheeks. She led the way back to the litters, and crawled into hers silently. Crassus walked; the litter-bearers set off back down the little road to Capua, and Caius still slept. Now the night was almost over, and the moon was losing its bright radiance. A new light touched the earth, and soon a common gray cloud would merge moonlight with daylight. Crassus, for some reason, felt a renewed vibrancy of life and power. A feeling came over him that he experienced but rarely, a feeling of life and vitality to such an extent that he half believed the old legends which claimed that a select few of mankind are seeded in mortal women by the gods. Was it not possible, he thought to himself, that he was one such? Only consider how he had been favored. Why was it then not possible that he was such a one?

His stride took him alongside Helena's litter, and she looked at him strangely and said,

"What did you mean before when you told me that the real thing was different? Am I not real? Why did you say such a terrible thing?"

"Was it so terrible?"

"You know how terrible it was. What is the real thing?"

"A woman."

"What woman?"

His brow clouded, and he shook his head. He fought valiantly to retain his feeling of splendor, and much of it stayed with him. At the Appian Gate, he left her litter, went to the gate captain, still struggling to see himself as one spawned by the gods. He told the captain, almost curtly,

"Send a detail to see her home safely!"

The captain obeyed, and Helena was shepherded off without even a goodnight. Crassus stood brooding in the deep shadow of the gate. The gate captain and the troops on duty there watched him curiously. Then Crassus demanded,

"What time is it?"

"The last hour is almost over. Aren't you tired, sir?"

"No, I'm not tired," Crassus said. "I'm not tired at all, captain." His voice softened somewhat. "It's a long time since I stood a dog watch like this."

"The nights are very long," the captain admitted. "A half hour from now, this place will be very different. The vegetable dealers will be coming in and the milkmen with their cows and the freighters and the fishermen and so forth and so on. This is a busy gate. And this morning, the gladiator goes up there." He nodded at the cross, which now was vague and gray and half visible in the morning darkness.

"Will there be much of a crowd?" asked Crassus.

"Well, sir—not so much at the beginning, but there will be as the day goes on. I must admit that there's a peculiar fascination in watching a man crucified. By noontime today, the gate and the walls around here will be packed. You would think that having seen it once, it would be enough, but that's not the way it works out."

"Who is the man?"

"That I can't say. Just a gladiator, as far as I know. A very good one, I suppose, and I could almost feel sorry for the poor devil."

"Save your sympathy, captain," Crassus told him.

"I didn't mean it that way, sir. I only meant that one always feels something for the last of a *munera*."

"If you enjoy mathematical probabilities. Their *munera* began a long time ago. There had to be a last man."

"I suppose so."

The last hour was over. With daylight, the first hour began. The moon had faded and the sky was like dirty milk. The morning mist lay fallow everywhere, except where the dark line of the great road stretched endlessly toward the north. Stark and gaunt stood the cross against the lightening sky, and over to the east, a pale pink radiance was a harbinger of the rising sun. Crassus was glad he had decided to remain awake. His own mood welcomed the tantalizing bitter sweet of the first dawning. Dawn is always a mixture of sorrow and glory.

Now a little boy of about eleven years came walking up, carrying a jug in his hand. The captain of the gate greeted him and took the jug from him.

"My son," he explained to Crassus. "He brings me hot wine each morning. Would you greet him, sir? It will mean a great deal to him. Afterwards he will remember it. His gentile name is Lichtus and his own name is Marius. I know it is presumptuous of me to ask it, sir, but it would mean a great deal to him and to me."

"Hail Marius Lichtus," Crassus said.

"I know you," the little boy told him. "You're the general. I saw you yesterday. Where is your golden breastplate?"

"It was brass, not gold, and I took it off because it was very uncomfortable."

"When I have one, I will never take it off."

"So Rome lives, and the glory and traditions of Rome will live forever," Crassus thought. He was very touched—in a certain way—by the scene. The captain offered him the jug.

"Will you have a drink, sir?"

Crassus shook his head. Now, in the distance, there sounded a drumbeat, and the captain gave the jug to the boy to hold and shouted orders at the gate detail. The soldiers lined up along either leaf of the open gates, their shields grounded alongside of them, their heavy spears presented and upended in the air. It was a difficult position to hold and it annoyed Crassus, for he suspected that if he had not been there, the fancy play of arms would not have been indulged in. The beat of the drums increased, and presently the first ranks of the military band came in sight on the broad avenue which ran from the gate to the forum. Now the rising sun touched the tops of the taller buildings, and almost at the same time a trickle of people appeared in the streets. They moved toward the gate and the sound of the military music.

There were six drums and four fifes; then six soldiers; then the gladiator, naked and with his arms bound tightly behind his back; then a dozen more soldiers. It was a considerable detail for a single man, and this man did not look very dangerous or very strong. Then, as he came closer, Crassus revised his opinion; dangerous, certainly—such men are dangerous. You saw it in his face. In his face was none of the open warmth or frankness that one sees in the face of a Roman. He had a face like a hawk, a jutting nose, the skin stretched tightly over high cheekbones, thin lips, and eyes that were green and hateful as a cat's. His face was full of hate, but the hate was unexpressive, like the hate of an animal, and the face was a mask. In form he was not large, but his muscles were like leather and whipcord. He had only two fresh cuts upon his body, one across the top of the chest and one on the flank, but neither was very deep and the blood had clotted hard on them. Yet under the cuts and all over him was a veritable tapestry of scar tissue. A finger was missing from one hand and one ear had been sliced off close to the skull.

When the officer who was leading the detachment saw Crassus, he held up his arm for his men to halt and then strode over and saluted the general. He was obviously full of the meaning of the moment.

"I never dreamed it would be my honor and privilege to see you here, sir," he said.

"It's a fortunate accident," Crassus nodded. He too could not escape the fitting juxtaposition of himself and this last of the servile army. "Are you going to place him on the cross now?"

"Those were my instructions."

"Who is he? The gladiator, I mean. It's quite obvious that he's an old hand in the arena. The mark of the sword is all over him. But do you know who he is?"

"We know a little. He was an officer, and he commanded a cohort or perhaps even more than that. Also, he seems to be a Jew. Batiatus had a number of Jews, who are sometimes better than Thracians with the *sica*. As a matter of fact, Batiatus made a deposition concerning a Jew called David, who was, along with Spartacus, one of the original leaders of the insurrection. This may be him or it may not be. He never spoke after he was brought here to participate in the *munera*. He fought very well—my god, I've never seen such work with the knife. He fought in five pairs and here he is with only two cuts on his body. I saw three of the pairs myself, and I never saw anything better with the knife. He knew in the end he would go on the cross, yet he fought as if his victory would be signed with freedom. I can't understand that."

"No—well, life is a strange business, young man."

"Yes, sir. I can agree with that."

"If he is the Jew, David," said Crassus thoughtfully, "then there's ironic justice after all. May I speak with him?"

"Of course—of course. I don't think, though, that you will get any satisfaction out of him. He's a sullen, silent brute."

"Suppose I try."

They went over to where the gladiator stood, surrounded now by a growing crowd of people whom the soldiers had to press back. Rather pompously, the officer announced,

"Gladiator, you are singularly honored. This is the Praetor, Marcus Licinius Crassus, and he condescends to talk with you."

When the name was announced, the crowd broke into

cheers, but the slave might have been deaf for all the reaction it brought from him. Unmoving, he stared straight ahead of him. His eyes gleamed like bits of green stone, but no other sign or motion appeared on his face.

"You know me, gladiator," said Crassus. "Look at me."

Still the naked gladiator did not move, and now the officer in command of the detachment strode up and struck him across the face with his open hand.

"Who is addressing you, pig?" he cried.

He struck him again. The gladiator made no attempt to avoid the blow, and Crassus realized that if this continued, he would derive precious little from it.

"That's enough, officer," Crassus said. "Leave him alone and get on with what you have to do."

"I'm terribly sorry. But he hasn't spoken. Maybe he can't speak. He was never seen to speak even to his own companions."

"It's of no consequence," said Crassus.

He watched them as they marched on through the gate to the crucifix. A steady stream of people now were pouring through the gate, spreading out along the road where they had a high, uninterrupted view of the proceedings. Crassus walked through the crowd to the base of the cross, curious in spite of himself as to how the slave would react. The man's stony reticence had become a sort of challenge, and Crassus, who had never known a man—no matter how hard he was—to go onto the cross in silence, began to speculate on what sort of reaction this would provoke.

The soldiers were old hands at a standing crucifixion, and they went about their work quickly and expertly. A rope was passed under the arms of the slave who was still trussed and bound. The rope was drawn through until the two lengths were equal. The ladder, which the slaves had left there the night before, was placed against the back of the cross. The two lengths of rope were tossed over the arms of the cross, and a pair of soldiers seized hold of each end. Then, with quick dexterity, the gladiator was drawn up almost to the crossbar. Now another soldier mounted the ladder and eased the gladiator up while those below drew on the ropes. Now he hung with his shoulders just below the point where the two wooden beams met. The soldier on the ladder leaped up onto the crossbar, and another, carrying a hammer and several long iron spikes, went up the ladder and straddled the other arm of the crossbar.

Meanwhile, Crassus observed the gladiator with interest. Though his naked body twisted when it was drawn up against the rough wood of the cross, his face remained impassive, even as it remained impassive under the painful bite of the rope. He hung motionless and inert while the first soldier took a turn of rope around his chest and under his arms, knotting the rope above the crossbar. Then the first rope was pulled through and back to the ground. Then the cord that bound his hands together was cut and each soldier drew up one of his arms and tied it with a twist of rope around the wrist to the crossbar. Not until the second soldier forced open his palm, laid the spike on it, and drove the spike into the wood with a single hard blow, did the gladiator actually react in pain. Even then, he did not speak or cry out, but his face contorted and his body twisted spasmodically. Three more blows buried the spike five inches into the wood, and a final blow bent the head, so that the hand could not slip off. Then the same process was repeated with the other hand, and once again the gladiator twisted in agony, and once again his face contorted as the spike bit through the muscles and tendons of his hand. But still he did not cry out, even though tears ran from his eyes and saliva dripped from his open mouth.

Now the rope around his chest was cut, so that he hung entirely by his hands, with only the support of the cord around each wrist to lessen the weight on the spikes. The soldiers came down the ladder, which was then taken away, and the crowd—which numbered hundreds of people by now—applauded the skill that had crucified a man in just a few minutes . . .

Then the gladiator fainted.

"They always do," the officer explained to Crassus. "The shock of the spikes does it. But they always regain consciousness, and sometimes it's twenty or thirty hours before they faint again. We had a Gaul who remained conscious for four days. He lost his voice. He couldn't scream anymore, but he remained conscious. There was never anything like that one, but even he sounded off when they put the spikes into his hands. God, I'm thirsty!" He opened a flask, drank deeply, and offered it to Crassus. "Rose water?"

"Thank you," said Crassus. He was suddenly dry and tired. He drank all that was left in the flask. The crowd was still increasing; and nodding at them, Crassus asked, "Will they remain all day?"

"Most of them only until he recovers consciousness. They want to see what he'll do then. They do funny things. Many of them cry for their mothers. You never think of slaves in that way, do you?" Crassus shrugged. "I'll have to clear that road," the officer went on. "They block up traffic. You'd think they'd have enough sense to keep part of the road open—but no, never. They're all the same. A crowd doesn't have any sense at all." He detailed two of the soldiers to clear enough of the road to let traffic pass.

"I wonder—" he said to Crassus. "I wonder whether I could trouble you about something, sir. It may be none of my business, but I'm terribly curious to know why you said before that if this is the Jew, David, there was ironic justice concerned. Or something like that—"

"Did I say that?" Crassus asked. "I don't know what I meant or could have intended." It was done, and much of the past had to lie quietly, and there was little glory in servile war. The triumphs and mighty devotions were for others; for himself, there were petty slaughterhouse satisfactions of the crucifix. How tired he was of killing and death and torture! Yet where did one go to escape it? More and more, they were creating a society where life rested on death. Never before in the whole history of the world had slaughter been elevated to such a plane of precision and quantity—and where did it end and when would it end? He remembered now an incident that happened shortly after he had taken command of the defeated and demoralized forces of Rome. He had given three legions to his friend and childhood companion, Pilico Mummius, a man who had already participated in two important campaigns, and he had instructed Mummius to harass Spartacus and see whether he couldn't cut off a part of his forces. Instead, Mummius blundered into a trap, and his three legions, confronted suddenly by the slaves, fled in one of the blindest and most shameful panics ever to overtake a Roman army. He remembered how he had given Mummius an indescribable tongue-lashing; he remembered the names he had called him, the charges of cowardice he had hurled against him. But one went no further with a man like Mummius.

With the legions, it was something else. Five thousand men of the Seventh Legion were lined up, and every tenth man was taken out of the ranks and put to death for cowardice. "You should have killed me," Mummius said to him later.

Now he thought of that so clearly and so well—for it was Mummius and the former consul, Marcus Servius, who symbolized for him his deepest hatred against the slaves. The story came back to him, but like all stories from the camp of slaves, one could not separate truth from falsehood. Marcus Servius was to some extent responsible for the death of the beloved companion of Spartacus, a Gaul named Crixus, who was cut off, surrounded, and who perished with his army. So when, much later, Servius and Mummius were captured by Spartacus and tried by the slave tribunal, it was said that a Jew called David had argued for the manner of their death. Or perhaps the Jew called David had argued against the manner of their death. Crassus was not certain. They had died as a gladiatorial pair. They were stripped naked, these two middle aged leaders of Roman armies, and they were each given a knife and put into a makeshift arena to fight each other to the death. That was the only time Spartacus had done such a thing, but Crassus never forgot and never forgave.

Yet it was not anything he could tell the officer, standing here in the shadow of the crucifix. "I don't know what I could have meant," Crassus said. "It was of no importance."

He was tired, and he decided that he would return to his villa and sleep.

III

The essence of it was that Crassus did not very much care whether this crucifixion of the last of the gladiators represented justice in the light of these specific facts or not. His sense of justice had been blunted; his sense of revenge had been blunted; and death retained no novelty whatsoever. In his childhood, as with children of so many of the "better" families of the Republic, he had been filled with the heroic legends of the past. He had fully and wholly believed that *Roma supra hominem et factiones est.* The state and the law served all men, and the law was just. He could not

have said exactly at what point he ceased to believe this—
yet never wholly. Somewhere within him, a little of the
illusion was retained; yet he who had once been able to
define justice so clearly could no longer do so today. Ten
years before, he had seen his father and his brother coldly
put to death by leaders of the opposition party, and justice
never avenged them. The confusion concerning what was
just and what was unjust increased rather than decreased,
and it was only on the basis of wealth and power that he
was able to make a rationale. In all reason, justice came
to mean that wealth and power were undisturbed; the importance of the ethics concerned gradually disappeared. So
that when he actually saw the last gladiator crucified, he
felt no grand sense of godly fulfillment. In essence, he felt
nothing at all. He was simply not moved.

Yet in the mind of the gladiator, there were questions of
justice and injustice—and they were mingled in the unconsciousness that came of pain and shock and weariness.
They were mingled in the numberless threads of his memory. They might have been unraveled; they might have been
sorted out of the blinding and stabbing waves of agony.
Somewhere in his mind, the memory of the incident Crassus
had referred to was preserved, clearly and precisely.

It was a question of justice with the gladiators even as it
was with Crassus; and afterwards, when the history of what
the slaves did was written down by those who most bitterly
hated the slaves and by those who knew least of what they
did, it was said that they took the Roman captives they held
and made them kill each other in a great orgy of reversed
gladiatorial combat. So it was taken for granted—as the
masters have always taken it for granted—that when power
came to those who were oppressed, they would use it just
as their oppressors had.

And this was in the memory of the man who hung from
the cross. There had never been an orgy of gladiatorial
slaughter—only the single time when Spartacus, in a cold
passion of rage and hate, had pointed to the two Roman
patricians and said,

"As we did, so you will do! Go onto the sand with knives
and naked, so that you may learn how we died for the
edification of Rome and the pleasure of its citizens!"

The Jew had been sitting there then, listening silently,
and when the two Romans had been taken away, Spartacus

turned to him, and still the Jew said nothing. A great bond, a deep connection had grown between them. In the course of years, in the course of many battles, the small band of gladiators who had escaped at Capua dwindled. A special toll was taken of them, and the handful who survived as leaders of the huge slave army, were welded together.

Now Spartacus looked at the Jew, and demanded, "Am I right or am I wrong?"

"What is right for them is never right for us."

"Let them fight!"

"Let them fight, if you want to. Let them kill each other. But it will hurt us more. It will be a worm eating our insides. You and I are gladiators. How long ago did we say that we would wipe even the memory of the fighting of pairs from the face of the earth?"

"And we will. But these two must fight . . ."

So it was there, a little bit of the memory of a man nailed to a cross. Crassus had looked into his eyes and Crassus had watched him crucified. A great circle was completed. Crassus went home to sleep, for he had been up all night, and as might be expected, he was tired. And the gladiator hung unconscious from the spikes.

IV

It was almost an hour before consciousness returned to the gladiator. Pain was like a road, and consciousness travelled down the road of pain. If all his senses and sensations were stretched out like the skin of a drum, then now the drum was being beaten. The music was unbearable, and he came awake only to the knowledge of pain. He knew nothing else in the world of pain, and pain was the whole world. He was the last of six thousand of his comrades and their pain had been like his; but his own pain was so enormous that it could not be shared or subdivided. He opened his eyes, but pain was a red film that separated him from the world. He was like a grub, a caterpillar, a larva, and the cocoon was spun out of pain.

His awakening was not all at once, but in waves. The vehicle he knew best was the chariot; he was riding a bumping, lurching chariot back into consciousness. He was a little boy in the hill country, and the great ones, the lords from afar, the civilized ones, the clean ones, rode occasionally in chariots, and he ran along the rocky mountain path pleading for a ride. He cried, "Oh master—master, let me ride?" None of them spoke his language, but sometimes they let him and his friends sit on the tailboard. Generous were the great ones! Sometimes they gave him and his friends sweets! They laughed at the way the little, sunburned, black haired children clung to the tailboard. But often enough they would whip the horses ahead, and then the sudden lurch and motion would send the children flying. Well, the great ones from the western world were unpredictable, and you took the good with the bad, but when you fell off the chariot, it hurt.

Then he would realize that he was not a child in the hills of Galilee, but a man hanging from a cross. He would realize it in areas, because all of him did not belong to himself at once. He would realize it in his arms, where the nerves were white-hot wires and the hot blood flowed along his arms and down to the twisted hump of his shoulders. He would realize it in his belly, where his stomach and intestines had turned into furious knots of pain and tension.

And the crowds of people who watched him were rippling waves, real and unreal. His sight was not quite normal at this point. He was unable to focus properly, and the people he saw folded and unfolded, as an image does under a curved glass. The people, in turn, saw that the gladiator was returning to consciousness and they watched him eagerly. If this had just been another crucifixion, there would have been no novelty to the occasion. Crucifixion was very common in Rome. When Rome conquered Carthage, four generations before this, she took the best of what she had conquered, the plantation system and the crucifix being prominent among the spoils. Something about the cross with the man dangling from it took the fancy of Rome, and now the world had forgotten that it was Carthagenian in origin, so universal a symbol of civilization had it become. Where the Roman roads went, there too went the cross and the plantation system and the fighting of pairs and the enormous contempt for human life in bondage and the enormous drive to squeeze gold from the blood and sweat of mankind.

But even the best of things pall in time, and the best

wine becomes a bore when too much is swilled, and the passion of one man becomes lost in the passion of thousands. Another crucifixion would not have brought out the crowd; but here was the death of a hero, a great gladiator, a lieutenant of Spartacus, a gladiator of all time, a mighty gladiator who had survived the *munera sine missione*. Always, there had been a curious contradiction in the role of the gladiator, the slave who is marked for death, the fighting puppet, the most contemptible among the contemptible —yet at one and the same time, the survivor on the bloody field of battle.

So they came out to see the gladiator die, to see how he would greet that great mystery in which all men share, and to see how he would conduct himself when the spikes were driven into his hands. He was a strange one who had turned in on himself in silence. They had come to see whether the silence would be broken, and when it was not broken with the driving of the spikes, they lingered to see whether it would be broken when he opened his eyes on the world again.

It was broken. When he saw them finally, when the images of sight ceased to swim before his eyes, he cried out, a terrible cry of pain and agony.

Apparently no one understood his words. There was speculation on what he had said in the agonizing burst of sound. Some had bet on whether he would speak or not, and the bets were paid or not paid among angry squabbles as to whether he had spoken words, or whether it was merely a moan, or whether he had spoken in a foreign tongue. Some said he called upon the gods; others said he whimpered for his mother.

Actually, it was neither of the two. Actually, he had cried out, "Spartacus, Spartacus, why did we fail?"

V

If in some miraculous manner, the minds and brains of the six thousand men who were taken prisoner when the cause of Spartacus went down into the dust of history could have been opened and laid bare and mapped out, so that one could trace back from the crucifix the tangled web and skein which had brought them there—if six thousand maps of human lives could have been drawn, it might have been seen that the pasts of many were not too different. In that way, perhaps their suffering at the end was not too different; it was a common suffering and it blended, and if there were gods or a God in the heavens and the tears of such were rain, then surely it would have rained for days and days. But instead, the sun dried out the misery and the birds tore at the bleeding flesh, and the men died.

This was the last one to die; he was a summation of the others. His mind was filled with the sum of a human life, but in such pain a man does not think, and the memories are like nightmares. His memories could not be set down as they came to him, for they would have no meaning apart from the reflection of pain. But a tale could be sorted out of his memories, and the memories could be reshuffled to make a pattern—and in that case, the pattern would not be too different from the patterns of the others.

There were four times in his life. The first was a time of not knowing. The second was a time of knowing, and it was filled with hatred, and he became a creature of hatred. The third was a time of hope, and his hatred passed away and he knew a great love and comradeship for his fellow men. The fourth time was a time of despair.

In the time of not knowing, he was a little boy, and in that time there was happiness and the radiance of pervading sunlight all about him. When his tortured mind on the cross sought for coolness and flight from pain, he found that blessed coolness in remembering his childhood. The green mountains of his childhood were cool and beautiful. The mountain streams tumbled and sparkled, and the black goats grazed on the hillside. The hills were terraced and cared for with loving hands, and the barley grew like pearls and the grapes grew like rubies and amethysts. He played on the hillsides; he waded in the brooks, and he swam in the great, beautiful lake of Galilee. He ran like an animal, free and wild and healthy, and his brothers and sisters and his friends provided a society in which he was free and assured and happy.

Even in that time, he had known about God, and he had a clear and certain and delineated picture of God on his childhood vision. He came of a mountain folk, so they had placed God on a peak where no man could live. On the highest mountain of all, where no one had even climbed, God lived. God sat there all alone. There was one God and no other. God was an old man who never grew older, and his beard swept down across his breast and his white robes billowed out like the white clouds which suddenly fill the sky. He was a just God and occasionally a merciful God, but always a vengeful God; and the little boy knew this. Night and day, the little boy was never free from the eyes of God. Whatever he did, God saw. Whatever he thought, God knew.

He came of a pious people, an exceedingly pious people, and God was woven in and out of their lives just as a thread is woven in and out of a cloak. When they tended their flocks, they wore long striped cloaks, and every tassel of those cloaks signified some part of the awe they had for their God. Morning and night, they prayed to God; when they sat down to their bread, they prayed; when they took a glass of wine, they gave thanks to God; and even when misfortune came upon them, they blessed God, so he might not think they resented their misfortune and thereby surrendered to arrogance.

Therefore, it was not surprising that the boy, the child, who was now a man and who hung from a cross now, was full of the knowledge and presence of God. The child feared God, and his God was a God to be feared. But the fear was a minor note in the pervading sunlight, and in the coolness of the mountains and the mountain streams. The child ran and laughed and sang songs and tended goats and sheep, and watched as the older boys threw the razor-edged Galilean knife, the *chabo* that they wore so proudly at their sides. He had one of his own he had carved out of wood, and often with this he engaged in mock knife duels with his brothers and friends.

And if he did particularly well, the older boys would nod grudgingly and say, "Like a Thracian, little one, monkey, pimple!" The *Thracian* was all things evil and all things in fighting as well. A long, long time before, mercenaries had come into the land, and there had been many years of fighting before they were killed and driven out. *Thracians*, these mercenaries were called, but the little boy had never seen one.

He looked forward to the day when he would wear a knife by his side, and then they would see whether he wasn't as fierce as a Thracian. Yet he wasn't very fierce; he was a gentle little boy, and to a great degree a happy one . . .

That was the time of not knowing.

In the second time of his life, in the time of knowing, he stopped being a child and the pervading sunshine gave way to a chill wind. In time, he drew a cloak of hatred around him to shelter and shield himself. That was the time that stabbed through his mind in sharp flashes of red agony as he hung from the cross. His thoughts of that time were wild and twisted and terrible. The recollections were as scrambled as the pieces of a jig-saw puzzle. He saw that second time of his life in the undulating masses of people who watched him, in their faces, in the sounds which came from them. Again and again as his passion endured, he was shunted back through his memory to that second time of his life, the time of knowing.

In that time, he became aware of things, and in this awareness his childhood perished. He became aware of his father, a brown-faced, work-hardened man who toiled from morning to night—yet the toil was never enough. He became aware of sorrow. His mother died and they wept for her. He became aware of taxes, for no matter how much his father toiled, there was never enough to fill their bellies, yet the land was as fruitful as any land could be. And he became aware of the great gulf that separates the rich from the poor.

The sounds were the same as before; the difference was that he heard the sounds and understood them, whereas before he had heard them without understanding. Now when the men talked, they permitted him to stand at a little distance and listen; before, they had urged him out of the house to his play.

Also, he was given a knife, but the knife brought no gladness with it. He went one day with his father across the hills a full five miles to where there was a man who worked with iron, and there they stayed for three long hours by the forge while the smith hammered out a knife for him. And all the time his father and the smith talked about the sorrows that had fallen upon the land and how the small man was squeezed. It was as if his father and the iron worker were in competition, each to demonstrate to the other how he was squeezed more than the other.

"Take this knife," said the smith. "My price to you is four *denarii*. From that, one fourth will be taken by the Temple collector when he comes for his dues. One fourth will be taken by the tax collector. That leaves me two *denarii*. If I am to make another knife, I must pay two *denarii* for the metal. Where is the price of my labor? Where is the price of the horn I must buy for the hilt? Where is the price of food to feed my family? But if I should charge five *denarii*, then everything else goes up accordingly, and who will buy when they can get a knife elsewhere for less? God is kinder to you. At least you take your food from the ground and you can always fill your belly."

The boy's father, however, had another argument. "At least you have a little hard money in your hands sometimes. My own case is like this. I reap my barley and I thresh it. I fill the baskets, and the barley gleams like pearls. We give thanks to the Lord God of Hosts, because our barley is so beautiful and so full of sustenance. Who can have troubles when his storehouse is so filled with baskets of pearly barley? But then the Temple collector comes, and one quarter of the barley he takes for the Temple. Then the tax collector comes, and he takes one quarter for taxes. I plead with him. I point out to him that there is only enough barley to feed my animals through the winter. Then eat your animals, he tells me. And this is the awful thing we must do. So when the time comes that there is neither meat nor grain and the children whimper for food, we string our bows and think of the hares and the few deer left on the mountainside. But this is unclean meat for a Jew unless it is blessed. Unless there is a dispensation. So last winter, we sent our rabbi to Jerusalem, to plead at the Temple. Our rabbi is a good man. His hunger is our hunger. But five days he lingered in the Temple court before the priests would see him, and then they listened with contempt to his pleading, nor did they give him even a crust of bread to ease his awful hunger. When shall we hear the end of this Galilean whining? they said to him. Your peasants are lazy. They want to lie in the sun and eat manna. Let them work harder and plant more barley. Such is their advice, but where does a peasant find more land for more barley, and if we found more and planted more, do you know what would happen?"

"I know what would happen," the smith said. "In the end you would have no more. That way, it always happens. The poor get poorer and the rich get richer."

This happened when the boy went to get his knife, but at home it was no different. At home, in the evening, the neighbors came to his father's little house, the house where they all lived crowded into one single room, and there they sat and everlastingly talked of how difficult it was for a man to live and how they were squeezed and squeezed and squeezed—and how far could it go, and could you squeeze blood from a stone?

Thus thought the man on the cross, and these were stabbing fragments of memory which connected with his suffering. But even as he suffered, even as the pain rose in waves beyond endurance and then subsided into waves only endurable, he desired to live. Dead already, given to the cross, still he desired to live. What a power life is! What a drive life is! What things people will do when it becomes necessary to the simple fact of existence!

But why that was so, he did not know. In his suffering, he did not call upon God, because in God there was no answer and no explanation. He did not believe any more in one God or in many gods. In that second time of his life, his relationship with God changed. God answered only the prayers of the rich.

So he did not call on God. Rich men do not hang on crosses, and his whole life had been spent on a cross, an eternity with spikes through his hands. Or had that been another? Or had that been his father? His mind worked poorly now; the beautiful and precise and orderly impulses of his brain were being disarranged, and when he remembered how his father had been crucified, he confused his father with himself. He searched his poor, tortured brain to recall how that had come about, and he remembered the time when the tax collectors came and were turned away with empty hands. He remembered the time when the priests came from the Temple, and they too were sent packing with their hands empty.

There was a brief moment of glory after that. There was a shining memory of their great hero, Judas the Maccabee, and when the first army was sent by the priests against them, the hill farmers took up their bows and knives and destroyed the army. He had been in that battle. Only a stripling of fourteen years, yet he had used his knife and he had fought alongside of his father and he had tasted victory.

But the taste of victory did not last long. Great columns of armored mercenaries came marching against the Galilean rebels, and there was a bottomless well of gold in the Temple treasury to buy more and more soldiers. The farmers with their knives and their naked bodies could not fight a great army. The farmers were smashed, and two thousand were taken prisoner. From among the prisoners, nine hundred men were selected for the cross. This was the civilized way, the western way, and when the crosses were strung like beads over the hillsides, the priests from the Temple came to watch and with them came their Roman advisers. And the boy, David, stood and saw his father nailed to a cross and left there to hang by his hands until the birds ate his flesh.

And now he was on the cross himself. As it began, so it had ended, and how tired he was, and how full of pain and grief! As time passed on the cross—time which had no connection with time as known to mankind, for a man on a cross is no longer a man—he asked himself endlessly what was the meaning of a life which came from nowhere and moved into nowhere? He began to lose that incredible grip on life which had sustained him for so long. For the first time, he wanted to die.

(What had Spartacus said to him? *Gladiator, love life. There is the answer to all questions*. But Spartacus was dead, and he lived.)

He was tired now. Weariness contested with pain, and so his ragged memories were of weariness. After the revolt failed, he and seven hundred other boys were chained neck to neck and marched north. How long they marched! Across plain and desert and mountain, until the green hills of Galilee were a dream of paradise. Their masters changed, but the whip was always the same. And at last they came to a land where the mountains towered higher than any mountains in Galilee, where the tops of the mountains wore a mantle of snow in summer and in winter.

And there he was sent into the earth to dig copper. For two years he labored in the copper mines. His two brothers, who were with him, died, but he lived. He had a body of steel and whipcord. Others sickened; their teeth fell out, or they became sick and vomited away their lives. But he lived, and for two years he labored in the mines.

And then he escaped. He escaped into the wild mountains with the slave collar still on his neck, and there the simple, primitive mountain tribesmen took him in and sheltered him and removed the collar from his neck and let him live with them. All through the winter he lived with them. They were a kind-hearted, poor folk, who lived by hunting and trapping, growing almost nothing at all. He learned their language, and they wanted him to remain with them and marry one of their women. But his heart longed for Galilee, and when spring came, he set out southward. But he was captured by a band of Persian traders, and they in turn sold him to a slave caravan moving westward, and he was put on the auction block in the city of Tyre, almost within sight of his homeland. How he ate his heart out then! What bitter tears he wept, to be so near home and relatives and people who would love and cherish him—and yet to be so far from freedom! A Phoenician merchant purchased him, and he was chained to an oar in a ship which traded with Sicilian ports, and for a whole year he sat in the wet darkness and wet filth, dragging his oar through the water.

Then the ship was taken by Greek pirates, and blinking like a dirty owl, he was dragged up on deck and examined and questioned by the fierce Greek sailors. Short shrift was made of the Phoenician merchant and crew; they were flung overboard like so many bundles of straw. But him and the other slaves, they examined, and each was asked in turn, in the Aramaic dialect of the Mediterranean, "Can you fight? Or can you only row?"

He feared the bench and the darkness and the bilge water as he might have feared the devil himself, and he answered, "I can fight. Only give me a chance." He would have fought an army then, only not to be sent down below decks to bend his back over an oar. So they gave him a chance on deck and taught him—not without many a blow and curse—the craft of the sea, how to furl a sail and run up the rigging and steer with the thirty-foot steering oar, how to splice a rope and hold a course on the stars at night. In their first fight with a fat Roman cog, he showed a quickness of motion and a skill with the long knife that won him a secure place in their wild and lawless band; but there was no happiness in his heart, and he came to hate these men who knew only slaughter, cruelty, and death. They were as different from the simple peasants among whom he had lived his childhood as night was from day. They believed in no God, not even in Poseiden, the lord of the sea, and though his own faith had been shaken, the good years of his life were among those who believed. When they stormed onto shore, it was to kill and burn and rape.

It was in this time that he built around him a hard wall in which he encased himself. Within that wall, he lived, and the signs of youth disappeared from his face with its cold green eyes and its hawklike nose. He was a little less than eighteen years old when he joined them, but his appearance became an ageless one, and already there was a sprinkling of white hair in the black mop that covered his head. He kept to himself, and sometimes for a whole week he would speak no word at all; they left him alone. They knew how he could fight, and they feared him.

He lived on a dream, and the dream was wine and sustenance to him. The dream was that one day or another, sooner or later, they would raise the coast of Palestine, and then he would slip over the side, swim ashore, and make his way on foot to the beloved Galilean hills. But three years went by, and that day never came. They raided first on the African coast, and then across the sea along the Italian coastline. They fought on the coast of Spain and burned Roman villas and took the riches and the women they found there. Then they crossed the sea again and spent a whole winter in a walled and lawless city near the Pillars of Hercules. Then they sailed through the Strait of Gibraltar and came to Britain, where they beached their galley and cleaned and repaired it. Then they sailed to Ireland, where they exchanged bits of cloth and cheap jewelry for the golden ornaments of the Irish tribesmen. Then to Gaul, and up and down the French coast. And then back to Africa. Thus three years went by—and never did they raise the coast of his native land. But the dream and the hope remained with him—the while he became harder than a man has a right to be.

But he learned much in that time. He learned that the sea was a road upon which life flowed, even as blood flows through the body of a man. He learned that the world was great and boundless, and he learned that everywhere one went, there were poor and simple folk, people like his own people, people who scratched away at the soil for a living for themselves and their children—only to give over most of what they took out of the soil to chief or king or pirate. And he learned that there was a chief, king and pirate above everything else—and that was called Rome.

And in the end, they went down to a Roman warship, and he and fourteen others of the crew who survived were taken to Ostia to be hanged. So the sands of his small cup of life seemed to have run out, but at the very last, an agent of Lentulus Batiatus bought him for the school at Capua . . .

Such was the pattern of the second part of the gladiator's life, the time of knowing and hating. That part was completed at Capua. There he learned the ultimate refinement of civilization, the training of men to kill each other for the amusement of Roman idlers and for the enrichment of a fat, dirty and wicked man who was called a *lanista*. He became a gladiator. His hair was clipped close to his skull. He went into the arena with a knife in his hand, and he killed not those he hated but those who, like himself, were slaves or doomed men.

Here was where the knowing was combined with hating. He became a receptacle for hatred, and day by day the receptacle filled. He lived alone in the hideous bareness and hopelessness of his cell; he turned inward upon himself. He no longer believed in God, and when he thought of the God of his fathers, it was only with hatred and contempt. He said to himself once,

"I would like to go into the arena with that damned old man of the mountain. I'd pay him back for all the tears and broken promises he brings on men. Give him his thunder and lightning. All I want is a knife in my hand. I would make a sacrifice for him, all right. I'd teach him something about wrath and anger."

He had a dream once, and in the dream he stood at the throne of God. But he wasn't afraid. "What will you do to me?" he cried mockingly. "I have lived twenty-one years, and what more can you do to me than the world has done? I saw my father crucified. I labored like a mole in the mines. For two years I worked in the mines, and for a year I lived in the filth and the bilge water, with the rats running across my feet. For three years I was a thief who dreamed of his homeland, and now I kill men for hire. Damn you to hell, what will you do to me?"

That was what he became in the second time of his life, and during that time, a Thracian slave was brought into the school at Capua, a strange man with a gentle voice and a broken nose and deep dark eyes. That was how this gladiator came to know Spartacus.

VI

Once, long after this time, a Roman slave was placed upon the cross, and after he had hung there for twenty-four hours, he was pardoned by the emperor himself, and somehow he lived. He wrote an account of what he had felt on the cross, and the most striking thing about his account was what he had to say on the question of time. "On the cross," he said, "there are only two things, pain and eternity. They tell me that I was on the cross only twenty-four hours, but I was on the cross longer than the world has existed. If there is no time, then every moment is forever."

In that peculiar, pain-ridden *forever*, the mind of the gladiator fell apart, and the power of organized reason gradually ceased. Recollection turned into hallucination. He lived again through much of his life. He spoke to Spartacus again for the first time. He was playing over what he most desired to rescue from the meaningless ruin that was his life, the unimportant life of a nameless slave in the sweeping current of time.

(He looks at Spartacus. He watches him. He is like a cat, this man, and his green eyes increase his resemblance to a cat. You know the way a cat walks, with an everlasting tension. That is the way this gladiator walks, and you have the feeling that if you were to throw him up into the air, he would land easily on his two feet. He hardly ever looks at a man directly, though; instead, he watches from the corners of his eyes. That way, he watches Spartacus, day after day. He could not even explain to himself what quality in Spartacus commands his attention to this extent; but it is no great mystery. He is all tension, and Spartacus is all looseness. He talks to no one, but Spartacus talks to

227

all, and they all come to Spartacus and bring him their troubles. Spartacus is injecting something into this school of gladiators. Spartacus is destroying it.

(All except this Jew come to Spartacus. Spartacus wonders about that. Then, one day, in the period of rest between drills, he goes to the Jew and talks to him.

("Do you talk Greek, man?" he asks him.

(The green eyes stare at him unmovingly. Suddenly, Spartacus realizes that this is a very young man, hardly more than a lad. This is hidden behind a mask. He is not looking at the man himself, but at the mask.

(The Jew says to himself, "Greek—do I talk Greek? I think I talk all languages. Hebrew and Aramaic and Greek and Latin and many other languages in many parts of the world. But why should I talk in any language? Why?"

(Very gently, Spartacus urges him, "A word from me and then a word from you. We are people. We are not alone. The great trouble is when you are alone. It is an awful thing, indeed, to be alone, but here we are not alone. Why should we be ashamed of what we are? Did we do terrible things to bring ourselves here? I don't think we did such terrible things. More terrible things are done by those who put knives in our hands and tell us to kill for the pleasure of the Romans. So we shouldn't be ashamed and hate each other. A man has a little strength, a little hope, a little love. Those things are like seeds that are planted in all men. But if he keeps them to himself, they will wither away and die very quickly, and then God help that poor man because he will have nothing and life will not be worth living. On the other hand, if he gives his strength and hope and love to others, he will find an endless store of such stock. He will never run dry of those things. Then life will be worth living. And believe me, gladiator, life is the best thing in the world. We know that. We are slaves. All we have is life. So we know what it is worth. The Romans have so many other things that life doesn't mean very much to them. They play with it. But we take life seriously, and that is why we must not let ourselves be alone. You are too much alone, gladiator. Talk to me a little."

(But the Jew says nothing, and his face and his eyes do not change at all. Yet he listens. He listens silently and

228

intently, and then he turns around and walks away. But after he has walked a few steps, he stops, half turns his head, and watches Spartacus from the corners of his eyes. And it seems to Spartacus that something is there which was not there before, a spark, a plea, a gleam of hope. Perhaps.)

This was the beginning of the third period of the four times into which the life of the gladiator might be divided. This could be called the time of hope, and it was in this time that the hatred went away, and the gladiator knew a great love and comradeship for others of his kind. It did not happen all at once and it did not happen quickly. Bit by bit, he learned to trust a man, and through that man, he learned to love life. That was the thing in Spartacus which had captured him from the very beginning, the Thracian's enormous love of life. Spartacus was like a guardian of life. It was not merely that he relished it and cherished it; it absorbed him. It was something he never questioned and never criticized. To some extent, it seemed that there was a secret pact between Spartacus and all the forces of life.

From watching Spartacus, the gladiator David took to following him. He did not do this ostentatiously; he did it almost secretively. Whenever the occasion arose and it was not too directly noticeable, he placed himself near Spartacus. His hearing was as keen as the hearing of a fox. He would listen to the words of Spartacus; he would take those words with him and repeat them to himself. He would try to learn what lay within those words. And all this time, something was happening inside of him. He was changing; he was growing. In something of the same way, a little of change and a little of growth was happening inside of every gladiator in the school. But for David it was singular. He came of a people whose life was full of God. When he lost God, there was a hole in his life. Now he was filling this hole with man. He was learning to love man. He was learning the greatness of man. He did not think of it in this way, but this was what happened to him—and to some extent to the other gladiators.

This was not anything which could be encompassed by the understanding of either Batiatus or the senators at Rome. To them, the revolt sprang full blown and unpremeditated. To their knowledge, there was no preparation and no prelude, and so they had to record it. There was no other way for them to record it.

But the prelude was there, subtle and strange and growing. David never forgot the first time he heard Spartacus recite verses from the Odyssey. Here was a new and enchanting music, the story of a brave man who endured a lot but was never defeated. Many of the verses were wholly understandable to him. He had known the frustrating agony of being held away from a homeland he loved. He had known the tricks capricious fate plays. He had loved a girl in the hills of Galilee whose lips were as red as poppies and whose cheeks were as soft as down, and his heart had ached for her because she was lost to him. But what music this was, and how splendid that a slave, a slave who was the son of a slave and never a freeman even once, could recite endless verses of this fine story all by heart! Was there ever such a man as Spartacus! Was there ever a man so gentle, so patient, so slow to anger!

In his mind, he identified Spartacus with Odysseus, the patient and wise Odysseus; and forever after the two were one so far as he was concerned. Boy that he was then, underneath all, he found his hero and pattern for life and for living in Spartacus. At first, he was mistrustful of this tendency in himself. Trust no man and no man will disappoint you, he had said to himself often enough, so he waited and watched and looked for Spartacus to be less than Spartacus. And gradually, the realization grew upon him that Spartacus would never be less than Spartacus—and the realization was more than that, for there came to him an understanding that no man is less than himself, not the whole understanding, but a glimmering of knowledge of the wealth of wonder and splendor that lies in each separate and singular human being.

So when he was chosen as one of four gladiators to satisfy the caprice of the two perfumed homosexuals from Rome, to fight in two pairs to the death, he was torn by such a struggle and unholy contradiction as he had never experienced before. It was a new struggle, and when he conquered in that struggle, he made the first real penetration of the protective covering with which he had encased himself. That moment too, he lived through now on the cross. He was back again, and fighting with himself, and from his parched lips on the cross came the agony of words he had spoken to himself four years before.

(I am the most cursed man in all the world—he says to himself—for see how I am chosen to kill the man I love better than any man who lives. What a cruel fate this is! But it is just what one would expect from a God or gods or whatever they are who have no other purpose but to torture man. That is their whole mission. But I will not satisfy them. I will not perform for them. They are like those perfumed Roman swine who sit at the arena and wait for a man's guts to roll out on the sand! Well, I won't satisfy them this time. They will miss the pleasure of watching pairs fight, those miserable and corrupt people who can find pleasure in nothing else. They will see me killed, but it will be no satisfaction to them to see a man killed. That they can see at any time at all. But I will not fight Spartacus. I would kill my own brother first. I will never do that.

(But what then? First there was only insanity in my whole life, and then the life here compounded insanity. What has Spartacus given me? I must ask myself that question and I must answer that. I must answer it because he has given me something of great importance. He has given me the secret of life. Life itself is the secret of life. Everyone takes sides. You are on the side of life, or you are on the side of death. Spartacus is on the side of life, and therefore he will fight me if he must. He will not just die. He will not allow them to put him to death, never saying a word and never striking a blow back at them. Then that is what I must do. I must fight Spartacus, and life will decide between us. Oh what a terrible decision to make! Was ever a man so cursed? But that is the way it must be. That is the only way it can be.)

He lived the thoughts and the decision over again, and he no longer knew that he was dying on a cross, that fate had been kind to him, that it was not his lot to fight against Spartacus. Piece by piece, his pain-wracked mind picked up the past and lived it out again. Once again, the gladiators killed their trainers in the mess hall. Once again, they fought the troops with knives and bare hands. Once again, they marched across the countryside, and from the plantations, the slaves poured out to join them. And once again, they fell upon the City Cohorts at night and destroyed them utterly, and took their weapons and their armor. All this he lived through once again, not rationally or chronologically or easily, but like a ball of hot flame flung back through time.

("Spartacus," he says, "Spartacus?" Their second great battle is behind them now. The slaves are an army. They look like an army. They have the weapons and the armor of ten thousand Romans. They are drawn up by their hundreds and their five hundreds. Their nightly camp is a wooden-walled, moated fortress, such as the legions build when they march. They practice for hours at throwing the Roman spear. The fame and the dread fear of what they have done is known all over the world. In every slave hut, in every slave barracks, there is a whisper of someone called Spartacus who has set the world on fire. Yes, he has done it. He has a mighty army. Soon he will march against Rome itself, and he will tear down the walls of Rome in his anger. Wherever he goes, he sets slaves free, and all the spoils he takes goes into a common treasury—as it was in the olden days when the tribe held all and no man had wealth. His soldiers have only their weapons and the clothes on their backs and the shoes on their feet. That is Spartacus now.

(He says, "Spartacus?"

(Little by little, speech has returned to this Jew, David. He speaks slowly and haltingly, but he speaks. Now he speaks to the leader of the slaves.

("Spartacus, I am a good fighter, am I not?"

("Good, very good. The very best. You fight well."

("And I am no coward, you know that?"

("I knew that a long time ago," says Spartacus. "Where is a gladiator who is a coward?"

("And I have never turned my back on a fight."

("Never."

("And when my ear was sliced off my head, I clenched my teeth and never cried out in pain."

("It's no disgrace to cry out in pain," says Spartacus. "I have known strong men to cry out in pain. I've known strong men to weep when they are full of bitterness. That is no disgrace."

("But you and I don't weep, and some day I will be like you, Spartacus."

("You will be a better man than I am. You are a better fighter than I am."

("No, I will never be one half of what you are, but I think I fight well. I am very quick. Like a cat. A cat can see a blow coming. A cat sees through his skin. I feel like that sometimes. Almost always, I see the blow coming. That is why I want to ask you something. I want to ask you this. I want you to place me by your side. Whenever we fight, I want to be at your side. I will keep you safe. If we lose you, we lose the whole thing. We are not fighting for ourselves. We are fighting for the whole world. That is why I want you to keep me at your side always when we fight."

("There are more important things for you to do than to stand by my side. I need men to lead an army."

("The men need you. Am I asking so much?"

("You ask very little, David. You ask it for me, not for you."

("Then tell me it is what you want."

(Spartacus nods.

("And you will come to no harm, ever. I will watch over you. Day and night, I will watch over you.")

So he became the right arm of the slave leader. He, who all of his young life had known only bloodshed and toil and violence, now saw shining and golden horizons. What would be as a result of their rebellion became clearer and clearer in his mind. Since most of the world were slaves, they would soon be a force that nothing could stand up to. Then nations and cities would disappear, and it would be the *golden age* again. Once upon a time, in the stories and legends of every people, it was the *golden age,* when men were without sin and without gall, and when they lived together in peace and in love. So when Spartacus and his slaves had conquered the whole world, then it would be so again. It would be ushered in with a great clashing of cymbals, a sounding of trumpets, and a chorus of all the voices of the people, giving praise.

In his fevered mind, he now heard that chorus. He heard the swelling timbre of the voice of mankind, a chorus that rocked back from the mountainsides . . .

(He is alone with Varinia. When he looks at Varinia, the real world dissolves, and there remains only this woman who is the wife of Spartacus. To David, she is the most beautiful woman in the world and the most desirable, and his love for her is like a worm in his belly. How many times, he has said to himself,

(What a contemptible creature you are, to love the wife of Spartacus! Everything you have in the world, you owe to Spartacus, and how do you repay him? You repay him by loving his wife. What a sinful thing! What an awful thing! Even if you don't speak of it, even if you don't show it, nevertheless it is an awful thing! And furthermore, it is a useless thing. Look at yourself. Hold a mirror up before your face. Was there ever such a face, sharp and wild, like a hawk's face, one ear missing, cut and scarred!

(Now Varinia says to him, "What a strange lad you are, David! Where did you come from? Are all your people like you? You are just a boy, but you never smile and you never laugh. What a way to be!"

("Don't call me a boy, Varinia. I've proven that I'm sometimes more than a boy."

("Have you indeed? Well, you don't fool me. You're just a boy. You should have a girl. You should put your arm around her waist and walk with her when the evening is early and lovely. You should kiss her. You should laugh with her. Aren't there enough girls?"

("I have my work to do. I have no time for that."

("No time for love? Oh, David, David, what a thing to say! What a strange thing to say!"

("And if no one put his mind to anything," he answers fiercely, "where would we be? Do you think it's just child's play to lead an army, to find food for so many thousands of people every day, to train men! We have the most important thing in the world to do, and you want me to make eyes at girls!"

("Not to make eyes at them, David. I want you to make love to them."

("I have no time for that."

("No time. Well, how would I feel if Spartacus said he had no time for me? I would want to die, I think. There is nothing more important than being a man, just a plain, ordinary, human man. I know you think Spartacus is something more than a man. He isn't. If he were, then he wouldn't be any good at all. There is no great mystery about Spartacus. I know that. When a woman loves a man, she knows a lot about him."

(He takes all his courage in his arms and says, "You do love him, don't you?"

("What are you saying, boy? I love him more than I love life. I would die for him, if he wanted me to."

("I would die for him," David says.

("That is different. I watch you sometimes, when you look at him. That's different. I love him because he's a man. He's a simple man. There's nothing complicated about him. He's simple and gentle, and never did he raise his voice against me or lift a hand against me. There are some men who are filled with sorrow for themselves. But Spartacus has no sorrow for himself and no pity for himself. He only has pity and sorrow for others. How can you ask if I love him? Doesn't everyone here know how much I love him?")

Thus, at times in his suffering, this last gladiator remembered with great clarity and precision; but at other times, the recollection was wild and horrible, and a battle became a nightmare of terrible noise, of blood and agony, of wild masses of men in wild and uncontrolled motion. At one point or another, in the first two years of their revolt, the realization had come upon them that the masses of slaves who peopled the Roman world would not or could not rise up and join them. They had then reached their maximum strength, but the power of Rome seemed to have no end. He remembered, out of that time, a battle they had fought, an awful battle, so great in its size, so vast in the numbers of men engaged, that for most of a day and a whole night, Spartacus and the men around him could only guess at the course the battle was taking. During the time of this recollection, the people of Capua who were watching the crucified gladiator saw how his body writhed and twisted and how white spittle flecked his lips and how his separate limbs jerked in convulsive agony. They heard the sounds come out of his mouth, and many among them said,

"He's not for long now. He's pretty well done in."

(They have taken position on a hilltop, a long hill, a long rolling ridge on either side, and their heavy infantry is spread out on the crest of the hill for half a mile in either direction. There is a pretty valley, with a shallow little river running through the center of it, a meandering little river that curves back and forth, with green grass on the valley bottom and cows heavy of udder munching the grass, and on the other side of the valley, there is a ridge of ground where the Roman legions have taken their position. In the center of his army, Spartacus has established his command post, a white pavilion on a hummock that overlooks the whole area. Here have been put into operation what are by now routine necessities of a battle command post. A secretary sits with his writing materials and paper. Fifty runners stand ready to dash at once to any part of the battlefield. A mast has been erected for the signal man, and he stands by his mast with his variety of brightly-colored flags. And on a long table in the center of the great tent, a large map of the battle area is being prepared.

(These are methods which belong to the slaves, and which they have worked out in the course of two years of bitter campaigning. Just as they have worked out their tactics of battle. Now, the leaders of the army stand around the table, looking at the map, and sifting information as to the size and quality of the force which opposes them. There are eight men around the table. At one end, Spartacus stands, David next to him. Looking at him for the first time, a stranger would say that this man, Spartacus, is at least forty years old. His curly hair is streaked with gray. He is leaner than before, and there are dark circles under his eyes from want of sleep.

(Time is catching up with him, an observer would say. Time is sitting astraddle of his shoulders and riding him . . . That would be a keen observation, for once in a while, once in a bag of years, of centuries, a man calls upon the whole world; and then as centuries pass and as the world turns, this man is never forgotten. So short a while ago, this one was just a slave; now who is there who doesn't know the name of Spartacus? But he has not had time to pause and fully reflect upon what has happened to him. Least of all has he had time to reflect upon what happened, in two years, inside of him, changing him from the man he was to the man he now is. Now he commands an army of almost fifty thousand men, and in certain ways it is the best army the world has ever seen.

(It is an army which fights for freedom in the most simple and unvarnished terms. In the past there have been armies without end, armies which have fought for nations or cities or wealth or spoils or power or control of this area or that area; but here is an army which fights for human freedom and dignity, an army which calls no land or city its own because the people within it come from all lands and cities and tribes, an army where every soldier shares a common heritage of servitude and a common hatred of men who make other men slaves. This is an army which is committed to victory, for there are no bridges over which it can retreat, no land which will give it shelter or rest. It is a moment of changed motion in history, a beginning, a stirring, a wordless whisper, a portent, a flash of light which signifies earth-shaking thunder and blinding lightning. It is an army which suddenly has the knowledge that the victory to which it is committed must change the world, and therefore it must change the world or have no victory.

(Perhaps as Spartacus stands brooding over the map, the question arises in his mind as to how this army came into being. He thinks of the handful of gladiators who beat their way out of the school of the fat *lanista*. He thinks of them as a spear thrown that sets a sea of life into motion, so that suddenly the enduring calm and stability of the slave world explodes. He thinks of the endless struggle to turn these slaves into soldiers, to make them work together and think together, and then he tries to understand why the motion stopped.

(But there is no time for much of such reflection now. Now they are going to fight. His heart is heavy with fear; it always is before a battle. When the battle starts, much of that fear will pass away, but now he is afraid. He looks around the table at his comrades. Why are their faces so calm? Don't they share his fear? He sees Crixus, the red haired Gaul, his little blue eyes sunk so deep and calm in his red, freckled face, his long yellow mustache curving down below his chin. And there is Gannicus, his friend, his brother out of bondage and tribal brotherhood. There is Castus and Phraxus and Nordo, the heavy shouldered black African, Mosar, the slight, delicate, keen-witted Egyptian, and the Jew, David—and none of them seems to be afraid. Why, then, is he afraid?

(He says to them now, sharply, "Well, my friends— what are we going to do, stand here all day, playing guessing games about that army across the valley?"

("It's a very big army," Gannicus says. "It's a bigger

army than anything we've ever seen or fought. You can't count them, but I can tell you that we've identified the standards of ten legions. They've brought down the Seventh and Eighth from Gaul. They've brought over three legions from Africa and two from Spain. I've never seen an army like that, not in all my born days. There must be seventy thousand men across the valley."

(Always it is Crixus who looks for fear or wavering. If it were up to Crixus, they would have conquered the whole world already. He has only one slogan, to march on Rome. Stop killing the rats and burn down their nest. Now he says, "You make me tired, Gannicus, because it's always the biggest army, always the worst time for a battle. I'll tell you what. I don't give two damns for their army. If it was my decision, I would attack them. I would attack them now and not an hour or a day or a week from now."

(Gannicus wants to hold it off. Maybe the Romans will split their forces. They have before, so maybe they will again.

("They won't," Spartacus says. "Take my word for it. Why should they? They have us all here. They know we are all here. Why should they?"

(Then Mosar, the Egyptian, says, "For once I am going to agree with Crixus. That is a very unusual occurrence, but this time he's right. That is a big army over there across the valley and we will have to fight them sooner or later, and it might just as well be sooner. They can outsit us, because they will eat, and after a while we'll have nothing to eat. And if we move, they will have the opportunity they want."

("How many men do you think they are?" Spartacus asks him.

("A lot—at least seventy thousand."

(Spartacus shakes his head somberly. "Oh, that's a lot—that's a devil of a lot. But I think you're right. We'll have to fight them here." He tries to sound light, but his heart is not light at all.

(They decide that in three hours they will attack the Roman flank, but the battle is joined before then. Hardly have the various commanders returned to their regiments when the Romans launch their attack at the center of the slave army. There are no complicated tactics, no skillful evolutions; a legion spearheads the attack on the slave center, like a spear thrown at the command post, and the whole mighty Roman army rolls to the attack behind the legion. David remains with Spartacus, but for less than an hour are they able to direct a coordinated defense from the command post. Then the fighting is on them, and the nightmare begins. The pavilion is smashed. The battle bears them along like a sea, and around Spartacus a cyclone rages.

(This is fighting. Now David will know that he has been in a fight. Next to this, everything else is a skirmish. Now Spartacus is not the commander of a great army, but only a man with a sword and the square shield of a soldier, and he fights like hell itself. That is the way the Jew fights. The two of them are a rock, and the battle churns around them. Once they are alone, and they are fighting for their lives. Then a hundred men come to their help. David looks at Spartacus, and behind the blood and sweat, the Thracian is grinning.

("What a fight!" he cried. "What a fight this is, David! Will we ever live to see the sun rise in a fight like this? Who knows?"

(He loves it, David thinks. What a strange man this is! Look how he loves battle! Look how he fights! He fights like a berserk! He fights like one of them out of that song he sings!

(He doesn't know that he too is fighting the same way. He must be killed before a spear can touch Spartacus. He is like a cat that never tires, a great cat, a jungle cat, and his sword is a claw. He is never separated from Spartacus. One would think that he is joined to Spartacus, the way he manages to remain always by his side. He sees very little of the battle. He sees only what is directly ahead of Spartacus and himself, but that is enough. The Romans know that Spartacus is here, and they forget the formal dance of the maniples that their soldiers train for years to perfect. They crowd in, driven by their officers, fighting and clawing to reach Spartacus, to drag him down, to kill him, to cut off the head of the monster. They are so close that David can hear all the vile filth pouring out of their mouths. It makes a sound above the clashing roar of the battle. But the slaves too know that Spartacus is here, and from the other side they pour into this center of struggle. They raise the name of Spartacus like a banner. It waves out over the whole battlefield like a banner. Spartacus! You can hear it miles away. At a walled city, five miles away, they hear the sound of the battle.

(But David hears without listening; he knows nothing but what he fights and what is in front of him. As his strength goes, as his lips become parched, the battle becomes more and more terrible. He doesn't know that it is spread over two miles of ground. He doesn't know that Crixus has smashed two legions and pursues them. He knows only his arm and his sword and Spartacus beside him. He is not even aware that they have fought their way down the hillside into the valley bottom until he begins to sink ankle-deep into the soft, grassy ground. Then they are in the river, and the fight goes on while they stand knee-deep in water that is running red as blood. The sun sets and the whole sky is red, a bitter salute to the thousands of men who fill the valley with their hatred and struggle. In the darkness, the battle lessens but it never pauses, and under the cold light of the moon, the slaves dip their heads into the bloody river water, drinking and drinking, for unless they drink they will die.

(With the dawning, the Roman attack breaks. Who has fought men like these slaves! No matter how many you kill, others come screaming and yelling to take their places. They fight like animals, not like men, for even after you have buried your sword in their guts and they go down on the ground, they will fasten their teeth in your foot, and you have to cut through the neck to make them let go. Other men crawl out of the battle when they are wounded, but these slaves go on fighting until they die. Other men break off a battle when the sun sets, but these slaves fight like cats in the dark and they never rest.

(With this kind of thing, fear creeps into the Romans. It grows in them out of an old seed long since planted. Fear of the slaves. You live with slaves, but you never trust them. They are inside, but they are also outside. They smile at you each day, but behind the smile is hatred. They think only of killing you. They grow strong on hatred. They wait and wait and wait. They have a patience and a memory that never ends. This is the seed which was planted in the Romans since first they were able to think, and now the seed bears fruit.

(They are tired. They hardly have the strength to carry

their shields and lift their swords. But the slaves are not tired. Reason goes. Ten break here, a hundred there. The hundred becomes a thousand, the thousand ten thousand, and suddenly the whole Roman army is swept with panic and the Romans begin to throw down their arms and run. Their officers try to stop them, but they kill their officers, and screaming in panic, they run from the slaves. And the slaves come behind them, evening old scores, so that the ground for miles around is carpeted with Romans who lie on their faces with the wounds in their backs.

(When Crixus and the others find Spartacus, he is still next to the Jew. Spartacus is stretched on the ground, sleeping among the dead, and the Jew stands over him, sword in hand. "Let him sleep," the Jew says. "This is a great victory. Let him sleep."

(But ten thousand slaves have died in that great slave victory. And there will be other Roman armies—larger armies.)

VII

When it became known that the gladiator was dying, interest in him slackened. By the tenth hour, mid-afternoon, only a handful of the most confirmed advocates of crucifixion remained to watch—they and a few such ragamuffin beggars and scabby loafers as would be unwelcome among the numerous fruitful pleasures which even a city like Capua provided in the afternoon. It was true that there were no races in Capua at that time, but there was sure to be something doing at one of the two fine arenas. Because it was so popular a city for tourists, it was a point of pride among the wealthier citizens of Capua to provide fighting pairs for a minimum of three hundred days of the year. There was an excellent theatre in Capua and a number of large public houses of prostitution, operating in a more open manner than would have been countenanced in Rome. In these places there were women of every race and nation, specially trained to enhance the reputation of the city. There were also the fine shops, the perfume bazaar, the baths, and the many water sports on the beautiful bay.

Therefore, it is not surprising that one dying, crucified

gladiator should be only a passing attraction. If he had not been the hero of the *munera*, not a second glance would have been given him, and even this way, he was no longer an object of great interest. In a letter addressed "to the full citizens of Rome who dwell at Capua," the three wealthy merchants who headed the small Jewish community disowned all knowledge of or responsibility for him. They pointed out that in their homeland, all elements of rebellion and discontent had been rooted out, and they also pointed out that circumcision was not proof of Jewish origin. Among the Egyptians, the Phoenicians, and even among the Persians, circumcision was quite common. It was also not in the nature of Jews to strike against that power which had brought a state of peace and plentitude and benign order over most of the world. Thus abandonded on every side, the gladiator was reaching his death in lonely indignity and pain. He provided no amusement for the soldiers and precious little for the onlookers. There was one wretched old woman who sat with her hands folded around her knees, staring at the man on the cross. The soldiers, out of sheer boredom, began to tease her.

"Now, beautiful," one of them said, "what are you dreaming about with that man up there?"

"Shall we cut him down and give him to you?" another asked. "How long is it since you had a fine young fellow like that in bed with you?"

"A long time," she muttered.

"Well, he'd be a bull in bed with you, all right. He'd be one to ride you. My God, he'd ride you the way a stallion rides a mare. How about it, old lady?"

"What a way to talk," she said. "What people you are! What a way to talk to me!"

"Oh, my ladyship, I apologize." One after another, the soldiers made sweeping bows to her. The few onlookers caught up with the game and crowded around.

"I don't give two damns for your apologies," the old woman said. "Filth! I'm dirty. You're filth. I could wash off my dirt in the baths. You couldn't."

They didn't like the game two ways, and their authority reasserted itself. They became hard, and their eyes glittered. "Take it easy, old lady," one of them said. "Keep a bolt on your tongue."

"I say what I please."

"Then go take a bath and come back. You're a sight, sitting here right at the city gates the way you look."

"Sure I'm a sight," she grinned at them. "I'm a dreadful sight, huh? What people you Romans are! The cleanest people in the world. Isn't a Roman who doesn't bathe every day, even if he's a loafer, as most of you are, and spends his mornings gambling and his afternoons in the arena. He's so damned clean—"

"That's enough, old lady. Just shut your mouth."

"It's not enough at all. I can't bathe. I'm a slave. Slaves don't go to the baths. I'm old and used up, and there isn't anything you can do to me. Not one blessed thing. I sit in the sun and bother no one, but you don't like that, do you? Twice a day I go to my master's house, and he gives me a handful of bread. The good bread. The bread of Rome that the slaves plant and the slaves reap and the slaves grind and the slaves bake. I walk through the streets, and what do I look at that hasn't been made by the hands of slaves? Do you think you frighten me? I spit at you!"

While this was going on, Crassus returned to the Appian Gate. He had slept poorly, as people often do when they try to make up in daylight the rest they should have had the night before. If someone had asked him why he was returning to the scene of the crucifixion, he might have shrugged his shoulders. But actually he knew well enough. A whole great era of the life of Crassus was finishing with the death of this last of the gladiators. Crassus would be remembered, not only as a very rich man, but as the man who had put down the revolt of the slaves.

This is an easy thing to say, but it was not an easy thing to do. As long as he lived, Crassus would never separate himself from his memories of the Servile War. He would live with those memories, rise with them, and go to bed with them. He would never say farewell to Spartacus until he, Crassus, died.

Then the struggle between Spartacus and Crassus would be over, but only then. So now Crassus returned to the gate to look again at all that was left and living of his adversary.

A new captain was in command of this shift, but he knew the general—as most people in Capua did—and he outdid himself in being personable and helpful. He even apologized for the fact that so few people had remained to see the death of the gladiator.

"He is dying very quickly," he said. "That's surprising. He seemed to be the tough, lasting type. He might have lived on there three days. But he'll be dead before morning."

"How do you know?" asked Crassus.

"You can tell. I've seen a great many crucifixions, and they all follow the same pattern. Unless the nails cut through a major artery, and then they bleed to death pretty quickly. This one isn't bleeding very much though. He just doesn't want to live any more, and when that happens, they die quickly. You wouldn't think it would be that way, would you?"

"Nothing surprises me," said Crassus.

"I guess not. I guess after all you've seen—"

At that moment, the soldiers laid hands on the old woman, and her shrill cries as she fought them attracted the attention of the general and the gate captain. Crassus strode over, took in the scene at a glance, and told the soldiers scathingly,

"What a fine lot of heroes you are! Leave the old lady alone!"

The quality of his voice caused them to obey. They let go of the woman. One of them recognized Crassus and whispered to the others, and then the captain came up and wanted to know what this was all about and whether they didn't have anything better to do with their time?

"She was insolent and filthy in her language."

A man standing by guffawed.

"Get out of here, the lot of you," the captain told the idlers. They retreated a few steps, but not too far, and the old crone peered shrewdly at Crassus.

"So the great general is my protector," she said.

"Who are you, old witch?" Crassus demanded.

"Great man, should I kneel in front of you or should I spit in your face?"

"Do you see? Did I tell you?" the soldier cried.

"Yes—all right. Now what do you want, old woman?" Crassus asked.

"I only want to be left alone. I came out here to see a

good man die. He should not die all alone. I sit and watch him while he dies. I give him an offering of love. I tell him that he will never die. Spartacus never died. Spartacus lives."

"What on earth are you talking about, old woman?"

"Don't you know what I'm talking about, Marcus Licinius Crassus? I'm talking about Spartacus. Yes, I know why you came out here. No one else does. They don't know. But you and I know, don't we?"

The captain told the soldiers to take hold of her and drag her away, because she was just a filthy old bag, but Crassus motioned them off angrily.

"Leave her alone, I told you. Stop showing me how brave you are! If you're so damned brave, maybe you'd all like to be in a legion instead of a summer resort. I can just take care of myself. I can just defend myself from one old lady."

"You're afraid," the old woman smiled.

"What am I afraid of?"

"Afraid of us, aren't you? Such a fear you all have! That's why you came out here. To see him die. To make sure that the last one is dead. My God, what some slaves did to you! And you're still afraid. And even when he dies, will it be the end? Will it ever be the end, Marcus Licinius Crassus?"

"Who are you, old woman?"

"I am a slave," she answered, and now she seemed to become simple and childish and senile. "I came out here to be with one of my people and to give him a little comfort. I came to weep for him. All the others are afraid to come. Capua is full of my people but they are afraid. Spartacus said to us, rise up and be free! But we were afraid. We are so strong, and yet we cower and whimper and run away." Now the tears poured out of her rheumy old eyes. "What are you going to do to me?" she pleaded.

"Nothing, old woman. Sit there and weep if you want to." He threw a coin at her and walked thoughtfully away. He walked over to the cross, looking up at the dying gladiator and turning over the old woman's words in his mind.

VIII

In the life of the gladiator, there were four times. Childhood was a happy time of not knowing, and the time of his youth was full of knowledge and sorrow and hatred. The time of hope was the time when he fought with Spartacus, and the time of despair was the time when it became known to him that their cause was lost. This was the end of the time of despair. Now he was dying.

Struggle had been his bread and meat, but now he no longer struggled. Life in him had been a fury of anger and resistance, a loud cry for a logic in the relationship of one man to another man. Some are made to accept and some are unable to accept. There was nothing he could accept until he found Spartacus. Then he accepted the knowledge that a human life was a worthy thing. The life of Spartacus was a worthy thing; it was a noble thing, and the men with him lived nobly—but now on the cross and dying, he still asked why they had failed. The question sought its answer in the confusion of reason that remained to him, but the question found no answer.

(He is with Spartacus when news comes that Crixus is dead. The death of Crixus was the logic of the life of Crixus. Crixus clung to a dream. Spartacus knew when the dream was finished and impossible. The dream of Crixus and the drive of Crixus was to destroy Rome. But a moment came when Spartacus realized that they could never destroy Rome, that Rome could only destroy them. That was the beginning, and the end was that twenty thousand slaves marched off under Crixus. And now Crixus is dead and his army is destroyed. Crixus is dead and his men are dead. The big, violent, red headed Gaul will laugh no more and shout no more. He is dead.

(David is with Spartacus when this news comes. A messenger, a survivor, brings the news. Such messengers have death all over them. Spartacus listens. Then he turns to David.

("Did you hear it?" he asks him.

("I heard."

("Did you hear that Crixus is dead and all his army is dead?"

("I heard."

("Is there so much death in the world? Is there?"

("The world is full of death. Before I knew you, there was only death in the world."

("Now there is only death in the world," Spartacus says. He is changed. He is different. He will never be as he was before. He will never have the precious relationship to life which he has had until now, which he had even in the gold mines of Nubia, which he had even in the arena when he stood naked with a knife in his hand. For him now, death has won over life. He stands with nothing in his face and with his eyes full of nothing, and then from the nothing the tears come and roll down over his broad brown cheeks. What a terrible, heart-breaking thing it is for David to have to stand there and watch him weep! This is Spartacus weeping. The thought goes through the Jew's mind, thus: *shall I tell you about Spartacus?*

(Because you will see nothing by looking at him. You will know nothing by looking at him. You will see only his broken, flattened nose, his broad mouth, his brown skin, and his wide-set eyes. How can you know about him? He is a new man. They say he is like the heroes of the olden times; but what do the heroes of the olden times have in common with Spartacus? Does a hero come from a father who is sired by a slave? And where did this man come from? How can he live without hate and without envy? You shall know a man by his bitterness and his gall, but here is a man without bitterness and gall. Here is a noble man. Here is a man who in all his life did no wrong. He is different from you—but also different from us. What we are beginning to be, he is; but none of us are what he is. He walked beyond us. And now he weeps.

("Why do you weep?" David demands. "It will be so hard for us now—why do you weep? They will give us no peace now until we are all dead."

("Do you never weep?" Spartacus asks.

("When they nailed my father on the cross, I wept. I never wept since then."

("You didn't weep for your father," Spartacus says, "and I don't weep for Crixus. I weep for us. Why did it happen? Where were we wrong? In the beginning I never felt a doubt. My whole life was for the moment when the slaves would have strength and weapons in their hands. And then I never had a doubt. The time of the whiplash was over. The bells were ringing all over the world. Then why did we fail? Why did we fail? Why did you die, Crixus, my comrade? Why were you headstrong and terrible? Now you are dead and all your beautiful men are dead!"

(The Jew says, "The dead are gone. Stop weeping!"

(But Spartacus goes down on the ground, all in a huddled heap, with his face in the dirt, and with his face in the dirt, he cries, "Send Varinia to me. Send her to me. Tell her I'm afraid, and death is all over me.")

IX

There was a moment of complete clarity before the gladiator died. He opened his eyes; the focus cleared; and for just a little while he was not conscious of any pain at all. He saw the scene around him plainly and clearly. There was the Appian Way, the great Roman road, the glory and bloodstream of Rome, stretching away northward all the distance to the mighty *urbs* itself. There, on the other side of him, was the city wall and the Appian Gate. There were a dozen bored city soldiers. There was the captain of the gate, flirting with a pretty girl. There, perched up on the edge of the road, were a handful of morbid idlers. Along the road itself there was a desultory flow of traffic, for the hour was already late and most of the city's free population were at the baths. Beyond the road, as the gaze of the gladiator lifted, he imagined he saw a gleam of the sea in that most beautiful of all bays. A cool wind blew from the sea, and its touch on his face was like the touch of the cool hands of a woman a man loves.

He saw the green shrubs that landscaped the edge of the road, the dark cypress trees beyond that, and northward, the rollings hills and the spine of the lonely mountains where the runaway slaves hide. He saw the blue afternoon sky, blue and beautiful as an ache for an unfulfilled longing, and dropping his eyes, he saw a single old woman who crouched only a few dozen yards from the cross and looked at him steadily and wept as she watched him.

"Why, she weeps for me," the gladiator said to himself. "Who are you, old woman, that you sit there and weep for me?"

He knew that he was dying. His mind was clear; he knew that he was dying and he was grateful that soon there would be no memory and no pain, but only the sleep that all men look forward to with absolute certainty. He no longer had any desire to struggle or resist death. He felt that when he closed his eyes, the life would go out of him, easily and quickly.

And he saw Crassus. He saw him and he recognized him. Their eyes met. The Roman general stood as straight and still as a statue. His white toga covered him from head to foot in its draped folds. His fine, handsome, sunburned head was like a symbol of Rome's might and power and glory.

"So you are here to see me die, Crassus!" the gladiator thought. "You came to watch the last of the slaves die on the cross. So a slave dies, and the last thing he sees is the richest man in the world."

Then the gladiator remembered the other time he had seen Crassus. He remembered Spartacus then. He remembered how Spartacus was. They knew it was over; they knew it was done; they knew it was the last battle. Spartacus had said goodby to Varinia. For all her pleading, for all her wild pleading to remain with him, he said goodby to her and forced her to go. She was heavy with child then, and Spartacus had hoped that he would see the child born before the Romans brought them to bay. But the child was still unborn when he parted from Varinia, and he told David then,

"I will never see the child, friend and old comrade. That's the one thing I regret. I regret nothing else, nothing else."

They were drawn up for the battle when they brought Spartacus the white horse. What a horse that was! A beautiful Persian steed, white as snow and proud and mettlesome. It was a fit horse for Spartacus. He had shed his worries, had Spartacus. It was not a mask he assumed. He was actually happy and youthful and full of life and vitality and fire. His hair had turned gray these past six months, but you never saw the gray hair now, only the vibrant youth of the face. That ugly face was beautiful. Everyone saw how beautiful it was. Men looked at him and were unable to speak. Then they brought him the fine white horse.

"First, I thank you for this splendid gift, dear friends, dear comrades." That was what he said. "First, I thank you. I thank you with all my heart." Then he drew his sword, and with a motion almost too quick to follow, he plunged it up to the hilt in the horse's breast, hung on to it while the animal reared and screamed, then tore it loose as the horse went down on its knees, rolled over and died. He faced them, the dripping sword in his hand, and they looked at him with horror and amazement. But nothing had changed about him.

"A horse is dead," he said. "Do you want to weep because a horse is dead? We fight for the life of man, not for the life of beasts. The Romans cherish horses, but for man they have nothing but contempt. Now we will see who walks off this battlefield, the Romans or ourselves. I thanked you for your gift. It was a fine gift. It showed how you love me, but I didn't need such a gift to know. I know what's in my heart. My heart is full of love for you. There are no words in the whole world to say what love I have for you, my dear comrades. Our lives were together. Even if we fail today, we did a thing that men will remember forever. Four years we have fought Rome—four long years. We never turned our backs on a Roman army. We never ran. We will not run from the battlefield today. Did you want me to fight on a horse? Let the Romans have the horses. I fight on foot, alongside of my brothers. If we win this battle today, we will have horses in plenty, and we will harness them to ploughs, not to chariots. And if we lose— well, we won't need horses if we lose."

Then he embraced them. Each one of his old comrades who remained, he embraced and kissed on the lips. And when he came to David, he said,

"Ah, my friend, great gladiator. Will you stay beside me today?"

"Always."

And as he hung on the cross, looking at Crassus, the gladiator thought, "How much can a man do?" He had no regrets now. He had fought at the side of Spartacus. He had fought there while this man who now faced him, this great general, reared his horse and attempted to smash through the ranks of the slaves. He had cried out, with Spartacus,

"Come to us, Crassus! Come and taste our greeting!"

He had fought until a stone from a sling laid him low. He had fought well. He was glad that he did not have to see Spartacus die. He was glad that he and not Spartacus had to bear this final shame and indignity of the cross. He had no regrets now, no cares, and for the moment, no pain. He understood that last youthful joy of Spartacus. There was no defeat. He was now like Spartacus, because he shared the deep secret of life which Spartacus knew. He wanted to tell Crassus. He tried desperately to speak. He moved his lips, and Crassus came up to the cross. Crassus stood there, looking at the dying man above him, but no sound came from the gladiator. Then the gladiator's head rolled forward; the last strength went out of his limbs and he was dead.

Crassus stood there until the old woman joined him. "He is dead now," the old woman said.

"I know," Crassus answered.

Then he walked back to the gate and through the streets of Capua.

X

That night, Crassus dined alone. He was not at home to any callers, and his slaves, recognizing the black mood which every so often came upon him, walked softly and carefully. He had disposed of the better part of a bottle of wine before dinner; another went with his dinner, and after the meal he sat down with a flask of *servius,* as they called a strong date brandy, distilled in Egypt and imported from there. He became very drunk, alone and moodily, a drunkenness compounded out of despair and self-hatred, and when he reached the point where he could only barely walk, he staggered to his bedroom and let his slaves help him into bed for the night.

However, he slept well and deeply. In the morning he felt rested; his head did not ache, and he had no memory of bad dreams which might have disturbed his slumber. It was his custom to bathe twice a day, immediately upon waking and in late afternoon, before dinner. Like many wealthy Romans, he made a political point of appearing in the public baths at least two afternoons a week, but this was a choice based upon politics and not upon necessity. Even in Capua, he had a fine bath of his own, a tiled basin twelve feet square, sunk below floor level, with a sufficient supply of hot and cold water. Wherever he lived, he insisted upon adequate bathing facilities, and when he built a house, the plumbing was always of brass or silver, so there would be no corrosion.

After he had bathed, his barber shaved him. He loved this part of the day, the necessary surrender to the keen razor on his cheeks, the childlike feeling it gave him, trust mingled with danger, the hot towels afterwards, the unguents rubbed into his skin, and the scalp massage which always followed. He was very vain of his hair, and very disturbed that he was beginning to lose it.

He dressed in a plain dark blue tunic, edged with silver thread, and he wore, as was his custom, knee-high boots of soft, white doeskin. Since these boots could not be properly cleaned, and since two or three days' wear would likely as not splatter them with mud, Crassus kept his own bootmaking establishment where four slaves labored under a journeyman. It was worth the expense, for the picture he made in the dark blue tunic and the white boots was an attractive one. He decided today, since the weather was growing warmer, that he would dispense with the toga, and after he had made a light breakfast of fruit and shortbread, he took a litter to the house where the three young folk were staying. He was a little ashamed and perturbed by his treatment of Helena, and after all, he had promised to entertain them at Capua.

He had been to this house once or twice before, and he knew Helena's uncle slightly; therefore, the senior door slave greeted him warmly and led him immediately to the plaza, where the family and their guests still sat at breakfast. The blood came to Helena's cheeks when she saw him and she lost some of her carefully-nurtured youthful composure. Caius seemed genuinely glad to see him, and the uncle and aunt were deeply appreciative of the honor the general was doing them and put themselves out to be hospitable. Only Claudia looked at him shrewdly and cynically with something of a malicious twinkle in her eyes.

"If you have not made plans for today," Crassus said, "I would like to be your host at a perfume factory. It would seem a shame to come to Capua and not to be inside one of the plants. Especially since our poor city is noted for little else than gladiators and perfume."

"A rather strange combination," smiled Claudia.

"We have no plans," Helena quickly said.

"She means that we have plans, but we will be glad to put them aside and go with you."

Caius looked sharply, almost angrily at his sister. Crassus explained that of course the older folk were included, but they begged off. Perfume factories were no novelty to them, and the matron of the house said that too much breathing of fumes tended to give her a headache.

A little later, they left for the perfumery. Their litters were carried into the older section of Capua. There the streets became narrower, the tenements higher. Evidently, even the mild housing ordinances of the *urbs* were not enforced here, for the tenement houses climbed up like a crazy jumble of children's blocks. Often enough, they seemed to meet at the top, where they were braced with wooden beams. Though it was morning and though the sky was clear and blue, these streets were gloomy with twilight. The streets were dirty; garbage was dumped from the apartments and allowed to lie until it rotted, and the foul smell of the garbage mingled increasingly with the sweet, sickening scent of the perfume oils.

"You see," Crassus said, "why our plants are here. The odor itself serves a useful purpose."

In these streets were none of the well-dressed, well-groomed house slaves so noticeable in the better parts of the city, nor were there many litters. Dirty, half naked children played in the gutters. Poorly-dressed women haggled for food at the sidewalk stands or sat in the doorways of the tenements nursing their babies. There was a babble of strange speech, and out of the windows came the odors of strange foods cooking.

"What a dreadful place!" Helena said. "Do you really mean that perfume comes out of this cesspool?"

"It does indeed, my dear. More and better perfume than

they make in any other city in the world. As for these people, most of them are Syrians, Egyptians, some Greeks and Jews. We've tried to run our factories with slaves—but it doesn't work. You can force a slave to work, but you can't force him not to spoil what he makes. He doesn't care about that end of it. Give him a plough or a sickle or a spade or a hammer and you can see what he does, and anyway tools like those are hard to spoil. But give him silk to weave or fine linen or delicate retorts or exact measurements and motions, give him a share of work in a factory, and sure as God, he will spoil the work. And it's no use to whip him; he still spoils the work. As to our own proletarians—what incentive do they have to work? In any case, there are ten of them for each job. Why should one work when the other nine live better on the dole and spend their days gambling or at the arena or in the baths? They'll go into the army because there's some opportunity for wealth if you're lucky, but even in the army we have to turn more and more to the barbarians. But they won't go into a factory for the wages we can pay. We smashed their guilds because we had to smash the guilds or give up the factories. So now we hire Syrians and Egyptians and Jews and Greeks, and even they work only until they can save enough to buy citizenship from some ward heeler. I don't know what the end will be. As it is, factories are closing, not opening."

They were at the factory now. It was a low wooden building, squat and ugly among the tenements. It was about one hundred and fifty feet square, shabby and run down, the wooden siding frequently rotten, and boards missing here and there. A forest of smoking chimneys poked out of the roof. Along one side there was a loading platform, and a number of wagons were drawn up to the platform. They were piled high with slabs of bark, baskets of fruit and earthenware crocks.

Crassus had their litters brought around to the front of the factory. Here, the broad wooden doors were thrown back, and Caius and Helena and Claudia had their first impression of the inside of a perfumery. The building was one great shed, with wooden beams supporting the ceiling, and much of the ceiling itself was shuttered, so that air and light could be admitted. The place was full of the heat and light of open ovens. Long tables held hundreds of crocks and crucibles, and the maze of condensing coils running out of the stills was like something from a weird dream. And through it all, there was the rich, nauseating smell of the perfume oils.

The visitors also got the impression of hundreds of workers. Small, brown-skinned men, bearded, many of them, naked except for loincloths, they watched the stills, stoked the ovens, stood at the cutting tables and chopped bark and fruit peel, or filled little silver tubes with the essence, ladling out the precious stuff drop by drop, sealing each tube with hot wax. Still others peeled fruit and chopped white strips of pork fat.

The manager of the place—a Roman whom Crassus introduced as Avalus, with no dignity of any other name—welcomed the general and his guests with a combination of unctuousness, greed and caution. A few coins from Crassus made him even more eager to please them, and he led them down one aisle and up another. The workers went on with their work, their faces hard and close and bitter. When they glanced sideways at the visitors, it was with no noticeable change of expression. Of all the things they saw there, it was the workers who were most strange to Caius and Helena and Claudia. They had never seen such men before. There was something different and frightening about them. They were not slaves—nor were they Romans. Nor were they like the dwindling number of peasants who still clung to bits of land here and there in Italy. They were different men, and their difference was worrisome.

"Our process here," Crassus explained, "is distillation. We have the Egyptians to thank for that, but they were never able to turn the distilling process into mass production. It takes Rome to organize a thing."

"But was it ever any different?" Caius asked.

"Oh, yes. In the olden times, men had to depend upon the natural production of scents—principally olibanum, myrrh and, of course, camphor. They are all gum-resins, and they exude from the bark of the trees. In the East, I have heard, the people have plantations of such trees. They gash the bark and collect the gum as a regular crop. For the most part, the scent was burned as incense. Then the Egyptians invented the still, which not only gives us brandy and a shortcut to drunkenness, but perfume as well."

He led them over to one of the cutting tables, where a worker was shaving lemon peel into paper-thin slivers. Crassus held one of these slivers up to the light.

"If you look carefully, you can see the oil sacs. And, of course, you know how fragrant the smell of the peel is. This is the basis—not only lemon, of course, but a hundred other fruits and barks—for the precious quintessence. Now if you follow me—"

He led them now to one of the stoves. There a great pot of bits of peel was being set on to cook. When it was set on the stove, a metal cover was bolted onto it. Copper tubing led out of the cover, twisting round and round to where it ran under a water spray. The end of the tube fed into another pot.

"This is the still," Crassus explained. "We cook the material, whether it be bark or leaves or fruit peel, until the oil sacs part. Then it goes up in steam and we condense the steam with the spray of water." He led them to another oven, where the still was feeding. "There you see the water coming over. When we have a pot of that, we chill it and the oil gathers at the top. The oil is the quintessence, and it is removed carefully and sealed in those silver tubes. What remains is the fine fragrant water, which is becoming so popular as a breakfast drink these days."

"You mean that is what we drink?" Claudia cried.

"More or less. It is cut with distilled water, but I assure you it is most healthful. Also, these waters are blended for taste, even as the oils are blended with each other for scent. As it is, the water is used for toilet water."

He saw Helena smiling at him and asked, "You think I'm not telling you the truth?"

"No—no. Only I'm filled with admiration for such knowledge. I can remember the times in my life when I heard how anything was made. I didn't think anyone knew how anything was made."

"It's my business to know," Crassus replied evenly. "I'm a very rich man. I'm not ashamed of that, as so many people are. A lot of people, my dear, look down upon me because I've devoted myself to making money. That does not concern me. I enjoy becoming richer. But unlike my colleagues, I don't look upon a plantation as a source of riches, and when they gave me a war, they gave me no cities to conquer, as they did Pompey. They gave me the

256

Servile War, which paid small profit indeed. So I have my own small secrets, and this factory is one of them. Each of those silver tubes of quintessence is worth ten times its weight in pure gold. A slave eats your food and dies. But these workers turn themselves into gold. Nor am I concerned with feeding and housing them."

"Yet," Caius speculated, "they could do as Spartacus did—"

"Workers revolt?" Crassus smiled and shook his head. "No, that will never be. You see, they are not slaves. They are free men. They can come and go as they please. Why should they ever revolt?" Crassus looked around the great shed. "No. As a matter of fact, all through the Servile War, we never stopped our ovens. There is no bond between these men and slaves."

Yet as they left the place, Caius was full of uneasiness. These strange, silent, bearded men who worked so quickly and expertly filled him with fear and misgiving. And he did not know why.

PART SEVEN

Which deals with the journey of Cicero and Gracchus back to Rome, of what they spoke of along the way, and then of the dream of Spartacus and how it was told to Gracchus.

Even as Caius and Crassus and the two girls went south along the Appian Way to Capua, so did Cicero and Gracchus, a little earlier, make their way north to Rome. The *Villa Salaria* was within a short day's journey of the city, and at a later time would be considered no more than a suburb. Therefore, Cicero and Gracchus proceeded at an unhurried pace, their litters travelling side by side. Cicero, who was inclined to be patronizing and something of a snob, forced himself to be respectful to this man who was such a power in the city; and as a matter of fact it was difficult for anyone not to respond to the political grace of Gracchus.

When a man devotes his life to winning the favor of people and avoiding their enmity, he is bound to develop certain attributes of social intercourse, and Gracchus had rarely met a person whose liking he could not win. Cicero, however, was not exceedingly likeable; he was one of those clever young men who never allow principle to interfere with success. While Gracchus was equally opportunistic, he differed from Cicero in that he respected principles; they were merely an inconvenience which he himself eschewed. The fact that Cicero, who liked to conceive of himself as a materialist, refused to recognize any aspects of decency in any human being, made him less the realist than Gracchus. It also allowed him to be somewhat shocked now and then at the bland wickedness of the fat old man. The truth of the matter was that Gracchus was no more wicked than the next person. He had merely fought somewhat more strongly against self-deception, having found it an obstacle to his own ambitions.

On the other hand, he had less contempt for Cicero than he might have had. To a certain degree, Cicero puzzled him. The world was changing; Gracchus knew that in his own lifetime a great new change had come, not only to Rome but to the entire world. Cicero was a harbinger of that change. Cicero was one of a whole generation of clever and ruthless young men. Gracchus was ruthless, but at least a recognition of sorrow, a sense of pity if no action on the basis of pity, crept into his own ruthlessness. But these young men could afford themselves neither pity nor sorrow. They seemed to have an armor without a crevice. There was some social envy concerned here, for Cicero was exceedingly well educated and well connected; but there was also an element of envy for the specific coldness involved. To some extent, Gracchus envied in Cicero an area of strength where he himself was weak. And on this, his thoughts turned and wandered.

"Are you sleeping?" Cicero asked softly. He himself found the motion of a litter lulling and productive of drowsiness.

"No—just thinking."

"Of weighty matters of state?" Cicero asked lightly, assuring himself that the old pirate was plotting the destruction of some innocent senator.

"Of nothing of any consequence. Of an old legend, as a matter of fact. A very old story, slightly foolish, as the old stories are."

"Would you tell it to me?"

"I'm sure it would bore you."

"Only scenery bores a traveller."

"In any case, it's a moral tale, and nothing is more tiresome than a moral tale. Do you suppose moral tales have any place in our lives today, Cicero?"

"They are good for little children. My own favorite concerned a possible distant relative. The mother of the Gracchi."

"No relationship."

"I was six years old then. At the age of seven I questioned it."

"You couldn't have been that nasty at seven," Gracchus smiled.

"I'm sure I was. The thing I like best about you, Gracchus, is that you never bought yourself a family tree."

"That was thrift and not virtue."

"And the story?"

"I'm afraid you're too old."

"Try me," Cicero said. "I've never been disappointed in your stories."

"Even when they are pointless?"

"They are never pointless. One has only to be clever enough to see the point."

"Then I tell my story," Gracchus laughed. "It concerns a mother who had only one son. He was tall and clean-limbed and handsome, and she loved him as much as a mother ever loved a son."

"I think my own mother found me an obstacle to her lurid ambitions."

"Let us say this was a long time ago, when the virtues were possible. This mother loved her son. The sun rose and set in him. Then he fell in love. He lost his heart to a woman who was as beautiful as she was wicked. And since she was exceedingly wicked, you can take it for granted that she was exceedingly beautiful. For the son, however, she had not even a glance, not even a nod, not even a kind look. Nothing at all."

"I've met such women," Cicero agreed.

"So he pined for her. When he had a chance, he told her what he would do for her, what castles he would build, what riches he would gather. These were somewhat abstract, and she said she was not interested in any of them. She asked instead for a gift which was entirely within his power to produce."

"A simple gift?" asked Cicero.

Gracchus enjoyed telling a story. He considered the question, and then he nodded. "A very simple gift. She asked the young man to bring her his mother's heart. And he did. He took a knife, plunged it into his mother's breast, and then tore the heart out. And then flushed with the horror and excitement of what he had done, he ran through the forest to where this wicked but beautiful young woman lived. And as he ran, he caught his toe in a root and fell, and when he fell, the heart was flung out of his hands. He ran to pick up the precious heart which would buy him a woman's love, and as he bent over it, he heard the heart say, 'My son, my son, did you hurt yourself when you fell?'" Gracchus lay back in his litter, placed the tips of the fingers of both his hands together, and contemplated them.

"So?" asked Cicero.

"That's all. I told you it was a moral tale with no point."

"Forgiveness? It's not a Roman story. We Romans are short on forgiveness. Anyway, this is no mother of the Gracchi."

"Not forgiveness. Love."

"Ah!"

"You don't believe in love?"

"Transcending all things? By no means. Nor is it Roman."

"Good heavens, Cicero, can you catalogue every blessed thing on earth in a category of Roman or un-Roman?"

"Most things," Cicero answered complacently.

"And do you believe that?"

"As a matter of fact, I don't actually," Cicero laughed.

"He has no humor," Gracchus thought. "He laughs because he feels it is a proper moment to laugh." And he said aloud, "I was going to advise you to give up politics."

"Yes?"

"However, I don't think my advice would affect you, one way or another."

"Yet you don't think I'll ever be a success at politics, do you?"

"No—I wouldn't say that. Have you ever thought of politics—what it is?"

"It's a lot of things, I suppose. None of them very clean."

"As clean or as dirty as anything else. I've spent my life being a politician," Gracchus said, thinking. "He doesn't like me. I hit him, he hits me. Why is it so hard for me to accept the fact that someone doesn't like me?"

"I've heard that your great virtue," said Cicero to the fat man, "is a memory for names. Is it true that you can remember the names of a hundred thousand people?"

"Another illusion about politics. I know a few people by name. Not a hundred thousand."

"I've heard that Hannibal could remember the name of every man in his army."

"Yes. And we will endow Spartacus with a similar memory. We can't admit someone wins victory because they are better than we are. Why have you such a fondness for the big and the little lies of history?"

"Are they all lies?"

"Most of them," Gracchus rumbled. "History is an explanation of craft and greed. But never an honest explantation. That's why I asked you about politics. Someone back there at the Villa said there were no politics in the army of Spartacus. But there couldn't be."

"Since you're a politician," Cicero smiled, "suppose you tell me what a politician is."

"A faker," Gracchus answered shortly.

"At least you are frank."

"My one virtue, and an extremely valuable one. In a politician, people confuse it with honesty. You see, we live in a republic. That means that there are a great many people who have nothing and a handful who have a great deal. And those who have a great deal must be defended and protected by those who have nothing. Not only that, but those who have a great deal must guard their property, and therefore those who have nothing must be willing to die for the property of people like you and me and our good host Antonius. Also, people like ourselves have many slaves. Those slaves do not like us. We should not fall for the illusion that slaves like their masters. They don't, and therefore the slaves will not protect us against the slaves. So the many, many people who have no slaves at all must be willing to die in order for us to have our slaves. Rome keeps a quarter of a million men under arms. These soldiers must be willing to go to foreign lands, to march their feet off, to live in filth and squalor, to wallow in blood—so that we may be safe and live in comfort and increase our personal fortunes. When these troops went to fight Spartacus, they had less to defend than the slaves. Yet they died by the thousands fighting the slaves. One could go further. The peasants who died fighting the slaves were in the army in the first place because they have been driven off their land by the *latifundia*. The slave plantation turns them into landless paupers; and then they die to keep the plantation intact. Whereupon one is tempted to say *reductio ad absurdum*. For consider, my dear Cicero, what does the brave Roman soldier stand to lose if the slaves conquer? Indeed, they would need him desperately, for there are not enough slaves to till the land properly. There would be land enough for all, and our legionary would have what he dreams of most, his plot of land and his little house. Yet he marches off to destroy his own dreams, that sixteen slaves may carry a fat old hog like me in a padded litter. Do you deny the truth of what I say?"

"I think that if what you said were to be said by an ordinary man aloud in the Forum, we would crucify him."

"Cicero, Cicero," Gracchus laughed. "Is that a threat? I'm much too fat and heavy and old to be crucified. And why are you so nervous about the truth? It is necessary to lie to others. Is it necessary that we should believe our lies?"

"As you state it. You simply omit the key question—is one man like another or unlike another? There is the fallacy in your little speech. You take it for granted that men are as alike as peas in a pod. I don't. There is an elite—a group of superior men. Whether the gods made them that way or circumstances made them that way is not something to argue. But they are men fit to rule, and because they are fit to rule, they do rule. And because the rest are like cattle, they behave like cattle. You see, you present a thesis; the difficulty is to explain it. You present a picture of society, but if the truth were as illogical as your picture, the whole structure would collapse in a day. All you fail to do is to explain what holds this illogical puzzle together."

"I do," Gracchus nodded. "I hold it together."

"You? Just by yourself?"

"Cicero, do you really think I'm an idiot? I've lived a long and dangerous life, and I'm still on top. You asked me before what a politician is? The politician is the cement in this crazy house. The patrician can't do it himself. In the first place, he thinks the way you do, and Roman citizens don't like to be told that they are cattle. They aren't—which you will learn some day. In the second place, he knows nothing about the citizen. If it were left to him, the structure would collapse in a day. So he comes to people like myself. He couldn't live without us. We rationalize the irrational. We convince the people that the greatest fulfillment in life is to die for the rich. We convince the rich that they must part with some of their riches to keep the rest. We are magicians. We cast an illusion, and the illusion is foolproof. We say to the people—you are the power. Your vote is the source of Rome's strength and glory. You are the only free people in the world. There is nothing more precious than your freedom, nothing more admirable than your civilization. And you control it; you are the power. And then they vote for our candidates. They weep at our defeats. They laugh with joy at our victories. And they feel proud and superior because they are not slaves. No matter how low they sink, if they sleep in the gutter, if they sit in the public seats at the races and the arena all day, if they strangle their infants at birth, if they live on the public dole and never lift a hand to do a day's work from birth to death, nevertheless they are not slaves. They are dirt, but every time they see a slave, their ego rises and they feel full of pride and power. Then they know that they are Roman citizens and all the world envies them. And this is my peculiar art, Cicero. Never belittle politics."

II

All this did not endear Gracchus to Cicero, and when they came finally to the first great cross, which stood just a few miles outside the walls of Rome, Cicero pointed to the fat man who sat dozing under his awning and remarked to Gracchus,

"Obviously a politician by look and training."

"Obviously. In fact an old friend of mine." Gracchus motioned for the litters to halt, and he laboriously climbed out of his. Cicero did the same, glad for a chance to stretch his legs. It was toward evening now and dark rain clouds were moving in from the north. Cicero motioned at them.

"If you wish to, go along," Gracchus said. He no longer had any desire to woo Cicero. His nerves were on edge. The few days at the *Villa Salaria* had left a bad taste in his mouth. What was it, he wondered? Was he getting old and insecure?

"I'll wait," said Cicero, and stood beside his litter and watched Gracchus go over to the man under the awning. Obviously, they knew each other. It was indeed a strange democracy in the wards and among the politicians. It was a world in itself.

"Tonight," Cicero heard Gracchus say.

The man under the awning shook his head.

"Sextus!" Gracchus cried. "I told you my offer. I don't give two damns for Sextus! Either you do as I say, or I'll never talk to you or look at you as long as I live—or as long as you live. Which won't be long, sitting under that rotten flesh."

"I'm sorry, Gracchus."

"Don't tell me you're sorry. Do as I say."

And Gracchus strode back to his litter and climbed in. Cicero asked no questions concerning what had just taken place, but as they were approaching the gates of the city, he reminded Gracchus of the story he had told earlier in the day, the story of the mother who loved her son too well.

"It was an amusing tale, but you lost it somewhere."

"Did I? Were you ever in love, Cicero?"

"Not the way the poets sing. But that story—"

"The story? Now, you know, I can't remember why I told it. I must have had a point, I suppose, but I have forgotten it."

Inside the city, they parted, and Gracchus went to his home. It was almost dusk when he reached there, and he had his bath by lamplight. Then he told his housekeeper that he would wait a while with dinner, since he was expecting a guest. The woman nodded, and then Gracchus went to his bedroom and lay down, staring blindly and moodily into the darkness. Death nudged him as he lay there. There was an old Latin saying about the darkness. *Spatiem pro morte facite.* Make room for death. Unless one lay with a woman he loved. But Gracchus had never done that. Not with a woman he loved. He bought his women in the market, old Gracchus did. Wicked old Gracchus did. When had a woman come to him, willingly and gladly? He forced himself to have a sense of possession and a current of identity with the women he purchased as concubines; but it was never there.

There came to his mind now that section in the Odyssey where Odysseus exacts his revenge after having slain the false suitors. Gracchus had not had the advantage of a Greek instructor in his childhood, to interpret the classics page by page. He came to them himself and read them the way a self-educated man reads such things. So he had always been puzzled by the fierce, almost inhuman hatred Odysseus displayed toward his female slaves who had bedded down with the suitors. He recalled now how Odysseus had forced the twelve women to carry the bodies of their lovers out into the courtyard and to scrape their blood from the dirt floor of the banquet hall. Then he sentenced them to death and instructed his son to carry out the sentence. The son outdoes the father. It was Telemachus who conceived the notion of twelve nooses on a single rope, of stringing them all up together like a line of plucked chickens.

Why such hatred, Gracchus wondered? Why such wild, terrible hatred? Unless—as had often occurred to him—Odysseus shared his bed with each and every one of the female slaves. So there were fifty women slaves in that household and fifty concubines for the moral man from Ithaca. And this was what the patient Penelopeia had waited for!

Yet he, Gracchus, did the same thing—too civilized perhaps to kill a slave woman who bedded elsewhere, less concerned perhaps—but essentially no different in his relationship to women. In all his long life, he had never greatly concerned himself with what a woman was. He boasted to Cicero that he was not afraid to recognize the essential truth of things—yet the truth of women in the world he inhabited was something he dared not face. And now, at long last—making truly a fine jest—he had found a woman who was not less than a human being. The difficulty was that he had yet to find her.

A slave tapped at the door, and when he spoke, told him that his dinner guest had arrived.

"I'll come in a moment. Make him at ease. He's dirty and ragged, but I'll have anyone whipped who looks down her nose at him. Give him warm water to wash his face and hands with, and then give him a light toga to cover himself with. His name is Flavius Marcus. Address him by his name and address him decently."

This was evidently done as ordered, for when Gracchus came into the dining room, the fat man who had sat under the awning at the first crucifix, was reclining on a couch, quite clean and respectable except that he needed a shave. As Gracchus entered, he rubbed his beard self-consciously. "If you could add a shave to all this—?"

"I'm hungry and I think we ought to eat, Flavius. You can spend the night here, and I'll have my barber shave you in the morning. It will go better after a good night's rest and a bath. I'll throw in a clean tunic and some decent shoes. We're just about of a size, so my clothes will fit you well enough."

They were of a size, a good deal alike; they might have been mistaken for brothers.

"That is—if you're not afraid Sextus will scold you for giving up his cheap sinecure and accepting a crumb from me."

"Yes, it's all very well for you to talk," Flavius said, a whining note in his voice. "Things have been good with you, Gracchus. Wealth, comfort, respect, honor, power. Life is like a bowl of cream for you, but it's been something else for me, I assure you. I assure you a man doesn't feel good or proud, sitting under a rotten corpse and making up lies so that travellers will grease his palm with a little something. It's a bitter, nasty thing to be a beggar. But at least, when I was at the end of my rope, I got a little something from Sextus. Now, when I go to him again, he'll say—Ah, you don't need me. Go to your great protector and friend, Gracchus. That's what he'll say. He hates you. He'll hate me."

"Let him hate you," Gracchus said. "Sextus is a frog, a cockroach, a cheap little ward boss! Let him hate you. Do what I ask you to, and I'll get you something here in the city, a clerkship, a wardenship, something where you can put aside a little money and live a decent life. You won't have to go crawling to Sextus again."

"I had a lot of friends at one time, when I was useful to them. Now I could die in the gutter—"

"You're useful to me," Gracchus interrupted. "Let's put it just on that basis. Now eat your dinner and stop whining. My God, good fortune is all over you. But you're afraid to say, how do you do, to it. I don't know what you're afraid of."

Food and wine mellowed Flavius. Gracchus had an Egyptian woman in his kitchen. Her specialty was to bone squab, and then to stuff the bird with pine nuts and fine barley. This was baked slowly and basted with brandy and fig syrup. It was served with tiny sausages which were made of chopped smoked lamb's tongue and citron peel, called *pholo,* and justly famous throughout the city. The meal began with melon, which was followed by these two dishes. Then a cream soup of minced lobster, flavored delicately with garlic. Then a sweet pudding of grapes and dates, with paper-thin slices of smoked ham on the side. Then broiled mushrooms on a base of glazed whitefish, and finally a tray of almond paste and sesame pastry for dessert. Hot white bread and good red wine kept pace with this, and when they had finished, Flavius lay back, smiling and comfortable, his big paunch heaving gently, and said,

"Gracchus, I have not eaten a meal like this in five years. Good food is the best balm in the world. My God, such food! And you eat this way every night! Well, you're a smart man, Gracchus, and I'm just an old fool. I suppose you deserve it, and I've got no right to be resentful. Now I'm ready to hear what you want me to do for you. I still know a few people, a few gangsters, a few cut-throats, a few pimps and a few madams. I don't know what I can do that you can't do yourself or find someone else who can do it better, but I'm willing."

"We'll talk over the brandy," said Gracchus. He poured a glass for each of them. "I think you have virtues, Flavius. I could have found someone else who knows everyone in Rome who deals in bodies and souls and suffering, but I don't want to bring into this anyone who has any call on me. I want something done quietly and well."

"I can keep my mouth shut," said Flavius.

"I know you can. That's why I'm asking you to take this on. I want you to find a woman for me. A slave. I want you to find her and purchase her, regardless of what the price is. And you have unlimited expenses to draw on in finding her."

"What kind of a woman? God knows, there are enough slave women on the market. With the end of the Servile War, there's a glut of them, and it's the exception which fetches any kind of a price. I suppose I could find you any kind of a woman you want, black, white, yellow or brown, virgin or slut, old or young, fair or ugly, blond, brunette, red head—anything at all. What kind do you want?"

"No kind," said Gracchus slowly. "I want a certain woman."

"A slave woman?"

"Yes."

"Who is she?"

"Her name is Varinia, and she was the wife of Spartacus."

"Ah—" Flavius looked searchingly at Gracchus. Then he took a sip of his brandy. Then he looked at Gracchus again. "Where is she?" he asked softly.

"I don't know."

"But you know her?"

"I do and I don't. I've never seen her."

"Ah—"

"Stop saying *ah* like a damned oracle!"

"I'm trying to think of something intelligent to say."

"I hire you as an agent, not as an entertainer," Gracchus growled. "You know what I want you to do."

"You want me to find a woman, but you don't know where she is and you've never seen her. Do you know what she looks like?"

"Yes. She's quite tall, well-built but slim. High-bosomed with full breasts. She is a German. She has that straw-colored German hair and blue eyes. Small ears, a high brow, a straight nose but not small, deep-set eyes and a full mouth with an underlip which is perhaps a trifle heavy. She would speak poor Latin and possibly pretend to no Latin at all. She speaks better Greek in the Thracian style. She has given birth to a child within the past two months, but the child may be dead. Even if the child were dead, she'd still have milk in her breasts, wouldn't she?"

"Not necessarily. How old is she?"

"I'm not sure of that. At least twenty-three and possibly as much as twenty-seven. I'm not sure."

"Maybe she's dead."

"That's a possibility. If so, I want you to find out. I want you to bring proof to me that she died. But I don't think she's dead. She is not someone who would ever take her own life, and a woman like that is not put to death quickly."

"How do you know she wouldn't commit suicide?"

"I know. I can't explain it, but I know."

"After Spartacus was defeated," Flavius said, "didn't they take his camp with some ten thousand women and children?"

"There were twenty-two thousand women and children.

270

Twelve thousand went as spoils to the troops. That's the rottenest scandal of the kind I ever heard of, but Crassus stood behind it, and he gave his own share of spoils to the public treasury to hush it up. That was no great gesture on his part, since his share was worth very little. He made a great gesture of taking no slaves himself. He knew what the market would be."

"And was Varinia among these women?"

"Possibly. Possibly not. She was the wife of their chief. They might have taken some special means for her protection."

"I don't know. The slaves made a fetish of equality."

Gracchus drained down his brandy and directed a stubby finger at the other. "Do you want to do it or don't you? You can't talk your way into any solution of this, Flavius. It means hard work."

"I know it does. And how much time will you give me?"

"Three weeks."

"Ah, now—ah—" Flavius threw his hands wide. "That's no time at all. She may not be in Rome. I'll have to send people to Capua, to Syracuse, to Sicily. Perhaps to Spain and Africa. Be reasonable."

"I'm being as reasonable as I intend to be. Damn it all, go to Sextus and take his charity."

"All right, Gracchus. There's no need to be so angry. But suppose I have to purchase a number of women? Do you know how many German women fit that particular description?"

"A great many, I'm sure. I don't want someone who fits that description. I want Varinia."

"And what shall I pay for her if I find her?"

"Whatever price is asked. I'll honor it."

"All right. I agree, Gracchus. Pour me another glass of that excellent brandy, will you, please." The brandy was poured. Flavius stretched on his couch, sipping it, and regarding the man who had employed him. "I have certain talents, don't I, Gracchus?"

"You do indeed."

"But I remain poor. I remain a failure. Gracchus, may I ask you one question before we leave this. Don't answer if you don't want to. But don't be angry."

"Ask it."

"Why do you want this woman, Gracchus?"

"I'm not angry. But I think it's time we both went to bed. We're neither as young as we used to be."

III

But in those times, the world was neither as large nor as complicated as it is today, and in less than the allotted three weeks, Flavius appeared at the home of Gracchus and announced the successful conclusion of his task. Money, as they say, has a soft surface and it rubs off on those who handle it. Flavius was different, well-dressed, clean-shaven, and self-assured since he had carried a difficult task through to the end. He sat with Gracchus over a glass of wine and toyed with his knowledge, and Gracchus himself restrained his impatience.

"I began," Flavius explained, "with the very puzzling job of reaching the officers who participated in the spoils. If Varinia was handsome and well built, I realized, she would be selected in that first group. But when you realize that the whole question of appropriating the slaves was illegal and that five or six hundred officers were concerned and that very few of them had any desire to talk, you can see that it was not easy. Well, luck was with us. People remembered. Varinia went into labor when news reached them that the slaves were defeated, and people remembered this woman who would not be parted from a new-born child. They didn't know it was the wife of Spartacus or that her name was Varinia. You must understand that Crassus sent a detachment of cavalry against the slave city, or camp or village or whatever you call it, immediately after the battle. Then the infantry followed. The slave women and the children there—there were some boys of thirteen and fourteen —did not put up much of a fight. They were dazed. They had just heard that the slave army was destroyed. But you know how soldiers are after a battle, and I suppose it's no picnic to fight with slaves. They—"

"I don't need a recapitulation of the mood of legionaries," Gracchus said. "Suppose you give me the facts."

"I'm only trying to describe the situation. I mean that there was a lot of senseless killing at first because our soldiers were angry and hot. Varinia had just given birth. Well, a slave child is hardly worth its weight in gold these days, and what gave me the clue to her was a story of a soldier who picked up this child by its leg and began the motion which would have dashed out its brains against a tent-post. Crassus himself stopped it. Crassus saved the child and beat the soldier half to death with his own hands. One would never suspect that of Crassus, would one?"

"I'm not interested in what one would or would not expect from Crassus. What sort of an old windbag are you, Flavius? Did you find Varinia? Do I own her? Did you buy her?"

"I couldn't buy her."

"Why?" Gracchus roared suddenly, rising to his feet in a burst of anger as frightening as it was unexpected. As he advanced toward Flavius, the other shrank back into his chair, and Gracchus hooked a hand in the neck of his tunic, twisted, and shouted, "Why? Why, you fat, useless tramp? Is she dead? If you bungled this, I swear I'll see you back in the gutter for good! For good!"

"She's not dead—"

"Oh, but you're so full of wind! Like a bag of wind that farts instead of talking! Why didn't you buy her?" He let go of Flavius, but continued to stand over him.

"Just calm down!" Flavius said suddenly and loudly. "You gave me something to do and I did it. Maybe I'm not as rich as you, Gracchus. Maybe I belong back in the gutter. But that doesn't give you any right to talk to me that way. I'm not your slave. It's bad enough when a man gets the way I do. You don't have to make it worse."

"I'm sorry."

"I didn't buy her because she's not for sale. That's all."

"Price?"

"Not price. There's no price at all. She belongs to Crassus. She lives in his house. And she's not for sale. Don't you think I tried? Crassus was at Capua, and while he was there, I took the matter up with his agents. Oh, no—nothing doing there. They wouldn't even discuss it. As soon as the conversation got to that particular slave, they closed up like clams. They knew nothing about such a slave. They wouldn't talk price. They wouldn't speculate. I let money trickle into their palms, but it didn't change things one bit. If I wanted the barber or the cook or the housekeeper, that

273

might be arranged. Why they were even willing to make a deal for a beautiful Syrian woman Crassus bought last year, and manage to turn her over to me. They were willing enough to do that for me, but not Varinia."

"Then how do you know it's Varinia, and how do you know she's there?"

"I bought that information from a wardrobe slave. Oh, don't think that Crassus's household is one happy little family. He has a son who hates his guts, and a wife—she lives apart from him—who would cut his throat, and the intrigue in that place is like something out of Damascus. Just fine. I could buy information, but I couldn't buy Varinia."

"Did you find out why he bought her? Why he keeps her?"

Flavius chuckled. "Indeed I did. Crassus is in love with her."

"What!"

"Yes. The great Crassus has found love."

Then Gracchus said, deliberately and slowly, "God damn you, Flavius, if you talk about this business, if it ever gets around, if I ever hear any of it repeated anywhere, so help me, I will see that you are crucified."

"What kind of a way is that to talk? You're not God, Gracchus."

"No. No, not even distantly related to any of the gods, as some of our better born halfwits claim. Not at all. But I'm as close to God as anyone has ever been in Roman politics, and I'm close enough to frame you, Flavius, and to see you on the cross. And if any of this gets out, I will. Mark my word."

IV

On the afternoon of the next day, Gracchus set out to go to the baths, an act of political expediency which was not without its rewards. More and more, the public baths were becoming political and social centers; senators and magistrates were made and unmade at the baths; millions of *sesterces* changed hands at the baths; they were stock exchange and political club combined, and to be seen at the baths at certain intervals was almost an obligation. There were three large and well-fitted bath houses which Gracchus patronized, the *Clotum,* which was rather new, and two others which were older but still elegant. While these were not free to all citizens, the admission price was exceedingly modest, not enough to keep even a poor man out; although a certain social status kept the rabble away from these particular places.

In good weather, all Rome was out of doors in the afternoon. Even the dwindling number of Roman workers were through by an hour past noon; longer hours would have made it easier not to work, to live by the dole. The afternoon was the time of the free man; the slaves labored; the Roman citizen took his ease.

Gracchus, however, had little interest in the games, and only occasionally in the races. He was somewhat different from his colleagues in that he could not see the drama of two naked men, each with a knife in his hand, who cut away at each other until they were horrors of torn flesh and pouring blood. Nor did he see the pleasure in watching a man squirm in a fish net, while his eyes were torn out and his belly perforated by a long fish fork. Once in a while he enjoyed an afternoon at the jockey races, but chariot races, which were becoming more and more a physical contest between the opposing drivers, with an audience never satisfied unless a head was broken or a body smashed, only bored him. It was not that he was more soft-hearted than the next man; it was simply that he hated stupidity, and to him these proceedings were exceedingly stupid. The theatre he did not understand at all, and he went only to formal openings where he had to appear as a city functionary.

His greatest pleasure in the afternoon was to walk to the baths through the dirty, twisting, endless streets of his beloved city. Rome, he had always loved; Rome was his mother. As he put it to himself, his mother was a whore, and he was cast out of his mother's womb into the filth of the street. But until now, he had loved this mother, and this mother had loved him. How could he explain to Cicero what he had meant by retelling that old legend? Cicero would have to love Rome first, and such love would have to be connected with a knowledge of how vile and evil this city was.

That vileness and evil was something Gracchus understood. "Why should I go to the theatre?" he once asked one of his intellectual friends. "Can they put on a stage what I see on the streets of the *urbs?*"

It was something to see, all right. Today, he did it almost ceremonially. As if he asked himself, "How often shall I do this again, ever?"

He went first to the day market, where the stalls would do business for another hour before they closed down. You had to force your way through the shrilling women to walk on this street, but he steered gently through, vast in his white toga, like a great warship under a slight wind. Here was what Rome ate. Here were mounds of cheese, round cheeses, square cheeses, black cheeses, red cheeses, white cheeses. Here were hung the smoked fish and geese, the slaughtered pigs, the sides of beef, the tender lambs, the eels and the herrings salting in their barrels, the barrels of pickles, smelling so pungent and good. Here were crocks of oil from the Sabine hills and from Picenum, the marvelous Gaulish hams, the tripe hanging everywhere, the big wooden bowls of chitterlings.

He lingered at the vegetable stands. There was a time, within his memory, when every peasant for twenty miles around had his own truck garden and when all Rome ate of the wonderful variety of vegetables that were at the market. But now the *latifundia* was interested only in cash crop, whether it was wheat or barley, and the price of vegetables had gone far beyond the reach of any but the ruling class. Still, one saw piles of radishes and turnips, lettuce in five varieties, lentils and beans and cabbage, squash and melons and asparagus, truffles and mushrooms —a great, colorful variety of vegetables, and fruit too, piles of African lemons and pomegranates, the yellow and red so bright and lush, apples and pears and figs, dates from Arabia, grapes and melons from Egypt.

"What a pleasure just to look at it!" he thought.

He walked on, passing through the edge of the Jewish quarter of the city. He had dealt with the Jews occasionally, as a politician. What a strange people they were—so long in Rome and still speaking their own tongue and worshipping their own God and still bearded and wearing those long striped cloaks of theirs, no matter what the weather! One never saw them at the games or the races;

one never saw them in court. One hardly saw them at all, except in their own quarter. Polite, proud, aloof—"They will drain more blood out of Rome in their own good time than Carthage did," Gracchus often thought when he saw them.

He came to a through street, and stood to one side against a shopfront as a City Cohort tramped by, drums beating and fifes blowing. As always, children ran after them, and as always, he could just glance from side to side and see, watching the parade, an Arab, a Syrian, a Sabaean.

He walked to where the towering tenements gave way to gardens and light, marble porticos and cool archways and broad avenues. In the Forum, the dice throwers were already at it. Gambling was like a disease in Rome, and dice was the worst brand of the disease. Every afternoon there were clusters of gamblers all over the Forum, rolling the dice, pleading with the dice, talking to the dice. They had a language all of their own. Loafers, off-duty soldiers, and the fourteen and fifteen year old girls who were everywhere in the city, doing nothing, bred in dirty little flats, living, as their parents had lived, on the dole, and making a little more out of indifferent prostitution. He had heard that many of these girls would go to bed with a man for as little as a glass of wine and a *quadrens,* the smallest coin in the currency. Once, he and so many others had considered it terrible and monstrous, but these days, when there was no shame cast on a virtuously married man who kept a dozen slave girls to spice his bedtime, it was no longer a matter for care or discussion.

"Little by little," Gracchus thought. "A whole world comes to an end, but we never stop to wonder at it. And why should we? It happens so slowly and man's life is so short!"

Here and there he paused to watch one of the dice games. He could remember rolling dice when he was a lad. You couldn't very well live on the dole then, and there were certain matters of ethics which made a proud man refuse the dole then, even if it meant starvation.

Now he walked on to the baths. He had planned it carefully. The odds were three to one that Crassus would be at the baths today, and that he would arrive at just about this time. And sure enough, when Gracchus entered the *apodyteria,* as the dressing rooms were called, Crassus was already there, stripped down and pausing a moment to admire his long, lean body in the tall mirrors. The rooms were filling up. Here was an interesting section of city life, a political mixing pot, few of the idle bluebloods, but enough political power to rock the city from its foundations, bankers and powerful merchants, ward bosses, slave importers, vote manipulators, a gallery of petty heelers and gang leaders, an important senatorial caucus, even a *lanista* or two, a trio of former consuls, a magistrate, one or two actors, and a round dozen of consequential military men. Interspersed with them were sufficient men of no particular importance to bear out the democracy of the baths—of which Rome boasted so importantly. Kings and satraps from the Eastern lands could never get over the fact that the rulers of Rome—which meant the rulers of the world—mingled so casually with the rank and file of the city and walked so indifferently upon the city streets.

Keeping an intermittent watch on Crassus, Gracchus sat down on a bench and let a slave undo his boots. Meanwhile he received greetings, nodded and smiled, let a word drop here, a word there. He gave advice when it was asked, briefly and decisively. He offered, also when asked, brief and certain opinions on the trouble in Spain, the African situation, the necessity of Egyptian neutrality—that eternal breadbasket of the city—and the problem of what to do with the incessant Jewish provocation in Palestine. He reassured dealers who were whimpering that the price of slaves would continue to fall until it wrecked the economy, and he squashed a rumor that the army in Gaul was planning a coup. But all the time, he watched Crassus, until finally the millionaire, still naked and displaying his lean fitness, ambled over and passed the time of day. Crassus could not resist standing there in public comparison as Gracchus undressed. When the slaves removed the politician's toga, the mountain of the man was revealed, but still impressive. When the tunic followed, the pathos of a very fat man was worse than any simple nakedness. Strangely, Gracchus had never before been ashamed of his body.

They walked together into the *tepidarium,* the lounging room and clubhouse of the baths. Here were benches and mats upon which one could stretch out and relax, but the general practice was to stroll back and forth between plunges. From this broad and handsome gallery, marble-paved, decorated with mosaics and statuary, one could go to the cold outdoor pool, the warm pool, the hot baths, the steam rooms, and through each of those to the various exercise and massage rooms. Then, wrapped in a cool sheet, one could indulge in the garden promenades, the libraries— a part of the baths—and the sitting rooms, the solariums. The whole routine was for those who had hours to spend at the baths. Gracchus usually satisfied himself with a cold plunge, a half hour in the steam room, and then a massage.

But now he tempered himself to Crassus. Harsh words and harsh feelings were evidently forgotten. Naked, fat and loose, he walked alongside the general, being charming and attentive—which he was most skillful at.

"Building bridges," people remarked who looked at them, and wondered what new political alliances were in the making here, since Crassus and Gracchus were not known for this kind of comradeship. Crassus, however, waited patiently, "Whatever he's up to," he said to himself, "it's bound to out." He became slightly insulting and asked the politician,

"Since when are you an authority on Egypt as well as other things?"

"You mean what I said before? Well, a few general words fill in a gap. It's a matter of reputation." This was a new Gracchus indeed.

"A reputation for knowing everything?"

Gracchus laughed. "You've been to Egypt haven't you?"

"No. And I don't pretend at it." ·

"Well—well. I don't know, Crassus. We snap and snarl at each other. We could be friends. Each of us is a friend well worth having."

"I think so. I am also cynical. There is a price on friendship."

"Yes?"

"Yes, indeed. What have I got that makes my friendship so precious? Money? You have almost as much."

"I don't care about money."

"I do. What then?"

"I want to buy a slave from you," Gracchus blurted out. There it was. Done.

"My cook, no doubt. If you had hair, Gracchus, I'd say

you wanted my hairdresser. A set of litter-bearers? Or possibly a woman. I hear you have nothing but women in your household."

"God damn it, you know who I want!" Gracchus cried. "I want Varinia."

"Who?"

"Varinia. Let's not play games with each other."

"My dear Gracchus, you're playing the games. Who has been peddling information to you?"

"I keep informed." The fat man stopped and faced the other. "Look—look, Crassus. No beating about the bush. No haggling. No bargaining. I'll put it to you straight. I will pay you the highest price ever paid for a slave in Rome. I will pay you one million *sesterces*. I will pay you that in gold coin, and turn over every bit of it to you immediately, if you will give me Varinia."

Crassus folded his arms and whistled softly. "Now, that is a price. That's a handsome price. They could write poems about such a price. When a man can go to market today and buy a ripe, big-breasted beauty for one thousand *sesterces,* you are ready to pay a thousand times as much for a skinny German girl. Now that is something. But how could I take such a sum? What would they say? They'd say Crassus is a damned thief."

"Stop playing with me!"

"Playing with you? My dear Gracchus, you are playing with me. I have nothing that you can buy."

"I made a serious offer."

"And I answer you seriously."

"I double my price!" Gracchus growled. "Two million."

"I never knew there was that much money in politics."

"Two million. Take it or leave it."

"You bore me," Crassus said, and he walked away.

V

"Varinia, Varinia, now you must dress. Now we must dress you, Varinia, because the master comes home and you are to sit with him and dine with him. Why do you make things so hard for us, Varinia?"

"I don't want to make things hard for you."

"But you do. You see how hard you make things for us, Varinia. You tell us that you are a slave. You don't want four slaves to wait on you, hand and foot. No, you are just a slave like we are. You tell us how wretched you are. You know how it is to be a slave. Or maybe when you were with Spartacus, conquering the whole world, you forgot how it was to be a slave. Then you were a queen, weren't you, Varinia? So—"

"Don't do that any more! Why do you do that? Have I ever set myself apart from you?"

"You don't have to, Varinia. The master sets you apart from us. We are something to have in his bed when he is bored. One, two, three. But he loves you, Varinia. That is why you make it hard for us. We get whipped if you are not dressed just so. You don't get whipped. We get whipped."

"Let him whip me!"

"Let him. Just let him. We can see him whipping you."

"All right. All right," she told them. "Now I'm nursing the baby. Let me finish nursing the boy. Then I'll get dressed. Any way you want me to get dressed. I won't make it hard for you. Only let me finish nursing my baby."

"How long?"

"He doesn't drink long. Just look at him. He's slowing down already. In a half hour, I'll be ready. He'll be asleep then. I promise you I'll do whatever you want me to. I'll wear whatever you want me to."

So they left her for a while. Three of them were Spanish girls. The fourth was a Sabine woman, and it was a cancer inside of her that her mother had sold her for debt. Varinia could understand that. It was a bitter thing to be sold by your own folk, and it made you bitter. Envy, jealousy, bitterness—it festered in this house. The whole house festered.

She nursed the boy, and sang to him softly.

"Sleep, my baby, sleep beloved,
    While your father in the forest,
    Seeks the otter, spears the otter,
    Brings the pelt, midnight softness,
    Never shall the cold of winter
    Touch my baby, my beloved . . ."

The sucking eased. She could feel the pressure on the nipple slacken. When he sucked strong and hard out of his hunger, a sharp current went through her whole body. And then bit by bit as his belly filled up, the sensation eased off. What a thing it was to have a baby suck!

She gave him the other breast, just in case he needed more milk, and she stroked his cheek to start the sucking reflex again. But he was finished. His eyes were closed, and he had the monumental indifference of children whose bellies are full. For a while, she cuddled him against her warm bare breast; then she put him in his crib and closed the front of her dress.

How handsome he was, she thought as she stood over him. Fat and round and strong—what a fine baby! His hair was like black silk, and his eyes were deep blue. Those eyes would turn dark later, as his father's eyes were, but there was no telling about the hair. When this black birth-silk fell out, it might grow in with dark curls or golden and straight.

Quickly and easily he fell asleep. His world was proper and right. His world was the world of life, ruled by life's own simple laws, undisturbed and uncomplicated. His world was the world which outlasted all others . . .

Now she left him and went to where they were waiting to dress her. Four slaves to dress her for dinner with the man who owned her. She stood obediently while they took off her clothes and sponged her naked body. It was still a very lovely body, long-legged, and lovelier for the fullness of her breasts with milk. They put a sheet around her and she lay down on a couch, so that the *ornatrix* might prepare her face and arms.

First a covering of fine chalk for her arms and brow, the chalk fading onto her cheeks. Then the rouge, light red on her cheeks, heavy red-brown on her lips. Then what they called the *fuligo,* a black carbon paste to bring out the brows.

When that was done, she sat up and allowed them to do her hair. The soft, straight blond hair was carefully built into a pile of fixed curls, held in place with pomade and little ribbons.

Then the jewels. She stood naked, without the sheet, obedient and listless, while the diadem was fixed onto her hair. Golden earrings were next, and then a gold and sapphire collar called the *monile*. Small matching collars were placed on her ankles and wrists, and a diamond ring was placed on the small finger of each hand. She was being dressed well and spendidly, dressed as the richest man in Rome would dress his mistress, not his slave. It was no wonder that these poor devils assigned to her wardrobe could not pity her. See how she wears the wealth of an empire just in jewels! How can one pity her?

At that time, the most precious material in Rome was not silk, but the delicate and wonderful sheer cotton, spun in India, and having a gossamer quality that no silk could equal. Now they slipped a cotton *stola* over her head. This was a long, simply-cut dress, which was gathered around the waist by a tied belt called a *zona*. The only decoration on the dress was a gold braid on the hem, and indeed it needed no decoration, its lines were so simple and so lovely. But Varinia could never be unconscious of the fact that every line of her body showed through; it was the nakedness which meant horror and degradation, and she welcomed the discharge from her breasts which wet the front and spoiled its looks.

Over all of this went a large, pale yellow silk shawl; Varinia wore it like a cloak. She covered the dress with it. Each time she appeared for dinner, Crassus said,

"My dear, my dear, why should you hide your beautiful body that way? Let your *supparum* fall free. The dress underneath cost ten thousand *sesterces*. At least I should have the pleasure of looking at it if no other does." He said it again tonight as she entered the dining room, and again tonight she obediently allowed the shawl to fall open.

"You puzzle me," said Crassus. "You puzzle me a good deal, Varinia. I think I told you once that I had the pleasure —or displeasure—of having to spend an evening in my camp in Cisalpine Gaul with that monstrous *lanista*, Batiatus. He described you to me. He described you as a wildcat. A very vivid description of a woman who couldn't be tamed. But I see no sign of that. You are unusually obedient and compliant."

"Yes."

"I wonder what has made the difference in you. You don't care to tell me, I suppose."

"I don't know. I can't tell you."

"I think you do know, but let it pass. You look lovely

tonight. Well-groomed, well-dressed—Varinia, how long does this go on? I've been very decent to you, haven't I? Grief is grief, but contrast this with the salt mines. I could take your child away and sell him for the three hundred *sesterces* he would bring on the market, and then send you off to the mines. Would you like that?"

"I wouldn't like it."

"I hate to talk this way," Crassus said.

"It's all right. You can talk any way you please. You own me."

"I don't want to own you, Varinia. As a matter of fact, you own me just as completely. I want to have you the way a man has a woman."

"I couldn't stop you—any more than any other slave in the house could stop you."

"What a thing to say!"

"Why is it such an awful thing to say? Doesn't anyone in Rome talk about such things?"

"I don't want to rape you, Varinia. I don't want to have you the way I have a slave. Yes—I've had the slaves here. I don't know how many women I've slept with. Women and men too. I don't want any secrets from you. I want you to know me as I am. Because if you love me, I'll be something else. Something new and fine. My God, do you know that they call me the richest man in the world? Maybe I'm not, but with you, we could rule the world."

"I don't want to rule the world," Varinia said, her voice level, toneless, a dead voice, as it always was when she spoke to him.

"Don't you believe I would be any different if you loved me?"

"I don't know. I don't care."

"But you would care if it came to that baby of yours? Why can't you take a wet nurse? Sitting there with milk running from your breasts—"

"Why do you always threaten me with the baby? The baby belongs to you and I belong to you. Do you think that by threatening to kill my baby you make me love you?"

"I didn't threaten to kill your baby."

"You—"

"I'm sorry, Varinia. We always talk ourselves into this same circle. Please eat. I do what I can do. I serve you a meal like this. Don't tell me that you don't care. One could buy a villa for the price of this dinner. At least, eat it. Nibble at it. Look—let me tell you something amusing that happened today. At least, you may find it amusing. And eat a little."

"I eat as much as I need to eat," said Varinia.

A slave entered and set down a duck on a silver platter. Another slave carved it. Crassus had a circular table—they had just come into fashion—with a continuous couch circling two thirds of it. The diners ate with their feet drawn up, pillowed on a pile of silk cushions.

"This duck, for instance. It's smoked, stuffed with truffles, and cooked with tart brandied peaches."

"It's very good," Varinia said.

"Yes—I was telling you before of an amusing thing that happened today. At the baths, Gracchus came in. He hates me so virulently that he can no longer hide it. Curiously enough, I don't hate him. I forgot—you don't know him. He's a senator and a great political power in Rome—or was. His power is very shaky today. He's one of the new crew who pulled themselves out of the gutter and made a fortune out of graft and block votes. A fat pig of a man. No pride—no body; that's usually the case. And no sensitivity either, so he will sit on his throne until it washes out from under him. Well, I could see immediately that he wanted something from me. He made a great display of parading his fat carcass back and forth in the *tepidarium* with me. And then finally, he came out with it. He wants to buy you. Offered quite a price too, and then, when I brushed him off, he doubled his price. Very determined. I insulted him, but nothing got under his skin."

"Why didn't you sell me?" Varinia asked.

"To him? My dear, you should see him once, walking around in his flesh. Or wouldn't that matter to you?"

"It wouldn't matter," Varinia said.

Crassus pushed his dish away and stared at her. He drained his glass of wine, poured another, and then in a sudden fury, hurled the glass across the room. He spoke now with considered control.

"Why do you hate me so?"

"Should I love you, Crassus?"

"Yes. Because I've given you more than you ever had out of Spartacus."

"You haven't," she said.

"Why? Why not? What was he? Was he a god?"

"He wasn't a god," Varinia said. "He was a simple man. He was a plain man. He was a slave. Don't you know what that means? You've lived your life among slaves."

"And if I took you out to the country and gave you to a plough-hand somewhere, could you live with him and love him?"

"I could only love Spartacus. I never loved another man. I never will love another man. But I could live with a field slave. He would be somewhat like Spartacus, even though Spartacus was a mine slave and not a field slave. That's all he was. You think I'm very simple, and I am, and I'm foolish too. Sometimes, I don't even understand what you're saying. But Spartacus was more simple than I am. Compared to you, he was like a child. He was pure."

"What do you mean, pure?" asked Crassus, controlling himself. "I've listened to so much of this rubbish from you! Spartacus was a lawless enemy of society. He was a professional butcher who became an outlaw murderer, an enemy of everything fine and decent and good that Rome built. Rome brought peace and civilization to the whole world, but this slave filth knew only to burn and destroy. How many villas lie in ruins because the slaves neither knew nor understood civilization! What did they do? What did they accomplish in the four years they fought Rome? How many thousands are dead because those slaves revolted? How much misery and suffering was brought into the world because this filth dreamed of freedom—freedom to destroy!"

She sat in silence, her head bent, her eyes cast down.

"Why don't you answer me?"

"I don't know how to answer you," she said quietly. "I don't know what those questions mean."

"I've listened to things from you which I would take from no one else on earth. Why don't you answer me? What did you mean when you said that Spartacus was pure? Am I less pure?"

"I don't know you," Varinia said. "I don't understand you. I don't understand Romans. I only know Spartacus."

"And why was he pure?"

"I don't know. Don't you think I asked myself that? Maybe because he was a slave. Maybe because he suffered so much. How can you understand the way a slave suffers? You were never a slave."

"But pure. You said pure."

"To me he was pure. He could not do a bad thing."

"And do you think it was good to raise that revolt and set half the world on fire?"

"We didn't set the world on fire. All we wanted was our freedom. All we wanted was to live in peace. I don't know how to talk the way you do. I'm not educated. I can't even talk your language too well. I get confused when you talk to me. I wasn't confused when I was with Spartacus. I knew what we wanted. We wanted to be free."

"But you were slaves."

"Yes. And why must some be slaves and some free?"

Crassus said, more gently, "You have been living in Rome now, Varinia. I have taken you through the city in my litter. You have seen the power of Rome, the endless, limitless power of Rome. The Roman roads stretch across the whole world. The Roman legions stands on the edge of civilization and hold back the forces of darkness. Nations tremble at the sight of the legate's wand, and wherever there is water, the Roman navy rules the seas. You saw the slaves smash some of our legions, but here in the city there was not even a ripple for that. In all reason, is it conceivable to you that a few rebellious slaves could have overthrown the mightiest power the world ever knew—a power which all the empires of antiquity could not match? Don't you understand? Rome is eternal. The Roman way is the best way mankind ever devised, and it will endure forever. This is what I want you to understand. Don't weep for Spartacus. History dealt with Spartacus. You have your own life to live."

"I don't weep for Spartacus. No one will ever weep for Spartacus. They will never forget Spartacus either."

"Ah, Varinia, Varinia—how foolish you are! Already Spartacus is only a ghost, and tomorrow that ghost will blow away. Ten years from now no one will remember his name. Why should they? Is there any history of the Servile War? Spartacus did not build; he only destroyed. And the world remembers only those who build."

"He built hope."

"Varinia, you repeat things like a little girl. He built

287

hope. Hope for whom? And where are those hopes today? Blown away, like ashes, like dust. Don't you see that there is no other way in the world and never will be—but for the strong to rule the weak? Varinia, I love you. Not because you are slave, but in spite of the fact."

"Yes—"

"But Spartacus was pure," he said bitterly.

"Yes, Spartacus was pure."

"Tell me. Tell me how he was pure."

"I can't tell you. I can't tell you things you don't understand."

"I want to understand him. I want to fight him. I fought him when he was alive and I'll fight him now that he is dead."

She shook her head. "Why do you keep after me like this? Why don't you sell me? Why don't you do what you want with me? Why don't you leave me alone?"

"I ask you to tell me a simple thing, Varinia. Was there such a man as Spartacus at all? Why can't anyone tell me of him?"

"I told you—" She stopped, and he said gently now,

"Go on, Varinia. Go on. I want to be your friend. I don't want you to be afraid to talk to me."

"I'm not afraid. I was never afraid again after I knew Spartacus. But it's hard to talk about him. You call him a murderer and a butcher. But he was the best and noblest man that ever lived."

"Yes—tell me how. I want you to tell me how. I want to understand what he did to make you think that. Maybe if I understand it, I can be like Spartacus." He had gone on drinking without tasting the food. His irony was quiet now. "Maybe I can be like Spartacus."

"You make me talk about it, but how can I explain? Men and women are not the same among slaves as with you. Among slaves, a man and a woman are equal. We work the same; we are lashed the same; we die the same, and we go into the same nameless graves. And at the beginning, we took up spears and swords and fought alongside of our men. Spartacus was my comrade. We were one. We were joined together. Where he had a scar, I had only to touch it and then it hurt me and it was my scar. And always, we were equal. When his best friend, Crixus, died, he put his head in my lap and cried and whimpered like a little boy. And when my first baby came still born in six months, I cried the same way, and he took care of me. In all his life, he never had another woman than me. And no matter what happens, I have no other man. The first time I lay in his arms, I was afraid. Then a wonderful feeling came over me. I knew I would never die. My love was immortal. Nothing could hurt me again. I became like him, and I guess he became a little like me. We had no secrets from each other. First I used to be afraid that he would see the blemishes on my body. Then I knew that a blemish was the same as pure skin. He loved me so. But what can I tell you of him? They want to make him a giant, but he wasn't a giant. He was an ordinary man. He was gentle and good and filled with love. He loved his comrades. They would embrace each other and kiss each other on the lips when they met. I never saw men among you Romans embrace or kiss, yet here men sleep with men as easily as they sleep with women. Whenever Spartacus said something to me, I knew what he meant. But I don't know what you mean. I don't know what the Romans mean when they speak. When the slaves would fight and bicker, Spartacus would call them together, and they would all talk, and then he'd talk to them and they'd listen. They did bad things, but they always wanted to be better. They were not alone. They were a part of something; they were a part of each other, too. At first they used to steal from the spoils. Spartacus showed me how they couldn't help that; they came from places where they saw stealing. But the common store was never locked or guarded, and when they saw that they could have all they needed without stealing, and no way to use what they stole, they stopped stealing. They lost their fear of being hungry and poor. And Spartacus taught me that all the bad things men do, they do because they are afraid. He showed me how men could change and become fine and beautiful, if only they lived in brotherhood and shared all they had among them. I saw this. I lived through it. But in some way, the man I had for my own was always like that. That's why he could lead them all. That's why they listened to him. They weren't just murderers and butchers. They were something like the world never saw before. They were the way people can be. That's why you can't hurt me. That's why I can't love you."

"Get out of here," Crassus said to her. "Get out of my sight, God damn you!"

VI

Gracchus called Flavius again. The two men were sharing a destiny. They looked more like brothers than ever, two fat, aging men. They sat and looked at each other with knowledge. Gracchus was aware of the tragedy of Flavius. Flavius had always attempted to be like other men who succeeded, but he never was. Gesture for gesture, he copied them, but in the end he was only an imitation. He was not even a fraud; he was only an imitation of a fraud. And Flavius looked at Gracchus and saw that the old Gracchus was gone; gone away and not to come back anymore. What awful thing had happened to Gracchus, he only suspected; but the suspicion was enough. Here he had found a protector, and now his protector could no longer protect him. This was something to happen, all right!

"What do you want?" asked Flavius. "Don't start in at me again. It's Varinia. I've got the confirmation of that, if you want it. The wife of Spartacus. What do you want from me now?"

"What are you afraid of?" Gracchus demanded. "I don't go back on people who've helped me. What on earth are you afraid of?"

"I'm afraid of you," Flavius said miserably. "I'm afraid of what you're going to ask me to do. You could call out the City Cohorts if you wanted to. You have your own gangs and your own plug-uglies, and there are whole wards where you can turn out every citizen to do a job for you. Then why don't you? Why do you come to an old has-been like me? Not has-been. I've never been anything but a cheap heeler, never. Why don't you go to your friends?"

"I can't," said Gracchus. "On this I can't."

"Why?"

"Don't you know why? I want that woman. I want Varinia. I tried to buy her. I offered Crassus a million *sesterces*, and then I doubled the price. He insulted me and laughed in my face."

"Oh—no, no—two million! Two million!" Flavius began to tremble at the thought. He licked his heavy lips and clenched and unclenched his hands. "Two million. That's the whole world. The whole world in a little bag. You carry it around with you, and you have the whole world. And you offered that for a woman. My God, Gracchus—why do you want her? I'm not just asking to pry into your secrets. You want me to do something for you, but I'm going out of here right now if you don't tell me. I have to know why you want her."

"I love her," Gracchus answered dully.

"What!"

Gracchus nodded. He had no dignity left now. He nodded and his eyes became red and watery.

"I don't understand. Love? What in the devil is love? You've never married. No woman's ever gotten her fingers into you. Now you say you love a slave girl enough to pay two million *sesterces* for her. I don't understand that."

"Do you have to understand it?" the politician growled. "You couldn't understand it. You look at me and I'm old and fat and you've always suspected I was a capon anyway. Make what you want of it. I never knew a woman who was a human being; how many of our women are? I've feared them and hated them. Maybe we made them that way—I don't know. Now I want to go crawling on my knees to this woman. I want her to look at me just once and tell me that I mean something to her. I don't know what Crassus is to her—but I can understand what she means to him. I can understand that, all right. But what can he mean to her? He's the man who destroyed her husband—the man who smashed Spartacus. How can she look at him without loathing and hatred?"

"Women can," Flavius nodded. "Crassus can raise the price indefinitely. You would be surprised."

"Oh, you're wrong as hell, you fat fool! You stupid fat fool!"

"Don't start that again, Gracchus."

"Then don't talk like an idiot. I want the woman. You know what the price is."

"You mean that you will pay—"

"Yes."

"You know what the consequences are?" Flavius said

carefully. "Not for me. If I bring it off, I'll take the money and go to Egypt and buy a villa and some slave girls in Alexandria and live there like a satrap the rest of my life. I can do that, but you can't, Gracchus. You're Gracchus; you're a senator; you're the most powerful force in Rome at the moment. You can't run away. What will you do with her?"

"I'm not concerned about that now."

"No? You know what Crassus will do. No one ever defeated Crassus. No one ever took anything from Crassus. Can you fight Crassus? Can you fight that kind of money? He'll destroy you, Gracchus. Right to death. He'll ruin you and kill you."

"Do you think he's big enough to?" Gracchus asked softly.

"Do you want the truth? Two million is more than I ever dreamed of, but the truth is yes. He can and he will."

"I'll take my chances," Gracchus said.

"And what will you have after you take your chances? Two million is a lot. I can pay to have her taken out of his house and brought to you. That's not hard. But how do you know she won't spit in your face? Why shouldn't she? Crassus smashed Spartacus. But who put Crassus onto it? Who maneuvered him into position? Who gave him the army and the job?"

"I did," Gracchus nodded.

"Precisely. So what will you have?"

"I can have her—"

"What can you give her? What? There's only one thing any slave wants. Can you give her that?"

"What?"

"Oh, you know what," Flavius said. "Why don't you face this?"

"You mean her freedom," Gracchus said calmly.

"Not with you. Her freedom without you. That means her freedom outside of Rome. That means her freedom outside the reach of Crassus."

"Do you think she would give me one night for her freedom?"

"One night of what?"

"Love—no, not love. Honor, respect, care. No—no, not that. Gratitude. Let me put it that way. One night of gratitude."

"What a fool you are!" Flavius said.

"The more so to sit here and let you say it," Gracchus nodded. "Perhaps I am—pehaps not. I'll take my chances with Crassus. You would have to convince her that I never break my word. I have lived on my word. Rome knows it, but could you convince her?"

Flavius nodded.

"You would have to make the arrangements for her to get out of Rome afterwards. Could you do that?"

Flavius nodded again.

"Where?"

"At least to Cisalpine Gaul. There she'd be safe. The ports would be watched and the roads south. If she went north to Gaul, I think she'd be safe. She's German. I suppose she could get to Germany if she wanted to."

"And how could you take her out of the house of Crassus?"

"That's no problem. He goes to the country three days each week. A little money judiciously spent will do it."

"Only if she wants to go."

"I understand that," Flavius nodded.

"And she will want to bring the child, I suppose. That will be all right. I can make the child comfortable here."

"Yes."

"You'll want the two million in advance, won't you?"

"I think I'll have to have it in advance," Flavius said, somewhat sadly.

"You can have it now. The money is here. You can have all cash, or you can have a draft on my bankers in Alexandria."

"I'll take cash," said Flavius.

"Yes—I think you're right. Don't walk out on me, Flavius. I'll find you if you do."

"Damn it, Gracchus! My word is as good as yours."

"Very well."

"Only I don't know why you're doing it! By all the gods that ever lived, I don't know why you're doing it! You don't know Crassus if you think he will take it lying down."

"I know Crassus."

"Then God help you, Gracchus. I wish I didn't feel that way. But that's the way I feel."

VII

Varinia dreamed this dream, She dreamed that she faced an inquisition of the noble Senate. There they sat, the men who ruled the world. They sat in their great chairs, in their white togas, and each and every one of them had a face like the face of Crassus, long and handsome and hard. Everything about them, the way they sat, leaning forward, chin in hand, the expression on their faces so grim and foreboding, their confidence, their assurance—everything about them added up to the sum of power. They were power and strength, and nothing in all the world could stand before them. They sat in their white stone seats in the great, vaulted Senate Chamber, and just to see them there was a very frightening thing.

Varinia dreamed that she stood before them and she had to bear witness against Spartacus. She stood before them in a sheer cotton dress, and she was acutely and painfully aware that her milk was staining it. They began to ask her questions.

"Who was Spartacus?"

She began to answer that, but before she could, the next question came.

"Why did he try to destroy Rome?"

Again she tried to answer, and again the next question came.

"Why did he murder all who came into his hands? Didn't he know that our law forbids murder?"

This she tried to deny, but before two words of her denial passed her lips, the next question came.

"Why did he hate all that was good and love all that was evil?"

Again she tried to speak, but one of the senators rose and pointed to her breast.

"What is that?" he asked.

"Milk."

Now anger was on every face, terrible anger, and she was more frightened than ever. And then, for no reason she could understand in her dream, her fear passed away. In her dream, she said to herself,

"This can only be because Spartacus is with me."

She turned her head then, and sure enough, he stood beside her. He was dressed as he had most often been dressed in the time of their struggle. He wore high leather boots. He wore a plain gray tunic and a small felt cap was perched on his black curls. He wore no arms, for he had always made it a point to be unarmed unless they faced battle. He wore no jewels, no rings, no bracelets. His face was clean-shaven, and his curly hair was cropped close.

His very stance was one of such ease and certainty! She recalled—in her dream—that it had always been that way. Spartacus would join a group, and that sense of ease would permeate everyone. But in herself, there was a different reaction. Always, when she saw him, it was with a feeling of joy. Like a ring which was broken open. When he appeared, the ring would close itself and become whole and complete. Once she had been in his pavilion. At least fifty people were there, waiting for Spartacus. Finally, he came; she stood to one side, letting him deal with the people who were waiting for him. She only watched him, but her happiness increased and increased, and every word he said and every motion he made was a part of this process of pleasure. A point came where she could not endure the addition, and she had to go out of the pavilion and find a place where she could be all alone.

Now, in her dream, she had something of that feeling.

"What are you doing here, my darling?" he asked her.

"They are questioning me."

"Who?"

"They." She pointed to the noble senators. "They make me afraid." And now she noticed that the senators were absolutely motionless, frozen, as it were.

"But you see, they are more afraid," Spartacus said. It was so typical of him! He saw a thing, and stated it simply and directly. Then she would always wonder why she hadn't seen it too. Of course, they were afraid.

"Let's go, Varinia," Spartacus smiled. He put his arm around her waist and she put her arm around his. They walked out of the Senate Chamber into the streets of Rome. They were lovers. They walked on and on through the streets of Rome, and nobody noticed them and nobody stopped them.

In her dream, Spartacus said, "Every time I'm with you,

it's the same. Every time I'm with you, I want you. Oh, I want you so much."

"Every time you want me, you can have me."

"I know—I know. But that's hard to remember. I suppose you should stop wanting something you can have. But I don't stop wanting you. I want you more and more. Do you want me that way?"

"The same way."

"Whenever you see me?"

"Yes."

"I feel that way. Whenever I see you." They walked on a while more, and then Spartacus said, "I must go somewhere. We must go somewhere and lie with each other."

"I know a place to go," Varinia said in her dream.

"Where?"

"It's the house of a man called Crassus, and I live there."

He stopped and took his arm away. He turned her to face him, searching her eyes. Then he noticed the stain of milk on her dress.

"What is that?" he asked, forgetting apparently what she had said about Crassus.

"The milk I feed my baby."

"I have no child," he said. He was afraid suddenly, and he backed away from her—and then he was gone. Then the dream was over, and Varinia awoke and there was nothing but the darkness around her.

VIII

The next day, Crassus went to the country, and when evening came, Flavius brought Varinia to Gracchus, just as he had agreed to do. They came as Gracchus sat alone at dinner. A slave came to Gracchus and told him that there were two people outside, Flavius and a woman. And the woman carried a child in her arms.

"Yes," said Gracchus. "Yes, I know. There is a place ready for the child. Bring them in." Then he said, "No. No. I'll do it myself." He almost ran from the dining room to the front door. He let them in himself. He was very polite, very considerate, and he welcomed them as one welcomes honored guests.

The woman was wrapped in a long cloak, and in the shadowed entranceway, he could not make out her face. But now he could wait to look at her. He led them inside, and told the woman that she could give him the child or take it herself to the nursery. The child was cradled in her arms, and Gracchus was afraid he might say or indicate something that would create apprehension in her concerning the child.

"I have a regular nursery for him," he said. "I have a little crib and everything you can want. He will be very comfortable and safe, and nothing at all can happen to him."

"He doesn't need much," Varinia answered. It was the first time Gracchus had heard her voice. It was a soft voice, but rich and deep, a pleasing voice. Now she threw the hood of her cloak back, and he saw her face. Her long, yellow hair was tied at the back of her neck. She wore no face paint—which, strangely enough, made the fine planes and contours of her face more noticeable and more handsome.

While Gracchus looked at her, Flavius watched Gracchus. Flavius stood to one side, interested, glum, and also puzzled. He was uncomfortable there, and as soon as he was able to get his words in, he said,

"I have to make the other preparations now, Gracchus. I'll be back at dawn. You'll be ready for me then, I hope."

"I'll be ready," Gracchus nodded.

Then Flavius left, and Gracchus led her to the room he had prepared for the child. A slave sat there, and Gracchus nodded at the woman and explained.

"She will sit here all night. She will never take her eyes off the baby. So you don't have to be afraid that anything can happen to your baby. If the baby cries, then she will call you right away. No need to worry at all."

"The baby will sleep," Varinia said. "You're very kind, but the baby will sleep."

"But you won't have to listen for the baby's cry. As soon as that happens, she'll call you. Are you hungry? Have you eaten?"

"I haven't eaten, but I'm not hungry," Varinia answered, after she placed the child in the crib. "I'm too excited to have any appetite at all. I feel like I'm in a dream. First I was afraid to trust that other man, but now I believe him.

I don't know why you should do this for me. I'm afraid I'm dreaming and that any moment I will wake up."

"But you'll sit with me while I finish my dinner, and perhaps you'll want to eat something too."

"Yes, I'll do that."

They returned to the dining room, and Varinia took the couch at right angles to the one Gracchus sat on. He couldn't recline. He sat there, rather stiffly, unable to take his eyes off Varinia. It occurred to him with some surprise that he was not disturbed in any way, not apprehensive, but rather filled with a greater happiness than he had ever known before in his life. It was a matter of contentment. In all his life before, he had never experienced this same feeling of contentment. It seemed to him that all was right with the world. The aching incongruities of the world had disappeared. He was at home in his house in his blessed city, in his wonderful *urbs,* and he was filled with a great outgoing love for this woman who faced him. He did not now attempt to trace the complex which had fixed the single act of love in his whole existence upon the wife of Spartacus; he thought he understood it, but he had no desire to probe in himself and lay hands upon it.

He began to talk of the food. "I'm afraid you'll find it rather simple after the table Crassus sets. I eat fruit and plain meat and fish for the most part and then sometimes something special. I have a stuffed lobster tonight that is very good. And a good white wine which I drink in water—"

She wasn't listening to him, and with unusual perceptiveness, he said, "You don't really understand, do you, when we Romans talk about food?"

"I don't," she admitted.

"I can see why. We never talk about how empty our lives are. That is because we spend so much time filling our lives. All the natural acts of barbarians, eating and drinking and loving and laughing—all these things we have made a great ritual and fetish out of. We are never hungry any more. We talk of hunger, but we never experience it. We talk of thirst, but we are never thirsty. We talk of love, but we don't love, and with our endless innovations and perversions we try to find a substitute. With us, amusement has taken the place of happiness, and as each amusement palls, there must be something more amusing, more exciting—

more and more and more. We have brutalized ourselves to a point where we are insensitive to what we do, and this insensitivity grows. Do you understand what I'm saying?"

"Some of it I understand," Varinia answered.

"And I must understand you, Varinia. I must understand why you are afraid this is just a dream. You have a great deal with Crassus. I think he would even marry you, if you wanted it enough. Crassus is a great man. He is one of the greatest men in Rome, and his power and influence are unbelievable. Yo know what an Egyptian Pharaoh is?"

"Yes, I know."

"Well, right now, Crassus has more power than a Pharaoh of Egypt. And you could be greater than a queen of Egypt. Wouldn't this bring you some happiness?"

"With the man who killed Spartacus?"

"Ah—but consider. He did not do this personally. He did not know Spartacus or have any personal hatred for him. I am equally guilty. Rome destroyed Spartacus. But Spartacus is dead and you are alive. Don't you want what Crassus can give you?"

"I don't want it," Varinia answered.

"What do you want, my dear Varinia?"

"I want to be free," she said. "I want to go away from Rome and never see Rome again as long as I live. I want to see my son grow up in freedom."

"Is it so much to be free?" Gracchus asked, genuinely puzzled. "Free for what? Free to starve, to be slain, to be homeless—free to labor in the fields the way a peasant does?"

"I can't tell you about that," Varinia said. "I tried to tell Crassus, but I don't know how to tell him. I don't know how to tell you."

"And you hate Rome. I love Rome, Varinia. Rome is my blood and my life, my mother and my father. Rome is a whore, but I would die if I had to leave Rome. I feel it now. Because you are sitting there, I am full of my city. But you hate it. I wonder why. Did Spartacus hate Rome?"

"He was against Rome and Rome was against him. You know that."

"But when he tore down Rome, what would he build instead of Rome?"

"He wanted a world where there were no slaves and no masters, only people living together in peace and brotherhood. He said that we would take from Rome what was good and beautiful. We would build cities without walls, and all men would live in peace and brotherhood, and there would be no more war and no more misery and no more suffering."

Gracchus was silent a long while now, and Varinia watched him with curiosity and without fear. For all of his gross exterior, the great fat hulk of him, he was a man she wanted to trust and different from any she had known before. There was a peculiar, inverted honesty about him. There was a quality in him that in some way reminded her of Spartacus. It was nothing she could pin down. It was nothing physical—not even a mannerism. It was more a pattern of his thinking; and sometimes—only sometimes —he said a thing as Spartacus would have said it.

He was silent for quite a while before he spoke again, and then he commented upon what she had said before, just as if not a moment had passed.

"So that was the dream of Spartacus," he said, "to make a world with no whips and none to be whipped—with no palaces and no mud huts. Who knows! What did you name your son, Varinia?"

"Spartacus. What else should I name him?"

"Properly Spartacus. Yes—of course. And he will grow up to be tall and proud and strong. And you will tell him about his father?"

"Yes, I will tell him."

"How will you tell him? How will you explain? He will grow up in a world where there are no men like Spartacus How will you explain to him what made his father pure and gentle?"

"How do you know that Spartacus was pure and gentle?" Varinia asked him.

"Is that so hard to know?" Gracchus wondered.

"It's hard for some people to know. Do you know what I will tell my son? I think you will understand me. I will tell him a very simple thing. I will explain to him that Spartacus was pure and gentle because he set his face against evil and opposed evil and fought evil—and never in all his life did he make his peace with what was wrong."

"And that made him pure?"

"I'm not very wise, but I think it will make any man pure," Varinia said.

"And how did Spartacus know what was right and what was wrong?" Gracchus asked.

"What was good for his people was right. What hurt them was wrong."

"I see," Gracchus nodded, "the dream of Spartacus and the way of Spartacus. I'm too old for dreams, Varinia. Otherwise, I would dream too much about what I did with the one life that is given to man to live. One life—and it seems so short, so pointless and aimless. It's like a moment. Man is born and man is dead, without rhyme or reason. And here I sit with this fat, gross and ugly body of mine. Was Spartacus a very handsome man?"

She smiled for the first time since she entered his house. She smiled and then she began to laugh, and then the laughter turned to tears and she put her face on the table and wept.

"Varinia, Varinia—what did I say?"

"Nothing—" She sat up and wiped her face with her napkin. "Nothing that you said. I loved Spartacus so. He wasn't like you Romans. Not like the men in my tribe either. He was a Thracian, with a broad, flat face, and once, when an overseer was beating him, his nose was broken. People said it made him look like a sheep, but to me he was as he should be. That's all."

The barriers had disappeared between them. Gracchus reached over and took her hand. He had never in all his life felt so close to a woman, so trusting of a woman. "My dear, my dear," he said, "do you know what I told myself? First, I told myself that I wanted one night of love from you. Then I rejected that myself. Then I wanted one night of honor and respect. That too I rejected. All I wanted then was gratitude. But there's more than gratitude, isn't there, Varinia?"

"Yes, there is," she said frankly. He realized then that there was no duplicity or artfulness in her. She knew no other way than to say exactly what was in her mind. He picked up her hand and kissed it, and she didn't draw it away.

"I want this," he said. "I have until daylight. Will you sit with me and talk with me and drink a little wine and eat a little food? There is so much I must say to you and so much I must hear from you. Will you sit with me until daylight—and then Flavius will come with the horses, and you will leave Rome forever? Will you do that for me, Varinia?"

"For myself too," she said. "I want to do it."

"I won't try to thank you, because there is no way I know how to thank you."

"There is nothing to thank me for," Varinia said. "You are making me happier than I ever thought I would be again. I never thought I could smile again after Spartacus died. I thought life would always be like a desert. Yet he used to tell me that life was important above all other things. I never knew what he meant as much as I do now. I want to laugh now. I can't understand that, but I want to laugh."

IX

When Flavius returned, it was the hour before the dawn, the gray, lonely hour when life ebbs and things have reached their lowest point before they begin again. Without saying anything, the housekeeper took him in to Gracchus and Varinia. Gracchus was sprawled in a chair, tired, his face pale yet not unhappy. Varinia sat on a couch and nursed her child. She too seemed tired, yet she was very beautiful as she sat there, giving suck to the fat, pink baby. When Gracchus saw Flavius, he put a finger to his lips, and Flavius waited quietly. He could not help but be caught up in admiration for the woman's beauty. As she sat there in the lamplight, feeding her child, she seemed to be something out of Rome's memory of long, long ago.

When she finished, she covered her breast and wrapped the sleeping child in a blanket. Gracchus stood up and faced her, and for a long moment she looked at him.

"I decided on chariots," Flavius told them. "That way, we can make the best time, and it will be a question of how many miles we put behind us whether we can bring it off or not. I filled one chariot with blankets and pillows, so you will be comfortable enough—but we must leave immediately. As it is, we've drawn it very thin. Exceedingly thin."

They didn't seem to hear him. They looked at each other, the beautiful wife of Spartacus and the fat, aging Roman

302

politician. Then Varinia turned to the housekeeper and said to her,

"Will you hold the child a moment?"

The housekeeper took the child, and Varinia went over to Gracchus. She caressed his arms and then reached up and touched his face. He bent toward her, and she kissed him.

"Now I must tell you this," she said to him. "I thank you because you are so good to me. If you come with me, I will try to be good for you too—as good as I can be for any man."

"Thank you, my dear."

"Will you come with me, Gracchus?"

"Oh, my dear, thank you and bless you. I love you a great deal. But I would be no good away from Rome. Rome is my mother. My mother is a whore, but with you she is the only woman I ever loved. I'm not unfaithful. And I'm a fat old man. Flavius there would have to search the city to find a chariot to carry me. Go, my darling."

"I told you we've drawn the time thin," Flavius said impatiently. "Fifty people know about this by now. Do you think that no one will blab?"

"You take good care of her," Gracchus said. "Now you will be a rich man, Flavius. Now you will live in comfort. So do this last thing for me. Take good care of her and the child. Take them all the way north until you reach the foothills of the Alps. The Gaulish peasants who live there in the little valleys are good, plain, hard-working people. She will find a place with them. But don't leave her until you can see the Alps—clear against the sky. And make time. Whip the horses. Kill them if necessary and buy new horses, but never stop. Will you do this for me, Flavius?"

"I have not broken my word to you yet."

"No, you haven't. Goodby."

He went to the door with them. She took the baby in her arms. He stood in the doorway, in the lightening gray of dawn, and watched them climb into the chariots. The horses were nervous and alert. They stamped on the pavement and champed at their bits.

"Goodby, Varinia!" he called to her.

She waved to him. Then the chariots were off, clattering through the narrow deserted streets, waking the whole neighborhood with their crash and clatter . . .

Gracchus went to his office now. He sat down in his big chair, very tired now, and for a while he closed his eyes. But he didn't sleep. His contentment had not passed away. He closed his eyes and let his thoughts wander and reflected upon many things. He thought of his father, a poor shoemaker back in that time which was apparently gone forever, when Romans labored and took pride in their labor. He remembered his political apprenticeship on the streets, the bloody gang wars, the training in the cynical buying and selling of votes, the use of the mob, his climb along the ladder to power. Never enough power, never enough money. In those days, there were still honest Romans who fought for the Republic, who fought for the rights of the people, who spoke bravely in the Forum of the injustice of expropriating the peasant and setting up the great slave plantations. They warned! They thundered! They set their faces against tyranny! Gracchus had understood them. That was his great gift—that he could understand them and acknowledge the justice of their cause. But he also knew that their cause was a doomed cause. The clock of history is not to be set back; it moves forward, and he had joined forces with those who put their faith in empire. He had sent his gangs to destroy those who spoke of ancient freedoms. He had slain the just and the principled.

He thought of it now, not with regret or pity, but with the desire to understand. They were fighting for ancient freedoms, those early enemies of his. But were there ancient freedoms? Here was a woman gone out of his house, and freedom was like a fire inside of her. She had named her son Spartacus, and he would name his own son Spartacus—and when would slaves be content to remain slaves? There was no answer for him, no solution he could pose for himself, and that too did not make him regretful. He had lived a full life, and he didn't regret it. He had a sense of history then, a sense of a sweep of time in which he was only a moment—and that comforted him. His beloved city would endure. It would endure forever. If Spartacus ever returned and tore down the walls, so that men could live without fear, they would understand that there were men like Gracchus once, men who had loved the city even though they accepted its evil.

He thought now of the dream of Spartacus. Would it live? Would it endure? Was the strange thing that Varinia had said true—that men could become pure and selfless by fighting against evil? He had never known such men; but he had never known Spartacus. Yet he had known Varinia. Now Spartacus was gone and Varinia was gone. It was like a dream now. He had only touched the edge of Varinia's strange knowledge. But for him it did not exist; it could not exist.

His housekeeper came in. He looked at her strangely. "What do you want, old woman?" he asked her gently.

"Your bath is ready, master."

"But I don't bathe today," he explained, and was amazed at her surprise and consternation. "Everything is different today, old woman, look," he went on to say. "Over there on that table is a row of bags. In each bag, there is a certificate of manumission for each of my slaves. In each bag, there are twenty thousand *sesterces*. I want you to give the bags to the slaves and tell them to leave my house. I want you to do that now, old woman."

"I don't understand you," she said.

"No? Why don't you understand me? What I said is perfectly clear. I want you all to go. You are free and you have some money. Did I ever allow you to disobey my orders before?"

"But who will cook for you? Who will care for you?"

"Don't ask me all those questions, old woman. Do as I say."

It seemed forever to Gracchus before they were all out of the house, and then the house was strangely silent, newly silent. The morning sun was rising. The streets were full of life and sound and clatter, but the house of Gracchus was silent.

He returned to his office, went to a cabinet and unlocked it. From there he took a sword, a Spanish shortsword, such as the soldiers carried, but beautifully wrought and held in a fine ornamental scabbard. It had been given to him years and years ago on some ceremonial occasion, but for the life of him he could not remember what the occasion was. How strange that he had such contempt for weapons! Yet not so strange when he considered that the only weapon he had ever relied on were his own wits.

He took the sword from the scabbard and tested its edge and point. It was sharp enough. Then he went back to his chair and sat down and contemplated his massive paunch.

He began to smile at the thought of killing himself. There was no dignity attached to it. It was utterly ridiculous. And he seriously doubted whether he had the strength to plunge the blade in—in the time-honored Roman manner. How did he know that he wouldn't merely cut into the fat and then lose his nerve and lie in his own blood and blubber and cry for help? What a time in a man's life to begin killing! He had never killed anything in his whole life—not even a chicken.

Then he understood that it was not a question of nerves. He had only occasionally been afraid of death. From his childhood, he had mocked at the ridiculous stories of the gods. As a man, he had easily accepted the viewpoint of educated people of his own class, that there were no gods and that there was no life after death. He had made up his mind what he intended to do; he was afraid only that he would not do it with dignity.

With these thoughts going through his mind, he must have dozed off. He was awakened by someone hammering upon the outside door. He shook the drowsiness from him and listened.

"What a temper!" he thought. "What a temper you have. Crassus! What righteous indignation! That this fat old fool should twist you around his finger and take your great prize of the war! But you didn't love her, Crassus. You wanted Spartacus to nail onto a cross, and when you couldn't have him, you wanted her. You wanted her to love you, to crawl before you. Oh Crassus, you're such a fool—such a stupid, blundering fool! Yet people like you are the people of the times. No doubt of that."

He looked for the sword, but couldn't find it. Then he got down on his knees and located it under the chair. He knelt with the sword in his hands, and then with all his strength he plunged it into his breast. The pain was such that he cried out in agony, but the sword went in, and then he fell forward upon it, driving it in the rest of the way.

That was the way he was when Crassus broke down the door and entered. It required all of the general's strength to turn him over. Then the general saw that the face of the politician was fixed in a grimace or a grin . . .

After that, Crassus returned to his own house, filled with anger and hatred. Never in all his life had he hated anyone or anything the way he hated the dead Gracchus. But Gracchus was dead, and there was nothing that he, Crassus, could do about it.

When Crassus entered his house, he discovered that he had a guest. Young Caius was waiting for him. Caius knew nothing about what had happened. As he immediately explained, he had just returned fom the holiday at Capua, and he had come straight to visit his beloved Crassus. He went up to Crassus and began to stroke his breast. And then Crassus knocked him down.

Crassus stormed into the next room and returned with a whip. Caius was just picking himself up off the floor, blood running from his nose, his face full of surprise and hurt and indignation. Then Crassus began to whip him.

Caius screamed. He screamed again and again, but Crassus went on whipping him. Crassus had to be held back finally by his own slaves, and then Caius stumbled out of the house, crying like a little boy from the pain of the whipping.

PART EIGHT

In which Varinia finds freedom.

Flavius carried out his agreement with Gracchus. Armed with the best of credentials, signed by Gracchus himself, the chariots dashed north and then eastward. Varinia did not remember too much of the journey. For most of the first day, she slept with the baby clutched to her breast. The Cassia Way was an excellent, smooth and hard-surfaced road, and the chariots ran smoothly and evenly. For the first part of the day, the driver drove the horses without mercy; a new team was harnessed at noon, and for all the latter part of the day they drove at a fast, even trot. By nightfall, they were better than a hundred miles north of Rome. They changed teams again in the darkness, and all night long in the moonlight, the chariots rolled on at an even, mile-devouring pace.

A number of times they were challenged by military patrols, but the senatorial mandate which Gracchus had given Flavius was always sufficient to take them through. During that night, Varinia stood for hours in the swaying chariot, the baby sleeping peacefully at her feet, swaddled in blankets and cushioned by pillows. She saw the moonlit countryside slip past. She saw torrents rush by below as they rolled over the splendid Roman bridges. The world slept, but they went on.

When the moon set, a few hours before dawn, they pulled off the road onto a little meadow, unharnessed and hobbled the horses, munched some bread and wine, and then lay down on blankets to rest. Sleep came hard to Varinia, but the exhausted drivers were asleep immediately. It seemed to Varinia that she had barely closed her eyes, when Flavius was waking her. She nursed the child while they harnessed the teams, working slowly and fretfully, as men do when they have hardly overcome their exhaustion; and then, in the faint light of dawn, they drove back onto the road and northward again. The sun was rising when they stopped at a mile station to stretch their limbs and to change horses once again. A while later, they bypassed a walled city, and all that morning the drivers lashed the horses and thundered on. Now the endless motion of the chariot was beginning to tell on Varinia. She vomited several times, and she was in constant fear that her milk would stop flowing. But at evening time Flavius bought fresh milk and goat cheese from a farmer—food Varinia was able to hold down—and since the sky was clouded, they rested for most of the night.

Again, they were up before dawn and out on the road, and by midday they came to where another great road met theirs and crossed it, like the top of a T. Now they were travelling north and westward, and when the sun was setting, Varinia saw for the first time the snowy tops of the Alps in the distance. There was a moon that night, and they went on without pushing the horses too hard. They halted once during the night to change horses for the last time, and then before morning they turned off the main road onto a dirt road which ran eastward. The road wound down into a valley, and when the sun rose, Varinia could see the whole length of the valley into the hazy distance, a pretty river flowing through the center of it, and rising hills on either side. The Alps were closer now.

They were unable to go very quickly now, since the chariots lurched from side to side in the rutted dirt road. Varinia sat among the pillows, holding her child in her arms. They crossed the river on a wooden bridge, and then began a slow pull up into the hills. All day long the horses strained against the traces over the winding mountain road. Gaulish peasants who saw them, stopped in their work to watch the two great chariots and the fine big-chested horses who drew them, and always there were tow-headed children to come running to the roadside and stare with wide eyes at this unusual sight.

Late in the afternoon, when the road had become only a rutted track, they topped the hills and saw a wide and lovely valley stretching before them. Here and there in this broad valley, Varinia could see a little town, a huddle of houses, and in other places, clusters of peasant huts. There were broad stretches of woodlands, many little streams, and vaguely in the distance, a suggestion of a large walled city. The city lay to the west of them; they took their own path down and northward, in the direction of the Alps, which still seemed far away.

It was as difficult to go down as to go up, for the horses had to be held back, and the road twisted and turned. It was dark already when they reached the valley bottom, and they stopped to rest and to wait for the moon to rise. They travelled a while that night in the moonlight, halted again, and then went on in the early light of the following day. All the roads were poor here. They went on and on— and finally they reached the rolling hills where the Alps began.

Here Flavius parted from Varinia, leaving her early one morning on a stretch of road where there was nothing in sight except fields and woods.

"Goodby, Varinia," he said to her. "I've done what I promised Gracchus I would do, and I think I've earned some of the money he paid me. I hope that neither you nor I will ever see Rome again, for that's not a healthy city for either of us from here on. I wish you luck and happiness—and for that little boy of yours as well. There is a little peasant village about a mile up the road. Better if they don't see you come by chariot. Here is a bag with a thousand *sesterces,* which will buy you food and shelter for a year if necessary in these parts. The peasants are simple people, and if you want to get across the mountains into your own land, they will help you. But I would advise you not to try that. There are wild people living in the mountains and they hate strangers. Also, you will never find your own folk, Varinia. The German tribes wander through the forest from place to place, and there's no telling where a tribe is from one year to the next. Also, those forests across the Alps, from all I've heard, are a dank and unhealthy place to bring up a child. I would make up my mind to live somewhere in this neighborhood, Varinia. I must confess that it wouldn't appeal to me, but this is what you wanted, isn't it?"

"This is what I wanted," she nodded. "I'm very grateful to you, Flavius."

And then they swung the chariots around, and Varinia stood there, the child in her arms, watching them as they drove off in the clouds of dust—watching them until a fold of the land hid them from her.

Then she sat down by the roadside and fed the baby. Then she set out along the road. It was a fine, cool summer morning. The sun was coming up in a clear blue sky and the birds were singing, and the bees went from flower to flower, drinking nectar and filling the air with their song.

Varinia was happy. It was not the happiness she had known with Spartacus; but he had bequeathed to her a knowledge of life and the rich reward of existence. She was alive and free, and her child was alive and free; so she was content after a fashion, and she looked upon the future with hope and anticipation.

II

This is what happened to Varinia. A woman cannot live alone, and in the village which she came to, a village of plain Gaulish peasant people, she found shelter with a man whose wife had died in childbirth. Perhaps the people knew that she was an escaped slave. It didn't matter. She had full breasts, and she gave life to one of their children. She was a good woman, and people loved her for her strength and outgoing simplicity.

The man whose house she came into was a plain peasant man, a man who could not read or write and who knew only the lessons of toil. He was not Spartacus, yet not so different from Spartacus. He had the same patience with life. He was slow to anger and loved his children deeply— his own and the child Varinia brought him.

Varinia herself, he worshipped—for she had come to him from the outside and had brought life with her. And in time, she came to know him and return some of his feeling. She learned their language easily enough, a Latin base with many Gaulish words mixed into it; she learned their ways, which were not so different from the ways of her own tribe. They tilled the land and brought forth a crop. They offered some of the crop to their village gods, and another part they paid to the tax collector and Rome. They

312

lived and died; they danced and sang and wept and married, and their lives went on in the ordinary cycles of the seasons.

Great changes were taking place in the world, but among them the changes were felt so slowly that nothing was really disrupted yet.

Varinia was fruitful. Each year brought another child out of her loins, and she had seven children by the man she married before she stopped conceiving. Young Spartacus grew up with them, tall and strong and straight, and when he was seven years old, she told him for the first time who his father was and the story of what his father did. It surprised her that he understood so well. No one in this village had ever heard the name Spartacus. Greater things had shaken the earth and passed this village by. And as the other children grew, three of them girls and five of them boys, Varinia told the story many times again—told how an ordinary man who was a slave put his face against tyranny and oppression, and how for four years mighty Rome trembled at the very mention of his name. She told them of the dismal mine in which Spartacus had labored, and she told them of how he had fought in the Roman arena with a knife in his hand. She told them how gentle and good and kind he was and she never put him apart from the plain people among whom she lived. Indeed, when she told of the comrades of Spartacus, she would single out this one or that one of the village as an example. And when she told these tales, her husband listened with wonder and envy.

It was not an easy life that Varinia lived. From daybreak to nightfall, she labored, weeding, hoeing, cleaning, spinning, weaving. Her fair skin was burned brown by the sun, and her beauty disappeared; but her beauty had never been something she set great store by. Whenever she stopped to think and contemplate the past, she was grateful for what life had given her. She no longer mourned Spartacus. Her life with Spartacus was like a dream now.

When her first son was twenty years old, she took a fever, and after three days, she died. Her death was quick and without too much pain, and after her husband and her sons and her daughters had wept for her, they wrapped her in a shroud and laid her to rest in the earth.

It was after she had died that the changes came home

313

to this place. Taxes began to be increased, and the increase was without an end. A dry summer came and most of the crop was ruined, and then came the Roman soldiers. Those families who could not pay their taxes were herded out of their houses and off their land, chained neck to neck, and marched off to be sold for payment in Rome.

But not all whose crops were ruined accepted this role meekly. Spartacus and his brothers and sisters and others in the village fled into the forests that grew to the north of them, the forests that rolled on up into the wild Alps. There they lived a poor and wretched life on acorns and nuts and what little game they could kill; but when a great villa was built on the lands which had once been theirs, they came down and burned this villa and took all it held.

Then soldiers came into the forests, and the peasants joined with the mountain tribes to fight the soldiers. Escaped slaves joined them, and year after year the war of the dispossessed raged. Sometimes their strength would be smashed by the soldiers, and sometimes the power of the insurgents would be such that they could sally down onto the plains and burn and harry and plunder.

With this kind of a life, the son of Spartacus lived and died—died in struggle and violence as his father had. The tales he told his own sons were less clear, less factual. Tales became legends and legends became symbols, but the war of the oppressed against those who oppressed them went on. It was a flame which burned high and low but never went out—and the name of Spartacus did not perish. It was not a question of descent through blood, but descent through common struggle.

A time would come when Rome would be torn down— not by the slaves alone, but by slaves and serfs and peasants and by free barbarians who joined with them.

And so long as men labored, and other men took and used the fruit of those who labored, the name of Spartacus would be remembered, whispered sometimes and shouted loud and clear at other times.

New York City

June 1951

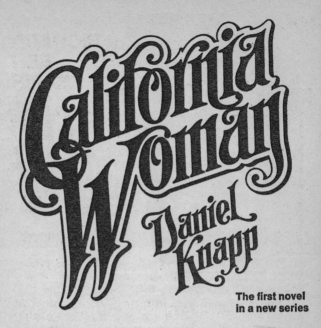

California Woman

Daniel Knapp

The first novel in a new series

A sweeping saga of the American West

Esther left New England a radiant bride, her future as bright as the majestic frontiers. But before she could reach California, she had lost everything but her indomitable courage and will to survive. Against the rich tapestry of California history, she lived for love—and vengeance!

A Dell Book $2.50   (11035-1)

RICHARD BEN SAPIR

THE FAR ARENA

"Moves like wildfire.
A marvelous read!"
—*Los Angeles Times.*

In a top security lab in Norway, an American
geologist delivers a frozen body buried deep in
glacial Arctic ice... a Russian specialist
achieves the ultimate cryogenic breakthrough
...and a beautiful nun witnesses a resurrection
beyond doubt. And Eugeni—premier gladiator
of Rome—awakens from a sleep of centuries to
face an utterly new and altered world.
"Riveting. Has all the earmarks of a bestseller."
—*Library Journal.*   A Dell Book $2.75   (12671-1)

Comes the Blind Fury

John Saul
Bestselling author of
Cry for the Strangers
and *Suffer the Children*

More than a century ago, a gentle, blind child walked the paths of Paradise Point. Then other children came, teasing and taunting her until she lost her footing on the cliff and plunged into the drowning sea.

Now, 12-year-old Michelle and her family have come to live in that same house—to escape the city pressures, to have a better life.

But the sins of the past do not die. They reach out to embrace the living. Dreams will become nightmares.

Serenity will become terror. There will be no escape.

A Dell Book $2.75   (11428-4)

Dell Bestsellers

- ☐ **COMES THE BLIND FURY** by John Saul $2.75 (11428-4)
- ☐ **CLASS REUNION** by Rona Jaffe $2.75 (11408-X)
- ☐ **THE EXILES** by William Stuart Long $2.75 (12369-0)
- ☐ **THE BRONX ZOO** by Sparky Lyle and Peter Golenbock $2.50 (10764-4)
- ☐ **THE PASSING BELLS** by Phillip Rock $2.75 (16837-6)
- ☐ **TO LOVE AGAIN** by Danielle Steel $2.50 (18631-5)
- ☐ **SECOND GENERATION** by Howard Fast $2.75 (17892-4)
- ☐ **EVERGREEN** by Belva Plain $2.75 (13294-0)
- ☐ **CALIFORNIA WOMAN** by Daniel Knapp $2.50 (11035-1)
- ☐ **DAWN WIND** by Christina Savage $2.50 (11792-5)
- ☐ **REGINA'S SONG** by Sharleen Cooper Cohen $2.50 (17414-7)
- ☐ **SABRINA** by Madeleine A. Polland $2.50 (17633-6)
- ☐ **THE ADMIRAL'S DAUGHTER** by Victoria Fyodorova and Haskel Frankel $2.50 (10366-5)
- ☐ **THE LAST DECATHLON** by John Redgate $2.50 (14643-7)
- ☐ **THE PETROGRAD CONSIGNMENT** by Owen Sela $2.50 (16885-6)
- ☐ **EXCALIBUR!** by Gil Kane and John Jakes $2.50 (12291-0)
- ☐ **SHOGUN** by James Clavell $2.95 (17800-2)
- ☐ **MY MOTHER, MY SELF** by Nancy Friday $2.50 (15663-7)
- ☐ **THE IMMIGRANTS** by Howard Fast $2.75 (14175-3)

At your local bookstore or use this handy coupon for ordering:

DELL BOOKS
P.O. BOX 1000, PINEBROOK, N.J. 07058

Please send me the books I have checked above. I am enclosing $_____
(please add 75¢ per copy to cover postage and handling). Send check or money order—no cash or C.O.D.'s. Please allow up to 8 weeks for shipment.

Mr/Mrs/Miss_____

Address_____

City_____ State/Zip_____